THE GREY ZONE

Jack Taggart Mysteries

Loose Ends
Above Ground
Angel in the Full Moon
Samurai Code
Dead Ends
Birds of a Feather
Corporate Asset
The Benefactor
Art and Murder
A Delicate Matter
Subverting Justice
An Element of Risk
The Grey Zone

THE GREY ZONE

A Jack Taggart Mystery

Don Easton

DUNDURN
TORONTO

Publisher: Scott Fraser | Acquiring editor: Kathryn Lane | Editor: Catharine Chen
Cover designer: Laura Boyle
Cover image: istock.com/dorioconnell
Printer: Webcom, a division of Marquis Book Printing Inc.

Library and Archives Canada Cataloguing in Publication

Title: The grey zone / Don Easton.
Names: Easton, Don, author.
Description: Series statement: A Jack Taggart mystery
Identifiers: Canadiana (print) 20190135166 | Canadiana (ebook) 20190135174 | ISBN 9781459745308 (soft-cover) | ISBN 9781459745315 (PDF) | ISBN 9781459745322 (EPUB)
Classification: LCC PS8609.A78 G74 2019 | DDC C813/.6—dc23

1 2 3 4 5   23 22 21 20 19

We acknowledge the support of the Canada Council for the Arts and the Ontario Arts Council for our publishing program. We also acknowledge the financial support of the Government of Ontario, through the Ontario Book Publishing Tax Credit and Ontario Creates, and the Government of Canada.

Care has been taken to trace the ownership of copyright material used in this book. The author and the publisher welcome any information enabling them to rectify any references or credits in subsequent editions.

The publisher is not responsible for websites or their content unless they are owned by the publisher.

Printed and bound in Canada.

VISIT US AT

 dundurn.com | @dundurnpress | dundurnpress | dundurnpress

Dundurn
3 Church Street, Suite 500
Toronto, Ontario, Canada
M5E 1M2

To the HQs — stay safe

CHAPTER ONE

"I'm eight. I should be allowed to ride in the front, not sit in the back like a baby."

Jia Chung braked to a stop and looked in the rear-view mirror. It was mid-May. The afternoon sun had broken through the clouds to shine on the Japanese plum trees lining the driveway of their White Rock estate. The trees were in full blossom and petals were falling, giving the appearance of pink snow swirling down.

Out on the main road she drove slower than the limit. Her car was a Mercedes-Benz S-Class that her husband, David, had purchased for her last month. They had a fifteen-minute drive to where Tommy had his music lessons.

"Mom, did you hear me?"

She glanced in the rear-view mirror again and focused on her son. "Tommy, we've talked about this. It's safer in the back. Maybe when you're ten."

"My friends get to ride in the front and they're eight."

Jia thought it funny how matter-of-fact, almost mature his voice sounded, but she hid her smile. "You're a bit smaller than your friends."

Tommy was silent for a moment. "Yeah ... I know."

"Children don't all grow at the same rate. I bet you'll have a big growth spurt soon."

"Do you think so?" He paused. "That'd be good. The boys at school tease me all the time."

"What do they say?"

"That I look like an elf 'cause I'm so little. And that my ears stick out and my hands are small, like a girl's."

Why are children so cruel?

"I know you said Asian people are shorter, but none of my Chinese friends are as small as me."

In the mirror she saw the forlorn look on his face. *Poor little guy.*

"It's okay, Mom," he said, as if reading her thoughts. "I don't let it bother me."

Jia hid her concern. "Your time will come. And as far as your hands go, none of your friends can play the piano as well as you." She turned off onto a residential lane that meandered through the neighbourhood, then added, "You're really good."

"You have to say that — you're my mom," Tommy said. But his face brightened.

"It's true! Ask Mrs. Finch. She told me that you're her favourite student."

"She said that? Really?"

"Yes, but don't tell any of the other students. That wouldn't be kind."

As Jia braked at a stop sign, the jolt of her car being bumped from behind ended the conversation. She glanced in her rear-view mirror at a white van. *Damn it. Is there any damage?*

The van's driver, an old man, pounded the steering wheel with his fist in apparent self-recrimination before getting out. Grey hair stuck out from under his fedora, which, like the long, dark topcoat he wore, had seen better days. His eyes peered at her from behind glasses with thick black frames, and his legs wobbled as he clutched the open door, seemingly afraid to let go.

"Stay in the car," Jia ordered Tommy. "I'll be right back."

She glanced at her rear bumper as she passed. *Is that a ding, or just dirt?* The old man bent over the driver's seat, probably looking for insurance papers.

She tapped him on the shoulder. "Are you okay?"

He turned quickly, grabbing her wrist with one hand and jabbing something into her stomach with the other. "Keep quiet and get inside. If you make any noise, we'll kill you and your kid."

Jia gasped when she looked down and saw the pistol. The man's voice sounded much younger than he looked. *He's wearing a mask!* She was startled further when the side door of the van slid open and another man wearing an identical mask peered out at her.

"My purse is in the car," she replied in panic.

"We don't want your fucking purse," said the man inside the van. "Get in here or you'll never see your kid again!"

She glanced at Tommy — he was peering out the back window, unaware of what was happening — then swallowed nervously and looked inside the van. It was made for hauling cargo; the only seats were up front. She put one foot inside, then was shoved from behind. Seconds later, she was face down on the floor with the man's knee on her back.

"Stay still and keep quiet," one of her attackers ordered.

"Please, don't hurt me," she begged in a whisper. "You can go ahead and take my car. The keys are still in the ignition. Just let me get my son out and you can have it."

"I'll get your kid," the man who'd been driving said. "You stay put. I'll tell Tommy you want to see him."

Oh, my God! "How do you know his name?"

"We know everything about you. Now shut the fuck up while I go get your kid."

Jia's worst fears were confirmed. These men had in mind something much more horrific than just stealing her car.

CHAPTER TWO

Constable Alicia Munday looked up from her desk in the bullpen when Sergeant Ned Hawkins came to the door of his office. She was a member of the Royal Canadian Mounted Police attached to the Major Crimes Unit working out of Surrey, British Columbia, which was a thirty-five-minute drive from their headquarters building in Vancouver.

Alicia had joined the RCMP seven years earlier, after obtaining a degree in political science. Her first five years were spent in uniform, until she was transferred into Major Crimes. She was the most junior member of the unit, but had a reputation of having the determination and ability to solve difficult crimes.

She was also single and spent much of her off-duty time working unpaid hours to bring criminals to justice. The fact that she seldom dated was her choice. She was an attractive brunette, and men were drawn to her like a magnet, but her advanced intellect sometimes limited the pool of people she'd want to spend time with.

"Everyone into my office!" Hawkins ordered with a wave of his hand.

Alicia and the six other officers in the bullpen glanced at each other, then got to their feet. She could tell from the look on Hawkins's face that it was more than the usual armed robbery or sexual assault. *This is something different.*

"All right," Hawkins started once everyone had crowded into his office. "I've had a call patched through from a David Chung, who says his eight-year-old son was kidnapped about twenty minutes ago."

"Has an all-points bulletin been issued?" asked Corporal Devon Bradley.

"No, I've decided not to put out an APB. The situation is dicey. Let me say first that this does not appear to be a domestic issue. He was calling on his way home from work and said his wife had just called him. She was apparently driving their son to piano lessons when her car was bumped from behind by a white van. When she got out, she discovered two men in the van, both wearing masks. They took her son and told her if she called the police, she wouldn't get her boy back in one piece. She was too rattled to even get the plate number."

It was probably stolen, regardless, thought Alicia.

"If we start stopping vans, it'll tip them off that we've been called," Hawkins continued. "Besides, it's probably already been dumped."

An eight-year-old kid. God, the parents must be sick with worry. How do you handle stress like that? "What's the boy's name?" Alicia asked.

"Tommy Chung. He's their only child."

"Where'd it take place?"

"A residential area in White Rock a few blocks from where they live on Marine Drive."

"Demands?" Alicia persisted.

"Getting to that, let me speak. The wife was given a map with a location that the husband is supposed to go to this Friday at four thirty p.m. He's to bring two hundred thousand dollars in hundred-dollar bills."

"Two hundred thou," Bradley commented. "Can he come up with that much money in two days?"

"The family moved into their home four years ago after paying fourteen mil for it, so there's no doubt he can pay. He's the chief executive officer of a company called Gamebest Technologies that makes computer software. He wants to pay, and I assured him we wouldn't make any overt moves until his son is safe."

"Fourteen million!" Bradley exclaimed. "Jesus, I'm surprised they only asked for two hundred K."

"Perhaps they were thinking the family would find that smaller amount easier to come up with without arousing attention and not worth the risk of calling the police," Alicia suggested.

"Same idea crossed my mind," Hawkins said. "The bad guys told his wife they were giving her husband two full business days to get the money. They made it clear that if he tried to stall, things would not go well for their son."

"Do you know what the location is?" Alicia asked.

"His wife just said it was in a park somewhere." Hawkins glanced at each of their faces. "There's no doubt they're going to run him through the hoops before making the actual drop-off. His wife was also told that they have scanning equipment to detect bugs and trackers. They said that if the police get involved, if anyone tries to follow them or to use bugs or GPS tracking equipment, they'll know."

These guys sound professional. What the hell do we do?

"I questioned Chung about the house and the staff," Hawkins continued. "They don't have any live-in help, but two maids come to the home Mondays, Wednesdays, and Thursdays. Today's Wednesday, but he says the maids will have left already. I tried to press him for details so we could start background checks, but he was anxious to get home to his wife. I did learn that his house is on one and a half acres of land, beachfront property. He says it's fairly secluded, but neighbours on the west side of his house can see part of his home. The entrance to the driveway is a different story. He says anyone can see who's coming and going to the house."

"So what do we do?" Bradley asked.

"We'll gain entry from the ocean. It'll be dark soon. He's going to slip outside to phone me. Later he'll meet us down by the water. I told him that any communication with his wife about us is to be in writing only until we've checked out his place for bugs. Providing we get the okay to talk, I'll interview him then."

"Could the maids be in on it?" Bradley suggested.

"Who knows." Hawkins paused, then addressed Alicia. "I want you with me in the Zodiac when we go in. If the house is clear, you'll stay to provide emotional support to the both of them. Bring a change of clothes and whatever else you need. You'll need to gain their confidence to allow us to do our job, and prepare the husband for what to expect when he delivers the money. Try as best you can to keep them from panicking and ensure they don't do or say anything stupid — like telling anyone else about what's going on."

Emotional support? Alicia frowned. *Crap. I'd rather be on surveillance when the time comes to take these scumbags down.*

Hawkins seemed to read her mind. "You're the only one who thought to ask Tommy's name. You care … and it'll show."

Everyone cares. You can see it in their faces.

"Your role is vital. If you're good at it, the parents will look to you over anyone else. In fact, they'll likely demand that you take part in supervising the money exchange because you'll be the one they'll trust with their son's life."

Alicia thought about her responsibility. With her limited experience, she wouldn't have a supervisory role, but the parents would be counting on her for their son's safety. "I understand. Thanks."

"Emotionally, it'll be difficult for you," Hawkins warned. He glanced at the other officers. "It will be for all of us, so keep a tight rein on your feelings and be professional. Our top priority is to get this kid home safe. Don't do anything to jeopardize that, even if it means letting the bad guys get away."

The idea that someone could get away with this made Alicia want to puke. *But he's right. Make sure Tommy's safe … then get the bastards.*

CHAPTER THREE

Darkness had fallen by the time the Zodiac's engine was turned off. Besides Alicia and Hawkins, on board there were four officers from the Emergency Response Team, all dressed in black, and four technicians specially trained in electronic surveillance, clutching their electronic detection gear like mothers clutching their newborn babies.

Two of the ERT officers slipped their paddles silently into the water while Hawkins talked on his cellphone. Soon Alicia caught the flicker of a flashlight from the shoreline.

"Okay, spotted you," Hawkins said.

Moments later, David Chung met them where the waves lapped at the shore, watching as everyone disembarked.

"Curtains, shades, blinds all closed?" Hawkins asked.

"Yes," David replied, staring at the ERT members, who stowed their paddles before equipping themselves with night-vision gear. "Where are they going?" he asked nervously as they disappeared into the darkness.

"Just a little reconnaissance of your grounds and neighbourhood to see if anyone is watching," Hawkins said.

Alicia put her hand on David's shoulder. "Don't worry, they know what they're doing and won't be seen," she said with assurance. "If they spot someone, all they'll do is report back to us. Our utmost priority is to get Tommy home safely."

"I've got security cameras on the driveway and around the house, but yeah, it'd be easy to watch us from lots of places."

"My name's Alicia, and I'll be with you every step of the way. Any questions, anything, just ask. I'm here for you and your wife."

"Thanks. I … I hope that calling you was the right thing."

"It was," Alicia replied confidently. "We don't want anyone else to go through what you two are going through now. These people must be caught."

He nodded for them to follow him.

After climbing a narrow path through some scrub brush, they skirted a tall hedge surrounding a tennis court, passed a swimming pool, then crossed a patio to a set of French doors.

"Guest room," David whispered as he reached for a door handle. "My wife, Jia, is inside, but she won't turn the lights on until you're all in."

"You're doing really well," Alicia whispered back. "We're going to get through this together."

"I, I just want Tommy back," he choked out in response.

He opened the door to let everyone inside. Once the lights were turned on, Alicia could see David and Jia clearly. The police database had revealed that neither had a criminal record, and according to their driver's licences, both were forty-two years old. If she'd been guessing their ages, though, she'd have added eight years. The stress was telling.

David looked at Alicia and turned his palms up to ask, *What now?*

Good, he was already turning to her for answers. She put her finger to her lips as a reminder to be quiet, then gestured for them to sit on the bed. She and Hawkins sat down in the only two chairs in the room.

The technicians immediately went to work. The room and hallway outside were given the all-clear, allowing them to talk while the technicians continued through the rest of the house.

Hawkins wasted no time conducting the interviews. Was there anyone whom they suspected? Any trouble at work or competitors who could be involved? Had anything unusual happened recently? Any salespeople come to the house? How long had Tommy been taking piano lessons, and was it always with this teacher, on this day? Could Jia better describe the men? Did they wear gloves? What about the white van? Was it dirty or clean? Old or new? Any decals or bumper stickers? Could it have been a rental? What did the inside look like? Any scratches on the floor?

The questions continued, but the answers were of little value. Jia remembered that the man who shoved a gun in her stomach wore latex gloves, but was too scared to remember if the other one did.

Hawkins made notes and had Jia repeat certain details to ensure accuracy or to help jog her memory. "You said one of them asked for your phone number as well as your husband's. Did you see him write them down?"

"He wrote the numbers on a piece of paper that looked like a sales receipt."

Too bad. If he'd used something like part of a cigarette package, that might have helped identify him later on.

"We'd like to put a tap on your phones immediately," Hawkins said.

Both parents agreed.

"Jia, you said you drive Tommy to school every morning," Hawkins continued. "Did you ever notice someone who might've been following you?"

Jia burst into tears. "No, I didn't! I should've been paying more attention!" she sobbed. "I let this happen. I let them drive away with my Tommy."

David put his arms around her and tried to comfort her. "It's not your fault. They had a gun. What were you supposed to do? Fight back? They said they'd kill you both if you didn't co-operate."

"You did the right thing," Alicia added firmly.

Hawkins cleared his throat. "Jia, you also said they took the keys to your car and chucked them out the window a block away, at the next intersection?"

Jia nodded. "They told me to wait three minutes before going to get them. I found them in the grass beside the sidewalk."

"You said they gave you a map?"

"As well as a note. They're upstairs on the kitchen table."

"A note?" Hawkins asked.

"Typewritten, giving David directions. They said they won't put up with any, uh, bullshit, like us asking for proof of life or going to the cops and having them send someone else to deliver the ransom. They said this isn't the movies, so no heroics. They'll release Tommy as soon as they have the money. That's not on the note — it's what they said. Their words."

"I see. Alicia will go with you to look at the map and the note. David, I have some questions for you while we're waiting. I'd like to properly identify everyone who comes to your property and the companies they work for. Maids, landscapers, pool maintenance, repairmen, tree pruning service, and anyone else you can think of. "

Alicia and Jia went upstairs. As they made their way through the living room, a technician came around from behind a grand piano to speak to Alicia.

"This level of the house is clear," he told her in a hushed voice. "It's okay to talk, but keep your voices low. I think the guys upstairs are almost finished, then we've got some rooms to do downstairs, including a media room. Shouldn't take long."

"Thanks," Alicia replied. She noticed Jia staring at a framed picture of Tommy on an antique desk.

Their eyes met. "Do you need it?" Jia whispered. "It was taken last month."

Tommy was smiling broadly in the photo. His ears protruded and his face seemed tiny in comparison to his two upper front teeth, which stood out like a beaver's.

"Cute kid," Alicia said. "I'll take a picture of it. Maybe you could hold it for me so there's no reflection or glare. Here, let's sit on the sofa." She took out her cellphone. Jia's hands shook as she held the picture. "Tell me more about Tommy," Alicia said, reaching out to steady the picture.

"The other officer wanted the map," Jia replied, looking toward the kitchen.

"There's no rush," Alicia responded. "We'll need to have it examined by Forensics later."

"I opened it, but David didn't touch it."

"That's okay. We'll get your prints if we need them and DNA swabs from the both of you. What's Tommy's favourite colour?"

"Red. It's a lucky colour in Chinese culture," Jia added blandly.

"I see. How about toys? Does he have a favourite? Or video games? Bet he spends a lot of time on the computer. Most kids do."

"Not really. What he really loves to do is play the piano. I know most children need a lot of prodding to practise, but not Tommy. He seems to have a natural love of music."

Alicia purposely stalled as they talked. One reason was to gain Jia's trust and try to calm her down. The other was to give Hawkins time to question David about his personal life — like whether there was a mistress or a past affair that could have made him an enemy. That conversation would be very intrusive, and it was unlikely he'd admit to any infidelities in front of his wife.

Alicia's instincts told her that David didn't have any such secrets, but the questions still had to be asked. Because Jia didn't work outside the home, they'd hold off asking her any questions in that regard until after they'd examined her phone records.

Eventually they went to the kitchen to examine the map. It was an enlarged copy of Queen Elizabeth Park in Vancouver. An *X* near West 33rd Avenue and Cambie Street indicated where David was to take the money.

A separate scrap of paper read:

> *Friday 4:30 p.m. — park car in lot. Walk to where the road branches off to 33rd Ave and the tennis courts. Wait at the park bench opposite that intersection. Carry $ in cloth satchel bag. NO SUITCASE!*

"Why not a suitcase?" Jia asked.

"Probably because a suitcase could easily hold a hidden GPS locator," Alicia replied. "A cloth bag would be harder to hide that in." She glanced up as Hawkins and David appeared.

"The techs are almost done," Hawkins said. "We can talk normally. Also got a text from the guys outside. They haven't spotted anyone."

Alicia stepped aside to speak to him privately. He made eye contact and shook his head subtly, indicating that David's personal life was apparently clean. *Yeah, I didn't get the feeling he was that kind of guy.*

Hawkins cleared his throat. "As soon as they finish, I'll round everyone up and head back to the office. David's provided me with thirty days' worth of security camera footage, which I'll have someone review at the office. Tomorrow he'll arrange for the money. He deals with a couple of banks, as well as financial investment places, so he'll split up where he gets the money from.

If anyone asks, he's going to say it's a bonus for someone who's assisting him with a foreign investment."

"In other words, a possible bribe," Alicia replied.

"Whatever works." Hawkins leaned over to view the map and the note.

"I'm pulling the location up on Google," Alicia said. She counted the potential exits from the park that a vehicle could take. "Thirty-two."

"Check out the bench where David's supposed to wait," Hawkins directed. Alicia went to Google Maps Street View and zoomed in on the bench. "Chain-link fence as a barrier to the golf course," Hawkins noted. "Looks to be a deserted part of the park for any pedestrians."

"Maybe David will be instructed to toss the bag over the fence to someone in a golf cart," Alicia suggested.

"Maybe." Hawkins paused. "I'll take the exhibit. I want to get back to the office as soon as I can." He rejoined David and Jia. "I'd like Alicia to stay in your house. Is that okay?"

"Yes, I'd feel better knowing someone is with Jia while I'm arranging the money tomorrow," David replied.

"You can use one of the spare bedrooms," Jia added.

"Thank you," Alicia replied, although she didn't suppose any of them would get much sleep tonight. She saw the pain on Jia's face. *We're all thinking the same thing: What kind of night will Tommy have … if he's still alive?*

CHAPTER FOUR

Back at his office, Hawkins and several subordinates worked through the night. The security camera footage that David had given him identified two pizza deliveries and a few other vehicles whose occupants were likely to be acquaintances. All would be identified and checked out.

Tommy's welfare wasn't the only priority. It was unlikely that the kidnappers knew when or where David would be collecting the money, but regardless, protection had to be provided for his security.

At 7:30 a.m. Hawkins held a meeting in the bullpen to outline what was to take place. Due to concern that the kidnappers had scanning equipment, no transmitters or GPS tracking equipment would be placed on David or in the satchel with the ransom. David was to be in the park at 4:30 p.m. It wouldn't get dark until around 9:00 p.m., but there was another concern: with nightfall, there'd be fewer people out, less traffic, making it easier for the bad guys to spot countersurveillance. For this reason, the satchel would be covered in an invisible ultraviolet spray that could only be seen through special goggles fitted with an ultraviolet filter. David's red Cadillac would also be marked with a large X on the roof.

An audio switch would be hidden in David's car. It was a one-way method of communication with the police, but was only to be used in an emergency. The audio would be encrypted to prevent potential eavesdroppers from hearing anything David said. However, equipment that could detect when transmissions were being made nearby existed and was available to the public. For that reason, all communication, even between police on cellphones, was to be kept to a minimum.

Hawkins reiterated an important point as he brought the meeting to a close. "Surveillance of David Chung will be maintained from the air," he declared. "I'll be the eye in the sky in the Cessna and relay what's happening. As far as you guys on the ground go, nobody — I repeat, nobody — is to come within three city blocks of Chung without my say-so. Got it?"

Nods and responses to the affirmative confirmed that they did.

* * *

For Alicia, the following day was long as she tried to comfort Jia while David was out arranging the money. Stress often brings people together; Alicia felt the two of them had connected, but eventually the conversation turned to small talk, and then silence took over.

At one point, when they were sitting on the sofa, Jia gave Alicia's hand a tight squeeze, and Alicia squeezed back. It wasn't necessary to ask what was going through Jia's mind. Alicia couldn't stop worrying, either.

At 5:30 p.m. the sound of the automatic garage door announced David's arrival.

"It's done," he said, once he'd met them inside. "Sergeant Hawkins will photocopy all the money tonight. He's arranged for someone to hand it off to me tomorrow morning in an underground parking lot."

Jia unexpectedly burst into tears, perhaps in relief that at least part of the ordeal had gone okay. Alicia stood back as David rushed to comfort her.

"It'll be okay," he said. "You'll see. Tomorrow night Tommy will be home and all this will seem like a bad dream."

More like a nightmare, Alicia thought.

"Did you remember to cancel the maid service for tomorrow?" David asked.

Jia nodded. "I said I have a migraine and don't want anyone around."

"Good. Are you hungry? Should we make some pasta?"

After dinner, Alicia pushed her plate back. "There's something you both need to know about tomorrow." She paused. "I'll be surprised if the drop takes place right away. It's a large park with lots of exits. They'll probably make you walk through the park or perhaps drive somewhere else. Don't get angry with them."

"Angry? Angry doesn't describe what I'd like to do to them," David said bitterly.

"I'm sure, but you'll need to keep your anger in check. It's important to maintain your cool. If anything, act subservient. It'll make them feel more relaxed and in control — which translates to less chance they'll do anything rash or react out of panic."

David nodded.

"Our goal is to get Tommy home safely," Alicia continued. "Once that's done, then we'll deal with the bad guys … which brings me to something else. Try and remember everything they say to you. Word for word, if possible. As soon as you're able, I want you to write it out. Court could be a long way off. You'll need a record to refresh your memory."

David swallowed, then nodded again.

Alicia turned to Jia. "I know you'll be watching every second that ticks by on the clock. Don't panic if the seconds turn into hours. The bad guys' nerves are going to be on edge, as well. They'll be paranoid and might suspect there's a cop behind every rock and tree. They could easily get spooked and pull back before working up the nerve to contact you again. Make sure your phone is fully charged. It may take a lot longer than you think … or hope."

"What if they get spooked and don't call back?" Jia asked.

"Greed is a strong motivation. Once they calm down, they'll likely realize that whatever spooked them shouldn't have. They've already taken a big risk and gone to a lot of trouble to set this up. They'll want it to be successful."

"I just want it over," Jia replied. "I want Tommy home with me."

"When I left the house yesterday morning, I was in such a hurry that I forgot to tell him I love him, like I always do," David said, his eyes welling. "I didn't even realize it until I was halfway to work."

"There's no doubt in my mind that Tommy knows you both love him," Alicia said. "And you can remind him how much when you see him."

"Will you be in the park tomorrow?" Jia asked. "I'd like it if you were. Then maybe you could let me know what's happening."

"That's up to my boss," Alicia said, pleased she'd been asked. Hawkins was right. *Maybe that's why he's a sergeant.* "I'll call him. I'm sure he'll agree. I'll be in touch with you every step of the way. I'll give you my cell number, as well. Feel free to call anytime."

"I could smuggle you out in the trunk of my car," David offered.

Alicia took out her phone and called Hawkins to make the request.

"No problem," he said. "I wanted you out there, regardless. Your gender is suited for the station wagon with the baby seat. Nobody would make you for a cop."

"Thanks, Ned."

"Doesn't mean you'll see much. I'll be watching from the air, and I don't want anyone on the ground closer than three blocks."

"You got it. David offered to smuggle me out in the trunk of his car."

"Take him up on the offer. I'll get him to smuggle someone else back in to stay with Jia."

Alicia joined David and Jia in clearing the dishes, then they all retired to the living room. She noticed that they were fidgeting and casting her occasional glances. "Anything you'd like to talk about?" she asked.

"What if you're spotted?" Jia blurted. "They told me not to call the police. What if they see you?"

"They won't, I can assure you," Alicia said firmly. "The surveillance will be done by someone with high-powered binoculars in an aircraft so high up it'll only be a speck in the sky. Nobody will know. I'll be helping out with the ground crew, but none of us are allowed to go within three blocks of wherever David might be."

"But still, what if you're seen?" David persisted.

"We'll be in unmarked police cars," Alicia replied. "For example, I'll be driving a blue Volkswagen station wagon with a toddler seat in the back and a *Baby on Board* sign. Does that sound like a police car?"

David looked surprised. "No, I guess not."

"It was brave of you to call us, though. I'm sure it was a tough decision."

David grimaced. "I wouldn't call it brave. In our minds it was the practical decision. We were both frightened out of our wits about what to do. Jia said that if we didn't involve the police, who was to say they wouldn't take the money and kill both Tommy and me? At least this way you'll have a better chance at catching them."

Alicia stared at David's grim face. *You're right. They could kill you. But it's not like we have a choice.*

CHAPTER FIVE

David drove into Queen Elizabeth Park at 4:15 p.m. He'd been keeping an eye on his rear-view mirror ever since he'd left home, but hadn't seen anyone following. He arrived at the parking lot early, so he waited in the car for about ten minutes, still looking around for anybody suspicious. He removed the satchel from the trunk and five minutes later was sitting on the bench the kidnappers had marked on the map. The only other people he could see were in the distance playing golf. He took out his cellphone and stared at it, willing it to ring.

Thirty minutes passed before he finally heard a ring — but it wasn't coming from his phone. The noise came from the crook of a tree behind the bench. He leapt to his feet, then stood on his tiptoes to grope around the branches. The ringing cellphone was in a Ziploc bag. He fumbled to open it and put the phone to his ear.

"Follow my instructions exactly," said a man's harsh voice. "Throw your own phone over the fence into the golf course, then go back to your car and drive north on Cambie. Cross the Cambie Street Bridge, take the Smithe exit, and keep going to Seymour. Turn right and you'll see public parking on your right side. Leave your car there, take the money, and walk down Seymour to Robson. Go right on Robson for a block and wait at the northwest corner of Robson and Richards, in front of the IGA. Stand close to the curb and be ready to toss the money into a passing car. Got it?"

"Cambie to Seymour, turn right and park, walk to the corner, go right for a block, and wait in front of the grocery store on the northwest corner of Robson and Richards?"

"You've got twenty minutes. Go!"

"Twenty? That's —" David realized the man had already ended the call. The location wasn't all that far away, but it was Friday and rush hour. *I'll never make it!* He grabbed the bag and started to leave, then remembered his own phone, ran back, and threw it over the fence before sprinting back to his car.

His heart beat wildly as he drove through traffic, cursing at every red light he came to. When he arrived at the parking lot on Seymour, he quickly pulled in. A moment later, he stood panting and trying to catch his breath in front of the grocery store, clutching the satchel in one hand and the phone in the other. He'd made it with two minutes to spare. Anxiously, he looked around the intersection. *Which direction will they come from?*

Throngs of people engulfed him, alternately waiting for traffic lights and swarming across the crosswalk. It was twenty minutes before the phone rang.

"Change of plans. Walk south on Richards to Nelson, turn right, then go six blocks to Nelson Park and find a bench to sit on. You're looking at a little less than one and a half kilometres. I'll give you another twenty minutes, which will make it six p.m. Go!"

Again, David made it with two minutes to spare. He sat panting on a bench in the park, hugging the satchel to his chest. The trees were sparse; he could see people and cars going past the park. At 6:10 p.m. he received his next call.

"You run fast. That's *real* good," the voice said mockingly. "Now go back to your car and drive to the Highstreet Shopping Centre in Abbotsford. Park in the lot."

"Abbotsford?" David questioned.

"Are you deaf? The Highstreet Shopping Centre in Abbotsford."

You piece of shit. I want to choke the life out of you so bad.

"Repeat it to me!" the voice snapped.

"The Highstreet Shopping Centre in Abbotsford. Yes ... sir," David replied, remembering Alicia's advice to act subservient.

"Sir ... I like that." The tone was less harsh. "Take your time. No speeding tickets. I expect to see you there by seven forty-five p.m."

"I'm on my way," David replied as he rose from the bench.

"One more thing. Quit looking in your rear-view mirror. It annoys me."

David found the comment chilling. *Am I being watched every second?*

He arrived at the shopping centre at 7:30 p.m. and parked in the lot. An hour passed. It was getting dark and he was bordering on panic when the phone finally rang again. "I'm here," he said, anxiously. "Why — why didn't you call me?"

"What're you so worried about? Have you done something you shouldn't have?"

"No! I — I … you said seven forty-five p.m. It's —"

"I know the time. We're almost done. Keep your phone on and listen to what I say, but don't repeat anything aloud."

"Okay."

"Pull out of the lot and drive south on Mount Lehman Road. Your next destination is inside the Abbotsford Airport. Bring the bag with you. You're about seven minutes away, so get going. Tell me when you're inside the terminal. In the meantime I won't say much, but I'd better hear you breathing. If I hear you talking, even to yourself … well, you don't want to think about what'll happen."

David did as instructed. Once inside the airport he said, "I'm here, inside."

"Good. Keep your phone on and go to one of the car rental agencies. Doesn't matter which one. Rent a car and put the bag on the seat beside you. Let me know when you've done it."

Minutes later, David toted the bag out to the car he'd rented, tossed it in the front seat, and said, "I've done it." By now it was after 9:00 p.m. and dark.

"Sounds like you got a Chevy Impala."

"Uh, yes."

"What colour?"

"Blue."

"Okay, pull out and drive south on Mount Lehman Road. In about a block you'll come to a T-intersection. Get going."

"I'm at the intersection," David said two minutes later.

"We're almost done. Turn right and drive for about five or six minutes. On your left you'll see the entrance to Aldergrove Park. The gate will be closed, but there's room to park in front of it. Wait there and I'll call you back."

· * * *

For Hawkins, the investigation was proceeding as he'd expected. When David first bolted out from under a tree in Queen Elizabeth Park and ran to his car, Hawkins guessed that the kidnappers had provided another cell-phone. From his vantage point up in the sky, he was able to see most of David's movements and relay that information to the surveillance teams on the ground, to ensure they kept their distance.

His job became even easier when darkness fell. The ultraviolet paint made the *X* on David's Cadillac stand out like a beacon. Likewise, Hawkins wasn't fooled when he caught sight of the satchel being placed in another car.

"Okay, everyone," he yelled into his phone over the noise of the aircraft. "This could be it. Our man is parked at the entrance to Aldergrove Regional Park. It's a little east of 272nd Street on 8th Avenue."

Moments later, the surveillance teams on the ground got into position. Alicia was assigned to wait at the Abbotsford Airport, approximately six kilometres away. The closest surveillance member was Corporal Bradley, who'd found a residential area to park in a kilometre from where David waited.

* * *

At 10:00 p.m. David got the call. A call he'd never forget.

"You obviously care a lot more about your money than about your own kid," the man snarled.

"What? What do you mean? I've got the money. It's right here beside me."

"Yeah ... along with the cops!" the man yelled. "We told you not to call them or your kid would face the consequences."

"I didn't call them! I swear I didn't."

"Bullshit. Tell the cop in the blue station wagon with the *Baby on Board* sign in the back window that he might as well go for a doughnut. You go home to your wife. The two of you can enjoy spending your money. We're not touching it."

"Oh, God, no ... please! Give me another chance! Please don't hurt him."

"We're going to make an example of you, David. Goodbye."

CHAPTER SIX

"Okay, something's happened," Hawkins reported. "Our man is heading back. It's possible he made the drop. Too hard for me to see; he was parked under the trees. Everyone hold your positions. The bad guys might have a motorcycle stashed in the park — it's something that could go around the gate. Doesn't matter, though, I'll still see when it leaves. If David has made the drop, once his son is safe, we'll send in the dog master."

He's got to have made the drop, Alicia thought.

"David's driving like a bat out of hell," Hawkins reported. Moments later he added, "Almost lost it coming around the corner back onto Mount Lehman. Okay, he's driving back into the airport. Any chance you see him, Alicia?"

"I can hear his tires … I see him," Alicia responded. "He's parked behind his own car. Out of the rental … into his own car. Maybe he forgot something. I'm about a block away, using the binocs, but it's hard to see —"

"Hello! Hello! Hello!" David's voice screamed over the emergency audio transmitter in his car. "Help me!" he pleaded. "I don't know what to do!"

"Alicia! Drive past him and see what the hell's going on!" Hawkins ordered.

Alicia's phone rang as she was backing her car up. She snatched it up.

"It's me, David!" he said shrilly. "They spotted you! They told me to keep the money!"

"Okay, David ... you need to try and calm down," Alicia replied, pulling back into the parking stall.

"Aren't you listening? They know! They told me to go home!"

"This could be a ruse to see what you do, test whether a bunch of police cars show up."

"No, they know it's you," David said adamantly. "They told me they saw you!"

"We talked about this. I told you, they'll be paranoid about everyone they see. It's no big surprise that they got spooked. I'm sure they'll call back."

"What should I do?"

"Return the rental. I wouldn't be surprised if they call you while you're doing that."

"But what if they don't?"

"Then get into your own car and drive home. Just unlock your trunk before you go back inside the airport. I'll sneak inside and go home with you."

"Okay. Okay. Should I phone Jia?"

Alicia sighed. "I've been updating her, but she might feel better hearing your voice."

"Not if I don't have Tommy with me."

"Not warning her before you get back isn't a good idea. Call her, and keep it short in case the bad guys are trying to call you. Tell her the bad guys got spooked. They might even make you sweat for a while, then call you back tomorrow."

"You think so?"

"Yes, I do," Alicia replied, doing her best to sound confident.

Her conversation with Hawkins was terse. "David called. The bad guys said they spotted our surveillance and told him to keep the money and go home."

"Christ. I don't believe we were spotted," Hawkins replied. "This has got to be a test. Either that or some citizen spooked them and they thought it was a cop."

"He's returning the rental now. I'm going to sneak back into his trunk and go home with him."

"Good idea. You should be there for support. I'll follow from above until you get home. We're running on fumes up here, so we'll have to land after that. I'll have Bradley and the rest of the team get to within a few blocks of the house until you're ready to call it a night. Let's hope we hear back tonight — and if not, let's hope they get over their jitters by tomorrow."

But the kidnappers did not call back. At 11:30 p.m., David and Alicia walked inside the house to meet Jia and Constable Vern Wales, who'd been detailed to stay with her.

Alicia gave them a moment to hold each other. "David, I'm sorry, but this is really important. I need you to go someplace quiet, without any distractions, and write down everything that happened. Or you can type it, if you like. Try to remember what they said to you, word for word. When you're done, initial every page and sign the last one. Also note the date and the time you start, as well as the time you finish."

David and Jia held each other a moment longer, then David headed upstairs. Alicia sat down on the sofa with Jia, and Wales sat across from them.

Jia turned to her angrily. "David told me they saw you. You promised you wouldn't be seen!"

"I told you that they might get spooked. Once they calm down, greed will take over. I'm sure they'll call back."

"If they don't, I'm holding you accountable!" Jia said, pointing her finger at Alicia's face.

Okay ... let it go. She's upset and lashing out. Who could blame her?

* * *

"We told the sitter we'd be home by midnight," the woman said.

"Seven minutes to go. We'll make it," her husband replied. The car tires sounded briefly as he rounded the corner onto a residential street.

"Hey, how much have you had to drink?"

"I dunno. Three or four glasses of wine."

"Bet it was more like six."

"You're the one bellyaching about the sitter."

"Being a few minutes late won't — look out!" she screamed. Their headlights shone onto a pathetic-looking figure directly in front of them. She saw the silver bands of duct tape across his eyes and mouth as he stumbled toward them, his hands tied behind his back.

She heard the screech of tires and smelled burning rubber as she shut her eyes.

* * *

It was 1:30 a.m. when David handed Alicia his several pages of typewritten notes. She flipped through to check that each page was initialled, then started reading.

When she reached the last page, she recoiled in horror and looked at David and quoted his notes: "'Tell the cop in the blue station wagon with the *Baby on Board* sign in the back window that he might as well go for a doughnut'?"

"Why are you looking so shocked?" David asked. "I told you they saw you."

"When you said *you* I thought you meant us, the police. Not *me* specifically."

"Well … it had to be you. Their description matches exactly what you said you were driving. Although he did say *he* instead of *she*."

Oh, God. Did I blow this?

"Was there a guy with you?" David asked. "Or did someone else drive the car sometimes?"

"No. I was alone the whole time," she admitted.

"Then it was you who tipped them off," David said, sounding matter-of-fact. "We trusted you. What —"

The flash of headlights through the drapes alerted them that someone was coming down the driveway. The four of them exchanged glances.

Alicia speed-dialed Bradley as she peeked through the curtains. "A vehicle is driving up to the house. What's going on?"

"It's not one of us," Bradley said hurriedly. "We're parked at least three or four minutes away."

"Wouldn't make sense for the kidnappers to come here," Alicia said. "Hang on, it's parking out front. Christ, it's a marked police car! I'm going out. Stay on the line with me."

"What's happening?" Jia said in a panic. "Are they bringing Tommy home or — or ..." She couldn't finish her sentence.

Oh, please don't be a next-of-kin call. "Stay here," Alicia ordered, rushing out the door. "I'll find out what's going on."

Two uniformed officers were getting out of the patrol car. "Hello, are you Mrs. Chung?"

"Constable Alicia Munday, Major Crimes," she said, showing her identification.

"Looks like the left hand doesn't know what the right hand is doing," the officer replied. "We didn't know you were already here."

Alicia felt a lump in her throat so big that she didn't think she'd be able to talk. Then the words came out. "Why are you here?"

"You don't know?"

"No, I don't fucking know! Is it about Tommy?"

"Yes."

"Is he alive or dead, damn it?"

The officer exchanged a glance with his colleague. "Okay, take it easy. He's alive."

Oh, thank God.

"He's been admitted to Langley Memorial Hospital. All we know is that someone found him in the middle of the street all tied up. Apparently he was almost run over. He's in shock, but gave his name as Tommy Chung and said some men took him from his mom Wednesday afternoon. We're here to take his parents to the hospital."

"They're both inside. I'll take them myself."

"We were told Major Crimes is being called in to interview them when they arrive — but you already know?"

"Yes."

"So this really is a kidnapping? How come we weren't told?"

"I don't have time to explain." Alicia didn't wait for an answer as she ran back inside.

David and Jia were waiting inside the foyer. Their eyes desperately searched Alicia's face.

"He's safe!" she yelled jubilantly. "We've got him!"

They burst into tears. Alicia gave them a moment to collect themselves. "He was found tied up on some street. Apparently he's in shock and he was taken to Langley Memorial. I don't think either of you is in any condition to drive. Lend me your keys and I'll drive you there myself."

David immediately held his keys out.

"Alicia! Alicia!" a far-off voice sounded.

She'd forgotten that she was still on the line with Bradley. She put her phone back to her ear. "Did you hear?"

"Yes, he's been found and is at Langley Memorial!" Bradley replied.

"You got it! I'm taking David and Jia," Alicia said, giving them a thumbs-up. "We should be there in about thirty minutes."

"Good. I'll have Hawkins meet us there."

* * *

Hawkins was waiting when Alicia, David, and Jia rushed inside Emergency. His face was grave. The jubilation Alicia felt quickly evaporated.

"Where is he?" Jia asked excitedly. "I want to see him."

Hawkins paused as Bradley arrived after them. He turned to Jia. "Tommy's in surgery."

"Surgery? I thought he was in shock!" David yelled. "What's happened to him?"

Hawkins motioned for them to follow him to an alcove away from other people.

David grabbed him by the sleeve. "What's going on? Is he … Is he going to … Tell me!"

"He was found staggering down a street with his eyes and mouth duct-taped. His wrists were taped behind his back and, uh, his hands were in a plastic bag also taped to his wrists." Hawkins swallowed. "Inside the bag, his right hand was taped up in a fist. Four of his fingers have been chopped off."

"No!" Jia screamed.

"He's lost a lot of blood, but his life isn't in jeopardy," Hawkins hurried to say. "He'll survive."

Jia burst into tears. David put his arms around her and they consoled each other. Her eyes met Alicia's. "How could you let this happen to our little boy?" she moaned.

CHAPTER SEVEN

On a mid-May Monday morning, Alicia walked into the Major Crimes Unit and sat down.

"Hey, you're back," Bradley noted. "How was it? Are you officially a trained undercover operator?"

Alicia had been away for six weeks. "Yup, I made it. One of the toughest and most gruelling courses I've ever had. They worked us day and night. Hardly got any sleep. The course ended Friday, and I flew back from Halifax on Saturday."

"Welcome back. Although I expect I-HIT will scoop you up now so you won't be around, regardless."

"That's a possibility," Alicia replied.

The Integrated Homicide Investigation Team was part of the Major Crimes Section. Up until now there had been only one trained undercover operative in the entire office. That was Constable Barry Short. He was good at what he did, so he was seconded by I-HIT to work on priority cases. This resulted in his spending most of his time testifying in court, leaving their office shorthanded.

"Maybe it won't be so bad with two operators … providing I-HIT doesn't get you transferred over to their unit entirely."

"Maybe," Alicia responded.

"Speaking of I-HIT, did you hear Connie Crane got her third stripe?"

"I didn't know. So it's Sergeant Crane now. That's great! I'm happy for her."

"A bunch of promotions came through last week," Bradley said as he walked away.

Alicia entered Connie's office a minute later. "I hear congratulations are in order."

Connie smiled. "Thanks. You missed the party, but I'd be glad to buy you a beer."

"I'll hold you to it."

"How was the course?" Connie sang part of the *Secret Agent Man* theme song.

Alicia giggled. It was actually true; to protect the identity of undercover operatives, headquarters assigned them numbers to be used instead of their real names in all reports. "Yes, I'm officially an HQ number. A bona fide secret agent."

"Congrats to you, too! We'll catch up over that beer later in the week."

As Alicia turned to leave, Connie again started signing.

"Ooh, don't quit your day job, Connie," Alicia teased.

"You witch! There'll be no beer for you!" Connie said, grinning.

Back at her own desk Alicia nodded a polite hello to a colleague at the next desk who was talking on the phone, then pulled out a well-worn file box from under her desk and sifted through its contents.

It'll be two years tomorrow, and we're still no closer to solving it.

Alicia came to Tommy's statement. She knew it by heart. Not a day went by that she didn't think about it.

He'd been hog-tied with tape the whole time, including over his eyes and mouth. He guessed that he'd been driven for an hour or more in the van, including a long stretch of time without stopping, the only noise the sound of cars and trucks.

Highway 99, or maybe the Trans-Canada? Those are only two of several possibilities, she thought, asking the same questions she'd asked herself repeatedly until her brain begged for them to be expunged, if only temporarily.

Once they'd arrived at their destination, Tommy was led into a building and put inside a trunk — he'd remembered hearing a lock snap shut. He wasn't given any food or water. Nobody spoke to him, but he sometimes heard a dog barking. It sounded like a big dog. He'd lain there in his own urine and feces until he was taken out.

God, how could they have done what they did to an innocent eight-year-old kid? She went over it again in her mind. Blindfolded, he was led down a porch, across a yard and into another building. He was told to hold on to a bench, with his thumb underneath the surface. He remembered the sound of crunching bone and the pain that followed as he tried to scream. He'd obviously lost consciousness, because his next memory was of being back in the van. When it stopped, someone cut the tape from his ankles, then tossed him onto the road.

Forensics matched paint and scratch marks on the back of Jia's car to a white Ford cargo van that had been stolen and abandoned. The interior had also been torched, so Forensics found nothing that could identify the culprits.

Alicia had also obtained copies of security footage from closed-circuit television cameras in the numerous locations where David had been sent with the ransom. Thousands of licence plates that appeared in the footage were checked out, as well as hundreds of pedestrians. Some had criminal records, but those leads eventually came to dead ends. Some pedestrians — who didn't have criminal records — could be seen talking on cellphones. *Could they have been doing countersurveillance?* Most of them, too, were eventually cleared.

The unmarked station wagon she'd been driving was visible in some of the footage, though never close to where David was. Still, she cringed at the thought of having being spotted.

She appreciated the support Hawkins had given her. An internal investigation into the handling of the case had focused on possible ineptitude or overzealousness on her part, but Hawkins's report had made it clear that Alicia was an extremely forthright, honest officer who followed policy as if it were gospel. Furthermore, he stated that he'd had a bird's-eye view of all the surveillance vehicles and was absolutely certain that everyone had followed his orders explicitly. He also noted that the kidnappers had referred to the driver of the station wagon as male. Hawkins suggested that they had seen someone in a similar car and that Alicia was being falsely accused.

It was good of him to say this, but in all the camera footage there wasn't another car that looked like the one Alicia had been driving. *It had to be me. I know it ... and so do David and Jia.*

There was another issue that haunted Alicia. The kidnappers had told David they were making an example of him. *An example to whom? Are they planning on doing more kidnappings? Maybe they intend to put other victims in touch with David to find out what would happen if they went to the police?*

Alicia had hoped to make amends with David and Jia and tell them of her concern that the parents of other kidnapped kids might be coming to their door, but they had refused to talk to her or any other investigators.

Later she had been notified by Internal Affairs that the Chungs were suing the Force, and they had named her in particular. All investigators had then been ordered to stay clear of them.

Tap, tap, tap, tap. Tap, tap, tap, tap. Tap, tap, tap, tap. The noise repeated.

Alicia glared at her colleague. He was still holding the phone to his ear, but he appeared to be on hold; he was absentmindedly drumming his fingers on the desk.

"Cut that out!" Alicia snapped.

He looked at her in surprise.

"I can't focus with you doing that!" she added.

The sight of my own whole, unmutilated fingers makes me lose focus — I sure as heck don't need yours to remind me of my failure, too.

CHAPTER EIGHT

Jack Taggart was putting his lunch dishes in the dishwasher Monday afternoon when his doorbell rang. *Here we go. How ticked off will she be when she finds out?*

He limped to the front door and let in Laura Secord.

Both Jack and Laura were trained RCMP undercover operatives assigned to the Intelligence Unit in the headquarters building in Vancouver. Officially, Jack was Laura's boss, but the two of them together had looked death in the face too many times over the years to be simply boss and subordinate. The fact that they were both still alive was a direct result of how well each knew the other. Their closeness was rivaled only by their relationships with their spouses.

Part of their mandate was to develop high-level informants within organized crime factions, then pass on information to appropriate RCMP sections or other law enforcement agencies as they saw fit. Their informants were involved in a variety of criminal activities including, at times, murder.

It was a recent murder that Jack had been brooding about. While Laura had been away on holiday, a biker informant of theirs had committed a murder after Jack had covertly given him the nod to do so. Their informant had introduced Jack as a trusted associate to a gun smuggler by the name of Erich Vath. Jack was investigating a white supremacist group. Unfortunately, his cover got blown. Vath's death ensured their informant's safety.

Dealing with informants was a perpetual balancing act. They had to ensure that the information they received was more valuable than the crimes being committed by their informants. Protecting informants from discovery by criminals and police officers alike was a delicate matter. The trust their informants had in Jack and Laura was vital. Often, informants would introduce them to criminal associates as trusted friends. To this end, Jack and Laura rarely went to court or took part in arrests. Their job was to remain in the shadows whenever possible.

"Hey, welcome back!" Jack exclaimed as Laura stepped into the foyer. "You look tanned. And relaxed."

"I should be. Two weeks in Hawaii … it was wonderful!" She hugged him and gave him a kiss on the cheek. "You miss me?"

"Actually, to tell you the truth, I did," he replied.

"Oh? That sounded serious. Are you okay?"

"I took last week off. Felt like I needed to unwind."

"You, unwind? That has to be a first. Were you that hungover from celebrating your promotion?"

Laura's tone was joking, but he caught her look of suspicion. *Yeah, something happened. I'll get to it in a minute.*

He forced a smile. "Natasha and I did have an olive soup to celebrate. How about you?"

"It was too hot for martinis, but after you called, my hubby brought a pina colada down to the beach for me."

Jack grinned. "I figured you wouldn't mind my interrupting your holiday to tell you we've both been promoted."

Laura looked at him with curiosity. "I never asked — why the afternoon shift? I thought with our new high and mighty ranks we'd be working more day shifts."

She was fishing to find out what was wrong. *First things first.* "About your promotion. Congratulations, Corporal Secord. I can't think of anyone more deserving."

"Likewise, Sergeant Taggart," Secord replied, pretending to sound official. She smiled and looked past him into the house. "Is Natasha home?"

"No, she's working an early shift at the clinic. One of the other doctors is undergoing another round of chemo, so she's been filling in more than usual."

"That's too bad. How are the boys?"

"They're good. Looking forward to summer holidays in six weeks. I told them we'd go camping."

"Okay …" Laura raised an eyebrow.

"Come into the kitchen and I'll fill you in on what happened while you were gone."

Laura took off her shoes and followed Jack. "Hey, what's wrong with your leg? Did you slip and fall on a wayward olive pit?"

"Grab a seat," Jack said, pulling out a kitchen chair for himself. His sombre expression dried up any levity Laura had felt.

"What's going on, Jack? What happened?"

Jack grimaced. "The gun smuggling investigation you and I were working on went sideways."

"Sideways?"

"Remember my friend Ferg?"

"The U.S. Customs agent? Yes, we met the day before I left for Hawaii. I talked to him and his wife at the border for a couple of minutes. They seem like a nice couple."

"He was murdered."

"Oh, my God!" Laura's mouth gaped open. "How? What —"

"He was killed by the same gun smugglers who we were trying to identify."

Laura closed her eyes and put her hand to her face for a moment. When she lowered it, her eyes flashed anger. "When you called me, you said everything was okay! You told me the gun smugglers were arrested in the States."

"I didn't say that everything was okay. I said arrests had been made and the investigation was over."

"You should've told me!"

"I'm sorry. I thought about it, but I didn't want to ruin your holiday. There was nothing you could do."

Laura appeared to think about it, then took a deep breath and slowly exhaled. "So the people who murdered Ferg were all caught and arrested?"

"There were four bad guys in the States —"

"They were the ones supplying guns to Erich Vath in Canada?"

"Yes. Two of them died in a truck after trying to run over me. One of them was the man who shot Ferg, and the other was his adult son. The other two men were arrested. They were already wanted by the FBI for other murders."

"So is that how you hurt your leg, when these guys tried to run over you?"

"No, it happened earlier, when they opened up on me with an AR-15. I was in a lookout tower. I had to use my belt to slide down a guy wire and sort of crash-land. It tore the ligaments in my knee."

"You slid down a wire to escape from a lookout tower?" Laura exclaimed.

"This white supremacist guy had set up his own survivalist camp on top of a mountain in Washington state. Had security cameras and sensors all over the place, as well as a lookout tower."

"And you were there undercover."

"Yes."

"How'd you find out who they were and get in with them?"

"Our friend introduced me to Vath as a member of the club. Then Vath took me to the States and introduced me to his suppliers. He returned to Canada while his associates took me to this compound where their main cache of guns was stored."

Laura knew that by "our friend," Jack meant their informant, Lance Morgan, president of the Westside chapter of Satans Wrath Motorcycle Club in Vancouver. For safety concerns, they never used his real name in conversation.

"So our friend really came through for us," Laura noted.

"Yes … but later my cover got blown, and things got hot."

Laura was quiet for a moment. "I thought your voice sounded funny when you called to congratulate me. When you told me the gun suppliers were arrested, I presumed it was on your info. You didn't even tell me you were involved in a UC." When he didn't respond, she said, "I knew I shouldn't have gone on holiday before the investigation was over."

"Then you'd never get a holiday. We're always investigating something. Besides, it wouldn't have made any difference. Ferg still would've been killed."

Laura looked glum as she eyed Jack. "You okay?"

"I'm okay. It's Ferg's wife who's hurting." He glanced at his watch. "Come on, let's head to the office. This is too depressing to be rehashing."

"Do you know when the two new constables will be arriving?" Laura asked on their way out the door.

Jack shook his head. "No. Neither one has even bothered to call our office."

"They'll be of little use, from what I hear. It seems one of them is too obese to leave the office and the other is on continual medical leave for a bad back. They're being dumped on us out of spite." Laura sighed. Her reference was clear: their former boss, Quaile, had been transferred due to incompetence in his handling of a file Jack and Laura had worked on. Unfortunately, Quaile was now a chief superintendent in Staffing and doing his best to screw over their unit.

Jack shrugged. "That's life. We've always handled things on our own. That's not going to change."

"No, but it would've been nice to get some extra help," Laura lamented. "We can only do so much on our own."

"True." Jack placed his hand on Laura's shoulder. "Don't get in your car yet. There's something I need to tell you." She turned to face him. "Erich Vath was shot and killed while I was wrapping things up in the States."

"Okay … that's good, isn't it? He was supplying guns to our local gangs."

"A Walther PPK was left at the scene."

Surprise registered on Laura's face. "The same type of gun our friend once offered to give us."

"Nobody else knows that. When I got back from the States, Rose met me at the border to question me about the murder. I suggested a white supremacist could have been responsible, as it was Vath who introduced me to them."

Staff Sergeant Rose Wood was their boss. Jack liked her, and sometimes he felt the need to protect her from knowing things that could land her in trouble.

"Let's hope she trusts you enough to swallow that. If it was our friend who left his piece at the scene, he would have known we'd recognize it as his. And yet he didn't bother trying to hide it." Laura paused. "You gave him the green light to do it, didn't you?"

Jack frowned. "I taught you better than to ask questions like that."

"It wasn't a question. I was only thinking out loud."

"Learn to keep some thoughts to yourself." He paused. "There was an element of risk in our friend introducing me to Vath, so I told him that if I nailed whoever killed Ferg, he'd be cut free. The plan was that once I discovered who killed Ferg, I'd tip off the U.S. My true identity would never be known. But then my cover got blown. If Vath blabbed about me — which he definitely would have done once he heard who I was — our friend would've been in jeopardy. I gave him my word that I'd protect him to the end."

"The end of Vath," Laura muttered.

"I felt that the deal I struck with him was worth it to catch whoever murdered Ferg."

Laura bit her lower lip. "You don't have to convince me."

"Which is why I've got us working an afternoon shift. We'll meet up with him this evening after he finishes work and say our farewells."

"Are you going to mention that we know he whacked Vath?"

Jack thought for a moment. "We'll play that by ear. He might want reassurance."

Laura mulled it over, then made a face. "Of course I-HIT will think you had something to do with it."

"Yup." Jack paused. "Connie got promoted, too, while you were away."

Laura's face brightened. "Sergeant Crane of the Integrated Homicide Investigation Team. That has a nice ring to it." She smiled. "It's about time. She deserves it."

"For sure. She's a good investigator — which is why I spoke to you outside."

Laura looked sharply at Jack, then glanced at his house. "Think you have a bug infestation?"

"Wouldn't be the first time."

CHAPTER NINE

Assistant Commissioner Irene Lexton was the criminal operations officer in charge of the Pacific region and worked out of the RCMP headquarters building in Vancouver. Her impeccable record as a police officer, coupled with her sharp mind, saw her excel rapidly over her peers. She had worked in I-HIT before doing a stint in Ottawa, where she had continued to climb the corporate ladder. Her latest promotion three months ago had resulted in her return to British Columbia. This time, because of her rank, she carried a mighty sword.

During her lunch hour she'd overheard Chief Superintendent Quaile telling another officer that an overly obese member who he'd scheduled to be transferred into the Intelligence Unit had just put in her papers to quit. Then Quaile had lowered his voice to make some comment before laughing. The other officer had looked disgusted and turned away, leading Lexton to suspect that

Quaile had said something crass or otherwise inappropriate. Quaile hadn't seemed to notice the other officer's response. *Likely lost in his own self-inflated ego.*

Quaile's mention of the Intelligence Unit had caused Lexton to reflect on another thorn in her side. A thorn by the name of Jack Taggart. During her days in I-HIT she'd heard many rumours and suppositions about him, so it was with particular interest that, after her return to B.C., she read an intelligence report Taggart had submitted which discussed the circumstances surrounding the unexpected resignation of her predecessor, Assistant Commissioner Mortimer.

The report mentioned the disappearance of Purvis Evans, the national president of Satans Wrath who had threatened Taggart's family. His disappearance and presumed death had fallen on the same day that a Satans Wrath hit team was apprehended outside Mortimer's house. The report said that an informant believed that Evans had ordered a hit on Mortimer to impress some high-level Russian cocaine traffickers. Taggart theorized that the capture of the hit team had spurred the Russians to kill Evans in order to sever any connection between them.

What wasn't in the report was an old operational plan that Mortimer had retained, but not approved. His handwritten scrawl on the back of the report noted a time and date when Taggart was ordered to turn over all his informants and never work undercover again. Six weeks later a hit team was waiting outside Mortimer's house.

And so Lexton had started her own file on Taggart. Now she went to the safe in her office and took out the file folder. Taggart had worked on more than a dozen cases in which criminals were killed. Too many to be coincidental.

She felt frustrated as she perused the reports. She'd amassed reports of numerous incidents from his past; clearly he was no stranger to Internal Affairs and Anti-Corruption investigations. Some of them had included surveillance and wiretaps, yet nothing had ever been uncovered to indicate he was involved in anything illegal or improper. *Doesn't mean you're not dirty. Just that you've never been caught.*

One document caught her eye: Project Birds of a Feather. U.S. authorities had planted a bug in the car of a suspected rogue agent and conspired with Ottawa to have the man work with Taggart on an investigation. Somehow Taggart's intuition had kicked in, and he warned the agent just as he'd been about to say something incriminating. *No doubt Taggart refrains from saying anything incriminating inside any vehicle or building.*

Lexton reread the notes she'd made a week previous concerning Taggart's most recent investigation, involving a white supremacist group involved in gun smuggling.

Taggart's informant had introduced him to Erich Vath, the white supremacists' Canadian contact. Vath, in turn, introduced Taggart to the supremacists. One week ago, Vath had been murdered within hours of Taggart's cover being blown.

Taggart had been in the States taking part in the arrests when the murder took place, but Lexton was betting that his informant had murdered Vath to protect himself. And if the murderer was the informant, how could he have known he was in danger — unless Taggart told him? *The*

*informant doing it on his own is one thing, but if Taggart
tipped him off, we're talking conspiracy to commit murder.*

On the day of Vath's murder, Lexton had felt that she
was in a delicate situation. She didn't want to risk exposing the informant to I-HIT in case he was innocent. At
the same time, she couldn't drop her suspicions, so she'd
chosen another route and ordered Internal Affairs to discreetly investigate whether there had been any communication between Taggart and his informant during the time
of the arrests in the States and Vath's murder.

That had been a week ago. She reached for her phone
and called Superintendent Weicker in Internal Affairs.
What have you got?

"I was about to call you," Weicker stated. "We've
obtained phone tolls on Taggart's phone for the night Vath
was shot and killed."

"And?"

"He made two calls. Both were from an area in
Washington several hours from the border. His first call
was made at three fifteen a.m. to his residence. It lasted for
slightly less than four minutes."

"So he called his wife," Lexton concluded. "What was
the other call?"

"He placed his second call at three nineteen a.m. to
Staff Sergeant Rose Wood. That call was also short."

"What about the informant? Were you able to trace
any calls to his residence?"

"Yes, at three fifty-five a.m. a call was placed to the
informant's house from a disposable mobile phone.
That call was less than a minute long and came from a
residential area in Burnaby, but we couldn't pin it to any

particular house. I suspect it was made from a vehicle or outside a house."

"Find out how far the location is from Taggart's house."

"Already did. It's about a twelve-minute drive. From Staff Wood's apartment the location is about fifteen minutes, but, uh, lots of members live in that area. From my own house I could be there in under ten minutes."

"You're not the person I'm interested in. Perhaps Taggart's wife placed the call. Have you pulled any available CCTV footage from gas stations and the like to see if you can spot a car belonging to the Taggarts?"

"Not yet. The area is residential, so I doubt there'd be any."

"Double check. Also check from the other end. Try and find out if the informant left his house."

"Concerning Staff Wood, do you want us to look at her? Good chance that her own apartment building has CCTV … but you asked that this be discreet. If we pull that kind of footage I can't guarantee she won't find out."

Lexton paused. "Yes, I want you to look at her, as well, but don't risk getting images from the apartment security. I doubt we'd have enough to support a warrant, anyway. I don't want the Intelligence Unit to suspect they're being looked at. I'm sure I-HIT will be throwing a few questions their way, but that's par for the course and nothing they won't expect."

"I understand."

Lexton gazed at her file after ending the call. Perhaps Sergeant Taggart was too smart to get caught through wiretaps and telephone records. She smiled grimly. *But Chief Superintendent Quaile despises you and the section. Time for him and me to have a chat.*

CHAPTER TEN

Quaile faked a smile as Lexton strode into his office and took a seat in front of his desk. *What the hell does she want? Surely she couldn't have heard that joke I made from where —*

"Did I hear you correctly at lunchtime?" Lexton asked.

Shit! She did hear.

"That the member who was to be transferred into the Intelligence Unit is quitting?" she continued.

"Oh!" He swallowed. "Uh, yes, she's put in her papers."

"Has a replacement been selected yet?"

"No … and we'll need two replacements. The other constable who was scheduled is being ousted from the Force due to medical problems."

Lexton was lost in thought for a moment. Then she made eye contact. "This conversation we're having stays between the two of us, do you understand?"

"Uh, yes … certainly."

"I have something of an interest in the goings-on of the Intelligence Unit." Her tone of voice belied her suspicion.

Goings-on? They're a bunch of idiots who'd rather waste their time catching criminals than be promoted. It's as if they don't respect rank.

"I'd like to see someone known for their integrity transferred into the unit," Lexton said firmly.

"Integrity?" Quaile asked.

"Someone who wouldn't remain silent if they witnessed or had knowledge of any miscarriage of justice. Someone with the guts to report it to a higher rank."

She wants a spy! Talk about making my day!

"Don't get me wrong," Lexton added, "I'm not looking to ask anyone to be an informer, but I'd like someone who'll be completely honest with me. Someone with the moral fibre to do the right thing, should a difficult situation arise."

"May I ask, is there a specific incident you're concerned about?"

"I'd call it more of a trend. A lot of good work has come out of the Intelligence Unit, but it appears to me that there've been an inordinate amount of murders connected to their files." Lexton grimaced. "Many are written off as coincidental to their investigations, but it's left me feeling somewhat uncomfortable."

Quaile leaned forward on his desk. "That's how I felt when I was running the section! Nobody listened to me when I said it needed to be cleaned out. It's the reason I finally left."

"I heard why you left," Lexton said icily.

"Oh, well, there was a misunderstanding with one file, but —"

"I'd like the replacement to be someone of high intelligence who is respected and trusted by their bosses. Preferably someone with undercover training, as they'll be more likely to be accepted with that credential."

Undercover training? Taggart and Secord are the only two undercover operators in the section. So they're the ones you don't trust! He made a conscious effort to hide his smirk.

"Think you could fill that order?"

"And two such people would be better?"

"Yes, it would."

"Give me a week. I'll see what I can come up with."

"I'm sure you will," Lexton replied, then left.

CHAPTER ELEVEN

Jack and Laura went into Rose's office to say hello. Their conversation was light. Rose congratulated Laura on her promotion, and eventually the discussion came around to trying to make room for the two additional constables the unit was scheduled to receive.

"Talk is the new headquarters building out in Surrey will be finished by the end of this year," Rose noted. "There'll be plenty of room then. Combining most of us under one roof will make things easier and more cost-effective."

"I don't know if having I-HIT under the same roof as us will be a good thing or not," Jack said facetiously. "Although I guess it will be easier for them to round up their suspects for lineups."

Rose didn't appear to be amused. "Speaking of, I got a call from Connie in I-HIT this morning asking when you'd be in. She wants to talk to you about Erich Vath."

"Gee, I don't know what more I could tell her that I hadn't already told you," Jack replied. "If I were Connie, I'd be looking to find out if any white supremacists crossed into Canada. Then again, I suppose the killer could be one of the ones up here."

"Gee, maybe she doesn't believe you," Rose retorted sarcastically.

Meaning that you didn't either when I tossed out that group as potential suspects.

"I had the distinct impression that she wants to talk to you in person," she added flatly.

Sure, she wants to read my body language to see if I'm lying.

Jack and Laura returned to their own desks, which butted up to each other in an office down the hall from Rose. They'd barely sat down when they had a visitor.

"Hello, Sergeant Taggart and Corporal Secord!"

"Well, hello to you, too, Sergeant Crane," Jack responded as he and Laura rose from their chairs.

Laura was first around her desk to shake Connie's hand. "Congratulations, Connie. You really deserve it."

"Back at ya, Laura," Connie replied. She looked at Jack. "You, I'm not so sure about ... but I'll shake your hand, regardless."

Jack gave a lopsided smile as he shook her hand. "Hey, haven't we made you look good over the years? I'm sure that's why you got your third hook."

"Unsolved murders don't make me look good," Connie retorted.

"Well ... look at it as job security," Jack replied.

Connie rolled a chair over to their desks as Jack and Laura sat back down. She then smiled at Jack. "There's one good thing: I'm senior to you. My promotion came out on the Friday and yours wasn't until Monday."

"That's good. If we do something together and any-thing goes wrong, it's the senior member who gets called up on the carpet."

Connie shook her head. "You're an asshole, you know that?"

"So I've been told." Jack paused. "What can we do for you?" *Damn it. Don't pretend you don't know why she's here. She knows Rose would've said she was coming.* "I pre-sume it's about Vath," he added quickly, "but I don't know how else we can help."

Connie studied his face. "Do you really think someone from the U.S. killed him?"

"It's logical, considering he introduced me into the group down there." *Okay, her gaze is on my hands. Palms toward her, portraying innocence. Then again, she knows I've also had interrogation training.*

Sure enough, she sighed. "Let's quit playing games."

Wish it were a game.

"How did you meet Vath and get him to introduce you to his connections in the States?"

"It was arranged through an informant."

"Once your cover was blown in the U.S., could your informant have killed Vath to protect himself?"

"He could have, but how could he have found out? There were only a couple of hours between my cover being blown and Vath's murder."

"Six hours," Connie stated.

"Okay, six, but there's no way my guy could have known." *Not if I hadn't had Natasha leave our house and call him on a burner phone.*

"Someone could have called him," Connie said, lock-ing eyes with Jack.

"Check my phone tolls," Jack replied. "It wasn't me."

"I already did."

Thought so. "Guess I can't get angry at you for being thorough. It's what I respect about you. However, even if my informant did find out my cover was blown, I don't think he'd have been worried."

"Bullshit. He introduced you ... which means he had to vouch for you."

"My informant is with Satans Wrath. It wouldn't be necessary for him to kill Vath. Nobody would take Vath's word over my informant's." *Nobody except Whiskey Jake, another chapter president who knows enough that he'd likely clue in.* "Not only that, Vath would have been too scared to point fingers, anyway, because of who my informant is. He wouldn't have been that stupid." *Actually, he would. The guy was as dumb as they come.*

"Okay, so let me clear your informant. Have him come in and take a polygraph."

"Sorry, Connie. That'd never happen. He'd tell you to take a hike. It's the biker code. His own guys would do a number on him if he co-operated with the police, because it would set a bad precedent for other bikers down the road."

"I'll bet you could convince him. Nobody would need to know."

"There's no way he'd go for it. Not only that, he's not an informant anymore. I told him we were square after he introduced me to Vath."

"Isn't that convenient," Connie replied skeptically.

Jack felt his phone vibrate — a perfect excuse. "Are we done? I have to take this call."

Connie nodded as Jack answered.

"So, I hear things worked out really well for you in the States … except for them finding out you were a cop," Lance stated.

Jack recognized his informant's voice and pressed the receiver tighter to his ear as he eyed Connie. *Come on, Connie. Get up and go, will you?* "Yes, it turned out okay."

"I know you said we're done, but I'd like to meet with you one last time to say goodbye and make sure there isn't any unfinished business."

"Hang on a sec." Jack made eye contact with Connie. "I thought we were done. Is there anything else?"

Connie locked eyes with Jack a moment, then said, "So if he's not your informant anymore, you won't care if he gets arrested. Right?"

"Be my guest. I doubt I'll ever see or hear from him again."

"All right … so be it," Connie said, then left.

"I'm back," Jack said into the phone.

"Were you talking about me?"

"Yes."

"You don't give a shit if I'm busted?"

"It's a moot point. You haven't done anything to get busted for. At least as far as I know."

"Yeah … right." Lance paused. "I'm retiring, by the way."

"I thought you might be," Jack replied. "I'll see if I can buy you a watch, paint it gold, and get it engraved on the back to thank you for all your help. Maybe even find a little Mountie emblem to stick on it."

"You know where you can stick that," Lance replied, "but we should meet and talk face to face."

"This sounds grave. What time?"

* * *

At 8:00 p.m., Jack and Laura saw Lance waiting up ahead in the cemetery.

"With him cut loose we'll be in the dark when it comes to Satans Wrath," Laura noted.

"I know, but he's paid his dues. He's been honourable, and he's more than stuck his neck out."

"That's for sure," Laura agreed.

"Not to mention, with his help we've done a number on the club, as far as British Columbia goes. It'll take time for them to sort things out. Hopefully by the time they do, we'll have a new source."

"I'm going to miss him in a way," Laura added.

"He's been an easy guy to handle. Always straight up with us."

"Easy except for the occasional murder."

"Now you're being picky."

"Hey, Laura, where'd you find the sun?" Lance asked as they neared.

"Hawaii," she replied.

"You're really brown. Show me your tan line," he said, pretending to attempt to look down her blouse. "Bet them headlights really stand out."

"Not as much as your nuts will after I kick them," Laura replied.

Lance guffawed and stepped back.

"Laura and I were discussing something interesting," Jack said. "A Walther PPK was found at the scene were Vath was murdered."

"Oh?" Lance said, feigning surprise. "Sounds professional. You wouldn't want to get caught with the murder weapon." He pinched his eyebrows together as if thinking. "You think I-HIT will bring James Bond in for questioning?"

"I-HIT are good at what they do," Jack cautioned. "Don't underestimate them."

Lance grew serious as he looked in their faces. "I know I can trust the both of you and that you'd never burn me. You've also told me before that I'm not immune from other cops. Is I-HIT focused on me, or am I one of many suspects?"

"You're one of many," Jack stated. "If I didn't have an alibi, they'd probably suspect me."

"Right, an alibi," Lance said, frowning. "Do you think they'd believe I was home in bed with my wife?"

"Not if they got your vehicle on a street camera going to and coming back from where Vath was shot."

"Did they?"

"I've no idea."

"I tried to be careful about that, but it was a long way to go. What about your wife?" Lance asked.

"Natasha stuck to residential streets. I'm fairly certain there weren't any cameras on her route."

"You actually think I-HIT would give you the hairy eyeball, too?"

"Last Monday when I came back from the States, I was questioned briefly by my boss. I reminded her that Vath was a white supremacist and that the people he'd introduced me to were all white supremacists. I suggested that one of them might've done the hit in retaliation."

"So they're not looking at me too seriously?"

"I didn't say that. I-HIT wanted to interview you. I said you'd refuse like any decent biker, but if they do think they have something on you, they'll bring you in. If they question you about a specific date or street you might've been on, don't deny it, but perhaps you won't remember the details, because some days you're out doing club business before you go to work and some days you're not."

"Actually, that's true," Lance replied.

"We know."

Lance's eyebrows furrowed, no doubt wondering how much they did know about him.

Jack cleared his throat. "If they ask who you might have met, I'd say it isn't any of their business. Or that you were finalizing club rides or charity runs or something and can't remember who you spoke to. They know you're a chapter president. That's an answer they'd expect even if you weren't guilty of anything."

"Gotcha. Enough said. Thanks."

"So you're finally retiring," Jack noted.

"First Saturday in June. The boys will be puttin' on a bash for me."

"Have you moved your money out of that account in the Caymans?"

"Not yet. I wanted to make sure I could do it without pissing you off. Also don't want to raise any suspicions from Whiskey Jake, seeing as he and I were laundering together."

"Like I asked Natasha to tell you last week on the phone, you and I are even. As far as I'm concerned, you can go ahead. Tell Whiskey Jake whatever story you want. You're retiring. Taking your money out now would make sense to him. The sooner, the better."

Lance raised his eyebrow. "Which will leave Whiskey Jake's account at the bank by itself. You'll still have evidence on him if you ever want to use it."

"I know."

"Are you thinking of replacing me with him?"

"Wouldn't that jeopardize you?"

"It would if Whiskey Jake found out my banking information had been discovered along with his. Especially considering all the busts I've given you since then. He'd know that I ratted. Especially if I transferred out my money before you talked to him."

"Exactly, so don't worry about it. We told you we'd protect you."

"Yeah, I know."

"Of course, if you get run over by a truck or something, then I'll approach him."

Lance eyed him suspiciously. "It better not be you driving, if I do."

Jack chuckled. "Enjoy your retirement."

"Thanks, I will." Lance looked uncomfortable, then stuck out his hand. "You're the only two cops I've ever wanted to shake hands with."

"Yeah, okay," Jack said, "but no kissing."

Jack and Laura shook hands with him, then Lance walked away.

Jack waited a moment, then hollered, "Don't forget to keep an eye on your rear-view mirror!"

"Fuck, I don't need a rear-view mirror anymore," Lance yelled back without turning around. "I'm done with all this bullshit!"

I-HIT might disagree with you.

CHAPTER TWELVE

Late the following morning, Rose approached Jack and Laura at their desks. "Possibly some good news," she said. "Lexton gave me a call and said that the two constables who were transferred to our unit aren't coming. One is quitting and the other is being terminated for medical reasons."

"I bet Quaile is scraping through the bottom of the barrel now," Jack replied pessimistically.

"Not if he doesn't want to piss Lexton off. She told me that she met with him and made it clear that our unit is important to her and she expects qualified replacements."

Jack could feel his mood brighten. "That sounds promising."

"Hopefully he'll listen to her," Laura added.

"I'm sure he will," Rose replied. "No doubt he's still squirming over getting caught trying to screw Jack out of his promotion."

Laura looked at Jack. "That was nasty of him."

"He's vindictive," Jack replied, "but I agree with Rose. He's a sycophant who'll go out of his way to curry favour. My only concern is that I doubt he has the cerebral ability to identify truly qualified members."

"Maybe he'll let Lexton peruse his selection," Rose suggested.

"Any idea on a time frame?" Laura asked.

"I expect it'll be soon," Rose replied. "Before summer is over, I think."

"Guess we better keep our fingers crossed," Jack said.

"So what are you two up to?" Rose asked. "Back to busting bikers?"

Jack leaned back in his chair and stretched his arms. "I cut loose our only source in Satans Wrath after he introduced me to Vath."

"So you're in the market for a new source. Anyone in mind?"

"Not yet. Laura and I need to do a little fishing before we decide who to work on. We got quite a few names from our ... old friend these last few months. Dealers, money movers, that sort of thing. At this stage we've got lots to do before selecting the best target."

* * *

Alicia Munday was pleased to get the call from Inspector Crimmins saying that he and Inspector Dyck wished to speak to her. Crimmins worked in Major Crimes, but Dyck worked on the I-HIT side of the office. She hurried to Crimmins's office, certain she knew what the meeting was about.

Now that I've passed the UC course, they'll want me in I-HIT with Connie. Perfect!

She sat down beside Dyck in front of Crimmins's desk. He stared at her briefly. Was he sizing her up?

"How would you feel about accepting a transfer into the Intelligence Unit?" he asked.

"The Intelligence Unit?" Alicia blurted. "I was thinking you'd want me to go over to I-HIT," she added, giving Dyck a quick glance.

"Believe me, I'd be happy to see you come over to our side," Dyck stated. "You have a stellar reputation. But first, listen to what we have to say."

"I received a call this morning from Staffing," Crimmins said. "They noted that you had the UC course and asked about you. I will say that you couldn't have received a higher recommendation from me."

"Thank you, sir, but ... you want me transferred?"

Crimmins exchanged a smile with Dyck. "No, on the contrary. You're an exceptionally dedicated, hard-working member. I told them that. I also told them that you have a reputation for being completely honest and going by the book, traits they were also interested in."

Then why do you want me to leave?

"You look a little dubious," Crimmins continued, "but let me assure you that the praise I passed along to Staffing was sincere. You're the type of officer I like to see in Major Crimes ... but I have to consider what is best for you and for the Force. In my opinion, you stand out as having the potential to go far. I can easily picture you having an important leadership role someday. With that in mind, I think it's in your best interest to have a background that's diverse in experience. Major Crimes and I-HIT aren't really all that different when it comes to experience."

"I see." *I don't even know what the Intelligence Unit does.*

"As much as I'd like to see you in I-HIT, I have to concur that a stint in the Intelligence Unit would be to your advantage down the road," Dyck added.

"Oh." Alicia wasn't sure whether she should be happy that she was being groomed to become a commissioned officer or sorry that she wouldn't be going to I-HIT.

"I was told that I could give you twenty-four hours to think it over, if you like," Crimmins said.

"I'm not quite sure what they do in there," Alicia ventured.

"With your new credentials as an undercover operative, I imagine you'd be working under Corporal Secord and Sergeant Taggart," Dyck stated. "I'm sure either one of them could provide you with an overview of what they do. Give them a call."

Taggart. She'd heard rumours both good and bad about him. *Come to think of it, Connie's mentioned his name more than once.* "Sir, I'd like to think about it for a day."

"No problem. It's your decision."

Alicia hurried over to Connie's office. "You got time to talk?" she asked. "It's sort of urgent."

Connie raised an eyebrow and gestured for Alicia to take a seat.

Alicia closed the door after her and told Connie about Crimmins's offer.

"Son of a bitch," Connie blurted, shaking her head when Alicia had finished.

"What? You don't think I should accept? You've worked with Taggart, right?"

Connie held up her hand for Alicia to slow down. "Give me a moment." She rubbed her temples. "Okay, first off, I know Taggart and Secord really well. I've had a lot of cases where they were involved. Cases that I'd never have solved without their input."

"So they're good? I've heard rumours that —"

"I didn't say they were good. I said they solve cases. The problem is, they play fast and loose with the rules."

"Rules? You mean Force policy?"

"Force policy? Christ, I wish that's all it was. No, I mean like statutes under the Criminal Code. I'm currently investigating the murder of a gun smuggler who I'm sure was killed because of Taggart."

"You think Taggart murdered him?" Alicia was astounded.

"No, but I think he gave the go-ahead. I suspect his informant did it, to protect himself from being found out."

"I see."

"It's stuff like that I have trouble with. There are numerous other incidents. Sometimes the brass even goes along with it. They call it 'the big picture' — which usually means that I don't get to see all of that picture."

"That actually sounds kind of interesting."

"Well, from what I've glimpsed, it isn't always pretty, especially when it comes to Taggart."

"Yet you say he and Secord have solved a lot of cases for you?"

"Yeah … to be honest, sometimes I don't know what to think about him. There're times I'd like to kiss him and times I'd like to shoot him."

"You're really not helping with this decision."

Connie made a face. "I can tell you one thing. Working with those two, you sure as hell would get the diverse experience they talked about."

"Maybe it'd be a good thing for me to learn about this big picture," Alicia suggested.

Connie looked thoughtful. "Staffing specifically said they were looking for someone who goes by the book?"

Alicia shrugged. "Inspector Crimmins mentioned they were interested in those traits. I presume there's concern about members being corrupted when working on organized crime."

Connie's eyes narrowed slightly. "Maybe you're being offered your first UC assignment."

"Do they do a lot of that over there?"

"Uh, that's —"

"I hope so. It really does sound interesting. And it probably would be a good career move."

"Sounds like you've decided to take the job."

"I think I will."

Connie nodded. "Good luck."

"Thanks."

Alicia rose to leave. "Listen," Connie said, "when something comes up that you're not sure about ... or that makes you uncomfortable, don't hesitate to give me a call if you want any advice. Nobody needs to know."

"When something comes up?" Alicia smiled. "You mean *if* something comes up."

"No, I mean when. With Jack, there's always something."

CHAPTER THIRTEEN

Two weeks later, Rose breezed into Jack and Laura's office, a smile on her face that said something was up.

"Why are you so happy?" Jack asked. "If you've been spiking your morning coffee with Baileys, how about sharing?"

"Lexton called. I know who one of our new constables will be."

"From the look on your face I presume it's a better choice than either of the last two," Laura noted.

"Sounds like it. Her name is Alicia Munday. She starts in a month. Lexton said she completed the undercover course recently."

"Never heard of her," Laura responded, then looked at Jack.

"Is she from the Major Crimes Unit?" Jack asked.

"Yes, do you know her?"

"No, but I've seen her. She stands out. Young, I'd say mid to late twenties. Long auburn hair ... very attractive. Bet her looks make it easy for her to meet and con the bad guys."

"She sounds promising," said Laura.

"Yes ... but MCU needs operators, too," Rose stated, "which made me wonder."

"They've only had one up to now," Jack said. "Barry Short. A really good guy, but from what I hear, he's run off his feet."

"Exactly," said Rose. "So I called Inspector Crimmins in MCU and asked him why they were pawning her off on us."

"And?" Jack prodded.

"He had nothing but great things to say about her. He said she's a real go-getter, single, spends most of her days off at work. He thinks she'll be commissioned some day, and he wants her to gain experience in different areas."

"Can't believe I'm agreeing with one of the white shirts," Jack replied, "but it'd be nice to have a commissioned officer with field experience, not some pencil-pusher out of Ottawa." He paused. "No idea about the other candidate yet?"

"Lexton said they're still looking. She hinted that with the type of work coming out of our unit, she'd prefer someone with undercover experience."

"That'd be perfect," Jack replied.

"Perfect?" said Rose. "Hell, I've a hard enough time with the two of you. Four would be a disaster!"

Jack and Laura smiled as Rose left.

"Give Munday a call," Jack said, "and welcome her to the section."

"A friendly little girl-to-girl chat?"

"Exactly."

"In other words, check her out and see if I can get a feeling of what she's like," Laura said knowingly. She reached for her phone.

Jack smiled at how well he and Laura knew each other and what close friends they'd become. He busied himself with administrative work while Laura was on the phone.

A few minutes later, Laura ended the call and smiled.

"Well?" he asked.

"You're right, she is young, but she sounds really eager. I told her we often work nights and weekends, and that didn't faze her. She asked a lot of good questions about what we do." Laura paused, then added, "She said she wants to learn all about 'the big picture.'"

"She's been talking to Connie."

"Yes, she told me Connie is a friend of hers and she asked her about us."

"Can't blame her, although I'm surprised Connie didn't talk her out of it."

"I get the feeling that Munday is going places. I don't think she'd let Connie slow her down."

"Sounds great."

"Now if our second constable has undercover experience, too, we'll be a force to be reckoned with," Laura said lightheartedly.

Jack grinned back. "If the new people are anything like us, what could possibly go wrong?"

CHAPTER FOURTEEN

Over the next few weeks Jack and Laura did a great deal of surveillance on the local Satans Wrath prospects.

Late afternoon on the third Monday in June, they discovered exactly how eager Alicia was to start work. When she found out over the phone that Laura and Jack were working afternoon shifts, she asked if she could work with them in the evenings, as her last seven shifts in MCU were all day shifts. Laura agreed, explaining that they'd likely be doing surveillance on some bikers.

At 6:00 p.m. Jack and Laura welcomed Alicia to their office. Jack was glad to see that she'd changed out of dress clothes into jeans and a T-shirt.

There was little room in the office to start with, but there was even less now that they'd brought in an additional desk and chair. They placed Alicia's desk along the sides of Jack and Laura's butted-up desks so that the three of them could easily talk and pass correspondence back and forth.

"Kind of cramped," Alicia noted, squeezing past a filing cabinet to sit down.

"We like to think of it as cozy," Laura said.

Alicia checked out her desk drawers before looking up. "So, what are we up to?"

"Tonight we're working on him," Jack said, sliding a surveillance photograph across his desk onto hers. "His name is Buster Linquist, and he's a prospect for Satans Wrath. His address is on the back of the photo."

Alicia flipped it over. "Out in Surrey," she noted. "Not all that far from MCU."

"Are you familiar with biker terminology?" Laura asked.

"A little. A prospect is like a probationary member, sometimes called a striker. Usually stuck doing the dirty work."

"You've got it," Jack replied. "You can identify them by the fact that they wear only the bottom portion of the club insignia on their backs. I'd like to see what Buster's up to. The guy I'm really after, though, is him."

Alicia accepted the next photograph Jack handed her.

"His name is Buck Zabat. He received his full patch in the club a year and a half ago and was promptly made a member of their hit squad. I don't think the hit squad is active at the moment, but he's someone I want to nail real bad."

"Because he's a member of their hit squad?"

"No, because he murdered an informant of mine — his father."

"His father!" Alicia's jaw slackened as she stared at the photo again.

"His father, Damien Zabat, was the national president of the club. He retired the same day Buck was made a full member," Jack said gravely. "Five days later Buck found out that Damien was my informant and put a bullet through his brain."

"How'd Buck find out?" Alicia asked.

Jack glanced at Laura. "Okay, before I tell you that, let me explain that coming into our unit means you're receiving a higher security clearance. Whether you know it or not, your background has recently been rescreened."

"I didn't know that," Alicia responded. "I thought I was already top secret."

"You were TS," Jack said. "But there's a level above that: SA."

"Special access," Laura explained.

"That's what allows you to access that bigger picture you've heard about," Jack said. "It also means that whatever you learn cannot leave this office without my consent. You're not allowed to tell anyone."

"Like your friend Connie, for example," Laura said.

"Or any of the inspectors over there," added Jack.

"Even an inspector won't have my clearance?" Alicia looked amused.

"Most commissioned officers aren't cleared for what you're about to see. Certain things are strictly on a need-to-know basis, and for most people, there's no reason for them to know."

Alicia looked at them in turn. "Holy shit, what do you do in here?"

"Part of our goal is to turn high-level criminals into informants," Jack replied. "One good informant in an organization is worth more than fifty cops on the outside peering in, not knowing what's going on."

"So how do you go about it? Offer them money?"

"We would if that worked, but a lot of the time they make more money from criminal enterprise than we could hope to offer."

"So you need to catch them doing something and then turn them," Alicia said.

"Generally that's how it works," Jack replied.

"Sounds relatively simple."

"Not as simple as you'd think," said Laura. "Jack has an expression: you don't catch sewer rats with church mice. Sometimes we have informants actively committing serious crimes, such as murder, yet we let them go because we have a greater objective."

"A criminal informant who belongs to an organization can't suddenly go straight, because everyone would clue in that they're working for the police," Jack added. "They have to continue their criminal activities."

Alicia was wide-eyed. "You really let them get away with murder?"

"Sometimes," Laura replied. "We make it clear to them that we won't bust them or burn them on things they tell us about, but at the same time, they know they're not immune from being caught by someone else."

"It's hard to grasp what could be more serious than murder," Alicia said.

"How about letting someone off for one murder in order to arrest someone who has committed multiple murders? Or allowing someone who murdered a drug trafficker to walk in exchange for someone who murdered an innocent person during a robbery?" Jack asked. "To me, not all murders are the same."

Alicia seemed to be thinking about it.

"So you see, it may not be as simple as you imagine," Laura said. "You have to consider the consequences of your actions carefully along with whatever guidance you provide your informants. Sometimes we're making life-and-death decisions."

"Which brings me back to your question about Buck Zabat and how he found out his father was our informant," Jack said.

"Yes, how? I'd also like to know what you used to turn the national president of Satans Wrath to be your informant."

"I'll show you," Jack said, unlocking a filing cabinet. He retrieved a USB flash drive, stuck it in his laptop, and opened the video that was stored on it. The shock on Alicia's face was obvious as she watched. The video showed Buck Zabat beating a man to death.

"Who gave you this?" she asked.

"We were outside the victim's window," Laura said. "Jack recorded the video."

"You took it yourselves? You didn't stop it?" Alicia looked appalled.

"The victim was the leader of a gang of street thugs," Jack replied. "We thought he was only going to get a beating, which I think is what Buck intended. The death was unexpected."

"Meaning that if he was convicted, he'd receive a lighter sentence," Laura said.

"If he was convicted," Alicia repeated slowly, thinking it. "Defence would go over your grounds for being there. Maybe have the video ruled inadmissible."

"Possibly. We believed that Satans Wrath was opening up a new cocaine distribution network into Europe. That was what we were after."

"Why didn't you turn Buck into the informant?"

"I knew he was too brainwashed to turn," Jack explained. "And he may not even have known about the European venture, as it would have been need-to-know at that point. So instead, we took the video to his father and mother."

"Damien and Vicki," Laura said.

"To make a long story short, Damien refused to help and said his son could go to jail. That riled up Vicki. She came to us later and gave up Damien's bank accounts, where he'd been laundering money. We busted him, but also made it look like Vicki was going to jail so that Damien wouldn't suspect her. That's when he agreed to help us in exchange for Vicki and Buck's freedom."

"We managed to arrange for the French authorities to seize a metric tonne of cocaine and arrest several full-patch members," Laura stated.

"The thing is, Vicki was still furious with Damien," Jack continued. "She blamed him for Buck getting into the club and wanted him out, so she tipped off the other bikers that Damien was responsible for our seizing the dope in France."

"Holy smokes," Alicia blurted. "She burned her own husband, who only informed to save her and their son."

"Yes," Jack said, making a concerted effort to keep his anger from showing. "Buck was enraged that his father had talked, and under the direction of the new national president, shot Damien in the head. Then Buck and his mother had a blowout because he wouldn't leave the club. The bikers feared Vicki would tell all to the police, so they had Buck lure her out to a prospect's house. Once there, she was murdered by two guys from their hit squad. They used plastic wrap to suffocate her."

Alicia stared at the two of them for a moment, apparently trying to collect her thoughts. "Did you tell I-HIT about all this?" she asked.

"I showed Connie the video," Jack said, "but she was told by the brass that she couldn't use it or tell anyone. We'd made a promise to Damien that his son and his wife would go free in exchange for the cocaine. Knowing Damien, I think that — despite the fact that his own son murdered him — he'd still have wanted us to honour that agreement."

"Wow," Alicia said quietly.

"So, how do you feel about working with us?" Laura asked.

Alicia gave what looked like a forced smile. "I feel like I need to catch my breath."

"I understand," Laura said. "I felt the same way when I first came in."

"Let's save Buster Linquist for tomorrow night," Jack said. "Laura and I have some administrative work to catch up on. If you feel up to it, I'd suggest you start by reading through past reports to get a feel for what goes on."

"I think I will need a history lesson," Alicia agreed.

Two hours drifted by before Alicia looked up from a pile of reports. "Do these guys do any kidnappings?"

"Which guys?" Jack asked. "The bikers, Vietnamese, Russians, Chinese, Eastern Europeans, Irish —?"

"I'm still reading about the bikers. I haven't gotten to any of those other groups yet."

"As far as bikers go, Satans Wrath is game for any criminal activity where money is concerned, but to my knowledge, any kidnappings they've done thus far relate to the dope trade and usually involve the wife or girlfriend of a dealer who's delinquent."

"Either pay up or the woman is forced into prostitution," Laura stated.

"Sometimes they'll grab other dealers and take them for a ride to convince them to buy their supply through Satans Wrath. Technically it's kidnapping, but I view it more as having a conversation."

"But they haven't ever taken a kid from an innocent family for ransom?" Alicia asked.

"Not that we know of," said Jack. "Why?"

"We had a kidnapping of a kid two years ago. I'm sure the parents were straight and were targeted because they're wealthy." Alicia grimaced. "Still unsolved."

"Too bad," Jack replied. "Sorry, I don't know of anyone specific that I could suggest to you. Biker or otherwise."

Alicia nodded and gestured to the reports. "There're lots of names in these files."

"On the first page we list all the names contained within the report, along with date of birth and indication of criminal record, if they have one," Laura said. "Sometimes the information is passed on to units such as Drug Section for whatever action they deem appropriate."

"I see that. But a lot of information, especially involving informants, isn't passed on."

"We have our own Intelligence database, but you're right," Jack said. "The protection of informants is crucial to what we do. There are a lot of cases we can't risk telling others about because it would jeopardize the informant."

"And a lot of the names don't have criminal records … meaning, they aren't known to regular police officers," Alicia observed. "They're simply noted as associates."

"Not having a criminal record makes them better suited to run under the radar when running drugs or doing something else to benefit the club," Jack said.

"Such as getting a job that gives them access to classified information," Laura added. "Motor vehicle branch, police station, city hall, or a company that keeps people's addresses on file, like a cable, phone, or power company. Knowing these associates' connections to certain criminals makes it easier for us to identify leaks."

"Which makes it particularly irritating if we learn about someone working in one of those areas, but can't do anything about it because it'd burn the informant," Jack said.

Alicia opened her mouth as if to say something, then changed her mind and went back to reading.

When their shift was coming to a close, Jack said, "Tomorrow night we'll do surveillance on Buster Linquist. If you'd like to join us, you could take one of our cars now and save having to drive back here tomorrow to get it. We could meet you around Linquist's place say, six p.m.?"

"That'd be great. Thank you."

"Good, put the reports back, but take Linquist's photo with you. I'll give you the keys to a blue Chevy Cruze hatchback. Tomorrow night Laura will be in a silver Dodge Ram pickup and I'll be in a black SUV Nissan Pathfinder."

"So what do you think?" Laura asked on the way out. "Still looking forward to coming here?"

"I am," Alicia said confidently. "You've opened up a whole new world for me. I think it's all fascinating ... and exciting."

"Yeah, it gets real exciting when someone's shooting at you," Laura said flatly. Alicia grinned. "I'm serious," Laura continued, seemingly irritated by Alicia's response. "Ask Jack why he's limping."

"I hurt myself zip-lining," Jack said. "Ignore Laura. She needs to work on her sense of humour."

"He crash-landed after using his belt to zip-line down a guy wire from a lookout tower because some guy opened up on him with an AR-15," Laura retorted. "Gee, I didn't realize that was supposed to be funny."

Jack saw the blood drain from Alicia's face. *It's okay, kid. I'll look after you.*

CHAPTER FIFTEEN

It was 6:00 p.m. Tuesday night when Jack, followed by Laura, drove past Linquist's house. Halfway down the block, Jack saw Alicia sitting in the blue Chevy hatchback and groaned as he grabbed his phone and dialed. "Get the hell out of there!" He caught her startled look through the window as he drove past. "Follow me, we need to talk."

Moments later, they were all parking at a convenience store. Laura got in the back of Jack's SUV, gesturing for Alicia to get in the front.

"What's going on?" Alicia looked at Jack. "You're angry. What did I do?"

Jack sighed. "I'm not angry at you. I'm ticked off at myself. I should've known you wouldn't know how to do surveillance."

"What're you talking about?" Alicia glanced down at her clothes. "I know how to fit in. I'm a trained under-cover operator. I completed the course last month."

"Yes, but that doesn't teach you how to do surveillance. You were far too obvious back there."

"No way I look like a cop! On the course in Halifax I made more dope buys than anyone —"

Jack put up his hand for her to stop. "No, you don't look like a cop. Far from it — but that doesn't matter to these guys. They've been around long enough not to go by anyone's appearance. Telling me you know surveillance because you completed the undercover course is like saying you took a first-aid course so you're qualified to do surgery. There's a lot to learn, especially when it comes to the professional criminals we work on. Sitting in a car halfway down the block makes you stand out like a sore thumb. The least you could've done was slide over to the passenger seat to make it look like you were waiting for someone."

Alicia looked crestfallen. "I hadn't thought of that."

"How long were you there before we arrived?"

"Uh, about an hour. Maybe a bit more."

"Sitting that long in the passenger seat wouldn't have worked, regardless." He caught Laura's eye in the rear-view mirror. "Linquist will be heated up. We better leave him alone for a couple of weeks."

"For sure," Laura agreed.

Alicia frowned.

"It's okay," Jack assured her. "Linquist isn't an important target. He may even be clean at the moment. There's lots of others I'd like to take a look at before deciding who to really go after."

"You seem pretty certain that I was seen."

"Not a hundred percent, but he's been well schooled to watch for police surveillance. Everyone in Satans Wrath is heat conscious. If he did see you, he'll be extra paranoid. It's not worth the chance he'll burn Laura's or my vehicle, too. It's better for us to select another target. Don't worry, we have lots to choose from."

"I'm sorry," Alicia said, upset.

"You'll learn," Jack said, trying to sound upbeat.

"We all had to," Laura added.

"To start with, you're going to have to change your way of thinking," Jack said. "You're coming from a reactive section, where the crime has already happened. I don't imagine you did much surveillance."

"I've done some."

"Laura and I do a lot. You need to look at things from a criminal's point of view. Imagine you're a criminal and you're worried about being busted. Someone sitting in a car where they can see your house will make you suspicious. Same thing if a van starts parking on the street. Imagine that you take a walk around the neighbourhood or send out one of your kids to do it. You see someone in a car and glance in and see ballpoint pens stuck in the sun visor or takeout food containers on the back seat. What would you think?"

"I guess it doesn't take a genius to figure out you've got heat," Alicia said.

"Exactly. You need to consider what you do through the criminal mindset."

"It doesn't help that the car you gave me is so plain," Alicia said, glancing at the hatchback.

"That's the idea," Jack responded.

"In MCU we had a station wagon with a toddler seat and a sign on the back window that said *Baby on Board.*"

"That might be okay if it was only seen once," Jack replied. "But the sign would stick in people's minds. It'd be better without it."

Alicia thought for a moment, then looked at Jack. "You're right. Of course you're right. I feel stupid."

He saw her eyes water. "It's no big deal," he said gruffly. "Like I said, we'll go back to the office and select a new target." But he couldn't help thinking that if she cried so easily over one little mistake, she probably shouldn't be working with them.

"You don't understand," Alicia sniffled. "Two years ago I blew another surveillance. Because of me, an eight-year-old kid had four of his fingers chopped off. That was the kidnapping I mentioned last night. The one that's still unsolved."

Okay, maybe I was wrong. This is a big deal.

"What happened?" Laura asked.

Alicia's voice was shaky as she outlined the Chung kidnapping, including how the kidnappers had identified her vehicle.

"I'm sorry," Jack said when she'd finished. "Until you mentioned it, I'd never heard about the kidnapping."

"It never made the news, and the parents didn't want anyone to know. They were under enough stress."

"What a horrible thing for you to have to live with," Laura said softly.

"I think about it every day," Alicia admitted. "I keep the file box under my desk and I've read the reports and statements so many times … but I always hit the same dead ends. Same thing for all the footage I obtained. Traffic cameras aren't allowed to record because of privacy laws, but I was lucky enough to find a couple of businesses with CCTV cameras where the plates on passing cars were visible. We identified some drivers as having criminal records, but none of those leads panned out."

"During the kidnapping, didn't you have Special O?" Jack asked. "They're an elite unit that specializes in surveillance. Drug Section uses them a lot, so —"

"Yes, I know what Special O is. We did use them that day, but even they didn't have the resources to cover what we needed. It started off in Queen Elizabeth Park. There are at least thirty-two exits vehicles could take leaving the park, never mind places where you could walk out on foot. We ended up using air surveillance, so everyone stayed back." Her face soured. "Including me ... but it was my car the bad guys saw."

And you'll live with that for the rest of your life. Jack changed the subject. "Last night when you were reading through our files, you looked like you were going to ask a question, but changed your mind. Was it about this case?"

"Uh, yes, but I was afraid of overstepping my bounds."

"You want to compare the names you've collected to the names in our database?" Jack asked.

"Right, but after what you told me about the special access security clearance and protecting informants, I didn't want to come across as obtuse. I thought I'd wait until we knew each other a little better."

"My name's Jack. My wife's name is Natasha and we have two sons, Mike and Steve. If you feel you know me well enough, grab your file box and meet us at our office."

Forty-five minutes later, Alicia walked into the Intelligence Unit carrying two large file boxes.

"Two?" Jack questioned. "I thought you said one."

"One is mostly reports, statements from possible suspects with alibis, and alphabetical lists of every name we could collect. The other is maps of the areas we were in, including the owners of nearby houses, and USB flash drives with CCTV footage, as well as comparison footage."

"Comparison footage?" Laura asked.

"It was rush hour when they had Mr. Chung going through the hoops. I wanted to see which vehicles regularly appeared in the vicinity at around that time each day so I could identify any ones that only showed up on the day I was burned."

"Time consuming, but a good idea," Jack said.

"Good idea, maybe, but nothing came of it," she responded.

"I'll sign in to a computer with my password to give you access to our database," Jack said. "How many names do you have to check?"

"About seven thousand."

"Are you kidding me?" Jack asked.

"No. Like I said, it was rush hour. I found one camera that caught plates on cars heading east onto the Trans-Canada. Not only that, we had a lot of surveillance teams, and I wanted to check out the areas where they'd parked. That included houses and apartment buildings. And particularly the area I was detailed to watch from," she added glumly. "When you think about it, seven thousand is only a fraction of the number of people who would've been in all the different areas."

Jack exhaled audibly. "Don't get your hopes up. Odds are we'll match some names, but they may not fit the profile you want."

"I'm used to that," Alicia replied. "We'd already identi-fied several dozen people with criminal records, and none of those checked out, either."

"One more reminder. If someone does match your list, you'll still need to clear it with me before telling anyone or taking any action. Understood?"

"I understand."

"You a good typist?"

"I can hold my own."

"We should each be able to check about two names a minute, which works out to 360 names an hour. Divide that into seven thousand and it'll take about twenty hours."

"Ouch. I hadn't done the math," Alicia responded.

"You still have your day shifts to put in at MCU." Jack paused. "Laura and I'll keep working on it while you're doing that. I'll also have our secretary help." He glanced around. "Let's get started. We should be able to wrap it up by Thursday."

"I — I don't know what to say," Alicia said. "Thank you."

"You don't need to thank us for trying to put bad guys away," Laura said. "It's our job, same as yours. We're on the same team."

And a monster who chops off a kid's fingers … I really want to put him away. Away someplace deep underground.

CHAPTER SIXTEEN

The next two days went as planned; on Thursday at 11:00 p.m., they finished checking all the names. There were a few matches, but none were viable suspects.

Alicia threw up her hands angrily. "Nothing works out. It never does," she fumed.

Jack leaned back in his chair and flexed his fingers. "I suggest we approach this from another angle."

"Tell me something we haven't already tried," Alicia replied skeptically.

"I reviewed the file," Jack said, pausing as his mind flashed to Tommy's statement. *Bound and blindfolded in a trunk. No food or water for two days. Lying in his own excrement. Then hauled out to have his fingers — this isn't helping. I need to focus.*

"Do you think we missed something?" Alicia prodded.

"I've got a couple of questions and observations to make first."

"Sure, go ahead."

Jack knew she would have rehashed the case countless times, and he appreciated that she at least tried to sound upbeat. "Your car was spotted, but you weren't. They presumed you were a man. That indicates to me that there's a good chance you were seen from above. When you were on surveillance by QE Park, did you park near any tall buildings?"

"I've thought of that," Alicia replied. "Near the park, I was in a strictly residential area — there were only houses. Anyone watching from a house would likely have identified me as a woman, especially if they were close enough to see the sign in the back window."

"The park was remote as far as people go. That's where they had the best opportunity to look for heat."

"Downtown Vancouver, on the other hand, is all tall buildings," Alicia reflected.

"And crowded," Jack noted. "You could've had a dozen members blending in on the crowded sidewalk without being made. These people did a lot of planning; they'd have known that."

"So if not to check for police surveillance, why did they send Chung downtown during rush hour?" Alicia asked.

"Good question. Worth giving it some thought."

"I have footage from a couple of cameras that picked up David Chung walking past carrying the ransom. One was on his way to the corner of Robson and Richards. I also have footage of him waiting there, as well as from another camera close to Nelson Park, where he was sent next. I didn't identify anyone who may've been following him."

"Too bad, but as I said, if they had him walking around in a crowd, I doubt they were doing countersurveillance. I have another question. Mr. Chung is the CEO of a computer software company. How closely have you looked at his associates and perhaps competitors?"

"Very close. Under a microscope, you might say."

"Okay, then I'll continue. In Chung's statement he says the last thing the kidnapper said to him was something about making him an example."

"Yes, right after he said that I should go for a doughnut," Alicia said, irate.

"He didn't mention you specifically," Laura noted. "He made a presumption that you were male."

"Whatever," Alicia replied. "He still meant me."

"Enough of that," Jack said, not hiding his irritation. "Saying they'd make an example of David suggests to me they were planning to do more kidnappings."

"Everyone is concerned about that," Alicia said, "but we've never received any indication that it has happened again."

"Is it possible that David and Jia Chung have been contacted by other victims since then? Have you spoken to them?"

"No, the Chungs hate the police now. Me in particular since I was the one who blew it. There's no way they'd co-operate or tell us."

"It's clear from everything you've said that you didn't blow it," Jack said. "You did what you were told, so quit blaming yourself." *Easier said than done, of course.* Alicia looked down, avoiding his eyes. "Believe me when I say I've played the self-blame game myself. But it doesn't help."

Alicia swallowed. "Sorry."

"Being sorry doesn't help, either."

From the corner of his eye, he noticed Laura frowning at him, but didn't relent. *If she isn't tough enough to handle the kind of stuff we've been through, we better find out — for her sake as well as ours.*

"As a matter of fact, the Chungs can't be approached," Alicia said, getting back on the subject. "They're suing the Force for what happened, and I've been named personally. I'm not even allowed in the same neighbourhood as them."

"That's awful," Laura said, "and a bit unfair."

"Personally, I think it's justified," Alicia said. "What happened to Tommy was …" She trailed off, unable to finish.

Jack looked at Laura. "Justified or not, I think we should do a quick undercover sting on the Chungs."

She shrugged. "Might work. Sure, why not?"

"Why not?" Alicia exclaimed. "Weren't you listening? There's no way an undercover operational plan would be approved. I was already warned by Internal Affairs to back off. Nobody's allowed to talk to them."

Jack brushed off her concern with a wave of his hand as he continued to talk to Laura. "Is their ethnicity significant? Perhaps Chinese Canadian couples are being specifically targeted. Chinese investors have bought up a lot of expensive homes in Vancouver. People tend to generalize. Maybe they went looking for a wealthy Chinese family. And if they thought the Chungs were recent immigrants, they might have assumed they'd be more likely to comply without contacting police."

"Many immigrants come from countries where the police are poorly trained and corrupt, and still carry a mistrust of them," Laura agreed. "It obviously didn't work with the Chungs, because they did call the police." She looked at Alicia. "They've been Canadian citizens for over twelve years, is that right?"

"Yes, but —"

"But the kidnappers might now be hoping that word of what happened to Tommy Chung will spread through the Chinese Canadian community, or something like that."

"Right," Jack said, still mainly addressing Laura. "I think it'd be better if I made the approach alone and portrayed the upset father. Sorry to cut you out, but I think I should use a little Asian heat for the role of mother."

"Asian heat? You mean Tina Chan on Drug Section."

"She speaks Cantonese, and I trust her to go along with it and keeper her mouth shut. She could play the terror-stricken mother waiting at home for a phone call, or for her husband to return."

"That makes sense. Don't be sorry, Jack. That doesn't help."

Nice dig.

"You guys!" Alicia cut in, perturbed. "You're not listening! It'll never be approved. They're suing us. There's no way —"

"I told you she was young," Laura said to Jack.

Alicia stopped talking and angrily folded her arms across her chest.

Jack eyed her for a moment before speaking. "That big picture you want to learn about often has a grey border around it. The scenario I'm suggesting could take place without the Chungs ever finding out my real identity. If you want to solve this case, I recommend we enter that grey zone. That means that nobody except the three of us and Tina will know about it."

"But it's not right. We could all get in trouble," Alicia replied.

Jack saw Laura roll her eyes, no doubt thinking the same thing he was. *Trouble? Hell, this is nothing.*

"I guess you'd have to weigh the risk against how badly you want to solve the case. If you have any other ideas, speak up now."

"You know I don't," Alicia replied, making a face. She appeared to be thinking it over.

"I don't think either of you would get in trouble, anyway," Jack said. "This is something I'd do alone. You and Laura could honestly deny ever seeing me go to the Chung home."

Alicia looked at him curiously. "So you're willing to risk getting into trouble alone just to help me?"

"You?" Jack was surprised, then angry. "This has nothing to do with you!" he said, pointing at her. "Your ego may be bruised over what happened, but that's nothing compared to how Tommy and his parents feel. I want justice for Tommy and I want to ensure that this vile, horrific act isn't done to anyone else." He paused to calm down. "In my opinion, that far outweighs a civil suit or any other trouble — so tomorrow night, I suggest you keep clear of what I plan to do."

"What if someone else finds out and questions me?" Alicia said. "Have you thought about that?"

"I presume you'll spill your guts, but I think it's worth the risk for what we might learn. Besides, how angry could the brass get with me?"

"Actually quite a bit," Laura noted. "You've been warned by Lexton before about not having an op plan. She doesn't strike me as the type to give repeated warnings. Also, if you did get sued, the Force wouldn't back you. Could cost you plenty."

That hurts, especially coming from you. "Et tu, Brute?"

Laura was grave. "You know I'm right."

"I know, but we're good at what we do. What are the chances of getting caught?"

Laura glanced at Alicia. "I'd say the chances are good."

"Let's get something straight!" Alicia snapped. "I know people think I was sent in here to rat, but that's not why I came. Two days with you two and I understand why, though," she seethed, glaring at Jack. "How dare you presume that I'd spill my guts if questioned!"

"Wouldn't you?" Jack asked. "I thought you were implying that you would. I'm a little curious — no, a lot curious — about who exactly thinks you were sent in here to inform?"

"So am I," Laura added tersely.

Alicia took a deep breath to compose herself. "Okay, maybe I exaggerated when I said people, but maybe not."

"We're listening," Jack said.

"Inspector Crimmins told me that Staffing wanted someone with a reputation for honesty and going by the book. At the time I thought it odd. After all, it should be taken for granted that all members do."

Good point.

"Then I thought he meant there was more opportunity for corruption when working on organized crime." Alicia looked at him for verification.

"The more money involved, the more risk there is," Jack replied.

Something stinks. First Quaile had tried to screw them by transferring in unfit constables, then Lexton appeared on the scene and suddenly there were new qualifications. Had Vath's murder pushed her over the edge? He glanced at Laura. *You thinking what I'm thinking?*

Laura gave a slight nod.

"After that I spoke with Connie," Alicia continued. "When I mentioned the bit about complete honesty and going by the book, she said maybe I was being offered my first UC assignment. I didn't get the connection at the time; I thought she just meant that you do a lot of UC work. But now I think she was suggesting that I was being transferred in to keep an eye on you guys."

"I suspect you were," Jack said. "I think Assistant Commissioner Lexton was behind the selection process. She's made it clear that she's had some doubts about me concerning previous cases. I thought it was all water under the bridge ... but maybe it isn't. I'm guessing Crimmins isn't aware of what's going on, otherwise he wouldn't have mentioned it at all. Maybe he thought the same as you, that the concern was about negating the possibility of corruption."

"If Lexton went to this much trouble, you can bet that if you get caught bending the rules even a little, she'll use it as a reason to have you transferred," Laura warned.

"Yeah, well ... what else is new?" Jack replied. "It wouldn't be the first time the brass have had a burr up their ass. I still think approaching David and Jia Chung is worth the risk." He eyed Alicia. "So, are you going to spill the beans?"

"Don't you think I want justice for Tommy? No, I'm not going to rat you out. Are you kidding?"

Jack smiled. "Okay, but like I said, I'll do it on my own. No need for either of you to be involved."

"I thought we were a team," Alicia said. "Like the three musketeers. All for one and one for all?" She looked at their faces. "Uh-uh. Bring it on. Nobody puts Baby in a corner. I'm dancing in the grey zone with you."

Jack smiled at her reference to the movie *Dirty Dancing* as he thought about the slippery slope Alicia was venturing down.

Sometimes the grey zone turns black ... but we can save that for another day.

CHAPTER SEVENTEEN

Early Friday evening, Jack stopped at a grocery store and bought a habanero pepper. Twenty minutes later, he approached the front door of the Chung residence and rang the doorbell.

"Who are you?" a man's voice asked over the intercom.

"You — you don't know me," Jack said, his voice wavering. "My name is Bruce. I was told to come here to talk to Mr. or Mrs. Chung about my son. Please, it's important. I beg you, I … I don't know what to do."

A moment later the door opened. "I'm David Chung."

Through his teary vision Jack saw the man staring at him.

"I think you'd better step inside," David said.

Jack entered the foyer and took a moment to blow his nose.

"My wife, Jia." David's tone was sombre.

She stepped forward to hold her husband's arm. Jack

nodded politely to her, then took a moment to look at each of their faces as if he was unsure how to start.

"This is about your son?" David prompted.

"Yes. This afternoon my wife, Tina, was driving Mikey to soccer practice and, and — oh, God." He covered his eyes.

"He was kidnapped," Jia said.

"You know?" Jack said, doing his best to look confused.

"We've been through it ourselves, and so have others," Jia said.

Others? Bingo!

"One look at you and I knew," she continued.

"They told my wife that if we call the police, they, they — I don't know what to do. They told her we should talk to you."

"I can't believe they did it again so soon," Jia said to David. "It's been less than a week."

Less than a week?

A cloud of suspicion appeared on David's face. He studied Jack closely.

Jack wiped his eyes. *At least my tears are genuine.* "You've been through this? They took your son or daughter?"

"Two years ago, our son was kidnapped." David's reply sounded matter-of-fact.

No sympathy. He's suspicious.

"Since then, you've been the third person to come to our house, but" — *I hate buts* — "the other two are of Chinese heritage, like myself."

Jack feigned surprise. "That's odd."

"Yes, it is," David said evenly. "It happened to us on a Wednesday, and they gave us until Friday — two banking days — to collect the ransom. And yet they took your son on a Friday?"

"Maybe because Fridays are the only day he has soccer," Jack said. "They gave us until Tuesday to pay."

"I see."

"My wife is Chinese Canadian," Jack said. "Why are they only going after Chinese people?"

David seemed surprised. "Uh, I don't know why. Maybe they assume we don't usually go to the police."

"So you're saying we shouldn't involve them?"

"Don't call them!" Jia said urgently.

"What about the person from last week, did they go to the police?"

"He took our advice and didn't," Jia said. "He called us back afterward and said that everything went okay and they'd returned his daughter. We have his number so if you want to —"

"Where's your wife now?" David interrupted.

"Waiting at home. She's terrified. Literally sick to her stomach. We didn't know what to do."

"Would you mind if I spoke to her?"

"Uh, I guess it would help if you could say something to calm her down. I'll call her."

Jack dialed, spoke briefly to Tina, then handed David his phone. He studied David's face as he spoke to Tina in Cantonese. He had no idea what David was saying, but could see the sorrow in his eyes. *Good job, Tina.*

David handed the phone back to Jack. "I'll be home as soon as I can," Jack said over the phone. "There've been others. Hopefully I can talk to one of them, too." He paused, glancing at David and Jia, then said, "No, they don't think we should go to the police. I don't know. We'll talk when I get home. I love you. Bye."

"I'm really sorry." David gave Jack's shoulder a squeeze. "Jia and I understand what you're going through. For us, it's like it happened yesterday."

"But you paid what they asked and everything went okay?" Jack asked.

"Come in and sit down," David said. "We'll tell you what happened."

"Coffee or tea?" Jia asked.

"Thanks, no," Jack replied. "I feel too sick."

She nodded.

Over the next twenty minutes, the Chungs gave Jack details that he already knew, grief, guilt, and sorrow washing over their faces as they spoke. Jack himself felt rage and sorrow on their behalf. Rage wouldn't be the right response for Bruce, the terrified father. At least not yet. But he allowed his sorrow to show on his face.

"Since then," Jia said, glancing upstairs, "Tommy seldom leaves his room."

"He's seeing a child psychologist, but so far there hasn't been much improvement. We're told it'll take time," said David.

"He rarely goes outside," Jia added. "He won't play with other children because he says he feels like a freak. I've had to start home-schooling him."

"I'm so, so sorry," Jack said. "Hopefully in time he'll be able to move past it."

David and Jia exchanged a silent look, no doubt hoping he was right.

"Would I be able to talk to the person from last week?

Tina's brother is a police officer in Toronto. I'm afraid that she'll tell him. But I don't want to hide what happened to Tommy from her, either. It's best for us to agree on the decision." Jack looked at their faces and swallowed. "I know she'd feel better if I could meet someone who's been through this and, uh, didn't have the same outcome as your son."

"I understand," David replied. "He was grateful for our advice. I'm sure he'll be willing to talk to you."

"And before that, what about the other person who came to see you? Did everything go okay for them?"

"I presume so," David replied. "I was so shocked when he showed up that I never thought to get his name or number. We never heard back from him. We wished we'd asked him to call us."

"It feels like we're all in it together," Jia added. "Like we belong to an exclusive club. Later, you'll want to talk to someone who really understands."

"Thank you," Jack said. "You're very nice people."

"But bad things can happen to nice people," David replied. "I'll make the call."

Moments later, Jack was speaking to a man called Andy Zhao on the phone. He said he didn't want Jack to come to his house because his family was still under a great deal of stress, but they could meet at the Kerrisdale neighbourhood Starbucks.

After assuring David and Jia that he'd be in touch, Jack returned to his SUV. He then called Laura, who was parked a couple of blocks away with Alicia.

"It went well," Jack said. "Need you to get to the Kerrisdale Starbucks on West 41st Avenue in Vancouver. I'm meeting a guy by the name of Andy Zhao. I want surveillance shots of him, as well as his plate number for an address."

"What's he got to do with it?"

"His nine-year-old daughter was kidnapped last week."

"No!" exclaimed Laura.

"It turned out okay. He paid up and got her back in one piece."

"Oh, man. Glad to hear that."

"See you there. I'm going to phone Tina. We owe her an olive soup, for sure. Maybe a couple."

At 7:30 p.m., Jack entered the coffee shop. It wasn't difficult to spot Zhao. He had noticeable dark circles under his eyes, and he was looking around nervously. *Huge trust issues.* Jack introduced himself as Bruce, shook Zhao's hand, and thanked him for the meeting.

Zhao trembled as he spilled out his story. Whenever he lifted his mug, coffee slopped out, and he soon gave up trying to drink it. He was clearly still in shock over what had happened. He didn't appear to notice Laura walking past with her cellphone in hand.

"So you paid them three hundred thousand dollars," Jack said. *A hundred thou more than Chung. They're getting greedier.*

"A week ago today. I'll never forget it." Zhao paused. "And you? Was it the same amount?"

Jack nodded.

"You should do everything they ask," Zhao stated. "Don't go to the police. I'm sure you heard what happened to —"

"I heard. I don't even want to think about it."

"The kidnappers warned me that if I went to the police afterward, they'd take revenge out on my daughter. I'm a business development manager for an international hotel chain. My work often takes me away from home. But after this, I don't think I could travel anywhere without my family with me."

Jack grimaced. "Will you tell me where they had you go with the ransom money?"

"Like I said, they made me go all over the place, for a couple of hours. I finally ended up out in Chilliwack. That's where I dropped off the money."

"But before then, where exactly did they make you go? How many street corners or parking lots were you told to wait in?"

Zhao gave him a curious look. "Why do you want to know?"

"A couple of reasons. My wife is really going to be so freaked out while I'm doing this. I want to be able to give her some idea of how long the whole thing'll take."

"Tell her to expect about three hours."

Jack let out a loud sigh. "It's not only her. I'm afraid of making a mistake, too. I have trouble hearing, especially when I'm stressed. It's like my brain goes into a fog. If I mess up one of their instructions, will they think I'm up to something?" He shook his head as if trying not to think about it, then put his hand on Zhao's arm and stared into his eyes, pleading. "What if they do something terrible to my son?"

Zhao sat back in his chair and thought for a long moment. "Okay. They'll probably send you to different places, but I'll describe what I had to do as best as I can."

He was warned not to talk to police or they'll exact revenge on his daughter. Jack pushed down his angst and gave a grateful smile. "Thank you."

CHAPTER EIGHTEEN

Jack met Laura and Alicia back at the office and told them everything he'd learned.

"It was almost identical," Jack said, "except it started at Pacific Spirit Regional Park in Vancouver. He was then sent downtown and told to park in the same lot where Chung did and take the money to the same corner, Robson and Richards. After that he walked about six blocks in a different direction before being called and told to return to his car. At that point he was sent to the Vedder Pointe Shopping Centre in Chilliwack. From there he was directed to a nearby path in Paradise Park where he dropped off the money before returning to wait in his car. An hour later, he was told where to pick up his daughter. She was duct-taped and lying in a ditch across from a bird sanctuary north of Abbotsford on Bateman Road."

"No car rental," Alicia noted, "but the pattern is roughly the same."

"More than roughly," Jack said. "There were two identical locations: the parking lot on Seymour and the corner of Robson and Richards. Also at the same time of day."

"Rush hour," Laura said. "Meaning crowds of people on the sidewalks."

"Exactly," Jack replied.

Alicia was deep in thought. "Too crowded for the bad guys to effectively check for countersurveillance, which begs the question, why do they keep sending victims there?"

"I suggest you get footage from CCTV in the vicinity of that street corner during Andy Zhao's drop-off last week and compare it with what you have from two years ago when David Chung was there," Jack said.

"There was a camera in a nearby restaurant that had been robbed before. It was facing the entrance, which was a glass door, and it also picked up the corner across the street. I could see David waiting there. I was also able to get footage from an apartment building on Seymour that showed David going past on the sidewalk after he'd parked his car."

"Good. Hopefully the same cameras are still operational. I'd like to compare."

"I compared footage from other CCTV cameras, too, including when David went to Nelson Park," Alicia stated. "I didn't find any repetition of people to indicate he was being followed."

"Maybe their intention at that point wasn't to follow him. The kidnappers told Jia they had scanning equipment. What if they used that crowded street corner as cover to scan David and the satchel?"

"Wouldn't David have noticed he was being scanned?"

"Not with current technology. Gone are the days of bulky equipment, waving a long wand back and forth while wearing headphones. These days anyone can purchase a bug detector the size of a cellphone and detect wireless microphones, as well as hidden cameras. The same goes for detecting GPS trackers." Jack paused. "Didn't they tell you all that on your UC course?"

"Yes, they said that in the past, wiring up a UC operator had its risks, but doing so today would be almost suicidal. Still, I'd presumed scanning would be obvious … like at the airport, when they check you from head to foot."

"Chung and Zhao were probably focused on watching for the vehicle they expected to toss the money into. They likely weren't paying attention to the people around them," Jack suggested.

"I believe some of the cameras hold their footage for thirty days," Alicia said, frowning. "I'll need to get a warrant. I might have copies of the footage in my hands by Monday afternoon."

"Why the face?" Jack asked. "You've gotten warrants before."

"It's not that. I'm not sure whether they can be entered into court if we do see something. There's case law on invasion of privacy. These cameras picked up people outside the vicinity of what they were intended for … or, in the eyes of the courts, where people could reasonably expect a degree of privacy."

"Yeah, like you can expect privacy on a busy Vancouver sidewalk," Laura said sarcastically.

"Fruit of the poisonous tree," Jack said. "I'm familiar with it. If it's ruled inadmissible, then defence could apply for any evidence that's obtained after that to be inadmissible." Jack paused. "You risked getting the CCTV footage before, though."

"I know, but with nothing else to go on, we thought we'd take a chance and hope for the best."

"Looks like we still need to hope for the best," Jack replied. "Can you do it without others in your office knowing about it?"

"Yes. Monday and Tuesday are my last days there. Nobody's going to be assigning me anything."

"Then do it," Jack ordered. "If you don't bring the footage of Zhao to anyone's attention, then no one will be going through court records to find out you obtained a warrant. When you turn in the file boxes on Tuesday, don't include any documentation of what we've done. As a matter of fact, I consider it part of an Intelligence file, to be treated as need-to-know, so keep the search warrant documents here. Also, make copies of all the CCTV footage you have and put that with our file, as well."

"I've already got extra copies," Alicia said. "What do we call this file? 'The grey zone'?"

"Now you're learning," Laura said. "Label the folder *GZ* for short."

"But if this does turn into something, won't we have to tell them? How will you explain where the information came from without admitting to being undercover at the Chung residence?"

Jack eyed Alicia. "We'll cross that bridge when we come to it."

* * *

At 11:30 a.m. Monday morning, Jack received a call at home from Alicia.

"Okay, so I've got it," she said, after the initial niceties.

"The camera footage?"

"Yes, a guy ran it off for me. Haven't seen it yet, but it picks up the sidewalk at the intersection where Zhao waited. Unfortunately the other camera close to where he parked his car has been adjusted out of fear of the privacy laws, so it no longer views the outside."

"You at your office?"

"No, I'm still downtown. I figured I could meet you at your office to compare footage."

"You haven't met our boss yet," Jack noted.

"Staff Sergeant Wood."

"You can call her by her first name, Rose."

"Okay."

"Our office isn't a good idea, though. Rose is a really good boss, but I don't see the need for her to venture into the grey zone. She always demands to know what's going on, but knowing about this would put her in a spot later on if word of what I did leaks out."

"So she doesn't know anything about what we've been doing?"

"I've told her that you've been working nights with us and that we gave you a hand comparing names of bad guys with names from an old file you had in MCU. If she sees us comparing footage, it might be hard to explain. She'd want to know what new lead we've developed ... and how."

"Maybe we should go to my place and use my computer."

"Where do you live?"

"Out in Langley."

"My house is closer, and so is Laura's. I also have my sons' laptops. If we put them side by side it'll be easier to compare images. Come on over. I'll call Laura and have her meet us here."

* * *

While Laura and Alicia sat at the kitchen table peering at the recent CCTV footage of Andy Zhao on the corner of Robson and Richards, Jack inserted a USB flash drive containing the footage of David Chung into the second computer.

"Yes! Yes!" Alicia screamed, stabbing her finger at the image on the screen of a man in the crowd behind Andy Zhao.

No way she lives in an apartment. She'd be written up for noise violation whenever she brought anyone home.

"Hurry!" she said, gesturing to the second laptop. "You'll see! It's the same guy!"

Jack brought up the footage of David Chung waiting at the same the corner.

"Fast forward about three minutes. Let me do it!" Alicia said excitedly.

Jack shoved his chair back. "Be my guest."

A moment later, Alicia paused the video. "There, there! It's the same guy, I'm sure of it! Look, both times it looks like he's talking on a cellphone."

Jack and Laura looked at the frame the video was frozen on. It was zoomed in and grainy, but it clearly showed the same man. He was taller than the people around him and had black, curly, well-trimmed hair. He was clean-shaven, wearing a suit and tie.

"Keep watching," Alicia said. "Look what he does!"

In both instances, the man bent down, seemingly to adjust his shoe or sock.

"And that's how he scanned them," Jack said, giving a thumbs-up sign. "Great, looks like we got —"

Alicia leapt from her chair and hugged him, then planted a kiss on his forehead before turning to Laura.

"No, I'm not into that," Laura said, putting up her hands to stay Alicia. "Might turn Jack on, but I'm not into exhibitionism." She winked at Jack.

"Thank you, thank you, thank you!" Alicia said. "Both of you, thank you."

Jack studied the picture. "Good news that he's wearing a suit and tie."

"Suit and tie ... five o'clock rush hour ... he probably works nearby," Alicia said thoughtfully.

"That'd be my guess. There are closer parking lots to that intersection than the one they were told to use. Perhaps our scanner didn't want to wait around on the sidewalk for fear of being remembered if there was a police investigation. He could work somewhere between the parking lot and the corner. Someplace where he can see his victims hurrying past with the ransom."

"Then he follows them to the corner," Alicia said. She glanced at her watch. "I'd better make an appearance at MCU. I've been gone most of the day. I want to stake out the area around Robson and Richards after, though."

"No worries. Laura and I'll be there by three thirty. If you're free at the end of your shift, pop over and help out."

"I'll be there," she replied adamantly.

"If we don't have any luck, we'll try tomorrow morning, and so on," Jack said.

"Thank you, this is, this is ... you don't know what this means to me."

"I've got a pretty good idea," Jack replied. "It's not just that the monsters chopped Tommy's fingers off — they also made it feel personal by singling you out."

Alicia sighed. "Sometimes I think David and Jia hate me more than they do the kidnappers. If I hadn't screwed up, their little guy wouldn't have been harmed."

"We all have to do our jobs. You were just doing yours. They may realize that in time."

"It'll help if we catch who did it. They might not forgive me, but at least they'd feel some sense of justice."

Jack eyed the man in the image. *There will be justice. One way or the other.*

CHAPTER NINETEEN

Jack and Laura staked out the area near the intersection of Robson and Richards at 3:30 p.m., and Alicia joined them at 6:00 p.m. Their surveillance continued until 7:30 p.m., then they met briefly in a nearby alley.

Jack saw the frustration on Alicia's face. "Hey, kid, cheer up. We've put a face to one of the monsters. It's only a matter of time. Laura and I'll be back out by six a.m. tomorrow. We'll keep returning until we find him."

Alicia's face brightened. "You're right, aren't you? We will find him."

"It's simply a matter of time," Jack repeated.

"I believe you. We've had the file for two years without getting anywhere. I met the two of you only last week and look what's been accomplished."

"There are peaks and valleys," Laura said. "We hit a peak. I agree with Jack. Bet we identify him within a month at most."

"Tomorrow's your last day at MCU," Jack noted.

"Yup, I'll be turning over all my files."

"Including this one," Laura said.

"Yes. Officially it's assigned to Sergeant Hawkins."

"Is he a good guy?" Jack asked.

"Really good. He stood up for me when the others were giving me dirty looks for being burned. He told everyone that he could see from the air that I hadn't done anything wrong." Alicia paused. "Sure feels like I did, though."

"Bet they'll want to take you out for drinks tomorrow night," Laura said.

"That's been planned, but I'd rather be with you guys."

"I'm surprised you're officially starting this Wednesday. Next Monday is Canada Day. It would have made sense for your transfer to start after the holiday."

"I'm excited to get started. I told them the sooner, the better."

Jack smiled inwardly. *The exuberance of youth.* "Well, don't worry about tomorrow. I guarantee you'll be working long hours with us soon enough. Enjoy your party tomorrow night."

"Besides, trying not to arouse suspicion is part of learning to operate in the grey zone," Laura said. She cast Jack a sideways glance. "That and developing a taste for olive soup."

"Olive soup?"

"You'll learn about that after we've identified this guy," Jack said.

Alicia looked bemused. "Thanks, guys."

* * *

Jack was blending in with a group of people at a bus stop a block and a half from the intersection of Robson and Richards when his phone rang. It was 8:15 a.m.

"I've got 'im," Laura said. Her voice was level, but Jack knew she was suppressing her excitement. "He's sitting in a Tim Hortons along with two other men and a woman. It's located on Robson slightly down the street from the IGA."

Jack's adrenalin surged. "Are you positive?"

"Yup. Suit and all."

Jack forced himself to sound calm. "Are you inside?"

"No, I went in to grab a cup to go and didn't spot him until I was leaving. I'll be watching from an alcove across the street and down a bit, in front of a burger place."

"On my way. ETA one minute. Keep the line open in case they come out before I get there."

Once Jack reached Laura, she gestured toward the entrance of the coffee shop. "He's still inside. They're sitting toward the back and won't be able to see us."

"You said he was with two other men and a woman?"

"Yes, I'd guess our target to be in his midthirties. Navy-blue suit with a light-blue shirt and a red tie. The other three I'd guess to be in their early twenties. They look like university students. Dressed casual. The woman is chubby, short blond hair, green top and — see for yourself, there they are."

The group came out of the coffee shop, then strolled down Robson Street, away from them.

"Take this side," Jack said, then rushed across the street to follow them.

At the intersection, the group crossed over to the opposite side of Robson, where Laura was approaching, before continuing along Robson.

Jack stayed on his side of the street. The group entered a three-storey building with stores on the street level and what appeared to be offices on the two floors above. He saw their target closing the blinds in a corner office on the second floor. *Gotcha!*

A minute later, Jack was scanning the building's directory. The name on the second-floor corner office made him flinch. Powers Security Consultant Service.

A security consultant? This asshole knows the game. He'll have all the toys for spying and countersurveillance.

CHAPTER TWENTY

Back at the office, Laura handed Jack a sheet of paper. "We have confirmation."

Jack smiled at the driver's licence copy. It was the man from the CCTV footage: Derek Powers. "Thirty-four years old and living in an apartment about ten blocks from his office," he noted.

"He has two vehicles, both registered to his company," Laura stated. "A blue Ford van and a black Ford Flex SUV. The Motor Vehicle Branch also lists another guy as living at the same address. Probably a brother." She handed him another copy of a driver's licence.

"Peter Powers, aged twenty-seven."

"He owns a red Mustang and has a record," Laura added, handing Jack more sheets of paper. "He was charged six years ago for trafficking in cocaine, but the charge was dismissed in court. Two years later he went to trial on another cocaine trafficking charge, was convicted, and received a fine."

Jack looked at the mug shot. Peter had a completely shaved head and a black goatee. He wore a gold earring in one ear. "Looks a lot different than his brother," he noted.

"Definitely. Derek looks like a businessman. Peter looks like a gangster. He definitely wasn't one of the two guys with Derek this morning."

"Derek and Peter could be connected to the same criminal element. This is exactly what I was hoping to find. We're off to a good start."

"Great way to start the day. Are you going to call Alicia or should I?"

"Let's tell her tomorrow. Today's her last day at MCU. I don't want to alert them yet, and she'd have a hard time acting like nothing was going on."

"You're probably right. After a few drinks at her fare-well party she might let something slip."

"My thoughts exactly." Jack studied the criminal record. "Let's get to work. I checked the Yellow Pages, and Powers is listed as doing both corporate and private secu-rity consultation."

"Sounds like he knows his stuff." Laura paused. "How do we gift-wrap all this for MCU? The Crime Stoppers route? Tip them off anonymously so that nobody knows about your visit to the Chung household?"

"That'd take us out of the picture completely," Jack agreed. "But there could be problems. If the tipster were to mention Zhao only, MCU would interview him, and I'm sure he'd crack."

"Then your role would come up, leading them directly back to Chung."

"Yes. I told them my name was Bruce, but going by my middle name wouldn't fool MCU if they dug a little deeper. Plus, with MCU appearing to know about Chung and Zhao but not me, Chung and Zhao themselves might clue in that there was something fishy going on."

"MCU would look for CCTV footage of Zhao and discover that Alicia had already done so."

"For sure. And Chung might blab about my Chinese wife. I don't want Tina in trouble, either."

Laura mulled it over. "So the tipster could only say that Powers was involved in the Chung kidnapping, making no mention of Zhao."

"Which would leave MCU basically where they are now. They'd have the CCTV footage of Powers standing behind Chung, but that wouldn't be enough. With privacy laws, they might not even be able to use it to apply for a wiretap. That leaves interrogation, but Powers has been around the block a few times. He wouldn't be the type to crack over that."

"MCU wouldn't know that there were others."

"Exactly. Even if MCU believed Powers was involved, they might think it was a one-time thing, and not attack the issue the way they should."

"Which is how?"

"We know the kidnappers are becoming greedier and, likely, more brazen. I'd run a UC op on him if I were them."

"Which could turn out to be a costly long-term project. Not something MCU would undertake without evidence to indicate Powers is still active."

"There's another worry. If MCU heats up Powers, there's always the chance that the kidnappers blame

Chung or Zhao and follow through with their threats to exact revenge on their children."

"Make examples of them, like they already did with Tommy," Laura said bitterly.

Jack nodded solemnly. "It would be better to say I had an informant who told me about Derek Powers being involved in a kidnapping. Unlike with the Crime Stoppers route, I'd be able to swear to the informant's reliability."

"You said *a* kidnapping, not two or three. Meaning you'd leave Zhao out of it?" Laura noted.

"For now, at least. I'd make it look like we were doing some preliminary investigation on Peter, and when Alicia came in she saw my informant notes indicating his brother may have been involved in a kidnapping. I'd say I initially presumed the kidnapping was to prod someone into paying up over a dope deal, but then Alicia looked into it further and matched the face in the CCTV footage to the Chung kidnapping. That would explain why this connection wasn't discovered until Alicia arrived. She'd be a genuine heroine her first day on the job."

"I wouldn't say genuine. Also, you'll look like an ass for not having investigated the allegation earlier."

"Hey, an ass is only half the word I'm usually called." Jack paused in thought. "No doubt the question will arise as to when I was given the information. I don't know if it would make much difference if they knew it was last week. I think MCU would be so thrilled that they wouldn't give it much thought."

"How do you come up with a believable informant to have given you the information? An imaginary person might not go over well — at least, not without a plausible cover story. Otherwise MCU might smell a rat. Same with Lexton. She'd definitely be taking a keen interest."

"You gave me the answer to that a minute ago. I'm sure Peter's still dealing dope. He wouldn't have been scared off it; he had one charge dismissed and only got a fine on the other. So we'll make it look like the informant is a dope dealer connected to him."

"In the event MCU uses your information to get a wiretap, and you're later called to court and cross-examined, what will you say?"

"I'll say I had someone give me information indicating that Derek Powers was involved in a kidnapping. Same as I'd tell MCU."

"I can see you lying to MCU, but I know you'd never lie in court."

"I wouldn't be lying. I'm thinking of Andy Zhao. It was his information that led us to the CCTV footage to identify Powers. Hell, I could even say I had two informants."

Laura smirked. "Hadn't really thought of Chung or Zhao as informants."

"Why not? Especially Zhao."

"And considering the threat made about his daughter, we'd be justified in protecting his identity."

"It would also work in our favour down the road, in court, when MCU reveals what prompted their investigation. The kidnappers will think it was one of Peter's dope-dealing associates who spilled the beans, and that'll take any heat off of Zhao or Chung."

"I see one flaw," Laura said.

"That we might get caught and lose our jobs?"

"No. What if Peter's dopey friends are the other kidnappers? They wouldn't rat out Derek, because they'd be ratting themselves out."

"Let's see who his friends are first. If we think it's a possibility, then we'll come up with another patsy, maybe someone lower on the dope-dealing chain. Peter lives with Derek, so I'm sure he knows about the kidnappings; he might even be involved. The others would likely think Peter was lying, even if he swore that he hadn't told anyone."

"So when do we pass it on to MCU?"

"I'd like to put together a bit of a package to make it look like Peter was connected to a group we'd considered working on. What we need to do is come up with a few criminal associates."

"Going by his appearance and his record, that should be easy," Laura noted.

"We'll make that our priority." Jack glanced at his watch. "I want you to go see if Peter's Mustang is at his apartment."

"To see if he's your regular doper who sleeps 'till noon, or if he has a legit job."

"You got it. Then take a look around Derek's office building to see if you can locate his van and SUV. In the meantime, I'll call Commercial Crime and see if they can find anything out discreetly. Maybe they could get a contact from some company to place a bogus call asking Powers for references to see who he's done work for."

"It would be interesting to see if he did any consultant work for the companies Chung and Zhao work for," Laura noted.

"That would tie in nicely. I'd do it myself, but Commercial Crime has the contacts when it comes to white collar people, and they can do a more secure cover story. Maybe I could get them to check City Licensing and Companies Branch, and also see if Derek or Peter owns any property. It'd be nice to get a peek at their money trail."

"What story will you tell Commercial Crime? We haven't yet come up with any chumps to take the heat for being your informant. What if MCU gets wind of it?"

"I'll think of something to prevent that." Jack paused as he thought of something else he needed to do.

"You're frowning. What's wrong?"

"I need to phone David Chung. He thinks I'm paying the ransom today. I promised I'd let them know how it went."

"Is that a problem? Tell them it went fine."

"I feel like an asshole. They're really nice people. I bet they've been worrying about me ever since Friday. That was four days ago."

Laura looked sympathetic. "Okay, I'm off to look for a red Mustang. Good luck."

Jack appreciated her giving him some privacy. He sighed as he picked up his phone.

CHAPTER TWENTY-ONE

"Hello, David? This is Bruce. I came over the other —"

"Oh, Bruce!" David sounded like he was on the verge of tears. "We've been on pins and needles. What's happening?"

Yeah, I'm an asshole. "Everything's okay. I paid up and about an hour ago I got my boy back. He hasn't been hurt … at least not physically. I think everything's going to be okay."

"Oh, what a relief. Jia and I have been sick with worry. We've hardly slept. Thank you so much for letting us know. Andy called me this morning to ask if I'd heard from you."

Now I really feel bad. "It's me who should be thanking you. We took your advice and everything went okay."

"Listen, now that your son is back, he may need to talk to somebody. If you like, I could pass on the name of the lady who's helping Tommy. You and your wife may need some counseling, as well. Jia and I found it really difficult

afterward. Damn near ruined our marriage. Blaming ourselves, blaming each other. It was —"

"Sorry, David, but I need to go," Jack interjected. "I
appreciate what you're saying, though. I'll talk it over with
my wife."

"Even if that's not the route you want to go, we should
still get together sometime," David suggested. "Andy, too.
Maybe everyone could come over for a barbecue."

"Maybe someday," Jack replied. "We need some time."

"I understand. If you ever feel the need to talk to someone, don't hesitate to call."

"Thank you. I — I need to get back to my family."

"No, I understand. Would you like me to pass on the
news to Andy?"

"Please, that'd be great. Listen, I want to get back to
hugging my son. I promise I'll keep in touch. The barbecue sounds like a really nice idea."

Jack stared blankly at his phone after he'd ended the
call. *Yeah, that'll be a real fun get-together.*

Jack's next call was to a Corporal Schneider in
Commercial Crime. Jack said he was checking out informant information that indicated Powers was involved in
a kidnapping.

It was lunchtime when Laura returned to the office.

"The red Mustang was still parked behind their apartment," she advised. "I found Derek's SUV in a parking lot
off the alley that goes past his office. No sign of his van."

"It would appear that Peter likes to sleep in."

"Which means, I presume, we'll be pulling some late
nights. How'd it go with your call to David? Do you still
feel like an asshole?"

"Like an even bigger one now."

"Is that possible?"

Jack gave his usual lopsided smile. "I want you to find out what led up to Peter's cocaine charges. While you're doing that, I'll try and track down which vehicles Derek and Peter have had access to in the last couple of years. Tomorrow I'll get Alicia to compare those with the CCTV footage she has from Chung's case. Could be another nail in Powers's coffin for down the road."

"That'll keep her busy," Laura noted.

Laura finished her call with Drug Section by mid-afternoon.

"How'd you make out?" asked Jack.

"The charge against Peter six years ago was for two kilos of coke that they seized from the trunk of his car. He took the stand and said he'd lent his car to his brother-in-law, who he suspected was involved with drugs. The judge bought it and dismissed the charge."

"That likely reinforced his confidence that it doesn't take much to outwit the courts," Jack replied cynically.

"Word is the judge also called the prosecutor to his bench afterward and gave her hell for charging an innocent person."

"No doubt the judge would never believe that an accused might lie in court. The police maybe, but not the accused."

"His conviction from two years ago stemmed from being caught by VPD uniform in possession of a quarter-pound of cocaine. An informant ordered the coke, and they busted Peter upon delivery. The informant then left town and Peter was later given a fine on a plea deal."

"I doubt that curbed his misguided ways."

"Seeing as most dopers are nocturnal, do you want to work a night shift?"

"Friday night would be good."

"A sergeant who works surveillance on night shifts? I'm truly aghast," Laura teased.

"If this thing goes sideways, we may both be constables again … if we're lucky."

Later in the afternoon, Jack received a call back from Corporal Schneider in Commercial Crime.

"Have a little bit of info for you," Schneider said. "I talked to a friend of mine who works for a company that hired Powers to check out their office security. He said it was basic kind of stuff. Ensuring use of identity cards, secure locks, alarms, cameras, passwords, that sort of thing."

"Any idea how many people work for Powers?"

"Not many. My friend told me that some of the guys who do the grunt work are young and don't have much experience. Mostly criminology students working part-time, or maybe full-time during summer break. That being said, he told me that Powers has a degree in criminology and also did a stint with the Military Police that included working in foreign countries. Apparently he comes off as a little cocky, but he's smart and knows his stuff. There's also a rumour that he does corporate espionage. I'll keep digging and see if I can get more."

"Much appreciated."

"You told me to keep this between us because what you're working on might involve a dirty cop."

"Yes, it's possible we have a member supplying info to the bad guys." *Okay, Laura, no need to raise an eyebrow.*

"Can you give me a hint as to who you suspect?" Schneider asked.

"I don't want to point fingers this early in my investigation, but uh, if anyone from MCU contacts you, don't mention this."

"MCU? Son of a bitch." Schneider paused. "If whoever it is does turn out to be dirty, I hope you nail 'em."

"You got that right."

Laura stared at Jack as he put his phone away. "What?"

"You told them that someone in MCU is dirty?"

"Hey, it's a stretch, but somehow Alicia got burned that day on surveillance."

Laura grinned, then glanced at her watch. "You mixing olive soup later on?"

"Let's hold off to celebrate when the new kid on the block can join us. I'm sure we can talk her into splurging for martinis after she sees what we got."

"Speak of the devil," Laura said, looking at the call display on her phone, "she's calling. What do I say?"

"Tell her to have a good time at her party tonight."

"So I shouldn't say that you started a rumour one of the MCU members is dirty," Laura retorted, then answered.

Jack listened to her exchanging pleasantries with Alicia.

"Hang on, I'll ask Jack." Laura put the phone down and looked up at him. "Are we meeting early tomorrow morning to set up surveillance downtown?"

"No, she hasn't been introduced to Rose yet. Tell her we'll meet her here at eight thirty a.m."

Laura relayed the message and ended the call. "She's going to be one excited puppy tomorrow when she discovers what we found out. We may have to hide her from Rose for a month until she settles down."

"Yes, about that. How do you feel about her? Do you like her? More importantly, do you trust her?"

Laura screwed up her face. "To start with, I didn't like or trust her. Perhaps because she's young and naive ... which I find annoying. When she asked if you'd thought what would happen if she was questioned about your UC, I wanted to smack her." Laura shook her head. "Can you imagine what she'd think about some of the things we've done?"

"At least she was honest."

"Then she talked about Staffing looking for someone with an honest reputation. I thought, oh, man, Lexton put her in here to spy on us. That's when I tried to talk you out of the UC."

"But after all that, she agreed to go along with it."

"She said nobody puts Baby in a corner." Laura smiled. "I kind of liked her after that."

"Me, too," Jack replied.

"So you trust her?"

"I trust her in the sense that she's being honest with us. I also get a sense that she's smart, but has no experience with the kind of work we do or its politics."

"Operating in the grey zone."

"Yes ... and how well would she disarm questions thrown at her by seasoned investigators out of Internal Affairs? Or, worse yet, by Lexton, who's clearly perceptive."

"I have the same concern, although in a way, she reminds me of myself when I was her age ... and I sur-vived." Laura paused as if making up her mind. "I think she shows good potential."

"I agree, she reminds me of you, as well, except I think of you as my kid sister, whereas she falls more into the daughter-figure category."

"A daughter? There's maybe fourteen or fifteen years' difference between you!"

"Just think what you and I've gone through. It ages you."

"Are you saying I look older than my age?"

"I didn't say we *look* older. I meant inside … maturity."

"Yeah, well, if you're my brother, you're a much older one. Much, much older."

Jack returned Laura's smirk. "Hopefully someday she'll be up to your standards. We'll tread lightly and take it slow until we've had more time to assess her."

"Tread lightly and take it slow?" Laura was indignant. "You sure as heck didn't do that with me!"

"Really? I thought I did. Guess you were young and naive and thought everything was a big deal back then."

"You ass," Laura muttered. "Don't even get me started about what you were up to the first time I worked with you."

Jack chuckled. "It troubles me about Lexton," he said, growing serious. "Particularly coming on the heels of Vath being murdered. If she's looking to develop a source in our unit, Rose ought to know."

"Everything?"

"Yup."

"This ought to be fun. I haven't had time to sew my stripes onto my red serge yet. Maybe I shouldn't bother."

CHAPTER TWENTY-TWO

Rose eyed Jack and Laura suspiciously across her desk. "What are you two up to?"

"What makes you think we're up to anything?" Jack replied.

"The way you looked at each other when you came in. Like kids caught with their hands in the cookie jar. Does it have to do with the kidnapping file?"

"Kidnapping file? You know about it?" Jack asked.

"The newbie left a couple of file boxes on her desk last week. I took a peek and saw the pictures. Bloody sadistic, what they did to that kid."

"Goes without saying," Jack said.

"So out with it. What do you want? Or worse yet, what've you already done without permission?"

"Laura and I have identified one of the kidnappers."

Rose's jaw slackened, then a look of delight crossed her face. "That's fantastic! How?"

"Let me give you a little history on the file that you likely don't know. The kidnappers threatened to harm the child if the police were called, but of course, David Chung did report it. Unfortunately, while the ransom was being delivered, the car Alicia was driving got burned."

"Oh, Jesus."

"It wasn't her fault, but she blames herself. In their last call to Chung, the kidnappers said they were making an example of him."

"And then they did what they did," Rose said.

"I took that comment to mean that there'd be other kidnappings, and that the Chungs would be given as an example to future victims of what could happen if they went to the police."

"And have there been more kidnappings?" Rose asked.

"Yes, but this is where things get a little tricky," Jack said.

"I knew it. What did you do?" Rose asked accusingly.

"Alicia told us that the Chungs hated the police for what happened to their son and ceased any co-operation since the day their son was mutilated."

"Uh-huh."

"So I did a very quick, very small UC on the parents by pretending my son was kidnapped."

"Quick, small, whatever you call it, you never submitted an op plan for authorization!" Rose's face darkened. "I was there when Lexton warned you the last time. If you wanted a transfer, there were easier ways to get it."

"I'll explain why I didn't in a minute. First let me tell you that the UC worked; Chung introduced me to a guy by the name of Andy Zhao whose daughter was kidnapped last week."

"Last week! So there was another one," Rose exclaimed.

"Actually Chung told Jack that there have been two others since Tommy was taken," Laura said.

Jack nodded. "So I continued the UC on Zhao. From him I discovered a downtown location where both victims were told to go before they were sent all over town with the ransom. After that, Alicia managed to get some CCTV footage from Zhao's run last week and compare it to footage from two years ago. We spotted a man who I think was using scanning equipment on Chung and Zhao without their knowledge. This morning Laura and I did surveillance in the area and spotted the guy. We've since identified him."

"Wow ... that's great." Rose's words were heartfelt, but she paused and looked at Jack. "Lexton isn't going to be happy. Hopefully your results will help, but why on earth didn't you submit a plan?"

"Yeah, about that," Jack said. "There's a little more to it. The Chungs are taking legal action against the RCMP for what happened to their son and have named Alicia in particular. Internal Affairs put out an order that nobody talk to them. The kidnappers also threatened retaliation if any of the parents went to the police after the fact."

"Oh, shit, I knew this was too good to be true. Lexton would have a bird if she knew. The kidnappers would never believe that you got the information the way you did. What if they follow through on their threat? Couple that with the ongoing civil action, and it would really put her in a bind. She'd have to take disciplinary action. A transfer would be certain."

"The thought has crossed my mind," Jack replied.

Rose looked exasperated, but conceded, "I guess I should be happy you told me. A few years ago you'd have kept your mouth shut and just tipped off Crime Stoppers or something."

"Uh, there's something else that you won't like."

"Something else?" Rose made a motion to reach for her purse. "That's it. I can't take it anymore. I'm going to shoot you."

Jack knew she was half joking, but that the other half was angry. "It's not about the kidnapping. At least not yet, providing nobody finds out what I did. It's about Lexton."

"Oh, Jesus," Rose cried, "what've you done to her?"

Jack put up his hands in protest. "Nothing, I swear!" He filled her in about what Alicia told them and his concern that Lexton was trying to get an inside look at what went on in their office.

When Jack was finished, Rose inhaled deeply and exhaled, then stared at him for a moment. "In my heart, I know your suspicions are right. Which makes me think she'd be happy to throw the book at you."

"I realize that."

"I should have been more suspicious when she said she'd spoken with Staffing on our behalf." Rose looked at both their faces. "Really, what officer in her position would bother to do that? I was so pleased about what she said that I never thought to question her real motive."

"Neither did we," Laura noted.

"At least Alicia wasn't asked to spy," Jack said. "If she hadn't said what she did, we wouldn't have been any the wiser."

"I think she went along with our plan due to her personal need to solve the kidnapping case," Laura said. "At the same time, it caused her to reflect on why she may have been selected. We're lucky that the circumstances led her to tell us about it."

Rose mulled it over. "Lexton likely didn't know about the kidnapping — she was stationed in Ottawa at the time. Even if she did, she couldn't have guessed it would lead to this conversation."

"Exactly," Jack said. "I feel we can trust Alicia because she was honest with us, but at the same time, because she's so honest, I doubt she'd last ten minutes if she were grilled on anything, uh, slightly untoward." He paused. "She thinks you don't know about the UC I did on Chung and Zhao. I think it'd be wise to keep it that way."

"So if her loyalty to you two falters, it leaves the door open for her to come to me."

"First line of defence," Jack said quietly.

Rose thought for a moment, then appeared to come to a decision. "Did you even think to have a plan before starting all this?" she asked pointedly.

"Of course I did. My plan is to catch whoever chopped off Tommy's fingers," he replied heatedly.

Rose nodded. "That sounds like a good plan."

CHAPTER TWENTY-THREE

It was Wednesday morning in Toronto when RCMP Constable Greg Dalton finished testifying and stepped down from the stand. He'd caught the look of jubilation from the defence lawyer, heightened further by the Crown prosecutor's look of consternation. He also caught the scowl directed at him from another Drug Section member sitting in the courtroom.

Dalton had been called in by the prosecution to offer expert witness testimony as to the evidence that had been seized. It was not his case, but due to his years of under-cover drug experience, his knowledge and expertise in the field were extensive. This gave him standing in court to offer an opinion about evidence, such as quantity and value of drugs, packaging, credit slips, coded conversations from intercepts, and anything else he felt was pertinent.

Today's case was not complex. An elderly Chinese man had been arrested in the Toronto airport after returning from Hong Kong with a quantity of opium secreted in cigarette cartons. Drug importation was a serious offence and could warrant a substantial length of time in jail.

Did he look like a drug trafficker? No, but Dalton explained that elderly people were often used as drug mules so as not to attract attention. He also noted that the opium appeared to be professionally hidden in the cigarette cartons; it was not an amateurish attempt in which tampering would have been found in a cursory examination.

"In your opinion, Constable Dalton," the Crown prosecutor had asked, "does the evidence put forward to you today suggest that this person is a professional smuggler, perhaps working for a drug distribution network?"

Probably, but there's a 1 percent chance that he isn't. Dalton cleared his throat. "There's other evidence that I feel needs commenting on. He was also found to have a small quantity of opium in his pocket."

"Uh, yes," the prosecutor had replied. "Is that of any significance?"

"It would be unusual for a paid drug mule to be caught over something as overt as having some of the drug in your pocket. It makes me question whether he is a professional smuggler, or someone who merely purchased the drugs from a professional network simply for his own use."

The prosecutor's mouth had flopped open. "You think that quantity is for personal use?"

"The quantity seized from him is large and would normally indicate that it was intended for redistribution, but the price of opium is much lower in Hong Kong. There is a remote chance he purchased it with the idea that it would last him for a very long time."

"I see. I have no further questions."

The defence lawyer stood. "I have no questions for this witness, your honour."

Smart. I've given you grounds to seek a much lower sentence. Questioning me might cause the judge to reject the 1 percent notion and go for a higher sentence.

Dalton ignored his colleague's continued scowl as he exited the courtroom. *Yeah, I know. He was probably busted from informant information and has been couriering drugs for years, but I can only comment on the evidence before me.*

Once outside the courtroom, Dalton checked his phone for messages. *A call from Staffing. Already?*

Dalton's father had recently died, and his mother, who suffered from arthritis, was now living alone in Burnaby. Two weeks ago he'd asked for a compassionate transfer to the Metro Vancouver area so he could help look after her. He'd said he was willing to accept any position, whether it be administrative, uniform, or whatever.

* * *

"Chief Superintendent Quaile from Staffing is on the line," the secretary said.

Lexton frowned. "Put him through."

"I have some great news," Quaile said. "I think you'll be delighted."

Why, are you retiring?

"I've come up with the perfect candidate to fill the open position in Intelligence. Get this, his performance records say he's forthright and always does the right thing, even if it puts him at odds with his peers."

"Where's he from?"

"Toronto Drug Section. All his service has been back east, so he won't have any, uh, alliances with anyone here to whom he might feel obligated."

"Thank you for keeping me informed."

"I knew you'd be happy."

Happy? You dumbass. I'd be happy if I didn't feel I had to do this.

CHAPTER TWENTY-FOUR

Jack and Laura greeted Alicia warmly at the start of her first official day in the Intelligence Unit.

"Hangover?" Jack asked.

Alicia smiled. "No, I behaved myself last night. I didn't want to show up my first day smelling like a brewery mouse. First impressions and all."

"Good. Come with us and we'll introduce you to Rose."

The introduction was both friendly and brief. On their way back to their office, Jack whispered to Laura, "Get ready. I bet she'll be dancing and singing 'Do You Love Me.'"

Laura smiled. "From *Dirty Dancing*."

A moment later they settled at their desks. Jack and Laura exchanged a look, suppressing their anticipation, then Laura turned to Alicia. "We thought we'd start you off with a case we've been working on." She slid a mug shot of Peter Powers onto Alicia's desk, along with his criminal record.

Alicia scanned it quickly. "Drug investigation, I presume?"

"Yes, but Jack came up with an informant who may alter the course of our investigation. It has to do with Peter's brother."

"This guy," Jack said, passing over a photo of Derek.

Alicia glanced at the photo, then did a double take. Her jaw slackened.

"My informant indicated that he was involved in a kidnapping," Jack added. "What do you think? Should we check him out?"

"It's — it's him!" Alicia stuttered. "The guy behind David Chung and Andy Zhao in the CCTV footage!"

"Let me see that photo again," Laura said, trying to keep a straight face. "I think you might be right."

Alicia gaped at each of them. "You found him! We — we know who he is!"

"Yes, Laura spotted him yesterday morning," Jack said. "We followed him and then —"

Alicia let out a sob. Her eyes brimmed over and she sat back, her arms hanging limp at her sides.

I wasn't expecting that.

Jack and Laura looked at each other, then got up and came around to her desk. Jack patted her on the shoulder. "We've identified the bastard. Now we need to find out who his friends are."

Alicia rose from her chair, first hugging Jack, then Laura, who this time hugged her back warmly.

"Thank you," Alicia said, choking out the words. "You don't know how much this means to me."

I think we do.

Once she'd calmed down, Jack and Laura went over the details of what they'd done yesterday.

"Is there a possibility that Derek was just hired to scan someone for a wire and didn't know it involved a kidnapping?" Alicia asked, pausing to blow her nose.

"Possible, but I don't think so," Jack replied. "Look how stressed and worried David and Andy were. With Derek's background, he would've realized it wasn't above board if he didn't already know. I think he's in on it completely."

"Look at the business he runs," Laura added. "This guy is a professional. We need to be extra cautious."

"Still, we've got one of them," Alicia said firmly.

"We've identified him," Jack said, "but as you know, knowing and proving are two different things."

"Maybe Derek is the brains behind it and his employees are the others," Alicia suggested, "including his brother."

"His brother, maybe," Jack replied, "but I doubt the others you mentioned are involved. They're young criminology students who work part-time and come and go. It's possible, and we'll keep an open mind, but Laura and I saw three of them yesterday. I didn't get the feeling that any of them would have the stomach to take part in what happened to Tommy."

Alicia's face momentarily reflected her angst over the grim possibility they wouldn't be able to obtain the evidence needed. Then she seemed to think of something else. "I wonder if Derek has done business with the companies that David and Andy work for?"

"Commercial Crime is looking into that for us," Jack replied.

"Aren't you worried that MCU will find out and wonder how you came up with his name?" Alicia asked.

"That brings us to the next step," Jack said. He explained how, to cover them legally, he'd use Andy Zhao as his informant, but in a report identify criminals associated with Peter in order to give the impression that one of them had squealed. He also told her what he told Commercial Crime, that someone in MCU might be dirty.

Alicia shook her head. "Oh, man, is this part of that grey zone you talk about?"

Both Jack and Laura grinned.

"When do we pass it on to MCU?" Alicia asked.

"As soon as we can identify someone connected to Peter whom everyone might believe to be the informant," Jack replied. "It won't take long."

Alicia looked downcast.

"What is it?" Laura asked. "We thought you'd be so excited that you'd get up and dance."

"Believe me, I'm super pleased. It's just that I have so much invested, and now that I finally know who one of the players is, we have to hand it over to MCU ... which is where I was working yesterday."

"Sort of a Catch-22," Jack said. "If you hadn't been transferred, Powers wouldn't have been identified. Now that you've done it, we have to turn the file over to them."

"I guess the important thing is seeing the kidnappers go to jail," Alicia said. "It doesn't really matter who gets to slap the cuffs on them."

"You got it," Jack said. "We try to remain anonymous and in the background as much as possible. Even so, there are times in our work when we feel a lot of job satisfaction." *Like when the bad guys take their last breath.*

"Well, from what I've learned and seen over the last week, I'm thrilled to be here," she said sincerely. "So when do we start looking for these criminal associates? I'm available tonight if you want to do surveillance."

"Not tonight," Jack said. "I think an early day shift tomorrow would be good so we can see what Peter is up to. If he isn't working at a legit job or with his brother, then we'll set up surveillance on him again at three p.m. on Friday."

"Sounds good to me," Alicia replied.

"It is a holiday weekend, though," Jack noted. "People may be travelling or not following their usual routine."

"We'll have to play it by ear as to whether or not to stay on him," Laura explained.

"Hold on, someone's calling me." Jack answered his cellphone.

"Hello, Jack. This is Constable Greg Dalton from Toronto Drug Section calling."

"Do I know you?" Jack asked.

"You don't know me yet. I got your number from Sammy Crofton in Vancouver Drugs. You likely haven't heard yet, but I'm being transferred to your unit."

"I hadn't heard. You're out of Toronto? How'd you manage that?"

"It's a compassionate. My mom and dad moved from Saskatchewan to Burnaby two years ago and bought a house. My dad died of a heart attack three months ago."

"Sorry to hear that."

"Thanks. Anyway, my mother is getting on in years and refuses to move out of the house. I'd like to be near to keep an eye on her. I'm putting my own house on the market this week."

"You married?" Jack asked.

"Two years. No kids yet."

"How do you know Sammy Crofton?"

"I did a UC operation in Vancouver about three years ago. He was in charge of the cover team. It was only a week long. Sammy had an informant who introduced me to four Lebanese brothers. Ended up taking them down with a few kilos of coke."

"I'm an operator, as well," Jack noted.

"Great. I've been doing UC for about seven years, mostly out east. Had a good time with Sammy, though. He looked after me and didn't leave me sitting in some hotel room by myself."

"Sammy's a friend of mine," Jack said. "He's a good guy."

"Good, then you can call him to check me out," Dalton replied.

I think you and I are going to get along really well.

After saying goodbye to Dalton, Jack did call Sammy.

"I've got nothing but good things to say about him," Sammy said. "He's smart, doesn't come across egotistical, like some operators do, plus he has a good sense of humour. You're lucky to be getting him. I wish he were coming here and not to your unit."

Jack was pleased. *Seems almost too good to be true.*

CHAPTER TWENTY-FIVE

At 6:30 a.m. on Thursday, Jack, Laura, and Alicia, each in their own vehicle, converged near Derek and Peter's apartment. It was on the ground level of a three-storey, red-brick Colonial-style building. Behind the building were designated parking stalls.

"I checked," Jack said, on conference call over his hands-free. "Derek's black SUV and Peter's red Mustang are parked beside each other. The only exit is alongside the apartment. My guess is Derek will be leaving soon to go to work. If Peter isn't with him, we'll stay and wait."

"Sure would be nice to have a tracker on his car," Alicia noted.

"Think about the business Derek is in," Jack replied.

"I know, he'll have gadgets for detecting trackers. I was just saying that it'd be nice."

At 7:30 a.m., Derek drove his SUV out onto the street. Laura did a loose surveillance and saw him drive to his office and park in the same spot where she'd seen his vehicle yesterday. She then returned to the apartment, where they waited for Peter.

At 1:30 p.m. Peter left through the front door of the apartment building and walked for ten minutes. Jack, Laura, and Alicia maintained surveillance from their vehicles.

"He's crossed Bute and is still walking southeast on Nelson," Jack reported when it was his turn to maintain visual contact. He saw Peter veer off into a park. *This can't be a coincidence.* "He's entered a park and is sitting on a bench. It's —"

"That's Nelson Park!" Alicia said excitedly. "The same park where Andy Zhao and David Chung were sent to during the ransom drop!"

"Yes, I realize that. I've got a place where I can see him through the binos. Laura, you set up to the east. Alicia, stay north."

A couple minutes later, a car arrived, and two men got out and approached Peter.

"Heads up," Jack said. "In the event that you didn't hear the loud music coming from down the street, two guys have arrived in a black Toyota Supra with a large spoiler on the back. They parked and are out talking to Peter. Both are dark skinned, maybe early to midtwenties. The driver is wearing a black do-rag and is clean-shaven. His passenger has dreadlocks and is sporting a horseshoe moustache."

"Can you see what they're up to?" Alicia asked.

"Only talking, from what I can tell. The newcomers are doing lots of nodding. From the body language, I'd say Peter's running the show. The Toyota is parked facing south on Thurlow. We'll try and follow it when it leaves, but stay loose. I'd rather lose them than heat them up."

"Copy that," Laura and Alicia echoed.

Five minutes later, the two newcomers returned to their car, and moments later, the team was following them onto the Trans-Canada Highway. The licence plate was registered to a Llanzo Brown with a Surrey address, but thirty minutes later, the car drove into an underground parking lot beneath a high-rise apartment building in Burnaby.

"Guess he forgot to change his address when he moved," Laura noted sarcastically.

"I'll go out and take a look at the intercom directory for names and see if I can come up with an apartment number," Jack said. A couple of minutes later, he reported, "The suites are simply listed as 'occupied.' Let's meet back at the office."

It didn't take long to confirm that Llanzo Brown, at twenty-four years of age, had amassed an impressive criminal record, including two drug trafficking convictions, two aggravated assaults, and one manslaughter conviction. Over the last six years he'd spent a total of four years in prison and was currently on parole.

"Wonder if he and his friend could be the other kidnappers," Alicia said.

"I really doubt it," Jack replied. "They've got nothing close to Derek's level of sophistication, which is probably why Peter met them in a park and not at his apartment."

Alicia nodded, then studied his mug shot. "Sweet boy. I wonder if my folks would like him."

"Hopefully you're not his type," Jack replied. "That being cokeheads."

"What about his friend with the dreadlocks?" Laura said. "He looks like a real prize."

"Yes, I saw him through the binos," Alicia replied. "Dreadlocks aren't my thing."

"We'll start by pulling everything we can on Llanzo," Jack said. "Get mug shots of every associate of his you can come up with."

"Do you want to talk to his parole officer?" Alicia asked.

"Not yet. If word does get back to Llanzo, I don't want him to realize it happened right after he met with Peter."

"You think the parole officer would burn us?" Alicia asked.

Jack shrugged. "In our work we've discovered dirty cops, dirty judges, and dirty parole officers. Why take a chance? Even if it's not intentional, certain questions or the wrong look and Llanzo might clue in that something has made his officer suspicious. He may be young, but you can bet he's hardened after prison. His street smarts are likely fine tuned."

At 5:00 p.m. Laura handed Jack a mug shot. "Dreadlocks is identified," she said.

"Yes, that's him," Jack confirmed.

"His name is Tarone Smith. He's twenty-three years old, and his driver's licence lists the same address in Surrey that Llanzo's does."

"Record?" Jack asked.

"Oh, yeah. Convictions for one count of trafficking, one aggravated assault, and one manslaughter. The same manslaughter involving Llanzo. They beat and kicked a man to death outside a nightclub."

"Drug deal gone bad?" Jack asked.

"Nope, they didn't know the guy. It stemmed from an argument inside the club when they accused the guy of looking at them."

"That certainly justifies it," Jack said. "I'm surprised they were convicted."

"Don't be so cynical," Laura responded. "I spoke to a VPD detective who was involved. He said a psychiatrist testified on their behalf that the young men were suffering from PTSD due to violent home lives caused by their fathers when they lived in Jamaica. Both apparently moved to Canada ten years ago with their mothers to get away from their fathers. The shrink said that given proper therapy and a chance, Llanzo and Tarone could become respected members of society. Hence, they each received a three-year sentence for that charge."

"Now I'm embarrassed I was so cynical," Jack replied, his voice dripping with sarcasm. "Where's my compassion?"

"Probably in your holster," Laura replied.

* * *

At 5:30 p.m. Friday, Jack followed a resident through the lobby doors of the Burnaby high-rise. Moments later he located the Toyota Supra in the underground parking stall, then went outside to his own car.

"The car is there," Jack reported. "The stalls are numbered, though not with apartment numbers, so we still don't know which one they're in."

"So we wait," Laura said.

It was 10:00 p.m. before the Toyota Supra emerged from the parkade, with the team following. Thirty minutes later, Llanzo and Tarone entered a men's club in Vancouver called the Hedonic Palace.

"Well, ladies, unless you want to pose as strippers, I suggest you let me do the inside coverage," Jack said.

"I don't know, maybe I could make enough in tips to buy us a fridge," Laura said.

Inside the club, Jack spotted Llanzo and Tarone seated close to the stage, ogling the stripper performing in front of them. He saw an empty table in a darkened corner and headed toward it. *I remember, you don't like it when people look at you.*

As the night progressed, Jack noticed the club bouncer joining Llanzo and Tarone at their table on several occasions, sometimes gulping down a shooter of liquor with them before returning to his post at the door.

On another occasion, Jack observed a stripper catching the bouncer's eye while he was at the door. She lightly touched her nose — the bouncer gave a nod, then followed her into the back.

Jack waited for the bouncer to return and take his position at the door before walking past him to leave. A neck tattoo that read *FTW* caught Jack's attention.

Once outside, Jack went over to where Laura and Alicia were sitting together in Laura's car and leaned in through the window. "They act like regulars and are friends with the bouncer, who's putting out coke to the strippers. His name tag identifies him only as Leo. About my height, husky, clean-shaven, with an FTW tattoo on his neck."

"FTW?" Alicia asked.

"Fuck the world," Jack replied. "Very common tattoo with bikers."

"There's staff parking in the back," Laura noted. "Want us to scoop some plates?"

"Do it, then we'll meet back at the office."

The bouncer was quickly identified as Leo Ratcliffe. He was thirty years old and had a record for assault and drug trafficking, and seven convictions for possession of stolen property. His address listed him as living in a suite in a house in Port Coquitlam.

"I've got something else," Alicia noted. "When I ran his name it listed him as being a member of the Devils Aces, an outlaw motorcycle club, out of Hamilton, Ontario."

"Interesting," Jack said. "I bet he keeps a low biker profile here. That club has been at war with Satans Wrath. If they caught him, he'd be in for a beating, or maybe worse. Could end up on the wrong side of the grass."

"So what's the next step?" Laura asked.

"It's a long weekend, so on Tuesday let's confirm if Ratcliffe lives at the address on his driver's licence. I'd also like to dig up background info on him out of Ontario."

"Do you have any contacts in the Ontario Provincial Police?" Alicia asked.

"I know someone in the OPP Biker Enforcement Unit," Jack replied. "After that I'll do a report on these guys and note that an informant identified Peter's brother as being involved in a kidnapping." He eyed Alicia. "That's where you come in. Around the end of next week I'll give you the honour of calling MCU to tell them you've identified one of the kidnappers and to arrange a meeting for us to turn over our file."

Alicia bit her lip, then nodded.

CHAPTER TWENTY-SIX

Alicia called Sergeant Hawkins on Thursday morning while Jack bent over her desk to listen in. She felt like the words were getting stuck in her throat. Was it from the excitement of having identified one of the kidnappers, or the pressure of knowing how they'd really obtained the information and the scam she was taking part in.

Alicia blurted out, "We've got a break in the Chung kidnapping!"

"What?"

"I've identified one of the kidnappers," she said quickly. "The Intelligence Unit had some info about a kidnapping, but hadn't connected it. They'd thought it was between drug dealers, but I checked. It wasn't. It involved David Chung."

"Are you sure?"

"Positive. My bosses, Sergeant Taggart and Corporal Secord, want to set up a meeting and turn their file over to you."

"Alicia, this is fantastic. I'll need to round up the people who've been involved. It's almost lunchtime now ... how about two p.m.? Can you come to our building? That would be easier, seeing as a lot of people here will want to sit in on the meeting."

Jack nodded. "No problem," Alicia said. "We'll be there."

* * *

A few minutes before the meeting was to start, Hawkins decided to pay a visit to Connie. She was all smiles until he told her Alicia's news.

"Son of a bitch!" Connie said angrily. "How long has Alicia been over there?"

Hawkins was surprised at her reaction. "She started a week ago yesterday," he replied. "I thought I'd stop by because you've worked with Taggart, right?" He eyed her curiously. "I've heard a few rumours about him over the years."

"I know him well," Connie stated. "Too well. That son of a bitch! He's already got her into something twisted or evil."

"What're you talking about? This is the break we've all been praying for."

"I guarantee you, if Taggart's involved, you'll end up transferring the file over to my side of the office."

"Homicide?"

"If you let him anywhere near it, at least one body will turn up eventually."

"They're turning the file over to us."

"Yeah, right. Turn around so I can see a monkey fly out your ass."

"You don't think they will?"

"He probably has to because it falls within your domain, but I'd be damned careful if he remains connected in any way."

* * *

Alicia returned a wave from her former colleague, Corporal Devon Bradley, as she sat down beside Jack and Laura in the conference room. She gave Hawkins a warm smile when he sat directly across from them. He was stone-faced. *Looks like you're as tense as I am. No worries, wait until you hear what we've got.*

"Shall we start?" Jack asked.

"By all means," Hawkins replied.

"Prior to Alicia's transfer to our unit last week, we were investigating a person by the name of Peter Powers, whom we suspect of being a cocaine trafficker."

Guess that's true, Alicia thought. *I hadn't officially started yet when we identified him.*

"As you can see in this copy of my report," Jack said, sliding it across to Hawkins, "Peter Powers is connected to two other people of interest to our unit."

"Those being Llanzo Brown and Tarone Smith," Hawkins said as he scanned the report.

"Correct," Jack replied. "We know Llanzo and Tarone are also connected to a fellow by the name of Leo Ratcliffe. We haven't confirmed if Peter knows Ratcliffe, but the person who'll be of interest to you is Peter's older brother … Derek Powers."

"Hold on a sec," Hawkins interjected. "Your report says that Ratcliffe is a small-time dealer putting out to strippers and living in a basement suite in Port Coquitlam." He eyed Jack suspiciously. "Are you telling me that your unit, which deals with organized crime, is interested in someone selling grams of coke to strippers?"

"We're always trying to look at the bigger picture," Jack replied.

Alicia struggled to keep her face neutral. She felt Jack's foot nudge hers.

"These three men may be only the tip of the iceberg," Jack continued. "Ratcliffe is a member of the Devils Aces out of the Hamilton, Ontario, chapter. They're spread throughout eastern Canada and have been at war with Satans Wrath for several years. If Ratcliffe has been sent here to see about opening up a chapter, then the war out east will be brought to our doorstep."

"That means shootings and bombings amongst innocent citizens," Laura noted.

"Furthermore, Llanzo and Tarone are both Jamaican," Jack added. "The Jamaicans also have a formable drug distribution network in many major cities across Canada. If they've joined forces with the Devils Aces, it is of definite interest to us."

"I see," Hawkins replied, looking embarrassed. "Sorry, I was simply curious. Thanks for explaining."

"Our information to date does not clarify whether any of this is taking place," Jack said. "Perhaps they are only low-level drug dealers not worthy of our time, but until we know for sure, they're definitely of interest to us."

"I take it your informant said that this group is involved in the Chung kidnapping?"

"My informant provided information to identify Peter's brother as being involved in a kidnapping. Upon reading

our reports, Alicia questioned me about kidnappings, and
I told her that it is not uncommon for bikers to grab someone, usually a wife or girlfriend, as collateral against some
drug dealer who's delinquent in paying them."

Yes, I remember that.

"Alicia told me she'd worked on an unsolved kidnapping and wished to compare some CCTV footage from
that case to a photo we had of Derek Powers." Jack turned
to her, smiled, and said, "Take it away, Alicia."

"It was a match!" Alicia stated. "CCTV footage of
David Chung standing on the corner with the ransom
money in a satchel shows Derek Powers behind him. In
the footage it appears that Derek may be talking on his
cellphone, but our theory is that he is actually checking
Chung and the satchel for GPS transmitters."

"Your *theory*," Hawkins reiterated.

Come on, quit being so stubborn. That's not like you.

"There's more," Alicia continued. "Derek's office is close
to that corner. It's called Powers Security Consultant Service.
Besides the usual corporate and private security concerns he
advertises, it's rumoured that he does corporate espionage."

"Holy shit," Hawkins exclaimed. "Then it makes sense.
You really are on to something!"

*Damn right we are. Too bad you don't know just how
big yet.*

"Without Alicia's persistence, this connection would
likely never have been discovered," Jack said.

Finally, Sergeant Hawkins offered her a smile.

"Is there a possibility that Peter Powers, Llanzo Brown,
Tarone Smith, and Leo Ratcliffe are the other kidnappers?" he asked.

"Peter may be involved," Jack said, "but I doubt the rest are. In my opinion, whoever orchestrated the kidnapping wouldn't trust people of Smith, Brown, and Ratcliffe's low calibre. Their records are attached to the report — they show a long history of drug trafficking and violence. On a cerebral level, they don't fit with the likes of Derek Powers."

"Let me ask you a direct question," Hawkins said sternly. "Was your informant involved in the kidnapping?"

Of course he was involved. He was the victim.

Jack appeared to be surprised by the question. "As stated in the report, my informant didn't even know Derek's name. It was Alicia who made the connection." He smiled knowingly. "I see where your concern is, though. You're afraid that once you identify and arrest all the kidnappers, my informant could be among them."

"Yes … and then you'd try to cut a deal or something."

"No fear," Jack replied. "The informant is clear of any arrest concerns, as far as kidnapping goes."

"What role do you see yourself and your unit playing?" Hawkins asked.

"None," Jack replied. "My informant is no longer in a position to assist with any of the names I've given you."

"None?" Surprise registered on Hawkins's face. "So that's it?" Surprise changed to suspicion. "You're turning the file over completely?"

"Yes. I'd like to be appraised if you gather any evidence to support whether or not the Devils Aces have linked forces with the Jamaicans. Or, likewise, if you hear that the Devils Aces plan to open a chapter in Vancouver — but even then I wouldn't take any action until you give the go-ahead."

"Of course. I understand. Thank you," Hawkins replied.

"Derek Powers sounds pretty sophisticated," Bradley noted. "I think the best way to proceed would be through the back door. Get Barry Short to do a UC on the dope dealers and meet Derek through Peter. Maybe in time Derek will trust him enough to talk about the kidnapping."

"Why not do a UC on Derek directly?" Jack suggested.

"Like I said, the other guys are dumb and violent. I'm sure they wouldn't have been selected to take part in something as sophisticated as —"

"Cutting off a kid's fingers is dumb and violent," Hawkins stated heatedly. He paused. "Thank you for your input. You can leave now."

Alicia waited until they were walking to the car before venting her anger. "Some gratitude! I can't believe how we were treated in there. He couldn't wait to toss us out," she fumed.

"It's okay," Jack replied. "Some people are a little territorial when it comes to their investigations. As long as the job gets done, that's all that matters."

"It's not like Hawkins to act like that," Alicia replied.

"You said he was a good guy," Laura noted.

"Usually he is. I don't know what got into him." She glanced at Jack. "What were you going to suggest in there? Doing a UC on Derek right off the bat?"

"Might save a lot of time," Jack replied.

"It'd be pretty hard," Alicia said skeptically. "Nobody would bat an eye if you asked someone where to score some dope, but you can't just go up to a guy and say, hey, I want to kidnap someone. Do you know anybody who could help me?"

Jack smiled. "Actually, what I'd do …" He stopped. "No, never mind, it's not our case. We need to move on. Maybe what they suggested will work."

It damn well better.

CHAPTER TWENTY-SEVEN

Constable Barry Short was an affable man with a stature befitting his name. He was a short, wiry individual who had a permanent happy-go-lucky smile on his face. It was these traits, perhaps, that helped make him a successful undercover operative. His size and good nature tended to put others at ease and he was never considered a threat to the hyper-masculine types with insecure egos.

He entered the Hedonic Palace and saw Leo Ratcliffe standing nearby, arms folded across his chest.

"Say, you don't happen to know if someone in here drives a black Toyota Supra with a big spoiler, do you?" Barry asked.

"Why?" Leo replied gruffly.

"I put a scratch on it and don't have a pen and paper to leave a note."

Moments later, Llanzo Brown, with Tarone Smith beside him, viewed the small scratch along the fender that Barry pointed out to them.

"I was runnin' across the street dodgin' a car when I tripped and my fucking watch strap hit it," Barry said, flashing the Rolex he was wearing. It, like the two heavy gold chains he was wearing, belonged to the RCMP. The gold earring he wore was his own.

He shook his head in apparent self-recrimination before gesturing to the car. "It's a beautiful set of wheels, man. I feel like shit for what happened."

Llanzo looked at the scratch. "It's not all that long … or deep."

Barry handed him his undercover driver's licence. It gave his name as Barry Alvin Randall, with a Calgary address. "Don't know what it'll cost, but of course I'll pay for it. You can write down my name and stuff if it'll make ya feel better."

"You're from Alberta," Llanzo noted.

"I moved out here a couple of weeks ago. Haven't changed it yet."

Tarone bent over for a closer look at the scratch. "They might be able to buff it out."

"Yeah, maybe," Llanzo replied.

"I'm really sorry," Short said. "Tell ya what, to start with, let me buy you guys a drink." He smiled. "My friends call me Bar because of my initials. Also fits with Barry."

"Yo, I'm Llanz and this here's Tarone. Sure, we'll take you up on that drink."

They headed back toward the club. "By the way, nice watch," Tarone said. "What ya do?"

"I, uh, invest in different commodities."

Llanzo and Tarone looked at each other and grinned.

"What's so funny?" Barry asked.

"That's what we do, too," Llanzo replied. He eyed Barry. "White or green?"

"White," Barry replied.

* * *

Almost two weeks later, early on a Thursday afternoon, Barry took a taxi to the Lougheed Town Centre, a location he knew was only a two-minute drive from Llanzo and Tarone's apartment.

So far his undercover operation had gone well. Although he had yet to meet Peter, Llanzo and Tarone believed his story that he was looking for a connection to ship a kilo of cocaine back to Calgary each month. They'd told him they could accommodate him in that regard, and two days ago, Llanzo had sold him an ounce as a sample.

Up until now all their meetings had taken place at the Hedonic Palace. Today was different. He was to buy a kilo. A quantity which he hoped would allow him to meet Peter. The RCMP brass, after some cajoling, had authorized him to spend the money despite no immediate arrests taking place.

As Barry waited outside the mall, he casually scanned the sky. He knew that Hawkins was watching from a plane circling above and was relieved that the dot he eventually spotted was far enough away not to be noticed on a casual glance. He was also well aware that the surveillance teams on the ground would be staying at least five blocks away. The Chung calamity, as it had become known, was not to be repeated.

Barry smiled when Leo drove up and talked to him from the driver's window.

"You got the thirty Gs?" Leo asked.

Barry jingled his car keys. "The money's in the trunk of a car, like we agreed. Once I see the coke, I'll give you the keys and tell you where it's parked."

Leo stepped out of the car. "What makes ya think we won't rip ya then?"

"Guess you could, but I figure there's a lot less chance of it if I see the dope. Not to mention, aren't you supposed to be driving me to where Llanzo and Tarone live? In my experience, people don't rip you off when you know where they live. At least, not if they know what's good for them."

Leo chuckled. "Okay, pull up your T-shirt so I can see, then turn around. Gotta check ya for wire and also make sure you're not packin'."

Damn. I was hoping Derek would show up to do that with a little more sophistication.

Five minutes later, Leo buzzed up to Llanzo and Tarone's apartment. Barry watched Leo push an elevator button. *Eighteenth floor.*

Loud music gave Barry an indication of which apartment they were going to. He wasn't wrong. Wearing his black do-rag, Tarone answered Leo's knock and motioned for them to enter.

Barry scanned the apartment. Facing him was the living room, where Llanzo sat on a sofa sucking on a crack pipe. Off to the right were two bedrooms divided by a bathroom. On his left was a closet and an adjoining wall that ran down the length of the living room to an entrance leading to the kitchen.

The carpet in the living room was covered in an array of grease and footprints of dried mud. Across from the sofa was a balding upholstered chair. The coffee table was cluttered with empty beer bottles and an overflowing ashtray. A large flat-screen television and stereo system looked new.

"You all set to do this?" Tarone asked, reaching for the crack pipe that Llanzo held out to him.

"Hell, yeah," Barry replied. "Maybe after this we won't have to play these games again. I hope you understand that I didn't exactly want to go with some guy the size of Leo with thirty grand in my pocket."

Llanzo glanced toward Leo, who was entering the bathroom, and smiled. "Don't blame ya for that, brother," he replied. "I'll make a call and it should be here soon."

Tarone took a suck on the pipe, then offered it to Barry.

"Not when I'm doin' business."

"Yeah? Whatever," Tarone replied.

"Wanna beer instead?" Llanzo asked, standing up.

"Yeah, I'll go for that," Barry replied. He followed Llanzo around the corner into the kitchen, which held a small table and two stainless steel chairs. The table and countertop were cluttered with dirty dishes. A glass door that opened onto a balcony between the kitchen and the living room was stained with a generous splash of what looked like dried cola.

Llanzo took a bottle of Budweiser from the fridge and handed it to him, then took out his phone.

Barry knew he wouldn't be able to hear the phone conversation from the living room due to the loud music, but to stand in the kitchen and listen would draw suspicion.

Instead, he pretended to admire the view, sliding open the patio door and stepping outside.

"Yo, man. It's me," he heard Llanzo say. "We're ready to go. Where ya at?" Llanzo paused. "Good. See ya."

Out on the balcony, Barry looked into the sky. *Wonder if Hawkins can see me? Probably not, since there are balconies directly above.* He looked down and automatically tightened his grip on the railing. *Christ, I hate heights.*

"Yo, Bar. Ten minutes tops," Llanzo said. "May as well come in and be comfortable."

Barry took a seat on the upholstered chair while Llanzo sat next to Tarone on the sofa. Leo exited the bathroom a moment later and opted to grab a kitchen chair and bring it into the living room.

Conversation for the next ten minutes was light, then finally, someone buzzed and Llanzo answered the intercom.

Barry tried to act nonchalant when he saw the man who entered. *Perfect. Hello, Peter Powers!*

Peter had a backpack slung over one shoulder. He gave Leo a friendly smile when he walked in, then his gaze took in Barry and he stopped short, enraged. "Llanz!" he ordered, nodding toward one of the bedrooms.

Barry tried to listen, but Llanzo had closed the bedroom door behind them. All he could hear was Peter saying, "Who the fuck is that!" Llanzo's murmured reply, then Peter again: "You didn't fuckin' tell me he'd be here!"

A moment later they came out. Barry raised his eyebrow at Llanzo.

"It's okay, it's okay," Llanzo said. "My friend doesn't like meeting new people. He needs to make a call, but everything's okay."

Barry shrugged.

Peter took a phone from his pocket, eyed Barry suspiciously, then turned the music up louder.

Don't want me to hear?

Peter glared at him, then spun on his heel, returned to the bedroom, and closed the door.

Barry looked at Llanzo. "You sure everything's okay?"

"Yeah, I guess I wasn't supposed to bring you here. But it'll be okay. I told him you were solid."

The next few minutes ticked past slowly. Barry decided to tell a joke, hoping to ease the tension. He was partway through it when Peter opened the bedroom door again and motioned for Llanzo to join him. A moment later, Peter walked out, glanced at Tarone, and said, "I gotta go. Llanz wants to talk to you."

Barry watched Tarone go into to the bedroom while Peter left. *Shit, now what?* It was obvious that Peter didn't want to be there when the deal went down. *Hopefully he'll trust me once it goes through okay.*

Barry tried to appear friendly when Tarone reappeared, followed by Llanzo. But his optimism vanished when Tarone stepped aside and Llanzo pointed a pistol at his face.

"What the fuck?" Barry exclaimed. "Is this a rip?"

Llanzo's lips curled in rage. "Hello, Constable Barry Short."

Oh, fuck.

CHAPTER TWENTY-EIGHT

Barry saw the green numbers on the clock on the stove from where he sat on the kitchen chair. He'd taken some comfort when Llanzo told him they were going to gag and tie him up, then take off.

Two-thirty. I arrived at two ... what time will it be before the cover team figures out something's gone wrong? Five, six, seven? Dope deals never go on time. They may think I'm sitting in here, sucking on a beer and waiting.

"Use his sock and T-shirt to gag 'im," Llanzo ordered.

Barry removed his T-shirt and placed it on his lap. Llanzo moved in behind him, and he felt the muzzle of the pistol at the base of his skull. Tarone and Leo then used the power cord from an electric skillet to tie his wrists together behind his back and secure them to the chair. Electrical cords, still attached to a toaster and a kettle, were used to bind his feet to each of the front legs of the chair.

Tarone yanked off Barry's shoe, then his sock. "Open up nice and wide, piggy. That's it."

Seconds later, Barry sat with his sock crammed in his mouth, his T-shirt rolled up and tied around his jaw to hold it in place. Tarone turned his back to him, and he heard the sound of utensils being moved around in a kitchen drawer.

Oh, God, no. Please don't …

Tarone turned back, grinning, and Barry writhed in pain as Tarone cut him with a paring knife, slowly drawing it down from the top of his shoulder, across his nipple, to his stomach, before ending with a sharp twist of the point inside his navel.

"How ya like that, piggy?" Tarone asked, holding the knife in his bloody fist close to Barry's face.

"That's enough," Leo said. "We're in enough shit. Come on, we better split."

"No fuckin' way Tarone an' I are goin' back inside," Llanzo said. "You can fuck off if ya want. But you'll be missin' out on a whole lotta fun."

"Yo, bro, it's school time," Tarone added. "Piggy is gonna get taught."

Leo glanced toward the living room, then back at Barry. His face said he wasn't happy about it, but he didn't leave.

"Yo, bro, let me show ya how it should be done," Llanzo said, shoving the gun in his waistband as he went to the kitchen drawer. "First of all, you did it too fast. Second of all, a fuckin' steak knife is better, 'cause it's serrated."

Barry knew his muffled cries brought on more slashes and more amusement on Llanzo and Tarone's faces, but it wasn't something he could control. On the fifth jagged cut, this time across his belly, the numbers on the stove read *2:47*. Then he blinked, and the numbers read *3:05*. The men had disappeared. He heard their voices from the living room.

I passed out.

The front of his jeans was sodden with blood and he felt his bare foot slip in a bloody puddle on the linoleum floor.

Llanzo's voice came from the living room. "We need to get rid of 'im. If we're grabbed we can say, yo, man, he was here but then he left."

Barry struggled with his wrists, trying to slide them up and down in a desperate attempt to free himself. *I can feel the cord in my fingertips. Work it … loosen the knot.*

"Figure he's got the thirty large?" Tarone asked.

"Fuck, if he does, you can bet the cops are watching his car," Leo stated. "I'd stay away from it."

"What we should do is gut 'im out in the tub," Llanzo said.

A moment of silence was broken by the sound of someone sucking on the crack pipe, then Tarone said, "That'd be good. Maybe one of us go out and get a hacksaw and some fuckin' garbage bags. Once he bleeds out we could cut 'im up and suitcase him outta here."

"You're readin' my mind," Llanzo said. "Also get a bottle of bleach to pour down the drain later. Maybe on the kitchen floor, too."

"You guys are fuckin' crazy," Leo said. "I ain't hangin' around to watch that shit."

Llanzo blurted out a laugh. "What, no stomach for it?"

"Yeah, don't ya wanna see what piggy had for lunch?" Tarone asked.

The door slammed, then Llanzo and Tarone laughed.

Leo's gone.

"That fucker givin' us the finger," Tarone said. "Next time we see 'im I'm gonna tell 'im what a pussy he is."

My hands are almost … yes, they're free!

"Let's go do it," Tarone said. "We can gut 'im and leave 'im to bleed out while we go get what we need."

Barry clenched his teeth in pain as he bent forward to fumble with the cords around his ankles.

"Yeah, yeah. Give me a sec," Llanzo said.

Barry heard the pipe crackling again as he slowly rose to his feet. His arms and legs were trembling from a combination of shock, fear, and blood loss. He knew he'd never be able to run past them in the living room and escape out the door alive. He looked at the balcony.

"We'll leave the hot water runnin' in the tub to help wash things down," Llanzo said, followed by the sound of the crack pipe being placed on the coffee table.

Barry slid open the balcony door and rushed out. He heard Tarone scream at Llanzo to grab him, but didn't look back as he swung himself over the railing, clinging to the wrought-iron balusters with his bloody fists and sliding down to the bottom rail. Briefly, he felt his body swing freely in the air, then Llanzo's face appeared above him and his fingers slipped from their hold.

CHAPTER TWENTY-NINE

Corporal Bradley was parked a kilometre away from Llanzo and Tarone's apartment when Hawkins phoned.

"I see two uniform cars with lights on heading toward the apartment," Hawkins reported over the drone of the airplane. "You hear anything?"

"My window's down," Bradley replied. "I can hear the sirens now, but I didn't hear anything leading up to it." *Nothing like a gunshot.*

"Call Telecoms and find out what the hell is going on."

Bradley's call to a woman in their Telecommunications office was short.

"Yes, we received a 911 call," the dispatcher said. "A woman reported a half-naked man covered in blood landing on her balcony. She's on the seventeenth floor, so —"

"Oh, fuck!" Bradley shouted as his adrenalin kicked into high gear.

"Listen, that sort of language isn't —"

Bradley disconnected to make a conference call while the tires of his surveillance car howled into action.

* * *

Alicia spent a good portion of the day on surveillance with Jack and Laura, following Satans Wrath member Buck Zabat around. Jack had said that although he didn't expect Buck to be up to anything conspicuously illegal, he still wanted to see how Buck put in his day.

Jack was right. Buck wasn't up to anything illegal. In fact, he didn't appear to be up to anything at all besides driving over to the Satan's Girls Entertainment Agency and returning to his apartment with a young woman.

"It's time to call it a day," Jack said when they met together in a mini-mall parking lot. "Tomorrow we'll pick another target."

"Maybe go back to Linquist and see what he's up to," Laura suggested.

Alicia's phone vibrated. It was Bradley. What he told her made her swallow hard to keep from being sick. When she ended the call, she saw Jack and Laura staring at her.

Jack's voice was sombre. "What happened?"

Her voice shook as she relayed what she'd been told. "Barry's condition is apparently not life-threatening. They say he'll require hundreds of stitches and I don't know how many blood transfusions, but he'll live."

"Llanzo Brown, Tarone Smith, and Leo Ratcliffe?" Jack asked tersely.

"In custody. They're not going after Peter because they don't want him to know that they know who he is. Solving the kidnapping case takes precedence over finding out how Peter found out about Barry."

Jack and Laura looked at each other for a moment.

"Maybe we should go to the hospital," Alicia suggested.

"No," Jack replied firmly. "We're undercover operatives. If the media gets wind of it, they'll be there filming. You stay clear. Got that?"

"Yes … I understand."

"Oh, man. I can't go home right now," Laura said, looking at Jack.

"Likewise," Jack replied.

"What are you going to do?" Alicia asked. "MCU is handling it."

"We're going for a drink," Jack stated.

"You feel like drinking?" *At a time like this?*

"We're both married," Laura explained. "We need to unload. Some … emotional baggage, especially concerning another HQ number, is best left outside the home. Our spouses suffer enough as it is."

"Are you coming?" Jack asked.

"Uh, do you want me to? I don't mind if —"

"Yes, we want you to." His voice softened. "You're an operator, too. We're like family. You'll feel that way, too, once you get some experience. What happened to Barry is personal. Personal to all of us."

* * *

At 9:00 a.m. the following morning, Assistant Commissioner Lexton gestured for Inspector Crimmins and Sergeant Hawkins to take a seat across from her desk.

"What is Constable Short's condition?" she asked brusquely.

"He's been given something to ease the pain and help him sleep," Hawkins replied, "but before that I was able to meet with him about three hours ago and get a statement."

At least he's alive. She looked at Crimmins. "Anything of particular interest that you didn't already know when you called me yesterday?"

"Nothing of significance."

"How's his wife doing?"

"Karen's understandably distraught, but managing to hold herself together," Hawkins replied. "She was with him until midnight, then came back again this morning while I was taking the statement. They have a four-year-old boy. I understand the neighbours are babysitting him."

"Okay, I'd like to hear what happened yesterday in detail. Start from the beginning."

Crimmins did most of the talking, turning to Hawkins once in a while for clarification. When they finished, Lexton focused her attention on Hawkins.

"Let me get this straight," she said. "You were — what? Two kilometres up in the air and the closest members on the cover team were a kilometre away when Constable Short was attacked?"

Hawkins removed his hands from the arms of the chair and clasped them over his groin, perhaps subconsciously.

Come on, Sergeant. I'm not going to castrate you.

"Yes, uh, that's uh, you see —"

"Two years ago our office worked on people associated to this group who'd kidnapped an eight-year-old boy," Crimmins stated. "At that time we conducted a similar surveillance with the cover team. Despite our precautions, we were spotted, and as a result, the child's fingers were chopped off. This time our members were slightly farther away. Bearing in mind what happened last time, I believe the action taken yesterday by Sergeant Hawkins was prudent."

Nice to see you back your men. "I'm familiar with the Tommy Chung kidnapping and the mutilation he suffered. You may've forgotten that I gave final approval for the expenditure to purchase a kilo of cocaine for this investigation."

"Yes, of course ... sorry," Crimmins replied.

Lexton refocused on Hawkins. "I'm not blaming you for what happened. I was simply trying to get a clear picture of events as they unfolded. Where do we stand on the investigation? Didn't you have wiretap on their phones?"

"We've had wire on Derek Powers's office phones for almost a week, but there haven't been any calls of interest, and no calls from Peter," Hawkins answered. "We're presuming that they're using disposable phones, and we don't know their numbers. Furthermore, if they do have cellphones, they'll likely be encrypted."

"What about the phones of those who were arrested?" Lexton asked.

"We think Llanzo Brown and Tarone Smith flushed their SIM cards down the toilet as they were about to be arrested," Hawkins said. "However, Leo Ratcliffe was arrested at his residence, and his phone was seized intact. It's early, but some numbers he called in Ontario belong to known members of the Devils Aces outlaw motorcycle gang. Many of the numbers haven't been identified yet. It'll take a few days."

"An outlaw motorcycle gang," Lexton mused.

"Yes," Crimmins said, "Sergeant Taggart from the Intelligence Unit first put us on to this investigation after receiving informant information indicating that Derek Powers was involved in a kidnapping."

Taggart. Oh, Christ.

"Actually it was Constable Alicia Munday who discovered the connection shortly after she was transferred into the unit," Hawkins noted.

"Did Sergeant Taggart or anyone else in the Intelligence Unit play a role in the investigation after providing you with the initial information?"

"No," Hawkins replied. "Sergeant Taggart only asked to be told if we heard that the Devils Aces were planning to open a chapter here. That and he was concerned about the Jamaicans hooking up with the bikers, as well."

I can't believe I'm going to say this. "Considering how your investigation ended up yesterday, I think it would be wise to include the Intelligence Unit going forward. There must have been a leak somewhere for them to have known Constable Short's real name."

"And I don't think the leak was accidental," Hawkins said bitterly. "Barry said everything was going fine until Peter Powers showed up. He believes Peter called someone who tipped him off. We have no idea who it could be. But God help the person if I ever find out," he added angrily.

"I trust, Sergeant, that you're referring to the sentence that would be handed down once the perpetrator is brought to justice in a court of law."

Hawkins sighed. "Yes, of course."

"Have you considered the possibility that your surveillance from two years ago may have been compromised by the same individual?"

"That's something we've discussed," Crimmins stated. "But there simply isn't anyone whom we suspect."

"All the more reason to work with the Intelligence Unit — a fresh set of eyes without any personal relationships that might cloud judgment."

"We're still optimistic about the kidnapping investigation and bringing the perpetrators to justice," Crimmins stated. "If we're successful, it'll no doubt result in a lengthy trial. But it's my understanding that the Intelligence Unit prefers not to be called to court to testify."

Lexton felt her anger rise. *I don't even want to think about what that poor man went through. Bleeding to death and clinging to life on a balcony eighteen floors above the ground.* She glared at Crimmins.

"What happened to our member yesterday was an atrocious act of violence! If the Intelligence Unit can assist in any way, I couldn't care less whether they have to testify or not!"

"Yes, uh, certainly. I agree," Crimmins replied.

Actually I don't know of a case where Taggart has ever testified. His suspects generally don't live that long.

"I'll call Sergeant Taggart to let him know," Hawkins said. "He's an undercover operative, too. I'm sure he'll want to help."

Want to help? Those bloody operators are like a family unto their own. It's how he'll help that concerns me.

Her intervention with Staffing had been well timed. *Perhaps now I'll discover what Taggart's really all about.*

"I'll also speak to Staff Sergeant Wood and make it clear to her that the Intelligence Unit is to co-operate fully," Lexton said. "Where do we stand with the three accused who were arrested yesterday?"

"Llanzo Brown, Tarone Smith, and Leo Ratcliffe are still in custody," Hawkins stated. "Today is Friday and I expect they'll be held over the weekend. After that, I've been told that the Crown prosecutor is confident that Brown and Smith will remain in custody, but there is a possibility that Ratcliffe could be released. His role in the matter was not as significant and his criminal record not as violent."

With Taggart involved, Llanzo Brown and Tarone Smith may be the lucky ones.

CHAPTER THIRTY

Jack was at his desk when Rose phoned. "My office. Come alone."

A moment later he entered Rose's office and shut the door behind him. "What's up?" he asked, taking a seat.

"Lexton called and told me she just had a meeting with Crimmins and Hawkins."

"That's no surprise after what happened yesterday."

"No, but what caught me off guard is she told MCU to include us in their investigation. She said she's particularly concerned that the bad guys called Barry Short by his real name; she suspects there's a leak. She also mentioned the possible biker involvement as a reason for us to get involved."

"You don't believe her?" Jack questioned.

"She's upset over what happened and wants to find out how Barry's cover was blown, but ..."

"But?"

"Considering the reason we think Alicia was selected to come into our section, I can't help but question whether Lexton has an ulterior motive for including us in the investigation."

"Maybe there is, but Lexton's not the only one upset. I'm glad for the opportunity to get involved. Someone must have tipped off Peter Powers."

"No doubt, but MCU doesn't want to heat up Peter yet. The Chung kidnapping is still their priority."

"I agree with that. My gut feeling is that Derek Powers has a connection who tipped him off, and he then warned his brother. Considering the type of work Derek does, I'm sure he has police connections. Makes me wonder if Alicia really was burned two years ago or if she was simply the fall guy."

"Then perhaps you should start off by focusing on Derek."

"Believe me, I hardly slept last night. If he's not already in MCU's sights, he sure as hell is in mine."

Rose stared at him for a moment. "I suspect you're also in Lexton's sights. Remember to tread carefully."

* * *

Later that morning, Jack received a call from Hawkins.

"I already heard," Jack said. "Lexton wants us to assist in whatever way we can."

"Yes, she made that clear to me and Crimmins when we spoke to her."

"I suspect Derek Powers had a hand in what happened to Barry. I'm thinking Peter called him when he saw Barry in the apartment."

"I agree," Hawkins replied, "but who told Derek who Barry really was? And was this leak the reason we blew our surveillance with Chung two years ago?"

"That's crossed our minds, as well. Anyone in your office you think is capable of it?"

"No one," Hawkins replied. "For the last week we've had wire on Derek's office phone, but his brother hasn't called him. We don't have a personal cellphone number for either Derek or Peter."

"They likely use disposable phones that they change regularly," Jack replied.

"That's what we figure. We did get Leo Ratcliffe's phone. When he left the apartment, he went home, and we bagged him there by surprise. Got some numbers that he called in Ontario identified. A couple came up on the system as being connected to the Devils Aces. Lots of other numbers we don't know about yet. I was wondering if you could help us with that?"

"I've got a contact in the OPP Biker Squad. I'll see what I can do. First, though, do you want to get together and discuss a strategy for how to proceed?"

"Today's not good — we're still giving statements over everything that happened yesterday and trying to piece it together. Next week would be better."

"I don't mind coming in with my people this weekend. We could sit down tomorrow."

"Uh, no, this weekend isn't good, either. I'll email those numbers to you, then call you early next week to arrange a meeting."

Why are you stalling?

* * *

It was 2:00 p.m. on Monday when Hawkins called Jack again. "Are you free to have that strategy meeting today?"

"Yes," Jack replied. "We can be there in a jiffy."

"Stay there. We'll come to you. I talked it over with Inspector Crimmins. We don't want anyone in here to know what's going on unless they have to."

Good.

Forty-five minutes later, Hawkins and Bradley arrived. Rose then wheeled a chair in from her office to join the meeting.

"Does your meeting us here mean that you suspect the leak came out of your unit?" Rose asked.

"Not necessarily, but we decided not to take any chances," Hawkins replied.

"How's Barry doing?" Jack asked.

"Still in hospital," Hawkins replied. "They're worried about infection, and he can barely move without triggering more pain. Says he'll never work UC again."

"I don't blame him for that," Jack replied. "Just to let you know, I don't yet have any feedback on those phone tolls you gave me for Ontario."

"Those aren't urgent at the moment," Bradley said.

"I do have a suggestion for how you could proceed," Jack noted.

"Oh? What would that be?" Hawkins asked.

"Have you thought about a UC operation on Derek, direct?"

"How would you go about that?" Bradley asked.

"By hiring him. Have an operator pose as a major drug dealer and say he wants Derek to check out some guys he's about to do business with. Then set up a situation where it looks like he was ripped off for a large amount of cash, and see if Derek takes the bait. If he does, I doubt he'd use a bunch of criminology students. I think he'd bring in whoever was involved in the kidnapping." He glanced at Rose for a response. She gave a nod.

"Well … maybe that'd work," Hawkins said, "but as of yesterday, we have a better idea."

Yesterday? Sunday? They cut a deal. That's why he wasn't in a hurry to meet us last Friday.

"We met with Leo Ratcliffe and he rolled," Bradley stated.

"He's a member of the Devils Aces," Jack noted. "Bet that wasn't an easy decision for him."

"You're right about that," Hawkins replied. "He has a sister who waitresses in some bar they hang out at. He's pretty concerned about her and said that if word leaks out to the Devils Aces that he rolled, they'll kill her if they can't find him."

"If word leaks out to Satans Wrath, he risks getting whacked, as well," Jack noted. "I'm surprised he's even out here."

"He told us he wants out of the club, but with the war on back east that isn't possible. His idea was to distance himself by bullshitting his buddies that he was going to do a little recon on Satans Wrath over here. He told his buddies that the Satans Wrath chapters in B.C. wouldn't be as paranoid as their chapters back east and suggested it might be easier to do reprisals out here." Hawkins frowned. "Then again, he might be bullshitting us and really he *is* doing recon for the Devils Aces, thinking about opening a chapter, as well."

"That's always a possibility," Jack replied.

"The good news is he's willing to do a straight introduction to Peter Powers," Bradley added, "and he has Peter's cellphone number. With that, we'll discover Derek's number and maybe find out who the leak is."

"Is Leo in tight enough with Peter to do an intro?" Laura asked.

"He says he is. He told us that, prior to last week, he'd already told Peter that his brother Ricky is coming out from Ontario, and that Ricky wants to put out coke to some guys he knows in the interior."

"Isn't Leo concerned that if he does a direct introduction, the Devils Aces might find out?" Jack asked.

"He said he wasn't worried because Peter doesn't have any connections back east," Hawkins replied. "He also said that if a rumour did start, the Devils Aces would take his word over Peter's."

"I see."

"But do you think Peter will still deal with Leo after what happened?" Alicia queried.

"Yes," Hawkins replied. "Leo was released this morning on his own recognizance. An hour ago he met Peter, and they went over what happened. Peter says he'll never do business with the Jamaicans again, even if they do get out of jail, and he told Leo that he was right to try and stay out of it."

"So Leo is still in tight with Peter," Rose mused. "That's excellent."

"I wouldn't say he's trusted completely," Bradley said. "They met in a park and Peter scanned him for bugs first. Still, he did warm up to him after he found out that Leo didn't get involved in the torture and that he took off soon after they started. Leo says Peter is still anxious to unload the kilo he didn't sell last Friday."

"Does Leo have any idea how Peter found out about Barry?" Alicia asked.

"No, but Peter did give him his cellphone number," Hawkins said. "Maybe Peter will phone later to check out whoever Leo introduces him to."

"Which park did the meeting take place in?" Jack asked.

"Nelson Park," Bradley replied.

"I know it," Jack said. "It's close to where Derek and Peter live and also to Derek's office. I'd be extra cautious with any surveillance in that area."

"We were," Hawkins said. "Nobody but Crimmins and those of us in this room know that we cut a deal with Leo." He eyed Bradley and added, "Only the two of us were in the vicinity of the park this morning, and we stayed well back."

"Good," Jack replied.

"Our next step is to get a UC operator for Leo to introduce as his brother," Hawkins stated. "We also want to run the UC operation without anyone else from our office knowing about it."

"I might have the perfect guy for you," Jack said. "Greg Dalton. He's currently stationed on Toronto Drug Section, so that'll help if he's questioned about details or locations back east. He hasn't been out here except for a one-week UC about three years ago on some Lebanese brothers, so he's basically unknown and won't have to worry about bumping into anyone who'd know him. I checked him out about a month ago with our Drug Section, and he was highly recommended." Jack paused. "There's only one problem: he's being transferred to our unit." He looked at Rose. "I don't know how you feel about it, because if he's successful, he'll be going to court afterward."

"Well —" Rose started.

"I can assure you, that isn't a problem," Hawkins stated. He gave Bradley a bemused smile. "Inspector Crimmins spoke to Assistant Commissioner Lexton an hour ago to tell her about Leo Ratcliffe and what we intend to do. She suggested using Dalton herself. For him, having to testify isn't an issue."

"Lexton knows Dalton?" Rose questioned.

Hawkins shrugged. "I don't think she knows him per se. All she said was that she'd heard your unit was getting a UC operator transferred in from Toronto, and what with our need to keep things secret, maybe he'd be suitable. That and it'd be more cost-effective down the road not to have to pay for someone to fly back and forth for court; by then he'd be stationed here."

"Let me phone him," Jack said. "He has his house on the market, so he may be hesitant to do it."

A moment later, Jack connected with Dalton and told him MCU was looking for an operator for an informant introduction.

"This have anything to do with the member who was tortured on Friday?" Dalton asked.

"Yes. Word spreads fast, considering it never made the news."

"I doubt there's an HQ number in Canada who hasn't heard about it," Dalton replied. "Of course I'll do it. I'd be honoured."

"Aren't you and your wife trying to sell your house?"

"Sally doesn't need me to hang around for that. She'll be glad to get me out. I can't move at home without her cleaning up or polishing something behind me."

Jack gave Hawkins a thumbs-up.

"When do you want me?" Dalton asked.

"As soon as possible. I want you to get a fake Ontario driver's licence in the name of Richard Ratcliffe. The informant, who's with the Devils Aces, is passing you off as his brother, Ricky."

"I'll contact the UC coordinator — could get it tomorrow. I've already got lots of Harley shirts and the like. I could be there by Friday."

"Hang on." Jack looked at Hawkins. "Friday?" Hawkins nodded. "Friday works."

"Good, I'm looking forward to working with you," Dalton stated.

Jack briefly filled Dalton in on the rest of the situation, then ended the call.

"So it's a go," Hawkins said. "Maybe set it up to have Leo do the intro on Saturday?"

"There are some things I'd like to discuss," Jack said. "First of all, it's obvious we can't have Dalton wired. At the same time, we can't have a cover team close enough that they'd actually be of any use if he did need help."

"So how do we protect him?" Bradley asked.

Jack grimaced. "I don't think we can. In my mind, having a cover team, whether in the air or on the ground, could jeopardize Dalton more than if he's on his own. It certainly hasn't worked so far."

"Policy won't allow us to send him out there on his own," Hawkins said.

"Yes ... and policy can get you killed."

"Lexton is also concerned," Hawkins said. "She told us she'd see to it that Special O teams are available to assist. They're the experts when it comes to surveillance." He paused. "We can't have Dalton going through what happened to Barry."

"Or worse," Bradley said.

"My thoughts are to let Special O take charge of Dalton's personal security, and the rest of us stay clear," Hawkins said. "They have enough people that the same faces won't be showing up."

Jack exhaled deeply. "Okay, but I'm also going to tell him to play up the angle that he's paranoid when it comes to doing any large drug transactions. No apartment buildings. Public spaces only. Places where Special O can be in position before he arrives."

"I agree," Hawkins replied. "I feel a hell of a lot better with that idea than sitting on my ass in some plane two kilometres up in the sky."

That's going to eat at you for the rest of your life.

"Anything else?" When nobody spoke, Hawkins said, "Good, then we're set."

As soon as Hawkins and Bradley had left, Rose turned to Jack. "I want to talk to you in my office."

Jack followed her and closed the door. "You're concerned about the fact that Lexton is recommending Dalton?"

"Yes, aren't you? Her reasons sound pragmatic, but again, it's highly unusual for someone in her position to become that involved."

"Maybe Alicia isn't the only mole she hopes to cultivate."

Rose stared at him in response.

Jack sighed. "Yeah, I know. I'll tread carefully."

CHAPTER THIRTY-ONE

On Friday morning Jack met Greg Dalton at a predesignated area in the Vancouver International Airport. He wasn't hard to spot. Greg was wearing a black Harley-Davidson T-shirt, a wallet attached to a chain on his belt, and several silver rings on his fingers, one of which was a skull.

"Hello, Greg. Welcome to Vancouver."

Greg smiled and shook his hand. "Glad to be here."

Jack sized him up. Greg was slightly shorter than himself, but had black hair pulled back into a ponytail and was sporting a moustache that grew down into his goatee. He guessed Greg to be in his early thirties and knew he'd be a good fit to play the role of Leo Ratcliffe's brother.

Moments later, they loaded Greg's luggage into Jack's SUV and headed out on the Trans-Canada Highway to Port Coquitlam.

"Do you know Vancouver very well?" Jack asked.

"Not really. I've been out to visit my parents a couple of times, but hardly left their house. If it's okay with you, in a few days or so I'd like to pop in on my mother."

"That'd be fine." Jack glanced at Greg. "You also worked with Sammy Crofton on Drug Section."

"Yes, but it was a quick in-and-out kind of thing. Back for court a few times, but that was mostly going from my hotel to the courthouse and back. Sammy did have me to his house for dinner a few times. He lives in Abbotsford."

"He spoke highly of you," Jack replied.

"Good. Better you spoke to him and not to the guys on my unit."

"Oh?"

"Ah, I probably shouldn't have said that. It's nothing. I gave expert testimony in court recently and pissed off some of our guys. I testified that there was some doubt in my mind that the dope was for trafficking as opposed to personal use."

"You're being asked to give your opinion. If you're not completely honest, where's your credibility?"

"Glad you see it that way."

Jack felt sure he'd get along with Greg. "I'm taking you out to a motel in Port Coquitlam. It's about forty-five minutes away. The motel is a bit of a dive, but Leo Ratcliffe, your new adopted brother, lives in a one-bedroom basement suite not far from there."

"Don't worry about it being a dive. I'm sure I've stayed in worse."

"We've also got another room in the motel to use for debriefings and for you to make your notes. Anytime you're in your room, day or night, somebody from the team will be in the debriefing room. When we get there, I'll introduce you to two others from my unit, Laura Secord and Alicia Munday. Secord has been doing UC for years and knows her stuff. Munday only recently finished the course and hasn't done any operations yet. She's a few years younger than you and recently transferred in from MCU."

"Secord. She's the corporal, right? Soon to be my boss?"

"Once your transfer is completed and you're working in our unit, you'll answer to her, yes. As far as this operation goes, myself and Sergeant Ned Hawkins from MCU will be running the show. Hawkins will be in charge of any investigative decisions, and I'll oversee any operational UC decisions."

Greg smiled. "In other words, you're along to protect my ass."

"You got it. Hawkins is also handling Leo. He'll bring him over to the motel to meet you this afternoon."

"Good. I'll need to talk to him about siblings, parents, where we went to school, what bars we drink at. You mentioned he was from Hamilton? I did a UC there a few years ago, so I know it fairly well."

"Leo's a bouncer at a strip club called the Hedonic Palace. He's working tonight, so he'll pick you up and you'll go there with him. I know you'll be tired, what with the time difference and the travel, but I'd like you to make an appearance."

"No problem. If he really was my brother, I would."

"Leo won't finish work before two a.m. at the earliest, but you can take a cab back to the motel before then if you want. Tomorrow you're to meet Peter Powers and talk coke."

"With the idea that eventually I'll meet Derek," Greg noted.

"Exactly. He's the number one target, although I suspect Peter had a hand in the kidnapping, as well."

"Got it." He paused. "Is Leo an agent? Is he going to be testifying?"

"No, he's only an informant. Once you're in tight with the targets, he plans on moving back to Ontario."

"So I'll try to cut him out of things as soon as possible."

An image of Barry Short flashed into Jack's brain, and he glanced at Greg. *Just try not to get cut yourself.*

* * *

It was 9:00 p.m. and the Hedonic Palace was crowded and noisy, its patrons becoming more vocal with catcalls and jeers the more they drank.

Greg had opted for a table away from the stage. He sipped on a Guinness while Leo worked the door.

Two short, overweight, balding men sat in what was commonly known as "pervert row" — the seats closest to the stage. Their plaid sports jackets hung open, and one had his tie loosened around his neck while the other one's tie hung from a side pocket.

As the stripper on stage finished her act, the man with the tie in his pocket abruptly stood, bumping the table and slopping his cocktail. He leaned over the stage, clenching a five-dollar bill between his teeth. The stripper obliged by cupping his face with her breasts to remove the money.

"Hey, Larry," his buddy chortled, "for that much money, ya should be able to bring her home ... and meet the wife!"

Larry appeared to think about it. "Think she'd mind?" he asked, before falling back into his chair.

Nobody noticed a moment later when Larry pretended to sip his cocktail … instead whispering into his sleeve.

* * *

Jack sat behind the wheel of his SUV, parked in a grocery store parking lot a kilometre away from the Hedonic Palace. Beside him sat Hawkins. Laura, Alicia, and Bradley were in the car parked next to them.

The phone rang. He was surprised to be getting a call so soon from Special O … and even more surprised at what they told him.

"What's going on?" Hawkins asked after Jack ended the call.

"Peter showed up. Leo is introducing him to Greg now."

"Even though the meeting was scheduled for tomorrow," Hawkins noted. "Maybe that's good. Shows Peter is anxious."

"Or suspicious and wanted to check him out right away," Jack replied.

At 11:00 p.m., Greg left the club and hailed a cab. Jack and the others went on to the motel and were waiting when Greg tapped on the door.

"Peter showed up," Greg said, upon entering.

"So we heard," Jack replied.

"He was still there when I left, but said he'd be heading home right after he finished his beer. Leo doesn't expect he'll be done work before three a.m."

"How'd it go with Peter?" Laura asked.

"I think it went well. He was friendly, but he was checking me out. Wanted to know if I was ready to meet and do a large one tomorrow morning."

"A large one?" Bradley asked.

"A full kilo. I turned him down, of course."

"But we've got the money for that. It was already approved," Bradley said.

"I told him I didn't have the cash yet." Greg glanced at Jack. "The story is I'm putting out to buddies from the interior, right?"

"Right," Jack replied. "Seeing as he's only just arrived," he explained to Bradley, "it's unlikely that he'd already have met his guys and arranged for a delivery."

"Oh."

"I'm sure he was testing me with that," Greg said. "I told him I had enough for a couple of ounces as a sample, but it'll take four or five days to get the rest of the cash."

"Perfect," Jack replied.

"He wants to meet me tomorrow morning to do a deal for two ounces."

"That's really, really good news," Hawkins stated.

"Hopefully it turns out. He asked if I was staying with Leo, and I told him I was staying here 'cause Leo only has one bed and he snores. He said he'd swing by about ten thirty a.m. Don't know if he'll have it with him or if we're going somewhere else. It's too early for Leo to be getting up, so Peter expects it'll be only the two of us."

"The sooner you can cut Leo out, the better," Hawkins said.

"So far that's not a problem. Leo was too busy tonight to be in on any pertinent conversation, anyway." Greg dug out his wallet and handed Hawkins a piece of paper. "Peter gave me his cell number. I told him I hadn't had time to pick up a phone yet, but that I'd buy a burner phone tomorrow, and also pick up a rental car."

Hawkins glanced at the number and handed it back. "Same number that Leo gave us already."

"He started to warn me about saying anything on the phone, then laughed and said seeing as Leo was my brother, he didn't need to counsel me on that."

"Sounds like he trusts you," Alicia said.

"Greed or trust — either one works for me," Greg replied. "He also mentioned he has a girlfriend in Abbotsford he'll probably be staying with tonight."

"You get a name?" Hawkins asked.

"Nope … it wouldn't have been cool to ask."

"Any calls between Peter and his brother?" Laura asked Hawkins.

"I checked with the monitors on the way over. None that we know of."

"Listen guys, I need to make my notes," Greg said. "After that I'll need some sleep. It's three a.m. in Toronto, and I've still got about three hours of work to do."

"We'll get out of your hair," Hawkins replied. "Bradley will stay here tonight."

"Special O and the rest of us will be in the vicinity by nine a.m.," Jack said. "Good luck tomorrow."

* * *

At 11:45 a.m., Peter arrived at the motel and went to Greg's room. A minute later, Special O reported that

Greg was sitting with Peter in his red Mustang, talking. The two men then went to the trunk of the car and then, seconds later, Peter drove away. Greg went straight to the debriefing room and grinned as he entered, then held up an ounce baggie of cocaine in each hand.

"Yes!" Alicia exclaimed, clapping.

"I agreed to meet him on Wednesday to buy a kilo," Greg said.

"Four days from now," Jack noted. "Where?"

"We're supposed to meet at noon for a drink in New Westminster, at a place called the Paddlewheeler Pub."

"I know the place. It's alongside the Fraser River and you can sit outside. Great place for beer and appetizers. It's a public spot, which is good if that's where the deal goes down. How do you intend to handle the cash?"

"I told him I'd rent a room nearby and that he wouldn't get the cash until I saw the dope. I told him I didn't care if he was packing a piece, because I'd trust him not to rip me off once I saw the dope. He said it's not his style to pack a gun and he has no problem showing me the dope first. I don't think we need to worry about a rip. Once I see the dope, we could complete the deal in the hotel room."

"Sounds good," Jack replied.

"The only bad thing is there's no hint of his brother being involved yet."

"No worries," Hawkins replied. "It sounds like Peter's in your pocket. That's all I'd hoped for at this point."

* * *

Hawkins was glad to hear that they finally had Peter placing a call to his brother's office an hour after he'd left the motel. Unlike their cellphones, which were encrypted, the office phone wasn't, so they were able to listen in on the conversation. He wasn't pleased when he heard the gist of the call:

"Hey, bro, what you up to?" Peter asked.

"Working. Some guy screwin' around on his wife. Took a few pics."

"I tried your cell."

"What? Oh, I must have left it in the van. Where've you been? Stay at your girlfriend's last night?"

"Yup. Got some good news, though. Got someone to take that, uh, big set of golf clubs off my hands."

"What? Who?" Derek asked testily.

"Leo's brother. He arrived from Ontario on Friday. Took two clubs from me this morning to try 'em out."

"Jesus fuck, Peter! Why didn't you tell me? You pull a stunt like that right after …" He paused. "After you know what."

"No, no. Leo was talking about his brother moving here long before last week. This isn't new."

"You still should've told me about it first."

"Maybe, but I need the bread. The clubs were, uh, on consignment."

"Where the hell are you?"

"At my girlfriend's."

"Get over here. We need to talk!"

CHAPTER THIRTY-TWO

It was 5:00 p.m. on Saturday when Greg called Peter to give him his new cellphone number and to let him know that he'd picked up a rental car.

"What're you up to tonight?"

"Still a little bagged from jet lag. Thought I'd have an early night."

"We need to talk about something. Are you at the motel?"

"Yup."

"I'm at home, which is in downtown Vancouver. How about we meet halfway? Say at the Starbucks at Brentwood Town Centre. You know where that is?"

"My car has GPS. I'll find it. Want to meet now?"

"No, uh, let's meet there in two hours."

"Yeah, okay. See ya then," Greg replied. A moment later he went to the debriefing room, which was being manned by Laura.

"What was his tone like?" Laura asked.

"He was cordial, but not as friendly as before. Judging by that call between Peter and Derek that Hawkins told me about, I think he caught shit. Hopefully he's not having second thoughts."

"He's already sold you two ounces," Laura noted. "A little late to be backing out. I'll phone Jack and alert the troops," she said, reaching for her cellphone.

"Maybe Derek wants to check me out personally," Greg suggested. "This might turn out to be a good thing."

* * *

Thirty minutes prior to the meeting, Special O was in position. As before, Jack was in his SUV with Hawkins a kilometre from the mall, and Laura, Alicia, and Bradley were parked beside them. They soon discovered that Derek was indeed attending the meeting — but not in the way they'd hoped.

Jack was alerted to Derek's arrival in a call from the Special O member in charge of his team. His name was Brian Rhodes, but he'd been nicknamed Bumpy due to acne scarring on his face from when he was a child.

"We've got a target vehicle that entered the lot and parked," Bumpy reported. "It's the blue Ford van belonging to T-1. The driver hasn't exited the vehicle."

Crap. "Hang on," Jack said, then turned to Hawkins. "Derek's van showed up and nobody got out."

"He's doing countersurveillance," Hawkins stated.

"For sure, but with what gadgets?" Jack replied. "In his line of work he could have cellphone detectors, bug detectors, radio-frequency detectors, you name it."

"We're looking at a busy mall on a Saturday evening," Hawkins replied. "There's bound to be a lot of cellphone usage."

"Yes, but how much coinciding with Peter or Greg's arrival, then their departure?" Jack turned his attention back to his phone. "Tell your team they're not to report anything until after the van has left, unless it's an emergency."

"I heard your concerns," Bumpy said. "No problem. I'll put out the word to cease all chatter and hold positions until after the van is gone."

Jack updated the occupants of the other car. Everyone waited in silence.

At 7:45 p.m. Bumpy called again.

"Okay, the HQ arrived on time, and T-2 arrived five minutes after in his red Mustang. They had a quick coffee, then came out together, got in their cars, and left. We can confirm that T-2 headed west on the Trans-Canada and HQ went east. The van waited for five minutes, then left heading west, as well. We also confirmed that T-1 was driving."

"Good, thanks. Did you have an eye on HQ's car the whole time?"

"Yes. Nobody went near it. Should be safe from bugs and trackers."

"Great. I'll call you back in a minute," Jack replied. He called Greg.

"Hey, Jack. Don't know if you know, but only Peter showed up. He said he was worried about whether I'd be able to get the cash together for Wednesday and wanted reassurance, otherwise he'd sell to someone else. I told him I'd definitely have it together, but uh, I don't know."

"Don't know what?"

"Seems a little fishy. I'd already assured him I'd have the money by Wednesday. And he knew I was tired. To meet just to reconfirm what we already talked about seems lame."

Jack told him that Derek had been in a van outside.

"Sounds like these guys know what they're doing," Greg said. "Guess we better do it better."

Thirty minutes later, Jack spoke to Bumpy again. Surveillance on Derek's office had spotted him returning with his van and parking it in a secure underground parking lot two blocks from his office. Bumpy also asked if Jack would like Special O to assist in planting a bug or tracker on it.

Jack was thankful for the information, but decided it would be too risky to do so, considering Derek had the equipment to scan for such items.

* * *

Greg entered the Paddlewheeler Pub at 12:00 p.m. on Wednesday and took a seat on the patio, then ordered a Kokanee and a plate of breaded calamari. Twenty minutes later, Peter called to say he was running a little late, but would be there in an hour.

At 1:00 p.m. Peter called again. "There's been a change. I'm at a lounge called Fraser's Nugget. I'm supposed to meet someone here shortly and the time is getting away from me. Can you pop over so we can talk? It's about a ten-minute drive from where you are, and there's parking in the rear. If you take Royal Avenue to —"

"Fraser's Nugget," Greg repeated. "I'll punch it into my GPS. Be there as soon as I can." *The RCMP should buy watches for all the dope dealers. Sure would save a lot of money if they could do things on time for a change.* As he returned to his car, he called Jack.

"The place is in Coquitlam, but not far from you," Jack said. "Drive slow. I'll make sure Special O has someone in there to cover you before you arrive."

"Any sign I'm being watched?" Greg asked.

"Not that we can tell. Special O saw Derek arrive at work this morning, and they called me a few minutes ago to say he's out with a bunch of young people who work for him. They're currently at a coffee shop near his office having lunch."

It was 1:20 p.m. when Greg entered Fraser's Nugget and approached Peter, who was sitting alone at a table. The lounge was quiet and dimly lit. The only other customers were a man and a woman cuddling in a darkened booth, holding hands and looking at each other like naughty children. Their wedding rings said they were married, but it didn't take much imagination to guess they weren't married to each other.

"So what's happening?" Greg asked as he sat down.

"Fuck all," Peter said angrily.

"What the hell? I thought you were ready to do this? I already rented a room for the cash. You should've at least called me earlier."

"Sorry. It's my fault. I unloaded the key I promised you to someone else after my connection assured me he had another one on hand. A few minutes ago he tells me that's gone, too, and he won't have any more before Saturday."

"Damn it," Greg replied. "I don't know if I can wait. I may need to go elsewhere."

"Yeah, well, that's your prerogative."

He says he'll have it in three days, but makes no attempt to get me to wait? Greg cleared his throat. "If I wait, is there a chance you'll come down on price a little?"

Peter glanced at his watch. "I don't know. I'll ask."

The waitress came to take Greg's order, but Peter said, "Listen, I'm supposed to meet the guy in a few minutes. He'll be ticked if you're here. Do you mind?"

Greg smiled apologetically at the waitress. "Sorry, looks like I'm on my way out."

Greg was halfway to the exit when Peter called after him.

"Hey, Ricky! Give me a call this evening. Maybe we can get together."

His tone was friendly and it gave Greg hope that everything would turn out okay. "I'll do that," he replied.

A moment later, he was walking across the parking lot at the rear of the building and fishing his car keys out of his pocket. He heard a woman call out to him.

"Greg! Greg Dalton! It is you!" she said as she approached. "What are you doing so far from Toronto?"

The woman was tall, attractive, in her midthirties, and had long, dark hair that hung to her shoulders. She wore skin-tight black leather pants and a red silk blouse that offered an ample view of her cleavage. A black leather purse with tassels was draped over one shoulder, and she carried a department store shopping bag in the other hand.

"I'm sorry. You think you know me?" he asked.

The woman smiled. "Jesus, Greg, how drunk were you that night? Are you saying you don't recognize me with my clothes on?" she teased.

Something moved in his peripheral vision, and Greg realized they weren't alone. He turned and caught a brief image of a baseball bat before the blow smashed his nose, cheekbone, teeth, and part of his eye socket.

Lying on the asphalt in a daze, he heard the woman's voice.

"Give him a few more whacks to make sure he's dead."

CHAPTER THIRTY-THREE

Jack wasn't concerned when he heard the ambulance siren. They were only a few blocks from the Royal Columbian Hospital in New Westminster, and since their arrival, it was the third siren he'd heard.

His curiosity was aroused when Hawkins received a call from Special O. Within seconds, the panic in Hawkins's voice told him something had gone horribly wrong.

"Make sure uniform secure the area!" Hawkins yelled. "What? Oh, fuck, oh, fuck. They've already notified my office?"

Hawkins ended the call and stared at Jack, his mouth hanging open.

"What happened?" Jack demanded.

"Greg left the lounge about ten minutes ago, but Peter stayed. Everyone held their positions and maintained silence for fear the bad guys have a cellphone detector. A few minutes ago some guy out walking his dog cut through the back parking lot and found a body."

No. Please, no. This can't be happening.

"They think it's Greg," Hawkins added.

"You mean it might not be him?"

"One of the Special O members got a look as the ambulance was loading him up. Said his face isn't recognizable. He was beaten with a pipe or a bat or something ... but he was wearing the same clothes that Greg was." Hawkins swallowed. "His car's still in the lot, too. It's, it's gotta be him."

This is my fault. I was supposed to be looking after him.

"Uniform's there?"

"Yeah, and they cordoned off the area. They already called my office. That's why Bumpy called me." Hawkins paused. "I-HIT is attending."

"So he's either dead, or they expect him to be."

"Yeah." Hawkins looked dazed. "I'll coordinate with I-HIT. Someone will need to attend the hospital. I — I gotta make some calls."

Jack clenched his jaw in an attempt to control his emotions as he lowered his window to speak to Laura, Alicia, and Bradley. *And I need to call Rose. Greg's wife will have to be notified.*

* * *

An hour later, Jack and Rose met Assistant Commissioner Lexton in her office.

"Any update?" she asked immediately.

"They found a weak pulse when he was admitted," Jack said. "He's in a coma. A neurosurgeon said that if they can keep him alive, he'll be in surgery for a lengthy period of time. A member from I-HIT is at the hospital and promised to keep me updated."

Lexton looked at Rose. "He's married, you said?"

"Yes," Jack replied for her. "I notified Toronto Drug Section and they sent someone to tell his wife. I gave them my number to call back to make arrangements."

"We'll pay for her flight out, of course," Lexton said. She eyed Jack. "Tell me everything from the time he arrived at the airport."

Jack went over in detail the events leading up to what had happened. When he finished, Lexton stared at him quietly. He grimaced. *I know. It's my fault. You don't have to tell me that.*

Lexton appeared to read his thoughts. "I don't see that anyone from our side is to blame for what happened," she said firmly. "Certainly not you. The decisions you made were reasonable given the circumstances."

There must've been something I could've done differently.

"Thank you for that comment," Rose said, glancing at Jack.

"What really concerns me is that this is the second undercover operative to be targeted by these people in less than two weeks," Lexton stated. "Granted, undercover work is dangerous, but this is unprecedented. Do we have any idea how their covers were blown?"

"Not a clue," Jack replied bitterly.

"Is there any chance it was a robbery? Maybe a drug addict who picked him at random?"

"I-HIT said he still had his watch and his wallet," Jack replied. "I don't think —" He was interrupted by his phone ringing. "It's Constable Jameson. She's the one I-HIT sent to the hospital."

"Answer it," Lexton prompted.

"No change," Jameson said as soon as Jack answered. "Still in surgery, but a doctor wants to know when his wife is arriving. They want to speak to her about, uh, how invasive the operation to try and keep him alive will be."

"I'm not sure whether she even knows about it yet," Jack replied. "She lives in Toronto. I'll get back to you as soon as I can."

"I've also got a picture of his face when he arrived," Jameson said. "It's, uh, unbelievable."

"Send it to me," Jack said abruptly. "I'm in a meeting. I need to go."

Jack relayed the message to Lexton and Rose as the picture came through on his phone. He looked at it and heard himself gasp. *I'm looking at a corpse. They'll never save him.*

"Show me," Lexton stated.

"It's gruesome," Jack warned, swallowing the bile rising up his throat.

"I used to work I-HIT. I've seen gruesome."

Rose leaned over for a look and winced, then Jack handed his phone to Lexton.

She turned the phone in her hands, apparently unsure of which way she was to look at the image. Her face showed little emotion, but her jawline rippled. Jack couldn't tell if she was clenching her teeth to control sorrow or outrage.

"The only times I've seen this much trauma inflicted on a victim were in crimes of passion," Lexton said sombrely. "Domestic situations, rejected lovers. People with a lot of repressed anger." She handed the phone back to Jack. "Still no weapon found at the scene?"

Jack shook his head. "It's within throwing distance of the Fraser River. The dive team has been called. If was a pipe, they should find it. If it was a bat it may've been carried downriver."

"What investigative steps have been taken so far in regards to Derek and Peter Powers?"

"Peter was brought in for questioning and immediately demanded a lawyer," Jack sighed. "He has a good alibi in that two members of Special O had him under observation in the lounge when it happened."

"An alibi which was planned, obviously," Lexton stated.

"Yes. As far as Derek goes, he was also under observation by Special O, having lunch in downtown Vancouver."

"Another planned alibi, no doubt," Lexton stated.

"It might've been a precaution, because we've never done anything to make him think we know he's involved. I spoke with Sergeant Hawkins. They'll be releasing Peter shortly, and we don't see any advantage in tipping Derek off as to our interest in him."

"What about the informant who made the introduction?" Lexton asked. "Could he have tipped them off?"

"Sergeant Hawkins and Corporal Bradley were on their way to pick him up twenty minutes ago. Considering the seriousness of the charges over his role in what happened to Constable Short, I'd be surprised if he tipped them off."

"We should find out shortly. I imagine Sergeant Hawkins will be putting him on a polygraph," Rose said.

* * *

Hawkins pounded on the door of Leo Ratcliffe's basement suite with his fist. There was no answer, no sound from within.

"I think that's his car," Bradley said, pointing to a green sedan parked in the alley behind a fence.

Hawkins tried the door. "Locked. I'll try calling him." He took out his phone and tapped in Ratcliffe's number. "No answer. Fuck it!"

The door smashed open on the first kick.

Leo was on his back inside the doorway with a bullet hole in his forehead.

CHAPTER THIRTY-FOUR

Jack had only just returned to his desk when Hawkins called to tell him that Leo Ratcliffe was dead.

"Oh, shit," Jack heard himself say. *This has got to be a nightmare. Wake up!*

"Yeah, my sentiments exactly." Hawkins sounded morose. "I've never lost an informant before."

"Do you think it happened before, during, or after the attack on Greg?"

"Connie Crane is here from I-HIT. She thinks it happened two or three hours ago."

"Before Greg was attacked," Jack noted.

"Yeah, if she's right, they may've popped him, then gone after Greg next. There was no sign of forced entry, and the door was locked when I arrived."

"But they shot Leo," Jack stated, "and Greg was attacked with a pipe or a bat."

"Yes, but according to Connie, the gun was a small calibre. Maybe a .22 or a .32. He lives in a basement and the landlord is at work all day. Not to mention, I saw freshly cut grass on the neighbour's lawn. Good chance that nobody heard the gunshot. Greg would've been a different story."

"They knew we would've been watching him," Jack replied. "All they needed was to catch him out of our sight and make it quiet."

"Exactly." Hawkins paused. "We're canvassing the neighbourhood for witnesses. I'll get back to you if we learn anything."

After telling Laura and Alicia what had happened, Jack was about to go and tell Rose when he received another call. He recognized the 416 area code for Toronto.

"Jack Taggart?" a man asked.

"Speaking."

"This is Constable Mason Stone from Toronto Drugs. I'm about a block from Greg and Sally's house and I'm about to tell her what happened. Is he still …" Mason's voice was croaky, and Jack agonized for him and what he was about to do.

"He's still in surgery."

The sigh was audible. "That's good, I guess." Mason paused. "He and I've done a lot of UC operations together, and I was best man at their wedding two years ago. Now I wish he'd stayed single, like I did." Mason paused again, then asked, "Can you give me some details?"

Jack relayed the gist of what had happened, his own role, and how serious the injuries to Greg's head were.

"Christ, what do I tell her? I don't want to give her false hope."

"I'd be as matter-of-fact as you can. She'll likely be in shock and it could take time to register, so hang in there with her."

"That's a given. Any progress on the arrests?"

"Not yet. I just found out that the informant who made the introduction was murdered shortly before Greg's attack. They grabbed one of the suspects who instructed Greg to go the area where he was attacked, but he demanded a lawyer and was subsequently released. Special O had him under surveillance when the attack occurred, so there's no chance that he did it himself."

"But he could have arranged it."

"Yes. His brother — another suspect who runs a security consulting business — was also under surveillance."

"So he has a solid alibi, too. Sounds like these guys are real pros."

"Which is why I stayed back and ordered only minimal communication."

"I'd have done the same. Still, you must feel like shit."

"Yeah, I do. Nothing compared to how Sally will feel, though. At least I can tell you that the brass have already okayed her to fly out here."

"I'll come with her. Don't care if it's on my own dollar." Mason paused. "I've never been to Vancouver before. Greg's mom lives in Burnaby, so I imagine Sally will want to break the news to her as soon as we arrive. Is that far from the hospital?"

"The hospital is in New Westminster, so depending where in Burnaby Greg's mom is, it's a fifteen- or twenty-minute drive."

"Okay … I'll rent a car when I get there. I suspect I'll stay at his mom's house, too."

"Don't worry about a rental. I'll pick you up at the airport myself … providing Sally wants anything to do with me, that is."

"I doubt she'll blame you. She'll take her cue from me. I've been doing UC for the last seven years. If I don't blame you, she won't either." Mason exhaled loudly. "Gotta say, though, the thought of telling her is making my stomach crawl up my throat."

Unfortunately, I know exactly how you feel. "Once you start talking to her, you'll forget how you're feeling."

"Because I'll be focused on her," Mason replied.

Your own feelings won't return until afterward. Feelings of sorrow, rage … and revenge.

* * *

At 10:20 a.m. the following morning, Jack spotted Mason and Sally in the arrivals area of the Vancouver International Airport. Neither looked like they'd gotten much sleep the night before.

Sally was a petite strawberry blond with mascara smudging her freckled cheeks. She was wearing a light-blue pantsuit and Jack guessed she was about thirty.

Mason, who was about the same age, wore blue jeans and a T-shirt. He was lanky, with a well-trimmed beard and dark-brown hair that hung to his collar. His eyes searched the crowd, then focused on Jack.

Jack approached and introduced himself. Mason was Jack's height, and his grip was firm. Considerably younger, Mason's face still had a youthfulness that Jack had long since lost.

He saw the anxiety on Sally's face when she shook his hand. "The surgery lasted seventeen hours, but Greg made it through," he said, knowing what was on her mind. "He's currently in an induced coma, and on a ventilator."

Sally nodded.

"I'm sorry, but I wasn't given any indication of how long he'd be —"

"It's okay. I understand," she said softly. "I'm a registered nurse."

"We'd like to go to the hospital immediately," Mason stated, "but maybe it would be best to rent a car here at the airport. Then I can drop it off when I fly back."

"I'm lending you mine," Jack replied. "I can use a company car."

"No, you don't need to —"

"It's not a problem. My wife has a car, as well. Plus a corporal on my unit lives close to me. She'll meet us at the hospital to pick me up. No worries. Keep it for as long as you need. It's got GPS, so you shouldn't have any trouble getting around."

Forty minutes later, they arrived at the Royal Columbian Hospital, where Jack introduced Laura to Mason and Sally. He left Mason with the keys, then returned with Laura to the office.

His first call was to Hawkins to let him know that Sally had arrived.

"I've got an update for you, too," Hawkins said. "The dive team recovered a stolen .32 calibre Beretta from the river. We'll need ballistics to confirm, but I'm betting it matches up with the slug in Leo Ratcliffe's head."

"Sounds like they brought it along as backup, but preferred not to use it because they knew we'd be close by. Afterward, they tossed it and whatever they used on Greg into the river."

"That's my guess. The dive team is still searching."

"A .32 Beretta," Jack mused. "I bought one of those for my wife years ago. Fits nicely into her purse should the occasion arise for her to carry it."

"Interesting you say that. We found a witness who lives across the back alley from Leo Ratcliffe. She says she saw a woman enter Leo's yard through the gate while a man waited by the fence. The woman was gone only a minute, then she returned and they both left."

"Could she identify them?"

"Even if she could, we couldn't use her in court. She's senile and not sure if it happened yesterday or perhaps last week. She has no idea what they were wearing. All she remembers is that the woman was good-looking and had either black or maybe blond hair."

"You're kidding."

"Wish I were." Hawkins paused. "I'd wondered if the killer walked in through an unlocked door, or if it was someone Leo knew. Maybe neither. He might've simply opened the door for a pretty woman."

"Any thoughts on how you'll proceed?" Jack asked.

"We'll keep digging and knocking on doors to look for witnesses. It'll also take time for Forensics to do their thing."

"I'll be surprised if any prints or DNA are found," Jack replied. "These people know what they're doing."

"I know. Both Derek and Peter's cellphones have already been disconnected. It's too bad. We never knew what was being said as the calls were encrypted, but at least we could record the numbers being called. Sometimes that gave us locations."

"Send me a list of every person and telephone number you can connect to these guys, and I'll see what we can do to find the leak."

"Will do. As far as the encrypted calls go, they've been passed on to the techies, but I'm fairly certain it won't help. I had another case recently with encrypted calls. Our people couldn't crack the code and sent it on to some other government agency that does cryptologic work. But apparently the code can't be deciphered."

"That'd be the Communications Security Establishment. The CSE is our national cryptologic agency headquartered in Ottawa." Jack paused. "If they could even come up with a location where the calls were made from, it would help."

"Like your building or ours," Hawkins said gravely. "It'll be nice to talk to Greg when he comes out of the coma. Unfortunately, the doctors can't say when that'll be."

"My priority will be finding out how they got burned," Jack said firmly. "Send me everything you have."

"Believe me, finding the leak would really make my day."

Finding the leak … and plugging it would make my day.

CHAPTER THIRTY-FIVE

On Sunday evening Jack received a call from Mason Stone thanking him for the use of his car and telling him Mason was flying back to Toronto late the following afternoon. Sally was staying with Greg's mother, but she didn't need the car.

"Despite the coma, Sally likes to sit and talk to him."

"Can he hear her?" Jack asked.

"The jury is still out on that."

"How's his mom handling it?"

"As you'd expect. A lot of tears. She lost her husband less than four months ago." Mason then said that the doctors might be bringing Greg out of his induced coma in a few weeks. "They've already warned us there'll be considerable cognitive dysfunction," he added glumly, "but we won't really know to what extent until then."

"I'm sorry. If Sally needs anything, you make sure she calls me."

"I'd also like a complete rundown on the file before I leave. Everyone on the section will be asking me about it when I get back. Could we meet for lunch tomorrow before I go?"

"You got it."

* * *

Late Monday morning Jack had Laura drive him to the hospital while Alicia stayed in the office trying to sort the names of people gathered through Powers's phone tolls into business contacts and friends. Friends who might work in sensitive areas.

"You sure you don't want to join us for lunch?" Jack asked, as Laura stopped near the main entrance to the hospital.

"No, I've got a doctor's appointment right after lunch. Her office is almost an hour away and I don't want to be late."

"You seem a little tense," Jack noted. "Everything okay?"

"Yeah, yeah. I'm fine. Routine stuff. See you back at the office later."

Bullshit, routine stuff. He eyed her carefully. "That night we went for drinks with Alicia after Barry Short was attacked, you drank cranberry sodas. At the time I thought maybe you were too depressed for alcohol."

Laura stared at him, then shook her head. "Damn you," she said, annoyed. "Yes, I'm way overdue and a home test indicates I am, but there's also such a thing as a false positive. I want you to keep it to yourself. A woman should be able to tell her husband first before he hears it through the grapevine."

Jack couldn't help but smile. "I know you guys have been trying for years. I'll keep my fingers crossed."

"I'm approaching the age where it could be menopause." She glared at Jack. "If you tell anyone that, so help me, I will shoot you!"

* * *

Thirty minutes later, Jack and Mason sat down on the patio at the Paddlewheeler Pub. It had been Mason's choice to go to the place where Greg had had lunch shortly before he'd been attacked.

They each ordered a Kokanee, then Mason ordered the breaded calamari and Jack the hot chicken wings.

Connie Crane called before the food arrived.

"Where are you?" she demanded.

"The Paddlewheeler Pub in New Westminster, having lunch with a narc from Toronto. Why?"

"I can be there in twenty minutes. Will you wait for me? I'll explain then."

Jack agreed and then told Mason that Connie was on I-HIT and the lead investigator in Leo Ratcliffe's murder.

"You don't know why she wants to see you?" Mason asked. "She didn't give you any hint as to what it's about?"

Jack frowned. "Connie and I have a long history together. She's one of the sharpest homicide investigators I know." He glanced at Mason. "I suspect she wants to be able to read my body language when she tells me whatever it is she wants to tell me."

Mason looked bemused. "I take it she isn't the trusting type?"

"Not with me, for some reason."

"Interesting. Why do you suppose that is?"

Jack shrugged. "Some people's personalities don't always mesh. Forget it. Let me tell you about the investigation and how it started."

Mason listened closely as Jack started with his story of having the informant who identified Derek Powers as being involved in the Chung kidnapping.

"They cut off the kid's fingers?" Mason interrupted.

"Yes, we're dealing with real animals." He continued up to the murder of Leo Ratcliffe and the senile witness who claimed that a woman had entered Leo's home from the alley while a man waited.

"Sounds like the man may've been standing six," Mason noted.

"Odd that he'd be the lookout. Usually it's the other way around."

"Maybe they thought Leo would be more inclined to open his door for a pretty woman," Mason suggested.

"Possibly. There's one other thing, but according to Hawkins it's a real long shot. Major Crimes had a wiretap on Derek and Peter's cellphones, but they were encrypted. The calls were passed on to the techies, but we're not optimistic that they'll be deciphered."

"It'll be passed on to the Communications Security Establishment," Mason noted.

"Yes, it already has been."

"I've got a friend who works there. I could make a call and maybe get them to prioritize it."

"Think they'd listen to you?"

"Are you kidding?" Mason gave a lopsided grin. "I think they listen to everybody!"

Jack smiled in response. He saw Connie arriving and waved to attract her attention.

"I'll make it short and sweet," Connie said after introductions had been made. She paused to order a glass of water from the waitress, then focused her attention on Jack. "Guess who visited me this morning?" Before Jack could respond, she said, "Carol Ratcliffe."

"As in Leo Ratcliffe's sister from Hamilton?" Jack asked.

"Yes."

"Wanting to know when her brother's body would be released, I presume?"

"That was part of it. Two guys were with her."

"Leo's brother, Ricky?" Jack asked.

"No. Carol mentioned a brother, but said he was somewhere in Quebec and she couldn't get hold of him yet. These were two other guys who wanted to know how my investigation was going ... and if we had any suspects. I said I couldn't comment on the investigation, let alone identify any suspects, for obvious reasons." Connie paused, looking perturbed. "Then one of them pointed directly in my face and said, 'It was Satans Wrath, wasn't it? Just tell us if it was Satans Wrath!'"

Jack and Mason looked at each other and simultaneously said, "Devils Aces."

"No shit. Tell me something I didn't know," Connie replied. "I told them I wouldn't disclose anything about the investigation, then I took a photo of the three of them sitting across from my desk." She held out her cellphone across the table and Jack and Mason leaned forward for a look. Both men were scowling. One of them, who had a jagged scar across his cheek, was holding up his middle finger. Carol Ratcliffe sat with her arms folded across her chest, also glaring.

"Did you get their names?" Jack asked.

"All they gave me was Zip-Head and Fat Boy."

"I take it the guy with the scar is Zipper-Head," Jack said.

"Abbreviated to Zip-Head, I guess. As you can see, Fat Boy isn't actually fat. With those muscles, he's gotta be on steroids," she said, putting her phone away.

"A Fat Boy is a type of Harley-Davidson," Mason noted. "It's probably the type of bike he rides."

"Maybe that explains it." Connie leaned forward, clasping her hands together on the table as she stared at Jack. "So tell me, did you know that Leo Ratcliffe was going to get whacked? Is this part of that big picture bullshit you're always winging at me?"

Jack felt his anger rise. "No, I didn't know! You're aware of what happened to Greg Dalton right after, aren't you?"

"Yeah, and Barry Short before him, but I'm talking about Ratcliffe. Bikers are your domain. Hawkins told me you're worried that the Devils Aces are opening up a chapter here. I know they're at war with Satans Wrath. I also know that it was your informant who put Hawkins on to Derek as one of the kidnappers."

"Yeah, so?" Jack replied. "Do you really think this big picture I speak of would include what happened to Barry and Greg?"

"No, I honestly don't think that about you … but shit happens. What I do know is that I've worked on about a dozen cases where bad guys ended up getting killed and you were somehow involved." She studied Jack's face.

"Christ, it's taken for granted in our office that if you're involved, there's never any court. Everything gets handed off to the coroner. Except not quite everything. Most of those unsolved murders end up in my office. I've lost count of how many you've been connected with."

"I have no idea who killed Ratcliffe," Jack stated. "Since the Beretta was found in the river near where Greg was attacked, I think it was the same person or persons who did both crimes. Believe me, I want to find out who that is."

"That's all I wanted to know," Connie said, getting to her feet. She paused and stared at Jack. "Considering what happened to Barry and Greg, I almost wish you do find them. But it wouldn't be right. Our motto is to defend the law … which is what I intend to do. You might want to keep that in mind."

Mason stared after her as she walked away, then gave Jack a curious look.

"Like I said, Connie and I have a bit of history."

* * *

Jack returned to his office after dropping Mason off at the airport. The intelligence database quickly identified Zip-Head as a prospect for the Devils Aces in the Hamilton chapter and Fat Boy as the sergeant at arms.

He was viewing their mug shots when Laura returned from her doctor's appointment. Her smile said it all, and he rose to meet her.

She wrapped her arms around him as he kissed her on the cheek.

"Congratulations," he whispered.

"I'm two months along," she whispered back. "Not a word to anyone other than Natasha for at least a month."

"Wow, you guys are really close," Alicia said. "Do you always greet each other like that?"

"Sometimes," Laura replied.

Jack felt giddy as he returned to his desk. He knew Laura had given up hope of ever having a baby. It was a spark of good news that he desperately needed to cheer himself up. *I almost feel like I'm the father,* he mused, as he answered his ringing phone.

"Jack, it's Ned Hawkins. I'm calling to let you know I've called off the dive team. Forensics found a chip of wood stuck to one of Greg's teeth, which they'd collected from the parking lot. The wood was identified as ash, so most likely they used a baseball bat on him."

Jack's giddiness turned to nausea.

CHAPTER THIRTY-SIX

The following week, Jack was roused from his sleep one morning by his cellphone vibrating on the bedside table.

"Jack, it's Mason from Toronto."

Jack glanced at the clock — *6:00 a.m.* He immediately sat up. "What's up? Is it Greg?"

"No ... not directly. Did I wake you?"

"Yes."

"Sorry, I thought guys your age got up early."

My age? Is he joking?

"I'm joking."

You asshole.

"I thought if I called when you weren't in an office environment, we could talk freely." Mason paused. "Although talking freely on the phone is not one of my strong suits."

He sounds a lot like me.

"In this case I'm going to chance it, but I need you to promise that what I tell you stays between the two of us ... unless I say otherwise."

"Not a problem. I've demanded the same of people myself."

"Yeah, I sort of figured you had." Mason paused. "How would you feel about saying you had an informant who identified the person responsible for burning Greg and Barry Short?"

"Are you serious? I'd feel great — if it were true."

"The information is true beyond any doubt."

How the hell did he find out? "If it's your informant, why don't you step forward and say so?"

"It's not actually an informant, but I do need to protect the source's identity. Coming from you out in B.C., and seeing as you're involved in the case, it'd throw people off as to the real origin of the information."

"Okay …"

"The trouble is, the information is so secret that nobody can know it, not even the judiciary, which means it can't be used to get a wiretap or even a search warrant."

His friend in CSE — son of a bitch, they've deciphered the calls! "I suspect I know where your information came from."

"Yup. They broke the encryption code several months ago, but don't want anyone to know because it'd tip off the bad guys around the world. They talked about that as the big picture … which made me think of you, because of what Connie said."

"Sounds like your friend trusts you quite a lot," Jack noted.

"A trust I never want to destroy. I told my friend about the little kid whose fingers were cut off, and also about what had happened to Barry and Greg. I was told that there are even worse things going on and that major investigations into terrorism around the world could be jeopardized if the bad guys find out their phones aren't safe. Globally they could be looking to stop thousands of murders."

"Sooner or later the bad guys will clue in," Jack noted.

"You're right. Then the world will become more dangerous. Regarding the kidnapping case you're involved with, at least it's covered with a legal wiretap order, which I suspect is the only reason I was given the information. However, let me tell you another concern my friend passed on. Once word gets out that government agencies or police forces have access to the technology to decode calls, it'll raise a red flag for civil liberties groups and probably get the service providers in trouble, simply on speculation of what police in different countries and jurisdictions might be up to."

"Undoubtedly."

"Currently super computers are programmed to listen for certain words ... like, perhaps the code name of a terrorist. Anyone mentioning the name would be of interest, but there's no way of knowing who they are without a computer monitoring calls. If legal documentation were required against the person in the first place, it'd be impossible, because no one would know who they were."

"Catch-22."

"Exactly, but that's someone else's headache," Mason replied.

"Providing it's not us or our loved ones who get gassed or blown up," Jack said.

"I know, so I'm caught between a rock and a hard place. Nobody can know who the source is, but if something isn't

done, more of our UC operators could be hurt or murdered. How do you explain that to the brass or to other
investigators without burning the source? They'll demand
to know who it is."

"I work with informants involved in organized crime,"
Jack said. "I often get information that can't be used in
court, but sometimes there're other ways to handle the
problem effectively."

"I gathered that from what Connie had to say to you
last Friday."

"I'd go to jail, if need be, rather than disclose who my
informants are."

"Yeah, I kind of had that feeling about you," Mason
replied.

"You're sure it can't be used to get a search warrant,
then have the grounds sealed so nobody would know?"
Jack asked.

"No, because people *would* know. Court clerks, judges,
prosecutors … eventually someone would blab." Mason
paused. "CSE knows word will get out someday. Some
horrific crime will be stopped or evidence used which will
spill the beans, but in the meantime, they're trying to stall
that day for as long as they can."

"I understand," Jack replied.

"It sure as hell is frustrating. From one cop to another,
this guy has to be stopped. The problem is how."

"Who is he?"

"His name is Miguel Hernández, and his address is in
North Vancouver. My guess is that he works in the courthouse. Three days before Greg was attacked, Derek Powers
sent him a photo of Greg outside a Starbucks. The next day

Hernández sent Derek an old picture of Greg with a text saying he positively identified him as Constable Gregory Dalton from Toronto. Before that it was the same scenario with Barry Short."

"The bastard's probably using computer facial recognition to match up the photos."

"Sure ... and sell them to bad guys. In both the photos Hernández sent Powers, Greg and Barry were wearing suits and ties. Greg was also clean-shaven, and it looks like he was in a courthouse. The last time Greg was clean-shaven was two years ago, before his wedding. The picture had to have been taken when he was out your way for court. I suspect Hernández has been taking pictures of all the UC operators when they testify."

"You're right, he needs to be stopped," Jack said tensely. "Has he been sending photos to other people?"

"Don't know," Mason replied. "Only Powers's phones were covered with a wiretap order. Hernández's phone can't be looked into, not even by CSE." Mason paused. "Sure would be nice if Hernández got run over by a bus."

"It wouldn't totally solve things. There could be photos of UC operators scattered out to who knows how many criminals," Jack noted. "If Hernández works in the courthouse, he's in the perfect spot to meet criminals and UC operators alike. Not only does he need to be stopped, someone needs to conduct an investigation into how many operators could be in jeopardy."

"Which is why I was thinking you could say you had an informant who told you about him. The thing is, to get the investigation going, you'd have to swear your informant was reliable. How could you do that without burning

CSE? The investigators, the brass, everyone would be out for Hernández's blood. They'd demand to know who the informant was. If you refused to tell them, you'd be charged with insubordination and bumped back to constable, with only a dogsled for transportation."

"We have to do something, though," Jack stated. "Lives are at risk."

"I want to grab Hernández by the throat so badly I'm shaking."

"His day will come, I promise," Jack said coldly. "I've got a suggestion, but I'd need to talk to our assistant commissioner and clue her in."

"The brass? No way! They're only interested in protecting their own asses. Can you imagine the shit that'd be raised in Ottawa if they found out a lowly constable like me got info from CSE that even they aren't privy to?"

"I feel much the same way as you about a lot of the white shirts, but she's backed me before with informants. Even she calls it the big picture. I think she'd go along with it, and she's in a position to shut down anyone from doing anything without my permission. Which in reality would be your permission."

Mason paused. "I don't know … I don't like it."

"I'm sure all the western intelligence agencies, such as the Five Eyes, know about this. I could tell her it came through them."

"The Five Eyes?"

"It's an alliance between western intelligence agencies from the United States, Canada, the United Kingdom, Australia, and New Zealand. Rumour is they spy on each other's citizens, then share the information in order to circumvent some of the legal restrictions imposed by the intelligence agencies' own countries."

"That's interesting," Mason noted.

"What if I indicate to the assistant commissioner that I received the information through someone with a contact in the Five Eyes? It wouldn't quite be a lie, and it would make her presume that the information came from one of the other countries. Even if our brass in Ottawa did hear about it, they'd be afraid to say much for fear of disclosing something that could cause a political backlash from our allies."

"So even if she did go to Ottawa, there wouldn't be an uproar over the fact that the information came from one of our own organizations."

"Right, but I don't believe she would tell them, in any case. She's impressed me so far as being able to think for herself without worrying about what Ottawa would say."

Mason was quiet for a moment, presumably mulling it over. "Okay, you've convinced me, but what about MCU and I-HIT?"

"The assistant commissioner has the power to stop them from using the information in any other way than how we want. They'd never go against her."

"No, but they'd sure be pissed off. They might assume it was the same informant who told you about Powers in the first place and be curious as hell why they couldn't use the info this time."

"I'd throw a spin on that, too. I'd insinuate that it's a different informant. Maybe indicate that Hernández is only the tip of the iceberg and that my investigation involves a court clerk, a couple of lawyers, and some judges."

Mason chuckled. "They'd be afraid to apply for a search warrant or a wiretap on Hernández because they wouldn't be able to trust anyone. It would drive them nuts."

"Exactly. I'd like to let Laura know what's going on. I might need her help, and I trust her completely. When it comes to my boss, Rose, I'd give her the same story as the assistant commissioner."

"I'll trust your judgment on who you need to tell what." Mason's tone brightened. "I'm glad I called you. Steps will be taken to ensure that any UC operators who have testified when Hernández was around are not working, plus no heat will come back on my source or CSE."

"Also, not arresting or hassling Hernández means that Derek Powers won't get paranoid before we identify the rest of the kidnappers."

"And then what? How do we deal with Hernández afterward? Are you thinking that he'll presume it was Derek Powers who ratted him out?"

"Without the evidence from your source, there might not be grounds to charge him with anything. Also, Powers himself would know that he didn't rat out Hernández, so that might get him to thinking about his phone. I've got an idea, but I'll need your help."

"Anything. You name it, I'll do it," Mason replied gravely.

"Do you plan on coming back out to B.C.?" Jack asked.

"Yes, I want to be there when Greg comes out of his coma."

"Then I'll tell you my plan when we're face to face."

CHAPTER THIRTY-SEVEN

One hour after his talk with Mason, Jack and Laura sat in the back of a surveillance van in an alley behind Miguel Hernández's apartment. They'd already identified his car as an older-model white Toyota Corolla.

"Not what you'd call a high roller," Jack noted. "Shoddy apartment complex and a car so dirty and dinged up it looks like he drives by Braille."

"Looks like a car driven by a drunk," Laura agreed. "I'd like to cram him in it and use it as a crab trap at the bottom of the ocean."

"Would be better to cut him up and put him in a real crab trap instead," Jack noted.

Laura cast him a sideways glance. "You know I didn't really mean it, right?"

Jack made a face. "Yeah, I know. Don't ruin my fantasy." He gestured at a large, beefy-faced man in uniform ambling toward the Toyota. "Grab the camera."

"B.C. Sheriff's Services," Laura noted.

* * *

They returned to their office at 8:45 a.m.

"Hey, you two," Alicia chided, looking at her watch. "Are you taking your annual leave fifteen minutes at a time?"

Laura held up her camera. "Nope, actually Jack and I started work two hours early."

Jack caught the downcast look on Alicia's face. "The only reason you weren't invited is because there wasn't time. I received some info about a guy early this morning and wanted some surveillance shots of him before he went to work. You wouldn't have made it in time from where you live out in Langley."

Alicia seemed to be appeased. "Who were you looking at? One of Satans Wrath?"

"No, I'd rather not explain twice — come with us while I tell Rose what I've learned."

The meeting was brief. Jack gave the story that a source of his in an intelligence agency with the Five Eyes was able to decode cellphone calls and had identified Hernández as the leak, but the information could not be used in any judicial capacity and was ultra secret.

"So now we know but can't do anything about it?" Rose stated.

"Can't do anything about who the leak is, but we can take steps to protect the UC operators and find out which ones have been in the courthouse where he works."

"But what about Barry and Greg?" Alicia cried.

"What about them?" Jack asked.

"You can't let Hernández get away with it!"

"Welcome to the big picture," Jack said. "For now, that's all we can do."

"Maybe down the road, once word gets out that the encryption can be deciphered, we'll be able to use the info," Rose suggested.

"That could be a couple of years," Alicia said.

"Even if he were charged," Jack said, "what do you think he'd receive if convicted? A fine? Probation? He'd swear that he didn't think anyone would get hurt, that he'd been told the UC operator would only be shunned or avoided."

"Defence would argue that losing his job was punishment enough," Laura agreed.

Alicia stared, open-mouthed, then blurted, "You're right, aren't you? God, that pisses me off!" Her face was red. "Doesn't it bother you guys? How can you be so nonchalant?"

"You just have to believe in karma," Jack said. *Come on, Rose, don't give me the stink eye.*

"I'd better make an appointment for you and me to see Lexton," Rose said. "No talk of karma when we do," she warned.

* * *

Lexton sat stone-faced behind her desk as Jack repeated the information he'd just given Rose.

"You said he's with the B.C. Sheriff's Services," Lexton noted. "Do you know for how long?"

"Not yet," Jack replied. "I'd like to investigate further, but I'm concerned about the ramifications."

"Ramifications?" Lexton asked.

"The source needs to be protected. Considering how significant the revelation that that cellphone encryption can be decoded is, Ottawa, if they learn of it, will take a keen interest and perhaps demand to know who the source is."

"I take it your source is concerned that word would then get out and jeopardize international investigations?"

"Exactly. If Ottawa demands to know, I'm willing to say my source is connected to the Five Eyes, but that's all."

Lexton gave Jack a hard look. "Did you pick the Five Eyes because you thought Ottawa would be afraid to delve into things for fear of rocking the boat?"

Damn, she's sharp. "The thought had crossed my mind. But it happens to be true that the source is connected with the Five Eyes."

"As are the Canadian Security Intelligence Service and the Communications Security Establishment," Lexton noted, "but if it was one of those agencies that passed on the information, Ottawa might raise a stink ... which could potentially jeopardize things."

Okay ... she's on to me.

Lexton bit her lower lip as she thought things over. Then she focused on Jack. "I don't see any reason for Ottawa to be informed. Yes, your source would be of interest to a lot of people, but I understand the bigger picture. No need to stir up a hornet's nest if you don't have to. Especially if it would endanger the source ... and potentially a whole lot more people."

Yes, she gets it! "Thank you," Jack replied.

"MCU and I-HIT may not understand," Rose noted.

"It's not like I'll give them a choice," Lexton replied. "I'll order them to keep their hands off of Hernández. He'll be yours to investigate, not theirs. If his name does come up somewhere else in their investigation, I'll tell them they need to talk to you before taking any action."

"Thank you again," Jack said. "Considering the seriousness of what I've been told and the need to protect how the leak was discovered, it would be nice to put a stop to any theories the investigators may have that could conceivably hit upon the truth."

"And thus risk exposing the technology," Lexton said. "Yes, that'd be a concern. Do you have a solution?"

"I'd suggest there's a more important investigation taking place and indicate that it involves others at the courthouse besides Hernández." He studied Lexton's face for a reaction. *Is that the hint of a smile?*

"Seems like a reasonable suggestion," Lexton replied. "Let's convene a meeting this afternoon with MCU and I-HIT."

* * *

Jack looked around the boardroom. MCU was represented by Cummins and Hawkins, while Dyck and Connie represented I-HIT. Also in attendance were Lexton, Rose, Laura, and Alicia.

Jack gave his story of having received confidential information positively identifying Miguel Hernández as the leak. He went on to say that Hernández was only the tip of the iceberg and that an investigation was underway which precluded anyone interviewing Hernández or applying for wiretaps or search warrants.

"You mean there're others in the courthouse?" Crimmins exclaimed.

"The investigation is on a need-to-know basis, but let me say that Hernández is a small fish compared to the real targets. Hernández is — how should I say this — associated with a couple of judges, several lawyers, and some court clerks." *I mean, he's probably been seen around the courthouse by them.*

"Jesus," Hawkins muttered.

"Wait a minute," Crimmins said harshly. "Are you telling us you've identified the culprit, but we're not allowed to investigate or arrest him?"

"That's exactly what Sergeant Taggart is saying," Lexton said. "As heinous as the crimes committed against Constables Short and Dalton were, they pale in comparison with what else is happening."

"The big picture," Connie said, scowling.

"Investigation into Hernández will be handled by the Intelligence Unit," Lexton stated firmly. "Nobody is to take any action in regards to him without their permission."

"So where does this leave us?" Dyck asked. "We're fairly certain that whoever murdered Leo Ratcliffe was also responsible for beating Constable Dalton with a bat and leaving him for dead."

"Your investigation into the Ratcliffe murder can continue as before," Lexton said. "Hernández was complicit in identifying Constable Dalton, but in reality he may only have passed on his name to Derek Powers. You need to find out who Powers collaborated with to do the actual attack."

"Powers is our only lead to the other kidnappers," Hawkins stated. "We haven't been able to come up with any evidence other than CCTV footage of him standing behind Chung in a crowd of people once. The undercover operation was our best shot at solving it."

"Let's talk about undercover operations," Lexton said. "Could Hernández be taking photos of all officers because some may become UC operators later … or is he only taking photos of the UC operators?" She looked at their faces. "We don't know, do we?"

No, we sure as hell don't.

"Other than Powers, we really don't know who we're dealing with," Lexton stated. "Perhaps it's an organized crime ring operating on a national level. If so, they may be taking photos in courthouses right across Canada. Computerized facial recognition opens up whole new problems. We've had two UC operators seriously harmed in less than three weeks. I don't want it to happen again."

"I trust that current undercover operators will be warned?" Dyck asked.

"I've already contacted the undercover coordinator in that regard to have him alert his counterparts across Canada," Jack replied. "They're checking with all the UC operators to see who could be in jeopardy."

"Didn't that jeopardize your informant?" Dyck questioned.

"I said that I received information that an unidentified woman in the courthouse was passing on information to Satans Wrath. Hopefully the UC coordinators and operators will keep a lid on it, but if word does get back to Hernández, he'll think it's in relation to someone else."

"I see." Dyck turned to Crimmins. "Obviously our investigators will work together. Does anyone have any ideas for how to proceed, knowing what we know?"

"I still think an undercover operation by an experienced operator targeting Derek Powers might work," Jack said. "The problem is to find an operator who is experienced, but hasn't been to court. Usually the two go hand in hand."

"You don't go to court," Lexton observed. "Neither does Corporal Secord."

"Yes, but we're also on the Intelligence Unit," Jack replied. "Our mandate tends to exclude us from —"

"Your mandate be damned," Lexton interjected. "What happened to our two officers is far more serious."

"I couldn't agree more," Jack replied. *Not that she cares if I agree or not.*

Lexton eyed him. "How would you do the undercover operation?"

"At the moment, I expect Derek and Peter are extra paranoid," Jack noted. "To alleviate that, I'd recommend MCU conduct sloppy surveillance on Peter for the next two weeks, but stay clear of Derek. After that, I'd pull surveillance off of Peter, as well."

"So they'd think Derek was completely in the clear, and later, that we'd given up on Peter," Lexton mused.

"Right. Under the guise of a major drug trafficker from Alberta, I'd hire Derek Powers to check out some people I'm going to do business with. One of my alleged suppliers would be another undercover operative. As Powers is a professional, I'd prefer the second undercover operator be male, because illegal drug distribution at that level is usually male-dominated."

Laura nodded in agreement.

"Now that we know who the leak is, I'm sure a suitable candidate can be found," Lexton stated.

"I'd get Derek to think that the guy I'm buying drugs off of is from a wealthy family," Jack continued. "Then I'd set it up to look like he robbed me for say, five hundred thousand dollars. I'd act enraged and say I want to kill him. Hopefully Derek would suggest that we kidnap him to get the money back and bring in his accomplices to assist. We could set it up to have them arrested when they go to do it."

"Actually, that might work," Hawkins stated.

Lexton looked at Jack. "Then do it," she ordered.

CHAPTER THIRTY-EIGHT

"Good news," Jack said to Mason Stone over the phone. "The assistant commissioner is backing me completely. She wants to leave Ottawa completely out of it."

"Hey, are you sure she's a genuine white shirt?" Mason responded. "Sounds like an imposter to me."

"Once in a while a good one comes along."

"She sounds like a real cop. Didn't they send her on the hating constables course?"

"If they did, she must have slept through it. There's more. How'd you like to come out and do a UC with me targeting Derek Powers?"

"Are you serious? It kind of pisses me off that you even thought you had to ask."

"I was only being polite. The UC has already been given the go-ahead and it starts in about two weeks ... let's say right after the Labour Day long weekend."

"That'd make it Tuesday, September fourth."

"Yes. It may be a short-term, two-week project, but if it takes longer to gain his trust, it could last much longer."

"What role am I playing?"

"You're a major coke dealer from a wealthy family. Mother widowed. You were recently kicked off the family estate when she caught you coming out of the maid's quarters early one morning. That way we don't have to come up with a mansion for you."

"So a few silk shirts. No problem. I did a UC on Italian organized crime a while back. I've got the bling to go along with the image."

"Good. Basically I'm using you as bait to be kidnapped. Any questions?"

"Yeah, this maid I'm seeing, is she good-looking?"

Jack chuckled. "That's up to you because she'll be imaginary."

"Damn."

"What I want you to do is call your UC coordinator and say you've already been asked. Let him know an official request will be arriving on his desk in a day or two."

"I'll do it first thing in the morning." Mason paused. "Is this your way of arranging that face to face you spoke of?"

"I knew you wanted to be here when Greg comes out of his coma, but the real reason is I think you're the best choice because you're experienced, available, and you haven't testified in court in B.C. We're taking a chance that pictures aren't being taken in other courthouses across the country, but your role will be brief, and if anyone is going to be checked out, I think it'll only be me."

"So you didn't just pick me for my good looks and charm?"

"Nope. This case is too important to screw up. If I didn't think you were the best person for the job, I wouldn't be asking."

"I appreciate that," Mason said sincerely. "You know I'll do whatever it takes."

"One more thing. How well do you know your UC coordinator?"

"Not well. He transferred in from Winnipeg last spring. Why?"

"Does he know how close you are to Greg? That you were best man at his wedding?"

"I don't think so."

"Good. Keep it that way."

* * *

Two days later, Lexton summoned Rose and Jack to her office.

"It's been nine days since Constable Dalton was attacked," she stated when they sat down. "Are there any updates on his condition?"

"I've talked with his wife, Sally," Jack said. "The neurosurgeon told her that he'll suffer considerable and permanent cognitive dysfunction … to the point that he'll never be able to return to policing."

"Oh, God. How's his wife doing?"

"Still in shock. She spends all her time at the hospital, only going back to her mother-in-law's house to sleep. I invited her to join my family for dinner, but she declined. As for Greg, he's still in an induced coma." Jack paused. "The doctors might bring him out of it in two weeks, but that's still iffy."

Lexton grimaced. "Have you been able to learn anything further about Miguel Hernández?"

"A little," Jack said. "He's been married three times, but appears to be living on his own again. He's been with the Sheriff's Services for ten years, but applied to join the RCMP nine years ago. We've got his background history. Originally he was from Mississauga, Ontario. His parents still live there and his father's a retired plumber. According to his application, he came to Vancouver to be with his first wife. He took criminology classes when he first came out, which is interesting because Derek Powers studied criminology and hires criminology students to assist him, so that may be how they met. Hernández's application to join the RCMP was rejected when a background investigation revealed that he displayed bullying behaviour and that past neighbours reported he was verbally abusive to his wives ... if not physically abusive."

"It appears he harbours a grudge. Anything else?"

"Corporal Secord placed a bogus call to where he works, pretending to verify a credit rating. She was given his current cellphone number, which was only activated last week."

"Maybe he got rid of his old one as a precaution after what happened," Lexton suggested.

"Possibly. No phone tolls of interest, but he may be using office phones that we don't know about. I've also spoken with the UC coordinator, and they're still looking into which operators across Canada have testified in court here."

"Guess that's a start."

"I also asked the coordinator to come up with an experienced operator to act as my supplier when I do the UC sting on Derek Powers."

"Good." Lexton took a breath. "The real reason I called you both in has to do with my concern about our undercover operatives being burned. We don't know if Hernández's actions are being replicated elsewhere or if our own building is under scrutiny. With that in mind, Sergeant Taggart, I am going to approve a modest expenditure for you and the other two undercover operatives in your office."

It should be the other three, but I failed to protect one and now he's in a vegetative state in the hospital.

"I want you to rent an apartment or office space to work in." Lexton paused. "I realize there may be occasion for you or other members of your team to attend meetings and whatnot, but I'd like to limit the exposure of undercover operatives when it comes to frequenting known RCMP facilities. How do you feel about that?"

"I'd like that," Jack replied.

"As I said, it'll be a modest budget, so nothing fancy. I suggest you locate outside of Vancouver, as the cost will be lower. You'll still report to Rose or, in her absence, directly to me."

"There are some logistics required," Rose noted. "He'll need the rental space alarmed and to have some storage for classified materials and reports that will need to be secured in a safe."

"I'm aware of that. Currently there's a lull in the kidnapping investigation while MCU make themselves obvious by following Peter Powers around. Hopefully that'll give you enough time to set things up before you make your approach to Derek."

Jack nodded in agreement.

"I needn't remind you that you'll be in charge and accountable for the actions of all the undercover operatives under your command," Lexton noted, "including any who may be here on a temporary basis to assist you in your investigations."

"Their actions, and their safety, too," he snapped. *Shit, where'd that come from?* "I'm sorry," he quickly added. "That didn't come out right. I meant no disrespect."

Lexton gave him a stern look. "I don't hold you responsible for what happened to Constables Short and Dalton. You shouldn't, either."

* * *

Lexton eyed the next visitor she'd summoned to her office.

Chief Superintendent Quaile smiled nervously as he took a seat.

"You've heard, I take it, about what happened to Constable Dalton?" she asked.

Quaile slunk down in his chair and furtively looked around the room like a conspirator plotting a dastardly deed. His reply came in a whisper. "Do you think Taggart set him up and tried to get him killed?"

What the hell? "No, I don't think that!" Lexton replied, perhaps louder than necessary.

"Oh," Quaile responded, looking confused.

"Why would you?" she asked.

"Well … as you recall, you wanted people in there to spy on him. I can't help but wonder if Taggart suspected Dalton."

"I never told you that I wanted to put spies in the office," Lexton replied angrily. "I told you explicitly that I was *not* looking for anyone to inform, but simply wanted people known for their integrity and honesty."

"I'm sorry, yes, spying was the wrong word to use."

Lexton studied him briefly. "I'm told that Constable Dalton will not be returning to police duties. The Intelligence Unit is about to commence an undercover investigation of extreme importance. I'd like you to contact the undercover coordinator and see if you can find a suitable replacement to transfer in forthwith."

After Quaile left, Lexton sat with her elbow on the desk and her chin nestled in her hand, analyzing her own behaviour. The thought of her file on Taggart, hidden in her office safe, began to torment her.

Have I become like Quaile? So obsessed that I'd be willing to believe almost anything? She recalled the pain etched on Taggart's face when he said he was responsible for the safety of the people under him. Perhaps if she hadn't seen that, she, too, could have been suspicious and jumped to the wrong conclusion.

She removed the folder labeled *JT* from her office safe and scanned through the files, the most recent being that of the unsolved murder of the gunrunner Erich Vath. *Okay, I think I'm justified with these.*

She looked at the notations she'd made recently after he'd told her about his source in the intelligence community and his idea to divert suspicion, along with his plan to identify the kidnappers. She had written, "This member is devious and displays a ready willingness and natural tendency to lie." Lexton sighed. *Okay, maybe I went a little overboard.*

A moment later, Lexton returned the folder to her safe,

having amended the comment to read, "This member displays an aptitude for thinking outside the box."

Lexton brooded over the change she'd made. *Does he think outside the box, or does he see the boxes as coffins to be filled?*

CHAPTER THIRTY-NINE

The following week, Jack was scanning apartment and office space listings on his computer when he received a call from Mason.

"It's all set for me to come out for the UC," Mason said. "Approved by my boss and the UC coordinator."

"That's great."

"You want me there right after the Labour Day weekend?"

"Sally told me they're taking Greg off his induced coma on the Friday of that weekend," Jack noted. "I know you want to be there for that, so come earlier."

"Yeah, I'll be there for that, for sure. The problem is I've got a court case on the go, but the prosecutor swore she'd have me off the stand no later than the Wednesday."

"Then come as soon as you're able. I'm arranging an apartment for you, but I also want you to familiarize yourself with Vancouver, since that's where you're supposed to be from."

"I don't know the city at all," Mason admitted.

"Don't worry, your part won't involve much driving, and I don't expect the bad guys to even be talking to you. Simply trying to cover all the bases."

"Okay," Mason replied. "Looking forward to working with you."

Jack felt his stomach knot up. *That's exactly what Greg Dalton said.*

* * *

The next afternoon, Lexton received a call from Chief Superintendent Quaile.

"I'm not sure how urgent the Intelligence Unit's planned undercover operation is, but —"

"I told you it was of extreme importance," Lexton interjected. "Doesn't that reflect a degree of urgency to you?"

"Yes, yes. It was more a figure of speech. I'm reviewing a suggested candidate's file on my computer, but I thought I should get your thoughts about him."

"Keep your computer on. I'll be right there."

Moments later, Lexton took a seat across from Quaile and raised her eyebrow.

He cleared his throat. "I spoke to Staffing in Toronto. A person was suggested to them by their undercover coordinator. He's an experienced operator, single, lives in an apartment, and could transfer immediately."

"Okay, sounds good. What's the problem?"

"I wondered if there was an ulterior motive for their suggesting him, so I asked a lot of questions."

Now he's smiling like he expects a reward. "And?"

"I think they're trying to rid themselves of a bad apple," Quaile said smugly.

"What's his name?"

"Constable Mason Stone. He has a reputation for being a loose cannon and has had been investigated several times by Internal Affairs … although apparently nothing has stuck."

"What's his background?"

"He has ten years' service. Three in uniform in Regina, then seven in Toronto Drug Section."

"But he's an experienced operator?"

"Yes, the drug program coordinator said he's worked all through eastern Canada on some really heavy cases."

"Regarding the Internal Affairs investigations, were any for corruption or anything of a criminal nature?"

"They were policy related. It appears he has trouble following the chain of command."

Interesting. I wonder how Taggart would feel with some-one like that under him. The shoe would be on the other foot. "Do you know what Mason's exam scores were when he applied for the Force?"

"Give me a sec and I'll pull them up."

A moment later Quaile made a face.

"What's wrong?"

He gestured to the screen. "Likely a data entry error. They've got his score as 162."

"Isn't the average applicant score a 120? I understand that they're not the same as IQ tests, but 120 is basically the score of an average university grad, yes?"

"But we'll take less than 100 if their ethnic or cultural background would help us to fill political quotas. In this case I'm betting his score was actually 126. Someone probably mixed up the last two numbers." Quaile gave a quick smile as if to reassure that he knew what he was talking about. "A little high, but not uncommon."

"Out of curiosity, what was Sergeant Taggart's score?"

"I'll pull it up." Quaile's mouth gaped as he stared at his computer screen. "Uh, it says 171. There must be a mistake."

"You think whoever entered that score was dyslexic, as well?"

"I don't know what to make of it."

I do. I've interviewed him several times. You were once his boss. Doesn't say much for your intellect if you didn't realize you were dealing with someone far beyond your own capabilities.

"Maybe they're both wrong," Quaile offered.

"It's my understanding that people with high scores often are not hired because they don't tend to fit in well with the paramilitary discipline of the RCMP."

"Yes, there's another test we give to check that out. It's based out of 100. A score toward 100 means they're extreme radicals who fight all authority, while a score toward the bottom indicates they're basically doormats that anyone can push around."

"So the ideal score would be 50."

"Yes, but that exact score would be unusual. Most people fall somewhere in the 40 to 60 range."

"What did Taggart and Stone each get on this test?"

Quaile's fingers clicked away on the keyboard. He paused to frown, then clicked some more. Finally, he looked up, stunned. "They both got exactly 50."

I'm surprised neither of them adjusted their score slightly to make it less obvious that they'd seen through every question. Lexton cleared her throat. "Bring Stone in."

"Give them some rope to see if they hang themselves?" Quaile sounded optimistic.

"Let's hope that they don't, but if they do, I'll deal with it. It's often the hard workers who attract the most attention from Internal. Those who sit on their asses doing nothing never receive much attention." *Take yourself, for example.*

Quaile stared back blankly. Perhaps trying to digest what she'd said.

"I'll make it my business to keep an eye on the both of them," Lexton continued. "I'd like to clear up these rumours and innuendos about Sergeant Taggart once and for all. If either one of them is dirty, I'll see to it that they go down … and go down hard."

CHAPTER FORTY

Jack had barely settled in to work on Monday morning when Mason phoned.

"How's it going?" Mason asked cheerfully. "You find an apartment for me?"

"Yes, you'll be moving into it on Saturday, September first. Also have a car lined up for you. It's a Mercedes-Benz Cabriolet, a red two-door convertible. The plates will be registered to a company offshore but with a post office box in Vancouver."

"Sweet."

"That'll be temporary, though. You'll be falling on hard times, and after the bad guys see it once, you'll be driving something a lot cheaper."

"Damn, I hate these downturns in the economy," Mason joked. "What's the apartment like?"

"Luxury one-bedroom suite in Vancouver that over-looks a golf course on one side and the Fraser River on the other. Secure underground parking and secure access for all entrances, including a locked gate on a footpath leading into the property."

"Sounds nice. I can live in it while I'm looking for my own place," Mason added gleefully.

"Your own place?"

"Staffing called an hour ago. They wanted to know if I'd like a transfer to the Vancouver Intelligence Unit."

"You're kidding!"

"Nope. So I told them I'd like a month to think about it."

"Oh."

"That time I was kidding. Hell, yes, is what I told them! The transfer is effective immediately."

"That's great news!"

"I'll have a bit of running back and forth for court, but basically all I have to do is give my apartment manager thirty days' notice and pack my bags. Might sell my car, too. It's rusting out. Can't wait to get away from all the snow."

"We get some snow. You'll need an umbrella, for sure."

"Rain I can put up with. By the way, I've booked my flight for the UC. I'll be arriving Thursday morning. The flight gets in at ten."

"I'll have Laura and Alicia meet you at the airport and bring you your new set of wheels. I've got an appointment then to sign some papers and get the keys to a covert office we'll be using. It's a commercial space on the ground floor of an apartment complex in Surrey, which is close to Burnaby."

"Great." Mason paused. "When I arrive I'd like to go see Sally. She's stressed about how Greg's going to be when he's brought out of his coma on Friday. Me, too, for that matter. Maybe we could hold off getting together until after that?"

"Take whatever time you need." Jack paused as feelings of guilt came back to haunt him. "I've been wondering whether or not I should be at the hospital, as well."

"I don't think Sally wants anyone else around. She said she doesn't want everyone staring at him or to see other people's reactions until she's dealt with her own. Greg's mom will be there, of course … and Sally wants me there for support, but that's all."

"I understand."

Mason paused. "I sure am looking forward to being transferred out there," he said in a desperate change of subject.

"I'm pleased, as well. We could really use another experienced operator on our team. With you here, there'll be four of us."

"I'm still not certain exactly what it is you do."

"We're like a thorn in the side of organized crime families."

"A thorn, eh? Guess I'll have to change that. Wouldn't a dagger be better?"

Jack smiled. He and Mason were going to be good friends.

* * *

Mason arrived on schedule Thursday morning and was met at the airport by Laura and Alicia, who gave him the keys to his undercover car. It was almost noon the following day when Jack, Laura, and Alicia saw the arrival of the rented furniture for their new office. They were still putting it in place when Rose entered.

"Got you all a housewarming gift," she said, removing a coffee maker and half a dozen mugs from a shopping bag.

"Much appreciated," Jack said. "Although a fridge in my office to store olives would've been nicer."

"Yes, and a widescreen television for the rest of us," Laura added.

"Okay, you assholes, it's not too late for me to return this," Rose said, making a pretense of putting the coffee maker back in the bag.

"Only kidding," Jack said quickly. "Thanks, it's a thoughtful gift."

"Yes, thank you," Laura and Alicia chimed in.

"You're welcome." Rose looked around. The space consisted of a large front office with a smaller office toward the back. There was one washroom alongside a sink and a few cupboards. She nodded in apparent satisfaction. "Looks good. What did you tell the property management that you do?"

"I said we're a collection agency that works for lawyers tracking down people who've skipped out on their alimony payments."

"That'd cover your comings and goings at odd times," Rose noted.

"Exactly. I said I wouldn't be putting any name on the door because of threats we've received from the people we located, plus because we already have more business than we can handle and don't want to advertise."

"How'd they respond to that?"

"They promised to keep our business to themselves."

"Perfect. Your office number is 111, so I guess I'll start referring to you as the triple one team."

"Works for me," Jack replied. "Our guys are supposed to arrive soon with a safe and to install alarms. I'll get them to cut some extra keys and give you a copy."

"About the UC, did you arrange a meeting with Special O?"

"Yes. Monday's a stat holiday, so I booked the boardroom for Tuesday at one p.m., plus I invited MCU and I-HIT to attend. They won't be involved in any of the surveillance, but I figured they should be kept in the loop."

"Good."

"I'll make sure everyone is familiar with the areas we'll be in and give Special O a chance to figure out where they can watch from."

"Are you going to have Special O tail Derek?"

"No, I don't want to risk heating him up. On Thursday I'll call him to set up an appointment and get the ball rolling."

Rose nodded solemnly, then glanced at her watch. "Lunchtime. How about I spring for pizza?"

"Hey, buying us a coffee maker and lunch — sounds to me like you're missing us already," Laura said.

"Like a dog missing its fleas," Rose retorted.

* * *

Rose departed lunch, and the others waited for the RCMP members specializing in property security to arrive.

"Can we talk about the actual undercover operation?" Alicia asked.

"Sure," Jack said, leaning back in a swivel chair with his hands clasped behind his head. "Tomorrow Mason will move into his apartment, so I can fill him in then about what his role will be."

"What about Laura and me?" Alicia asked. "What parts do we play?"

"I'll tell you how I hope things will go," Jack replied. "On Thursday I'll rent a suite at the Pan Pacific Hotel. I've got a contact there, and she'll give me a good deal. Once there, I'll use a cellphone the UC coordinator got me from Alberta to call Powers at his office and arrange to meet him. Without coming out and saying it, I'll give him enough information to figure out I'm in town to buy dope and that the person I've been dealing with for the last few years has suddenly made me suspicious."

"That being Mason," Alicia noted.

"Yes. I'll say he has new business contacts who I want to identify. Then I'll meet with Mason someplace where it'll be easy for Powers to follow him afterward. The licence plate on his UC car is connected to a post office box, so that won't give Powers any info, presuming he can access that type of information."

"He'll have to follow Mason to find out his address," Laura said.

"Right. I want Powers to see that Mason lives in a very secure location. A location that wouldn't be suitable to try and kidnap him from. However, prior to Mason going to his apartment, I'll have him stop at a restaurant to help set up the story. Hopefully someplace that isn't crowded at that time of day and that has booths."

"Why booths?" Alicia asked.

"To make it easy for Powers or his people to sit nearby and listen," Jack said. "We'll make it nighttime and out of the city so there are fewer customers and it'll be easier to spot their surveillance and identify any new faces."

"Out near Langley would be good," Alicia said enthusiastically. "I know just the place: Jessie's Diner. I go there for dinner sometimes on my way home and it's usually half-empty."

Jack shrugged. "Jessie's Diner it is. Before Mason arrives, I'll make sure Special O has one of the booths so they can vacate it for Derek's people. Laura will already be waiting in the booth next to them, and she'll play the role of Mason's sister. Their conversation will confirm to Powers's mind that Mason comes from a rich family. Laura will also drop the name of the cemetery Mason will be visiting in a couple of days, the ideal spot to later kidnap him from. There will be minimal risk to the public, and our Emergency Response Team can easily move in and make the arrests."

"That's after you pretend that Mason ripped you for half a mil," Laura said, "to get Powers to suggest kidnapping Mason when he goes to the cemetery."

"Exactly," Jack replied.

"But what about me?" Alicia protested. "What's my role?"

"I'm going to get you to buy Mason's car from him so they won't be able to keep following him in the event they put a tracker on it."

"That's it? That's all I get to do? That's bullshit!" Alicia's face reddened. "This was my case from the beginning! There hasn't been a day over the last two years that I haven't thought about what happened to Tommy. Did you know the little guy was going to be a pianist? That is, until someone blindfolded him, kept him in a trunk for two days without food or water, then chopped off his fingers!" She glared at Jack. "It isn't fair to relegate me to being some background player. I've invested too much into this file. I should at least be able to play the sister."

"It's nothing personal," Jack said evenly, hoping to calm her down. "This is a serious case, and you don't yet have the UC experience that Laura does."

"I've had the course, and how the hell do I get experience if you cut me out of things? I've never testified in court as a UC operator, either. In fact, it's been over a year since I've been to court, and whenever I do go, I put my hair up in a bun. There's no way I'd be recognized, especially not just popping in for a moment to pretend to be Mason's sister."

"Listen —"

"And come on! Laura as Mason's sister?" Alicia looked at her. "No offence meant, but you're at least ten years older than Mason. He's only two or three years older than me," Alicia went on. "I'd be far more believable as his sister."

Laura's eyebrows knitted. She mauled her lower lip with her teeth, then looked at Jack. "She does have a point." *Damn it, Laura.* "And don't you be saying, et tu, Brute," she warned. "You know I'm right. Besides, it'd be like a cameo appearance. In and out. Give the kid a chance."

Maybe that's it. I feel like she is a kid. My kid … who I need to protect.

Alicia was staring at him, waiting for a reply.

"Okay, you can do it."

"All right!" Alicia shouted.

Jack smiled at her enthusiasm, despite his misgivings. "I've rented a BMW for you to drive. How does the name Ally Jenkins sound?"

"A Bimmer! That's great. I've always wanted to drive one."

"The name?" Jack reminded her.

"Sure, Ally Jenkins is fine."

"The story is that you're divorced, so if Derek searches for your rich mother, he may think Jenkins is your married name. The address on your plate will be another post office box."

"What colour is it?" Alicia asked.

"Don't know yet. Hang on, my phone."

"Jack, uh, this is Mason. I'm at the hospital. Greg's … oh, Christ …" He paused in an apparent attempt to control his emotions. "Greg's out of the coma. It's not good. He didn't recognize Sally, or his mother, or me. It's really bad. They're both bawling their eyes out."

Jack wanted to say something and opened his mouth, but couldn't find the words.

"The neurosurgeon said he may improve in time," Mason continued, "but he warned us that Greg may never even be able to feed himself."

"I don't know what to say," Jack said. "There aren't words enough express how bad I feel."

"I know. I feel the same whenever I look at Sally and his mom."

"Is there anything we can do?"

"I don't know. They want to … never mind. I'll need to arrange it myself."

"Arrange what?"

"A plastic surgeon spoke to us. It'll be some time before he's able to start his operations on Greg, but he's asked us for some recent photos to use as a guide in reconstructing Greg's face. Sally mentioned their wedding photographs. Maybe when I go back next I'll get them." Mason paused. "Fuck, I'm babbling. I don't even know what I'm saying, let alone why I'm telling you all this."

"I was going to have you move into the apartment and talk to you about the UC tomorrow, but all that can wait," Jack said. "Take a few days to —"

"I don't need a few days," Mason said vehemently. "What I need is to have that face to face you talked about."

CHAPTER FORTY-ONE

There was a knock at the door of the Pan Pacific Hotel's Bayview suite overlooking Vancouver Harbour. Jack answered it.

"Hello, I'm Derek Powers. Mr. Roberts, I presume?"

"You can call me Jack," he replied, accepted a handshake. "Come on in."

Derek entered and appeared to admire the room and the view. "Nice suite," he said.

Jack shrugged. "It'll do." He gestured to one of two sofas, each facing a Ming-style Cho-leg coffee table. "Have a seat. Would you like anything to drink? I'm thinking of ordering a beer."

"Uh, no, thanks. I'm fine," Derek replied as he took a seat.

Jack glanced at his watch. "I forgot you're an hour behind," he said, then adjusted his watch. "I want to thank you for taking the time to come over here. I drove out from Calgary and my engine started acting up, so I dropped it off at the Lexus dealership for them to look at. They said they'd drive it back to the hotel for me, so I wanted to wait."

"That's no problem. My office is only a fifteen-minute walk away. Have they delivered it?"

"A few minutes ago."

"A Lexus is a nice car. What model?"

"An RC. Turns out I got some bad gas. It's running smoothly now."

"So, what can I do for you, Jack? On the phone you said you wanted me to check someone out?"

"Yeah, I've got a bad feeling about this guy. I've been doing business with him off and on for a couple of years, but lately he's … I don't know. He's acting strange. I'd like you to take a look at him. Also find out who he meets after me."

"What sort of business are you in?"

"Uh, I'm an entrepreneur. I invest in different things. Sort of a cash-based business. I purchase different types of merchandise or property that I can turn for profit."

"I see."

Yeah, I bet you do, asshole. "Speaking of which, I prefer to pay you in cash. Don't know what you charge. One, two Gs a day?"

Derek's face brightened. "We can discuss that later. It'll depend upon what you want and how many of my people I'll need to use."

"Makes sense. Anyway, what I do isn't important," Jack said, giving a wave of his hand as if to brush the topic aside. "Mason, the guy I deal with, is one of these rich kids who has an overinflated sense of entitlement. About a month ago he told me his mom kicked him out of the house because she'd caught him coming out of the maid's quarters one morning. He was all indignant and pissed off. I laughed at him. The guy's gotta be thirty years old. What the hell is he doing living with his mommy, for fuck sakes?"

Derek shook his head as if in disgust.

"I think he may have a problem. Perhaps a little too much of this," Jack said, touching his nostril with his index finger. "If not that, maybe something else."

"Do you have his address?"

"I don't even know his last name, let alone his address. The kind of business we're in … well, no. I don't want him knowing anything about me, either, including where I'm staying. Where he hangs his hat is one of the things I'd like you to find out. I don't know where his mother lives, either, although I do have her number — Mason was switching phones one day and gave it to me. Mind you, it's a cellphone, so that doesn't really help. I'm supposed to meet him tomorrow night for a drink. I figured you could follow him after."

"That might work. What else can you tell me about him?"

"He was driving a red Mercedes-Benz Cabriolet convertible, which pisses me off because all it does is attract attention, which is not something I like. Not sure if he still has it. He was bellyaching about having to sell it because he's a little short on cash."

"If he does still have it, it'll be easy for me to spot," Derek noted.

"What has me worried is that he's offered me a really good deal on, uh, something. I think maybe it's too good of a deal. I asked him about it and he said he's got a new connection ... I mean, business partners, who can pass on a better deal. It'd be good if you could find out who they are, too."

"I'll see what we can do. Is there anything else you know about him that might help?"

"Not much. Mason says he's the black sheep of the family. He told me his dad had something to do with inventing computer software, but he died sometime back. I'd love it if you could find out where he lives and bug the place ... or maybe his car."

"Legally I can't do that, but who knows ... sometimes we overhear things." Derek paused. "What does he look like?"

"The guy's a pussy. You wouldn't know it to look at him, but he is. I bet he's never been in a fight in his life. He's about my height and build, but at least a dozen years younger. He has dark-brown hair that curls at his collar and wears a gold chain around his neck."

"Should be easy to spot."

Jack frowned, as if thinking of something.

"Is there something else?" Derek asked.

"Yeah, remembering what a pussy he is got me to thinking about these so-called new business partners. Is there any way you could tell if he was wearing a bug or something? You know, in case he's trying to double-cross me with, uh, his business partners and get me to say something I might regret later."

Derek appeared to stifle a grin. "I think I know exactly what you're concerned about. Yes, I have the capabilities to find that out."

"After tomorrow night I'm supposed to meet him again on Saturday for lunch. If you could check him out before I talk business with him, that'd be great. I'd also like you to watch and see if any of these business partners are around when I meet him."

"Yes, that can be arranged. I'll have my team ready for tomorrow night and all day Saturday."

Jack didn't have a hard time projecting relief and satisfaction. He felt both. "By the way, could you give me your cell number in case I need to reach you?"

"Sure, no problem."

Gotcha hooked, you bastard.

CHAPTER FORTY-TWO

On Friday night Derek's surveillance van arrived at a parking lot across the street from Central City Brew Pub in Surrey. Special O had been in position in the lot for an hour in their own van, and they noted his arrival.

A moment later a silver Nissan Altima sedan arrived. A man and woman got out, while another man remained in the driver's seat. Special O recognized them from previous surveillance photographs as the criminology students. Derek spoke with them briefly, then the couple concealed themselves in the back of his van while he got out and sat in the Nissan with the other man.

Twenty minutes later, Jack arrived in a white Lexus RC with Alberta licence plates and parked in the lot. Derek was seen gesturing toward the car as he spoke to the man beside him. They watched as Jack crossed the street and entered the pub.

It was 9:05 p.m. when Mason arrived, driving the red Mercedes-Benz Cabriolet convertible. Derek was quick to follow him across the street and into the pub, while the man from inside the van snuck out and put a tracker under the rear of the Mercedes.

* * *

Mason joined Jack at the bar. He was engaged in small talk and ordering a beer when Derek strolled up behind them, appearing to be texting on his phone. A minute later, Jack met with Derek in the men's room.

"He's clean," Derek announced. "You're free to talk about, uh, whatever you want to talk about."

"Thanks, man," Jack replied.

"My guys also put a tracker on his car. I'll phone you later and let you know where he goes."

"Super. He's already told me he has to meet someone so he can only stay for one drink."

"I'll go back outside to wait, then phone you later."

* * *

Alicia tried not to show the excitement she felt as she sipped her coffee. It was 10:00 p.m., and she was sitting in a booth at Jessie's Diner, staring out the window. Excitement turned into a rush of adrenalin when she saw Mason arriving in his Mercedes.

That rush intensified when a van sped into the lot, and a couple got out and hurried toward the diner behind Mason. She recognized the couple from surveillance photos as Derek's employees.

Alicia heard the member from Special O getting out of the booth behind her. He made his way to the cash register.

"Hey, little sister! How ya doin'?" Mason called when he entered.

Alicia rose from her seat and gave him a hug, pretending not to notice the couple who quickly slid into the booth behind her.

"I'm doing okay, Mase. It's good to see you," she said, taking her seat again as Mason sat down across from her. She noticed peripherally that the woman behind her had put her jacket on top of the railing between them. *Bet she's recording.* A slight movement of Mason's eyes toward the jacket told her that he had noticed, too.

"No more hassle from your ex?"

"Nope, Mom's lawyers took care of him."

"Pretty goofy situation, Ally," Mason replied. "Usually in a divorce it's the wife demanding money, not the other way around."

"I should've known he was a gold digger," Alicia replied. "At least we never had kids."

"Yeah ... glad I never got married." He paused, then said, "So what else is new?"

"Not much. I called Mom the other day. Being all alone in that place has got to be lonely."

"Maybe if she hadn't kicked me out and fired the maid, she wouldn't be so lonely."

Alicia snickered. "You ass. I can't believe you did that."

"What? The maid was better-looking than the cook," Mason said.

"God, you're awful!" Alicia gave him a playful punch on the shoulder. She waited while the server came over and Mason ordered a coffee. "Mom misses you, you know."

"Yeah, I bet," Mason said sarcastically.

"No, really. She's already forgiven you for the whole thing."

"Forgiven me? More likely she's worried about what her friends will think. She wouldn't want them to find out that she threw me out, let alone that a son of hers would stoop to screwin' a maid."

"Well ... you're right about that. She'd be so embarrassed to see us in this diner."

Mason glanced around. "Yeah, it's not exactly fine dining."

Alicia shrugged. "It's homey. Not pretentious." She eyed Mason a moment. "Anyway, I mean it, Mom really does miss you. You're her only son, and you know she'd do anything for you. Don't ever tell her I told you, but she brought you up the other day and said something along the lines of boys will be boys."

"She said that?"

"Yes. You really should go see her. Especially if you're planning on moving."

"Yeah, I'm looking forward to that," Mason replied. "I need a fresh start. That's why I want to get away from here."

"How soon?"

"Could be real soon. I think I've found someone to buy my car. I owe some guys money, but I've got a business deal in the works with them. If it goes through, they'll be paid off and there'll be enough for me to take a break for a year or two. With luck, I could be gone within a week."

"Business deal? I know what sort of business you're in," Alicia said.

"Yeah, well, as Mom says, boys will be boys. This next deal will be the last one. I'm getting out of that business."

"Really? You promise?"

"Yeah, I thought it was cool a few years ago, but I've matured. I want out … which is why I need to get away from all the people I hang with."

"You don't know how pleased I am to hear that. Mom's not the only one who worries about you, you know."

"Aw, thanks. I love you, too, kid," Mason replied.

Wish they'd quit calling me kid. It's going to give me a complex.

Alicia eyed Mason. "God, if you're leaving so soon, you really do need to see Mom first."

"It's not like I won't fly back to visit once in a while. I have to do that to cover medical insurance."

"This coming Sunday, it'll be a year since Dad died," Alicia noted. "The anniversary's gonna be tough on Mom."

"How often do *you* visit her?"

"I call her every day and I see her once a week."

"You always were her favourite."

"And you were Dad's favourite. He'd be upset that you and Mom aren't talking."

Mason paused. "All right, fine, I'll call her tomorrow. See how it goes."

"She'll be so glad to hear from you!" Alicia waited a beat. "Speaking of Dad, do you ever go up there to see him?"

"Where, Silver Hills Cemetery? Yeah, actually I was thinking I'd go up Sunday afternoon with a mickey of Scotch and have a drink with him."

"That's nice. He'd like that."

"I know. I really miss him."

"Mom still can't bring herself to go back to the cemetery." Mason nodded.

"While you're up there, I'll go to the house and see her. Why don't you pop by after? Stay for dinner?"

"Yeah, okay. I'll be at Silver Hills about three p.m. I'll come over after that."

"Perfect."

Mason yawned loudly. "It's great to see you, sis, but I've got kind of a big day tomorrow. I need to go home and get some shut-eye." He gestured to the waitress for the tab.

Alicia hid her grin when the couple behind her hurried to the cash register. Mason then got up and kissed her on the cheek before wandering toward the cash register himself.

Moments later, she answered her phone.

"How'd it go?" Jack asked. "Special O says they're on their way out."

"I think it went well. The man and woman who work for Derek sat right behind me, and she put her jacket down close to me. I'm betting they recorded everything."

"Good."

"Mason is pulling out of the lot now, and the couple have returned to the van. Hang on ... yup, looks like they're going to follow him."

"Derek and some other guy are still outside in a silver Nissan Altima."

"I don't see him."

"Special O said that they're parked a little farther back. Also that they've been kissing and groping each other like teenagers."

"Maybe you'll think twice before having Derek come up to your hotel room again," Alicia teased.

"Oh, I don't know," Jack said, "he's so handsome and muscular. You don't get a body like that without working at it. I wonder if he'd like to watch *Brokeback Mountain* with me?"

Alicia laughed. "Okay, what do you want me to do now?"

"Head to your car and drive away. He probably only wants to see which car is yours and scoop the plate."

"How long do I get to hang on to my Bimmer?"

"A few more days at least. I may need you to make another cameo appearance if things don't go as planned. However, if he does follow you tonight, drive to a large apartment tower and park, then get out and lose him in the dark. He'll think that's where you live."

"No problem. I have a friend who lives in an apartment complex. I could even buzz her and go inside if need be."

"Good, as long as you don't live in the same vicinity, or your car could be spotted later."

"Nope, I own a townhouse in a quiet neighbourhood. Nobody could follow me home this time of night without me seeing them."

"All right, I'll get Special O to monitor, then call you right after you leave to let you know if he's following."

"And if he doesn't?"

"Then I expect Derek and his people will be breaking off in a few minutes, once Mason arrives at his apartment. If that's the case, we can all go home — except for me. I'll be going back to the Pan Pacific. Once Derek phones, I'll call Laura, and she can figure out when the two of you should meet at the triple one tomorrow morning."

"That's right, she's buying a convertible. I gotta say, I like my Bimmer better."

Alicia returned to her car and drove out of the lot. She was followed by the Nissan, but once they were out of the lot, it turned in the opposite direction. Moments later, Jack called back.

"It looks like you're clear, but take precautions, regardless. Derek drove off in the opposite direction, toward Mason's apartment."

"I saw him. Bet he got my plate," Alicia responded.

"No worries. Go home and get some rest. Tomorrow could be interesting."

I don't know if I could ever pull off what you're planning to do. "Jack?"

"Yeah?"

"Be careful tomorrow, will you? These people are evil. Tommy, Barry, Greg … I don't think I could handle another incident like that."

"Thanks, but don't worry. I've been dealing with these kinds of assholes for a long time. Some of them worse than any of this bunch."

Alicia felt apprehensive. *Who or what could be worse than these people? And can I handle it?*

* * *

Minutes after talking with Alicia, Jack received a call from Derek.

"Okay, we found out where Mason is living," Derek said. "He's in a high-end apartment building off of Southeast Marine Drive, across from the Fraserview Golf Academy. We don't know which apartment he's in, and there aren't any names on the directory, but give me a day or two and I might be able to pin it down."

"Terrific. I don't know Vancouver well enough to know the area you're talking about, but as long as you do, that's great. Anything else? Did he meet up with anyone after I saw him?"

"He met with his sister and talked about family stuff, then he said that he's planning to leave Vancouver in a week or so after doing a big deal with someone over the next couple of days. He said he's getting out of the business … uh, whatever business that is."

Jack grinned. *Like you don't know.* "I didn't know he was leaving, but guess it doesn't matter if the big deal he's talking about is the one he and I are doing."

"I'm sure it is. He also plans to sell his car and said he owes his business associates money, but expects to pay everyone off after the deal."

"Good. I'm supposed to meet him for lunch tomorrow to go over some things. A restaurant called Urban Fare on the corner of Bute and West Cordova. I thought I'd walk from my hotel. I scouted it out already and there's a boardwalk alongside the ocean I can take."

"I know the place. Walk along the boardwalk, then cut through Harbour Green Park, and you're right there."

"I was wondering if you could get someone to check him out before I get there? That and I'd like you to tag along behind me and make sure nobody is following me. That way I'll know it's you, since I don't know your people."

"Do you suspect you've been followed?"

"No, but I'd prefer not to meet the guys he's in business with. I want it to be one-on-one … that's what he told me it'd be, but I want to make sure."

"I understand."

"In case he has found out where I'm staying, I think it'd be best if we pretend not to know each other. How about you hang around the lobby or outside when I leave the hotel, then follow me?"

"Sure, I'll do that. Would you like me to have some of my people follow him when he leaves the apartment tomorrow, to see where he goes? We've got a tracker on his car, so it won't be difficult."

"Yes, I was about to ask you to do just that."

"I'll have my people there by seven a.m. Then I'll call you before you go for lunch."

Jack called Mason and Special O to update them. His next call was to Laura.

"Hey, I spoke with Mason," Laura said. "Sounds like the kid did good. He said she seemed like a natural."

"That's great. Have you talked with any of the monitors?"

"Still nothing on Derek's cellphone other than calls to you and to the people who he was working with tonight." She paused. "You be careful tomorrow."

"I will. I'm heading back to the hotel to try and get some sleep. Call Alicia and arrange when you want to meet her in the morning. Maybe pair her up with someone from Special O while you do your thing tomorrow."

* * *

Forty minutes later, Jack parked in the hotel parking garage, then sat in his car for a moment while his mind grappled with how the day had gone and what tomorrow would bring.

What could go wrong?

He opened his glove box, removed a hypodermic syringe, and slipped it into his jacket pocket.

CHAPTER FORTY-THREE

At 10:00 a.m. Saturday morning, Derek called Jack to report that Mason had left his apartment complex and parked near the intersection of Pacific Boulevard and Davie Street in downtown Vancouver.

"Now he's standing in front of a Royal Bank," Derek said. "Looks like he's waiting for someone."

"Still two hours to go before I meet him," Jack noted.

"Hang on, he met up with a woman … she's got some licence plates in her hand and they're going into the bank. He's selling his car — I gotta go get my tracker back!"

Thirty minutes later, Derek called again. "I was right. After they left the bank, they returned to the car, and he took his plates off. He left the woman putting her own plates on and headed off down the street. We're following him."

Not for long.

* * *

It was 11:40 a.m. when Derek called Jack to say that he was across the street from the Pan Pacific and that he had a guy waiting inside the Urban Fare to check out Mason when he arrived.

"Where's he now?" Jack asked.

"Unfortunately we lost him about five minutes after he sold his car."

"No worries."

"I've also got two people in a car on West Cordova about half a block past the restaurant, in case you end up going somewhere else."

"Super."

Jack put his phone away and rolled up his sleeve. He stuck the hypodermic needle into a vein and sucked back on the plunger.

Five minutes later, he walked out of the hotel's front entrance carrying what appeared to be a heavy sports bag. In reality, the bag held nothing but a few sticks of Styrofoam to make the sides bulge out. He'd barely started down the boardwalk when he saw Derek fall in behind him.

Jack's phone rang. It was Derek.

"You're too early," he said. "Mason's not at the restaurant yet."

"That's okay, I thought I'd take my time and wander a bit. I figured that would make it easier for you to see if someone is following me."

"Okay, but don't go to the restaurant until I let you know that it's okay."

"Yeah, no worries."

"What, uh, is the sports bag for?"

"Oh, just some stuff Mason wants. Call me when it's clear," Jack said, then ended the call.

Jack strolled along the boardwalk, and Derek followed about thirty seconds behind him. When he reached Harbour Green Park, he approached three flights of stairs which led up to Cordova Street. The park itself was bordered by tall hedges and decorated with cement pillars. An abundance of park benches were laid out amongst passageways through the trees.

Jack knew that once he reached the top of the stairs, it was only a short walk out of the park, across the street, and into the restaurant. He was pleased to see that there were few people around as he climbed the stairs.

Derek was quick to phone. "He's not there yet. Don't go in."

"I won't. I'm going to grab a seat near the top of these stairs and wait. Let me know when I can go in."

"Okay, I'll be close. So far it doesn't look like there's anyone following you."

"Good."

Jack took his time climbing the stairs, but once he reached the top and was out of Derek's sight, he ran to a park bench facing out from a tall hedge and took the syringe out of his jacket pocket. Seconds later, he tossed the sports bag containing the syringe over the hedge to a woman working for Special O, who crumpled it and stuffed it in her baby stroller before sauntering off.

Derek arrived at the top of the stairs a moment later and took a quick look around, then spotted Jack slumped over on the park bench. He ran over.

Jack pushed himself to a sitting position, then staggered to his feet as Derek grabbed his arm to steady him.

"Christ! What happened?" Derek yelled. "Are you okay?"

"They got it," Jack breathed. "Fucking Mason and some guys. They got it."

"You're hurt! I better call an ambulance."

"No, I'm okay," Jack mumbled. "Don't do that."

"You've got blood running out your ear and your nose. You've probably got a concussion. You should see a doctor."

"No, I gotta find them," Jack said, pushing Derek aside. "That was half a million bucks. I can't let them get away with —"

"You had five hundred thousand dollars in that bag?"

"Yeah."

Derek's mouth gaped open.

Jack looked around wildly as if he were desperate to see where his attackers had gone. He gawked at Derek. "I barely sat down and then Mason was like, right in front of me. I saw something out of the corner of my eye and turned to look back," he said, glancing behind the bench. "It happened so fucking fast ... but I think there were three guys. I knew something was up, and I turned toward Mason and was reaching for my piece, but I was too late. The next thing I know I'm lying on this bench, my head feels like it's about to explode, and you're running toward me."

"You've got a gun?" Derek asked.

"Hell, yeah. I'm not that stupid to be packing that much cash around without one. Got it right here," Jack said, flipping his jacket back and patting a holster attached to his belt, on the back of his hip.

"Your holster is empty," Derek observed.

"What? The fuckers took that, too! Shit," Jack mumbled, then sat down on the bench, pinching the top of his nose with his fingers.

"Are you sure you're going to be okay?"

"Yeah, give me a moment to stop the bleeding," Jack replied, not bothering to look up. "I feel like someone stuck an ice pick in the side of my skull." He gingerly touched his ear with his other hand, then gazed at the blood that stuck to his fingers.

"I'll phone my people," Derek replied.

Jack wasn't surprised by the news that Derek's people hadn't seen anything. Especially since Mason wasn't even in the downtown area, but booked into a hotel, out of harm's way.

"Come on," Derek said, putting his phone away. "Let me take you back to my office and clean you up. I might call in more of my people to help. Do you think you're okay to walk to my SUV? It's about a block away."

"Yeah, I can walk," Jack said, getting to his feet again. "But fuck going to your office. You know where his apartment is. That's where I wanna go. First, though, any chance you can get me a gun?"

"Maybe you didn't hear what I said on the phone. I already sent my people over to watch his apartment." Derek frowned. "Except he sold his car, so we don't know what he'll be driving if he shows up. Could be with his associates or in a taxi."

"Hope he's with his buddies. I'll do them all if I can get a piece. I want my money back."

"I know you're pissed off, but this isn't the time to be irrational. Not to mention, his apartment building is really high-end. Lots of security cameras and locked gates. Come on, we'll go to my office and see if we can figure something out."

"Yeah, you're right. Maybe we should talk," Jack replied.

CHAPTER FORTY-FOUR

Derek's office space consisted of a room with four desks and another, smaller room with one desk. This was where Derek went after directing Jack to a washroom. Jack left the door open as he stood over the sink, using paper towels to dab off the blood. In the mirror, he could see Derek using his computer.

When Jack entered the room, Derek gestured for him to sit down and took another cellphone from his desk.

"Two phones?" Jack asked.

Derek smiled. "Sometimes it pays to be cautious. I'm waiting for a call. Shouldn't be long."

Obviously not from the young people working for you. Bingo!

"You're looking way better," Derek commented. "You still feel okay? If you have a concussion, it could continue to manifest. You need to keep an eye on yourself."

"I'll be okay," Jack replied. "I've been thinking, though.

If Mason owed these guys, there's a good chance my money's already been divvied up."

"I expect it has. I wish you'd told me what you were doing. I'd have provided closer protection."

"I figured the fewer people who knew, the safer I'd be," Jack replied. "Anyway, I've kind of got an idea."

"Oh?"

"I've got his mother's phone number. From what I know, she's filthy rich and would freak out if she knew what Mason is involved in. If I call her and tell her who I am and what Mason has done, maybe she'll pay up to keep me from going after him."

"Uh, but if you tell her who you are, aren't you afraid she'll go to the cops?"

"I don't think she would. At least, not according to Mason. He once told me that she'd piss herself if word ever got out about what he did. Besides, it's her son who's been dealing blow to me for a couple of years, and him who robbed me." Jack shook his head. "Naw, a rich bitch like that won't be calling the cops. Maybe she'll decide not to pay me, but she won't want to rat me out. At the very least, she'll get hold of Mason and tell him to give me back whatever he's got left."

"I, uh, might have a better idea," Derek said. "One almost guaranteed to get all your money back."

"All of it? How?"

"Let me talk to someone first, then I'll tell —" Derek's spare phone buzzed, interrupting the conversation. "Could you, uh, let me take this call in private?"

"Sure," Jack said. He went to the outer office, closing the door behind him.

He did his best to listen, but Derek's words were mumbled. The only thing he heard Derek say clearly was, "No, no, you should've seem him. He was really messed up. Blood running out his ear ..."

A minute later, Derek opened the door and gestured for Jack to join him. He was still holding the phone to his ear.

"Listen, Jack, I didn't mention this last night because I didn't think it was important, but I think I know where Mason will be tomorrow afternoon."

"You do?" Jack exclaimed.

"What do you think about the idea of us grabbing him, then you calling his mother to demand your money back?"

"Christ, no problem! If we got Mason, I'm sure she'd pay up. Maybe take her a day or two."

"And you're comfortable with calling her?"

"Hell, yeah. It's my money he took. She's gonna know it was me, anyway. We could even put Mason on the phone. Bet she'd have the half mil for me by the next day."

"You hear that?" Derek said into the phone.

"Wait a minute," Jack said. "Kidnapping is kind of a big deal. How much would your cut be?"

"I'll ask," Derek replied.

So you're not the boss.

"You heard that, too?" Derek asked. "So what — okay." He looked at Jack and said, "Half for you and half for us."

Jack pretended to think about it.

"To do this right takes quite a few people," Derek urged. "We'll be ensuring security, doing countersurveillance when the money's delivered, checking for GPS tracking ... all sorts of things. Personally I think you're getting too good of a deal."

Jack waited a beat. "I didn't think of all that. You got people who'd do all this?"

"Yes ... people with experience."

"Then I'm in." *Hopefully you'll be in, as well. For about fifteen years.*

A moment later, Derek ended the call.

"So where's Mason going to be tomorrow afternoon?"

Derek hesitated. "Sorry, I was told not to tell you that for security reasons."

"You don't trust me? You think I might try to grab him on my own and get all the money for myself?"

"I'm not the one running the show, but I understand why you're angry. We don't want to take the chance that you'll do something reckless. The people I use are professionals, and it's their necks that'll be on the line."

Jack pretended to mull it over. "Fine. But how do we go about it?"

"Details need to be worked out. I'll talk to you about that later."

"Will you and I be involved?"

"When it comes time to pick up the ransom, I'll provide cover and monitor the situation from my van. I've got everything I need in there. Other people will be doing counter-surveillance, as well. Same for when we make the grab."

"What about me? What'll I do?"

"I figure you'll be with me, but like I said, that still needs to be worked out. I don't know if these people will even want to meet you."

"I have to be involved. Mason will know it's me. Besides, if his mother hears only my voice, it'll be safer for anyone else involved."

"I agree." Derek glanced at his watch. "Unfortunately there's not a lot of time. Usually we'd plan something like this over a period of weeks or months. Let me get going, and I'll either call you or stop by your hotel later." He eyed Jack, then added, "Guess in your line of work, I don't need to tell you not to say anything over your phone."

"I've never been busted yet and I don't intend to start now."

* * *

Jack returned to his hotel, on the way making a quick call to Laura to tell her what had transpired.

"You gotta love it when a plan comes together," Laura exclaimed. "Alicia and I are meeting with Connie and Ned at the moment. They've heard my end of the conversation, and they're so excited I think they might spring for that fridge we need."

"The show's not over yet. To reiterate, for tomorrow, let everyone know that Derek will be in his van and I might be with him. I saw him using another cellphone, so we know they cover all the bases. I'm sure his van is equipped to monitor cellphone transmissions and radio traffic. Basically everyone needs to get into place, wait, and keep as silent as possible. I don't want any heat on Derek. We can't afford to have him spot surveillance. We know where they're going, so have everyone in place at the cemetery."

"No problem. I've already gone over everything with everyone. We'll have our plane overhead and a full complement of Emergency Response Team guys ready to do the takedowns."

"Good."

"Do you think Hernández might be there tomorrow?"

"I don't know. It'd sure be nice if he was. Right now I need to spend a few hours making notes, which I'll put in the hotel safe. Call Rose for me. She's probably at home, but she told me she wants to be updated."

"Will do, but before you go, have you thought what'll happen if you're in the van with Derek and ERT starts swooping in on everyone? Things could get a little hot for you. He's probably going to be armed."

"Yeah, I thought about it," Jack replied sombrely. "I'll jump him before he pulls a gun. With luck, maybe he'll have a bat. I can use it on him like they did on Greg."

CHAPTER FORTY-FIVE

On Saturday evening Derek called Jack at the hotel. "How's your head?" he asked.

"It doesn't let me forget it's there, but I've got a feeling it'll feel a lot better tomorrow."

"Let's hope so. The business arrangement has all been worked out. My people would like to meet you."

You've no idea how glad I'll be to do that. "When?"

"Probably around noon. I'll swing by to pick you up."

"I'll be here."

* * *

Derek knocked at the door at 9:45 a.m. the following morning.

"Thought you weren't coming until about noon," Jack said. "Is everything okay?"

"Yes, it's happening. I'm taking you to meet the people I told you about."

To meet and hopefully yap about previous kidnappings. "Good, I'm all for that," Jack said, putting on his jacket.

"First let me say that they're feeling paranoid because they don't know you."

"Yeah, that goes both ways. I don't know them, either. Hope you don't have any rats in your midst."

"I guarantee that there aren't. All have proven track records. But before we go, you're to get the mother's phone number and write it down, then leave your phone here. They don't want the cops to ever be able to trace your movements, at least not to the place I'll be taking you."

"There's no way the mom would ever go to the cops. How about I simply shut it off? I'll need it to call her."

"No, leave it. Our, uh, team leader will give you a disposable phone. She also wants to go over what you'll say when you call."

"She?"

"Yes, she."

Jack recalled the witness who was interviewed after Leo Ratcliffe's murder who said a woman had entered Leo's yard through the back alley while a man waited by the fence. *Looks like I'm about to meet a lady killer. A real lady killer.* He shrugged, pretending he didn't care about his phone, and placed it on a bedside table.

"You'll need to write the mother's number down first," Derek said, with a nod toward the writing desk. "There's a pen and paper over there."

"Don't need to write it down," Jack said. "I memorized her number."

"You sure?"

"Like you said, trust is a bit of an issue. I want to make sure I don't get cut out of the action."

"Suit yourself. There's something else I need to do, so don't take it personal," he said, taking a scanner from out of his pocket.

Jack stood spread-eagled while Derek searched him. Minutes later, Jack was following Derek into the parking garage. They got into Derek's black SUV.

"Thought you said we'd be in a van," Jack said.

"They didn't want that. Don't worry, everything's okay. I'll let the boss lady explain."

It doesn't matter. I can't wait to see the looks on your faces when you're busted. Hope you all decide to put up a fight.

* * *

It was 11:15 a.m. when Derek pulled up to a mobile home on an acreage halfway between Abbotsford and Chilliwack and parked beside a van. Unlike Derek's blue Ford surveillance van, this was a black Dodge, so Jack memorized the licence plate. Near the mobile home was a hangar and a small runway with a windsock.

Son of a bitch. I wonder if the good guys aren't the only ones doing surveillance from the air?

A pit bull lunged at the end of its chain, barking and snarling at Jack when he got out of the SUV. At the same time, three men and a woman came out onto the wooden porch attached to the trailer and put on their shoes. One of the men had a shaved head. Jack recognized him as Derek's brother, Peter.

"Don't worry about the dog," Derek said. "He lives under the trailer. There's not enough chain for him to reach the steps on the porch. They only let him off at night, so don't go outside the trailer then without one of us."

"Diego! Shut up!" the woman yelled.

Diego snarled at Jack some more, then slinked back under the trailer.

The woman approached, not shy about giving Jack the once-over. She locked eyes with him and gave her upper lip a lick with the tip of her tongue, finishing with a pert little smile.

Okay, so you like to play games.

Normally Jack would've described her as attractive, in a sultry sort of way. She was tall — almost as tall as he was — and he guessed she was in her midthirties, with long, slender legs and a well-proportioned body. Her hair, which hung over her shoulders, was black with a tinge of red. She wore tight-fitting blue jeans and a frilly white blouse that exposed a black bra and plenty of cleavage. It was her demeanour that turned him off. *I can see why Leo would've opened his door for you, though.*

Derek cleared his throat. "Celeste, this is Jack."

"Pleased to meet you, Jack," she said, extending her hand.

Jack shook it and felt her thumb stroke the back of his hand while she maintained eye contact. *Wondering if I'll squirm?* He smiled, gripping her hand tighter and pulling her toward him slightly. A look of surprise crossed her face. She smiled, seemingly amused that he'd toyed with her.

"I hear you lost a little bit of money?" she said, letting go.

"Not a little bit to me," Jack replied.

Celeste tossed her hair back over her shoulder. "No, half a million isn't a little bit to me, either."

"Jack," Derek said, "this is Celeste's partner, Skye."

Skye was exceptionally short for a man and at least a head shorter than Celeste. He was thin with pointed features and had short brown hair. Jack guessed him to be in his early forties. He'd been watching Celeste with a bemused smile, but then he looked at Jack and nodded politely.

You're not angry about how your girlfriend is acting. If anything, you seem happy. What's the deal with you two?

"And this is my brother, Peter, and that's Horace," Derek continued.

Jack returned their nods. He knew that Peter was twenty-seven years old and guessed that Horace was a year or two younger than that. He had a massive chest and muscular arms. The sides of his head were shaved, leaving a short bristle of blond hair on top.

"We'll all stay together until we get the money," Celeste said. "Nobody makes any calls to anyone or goes anywhere without my say-so." She looked at Jack. "We've got a spare bedroom you can use. Derek can have the couch, and Peter and Horace will sleep on the floor in sleeping bags."

"Works for me," Jack replied.

"Good." Celeste gestured to the van. "We'll go for a little drive. I've got a phone that I'll give you to use once we get there." She gave him a hard look. "I obviously don't have to tell you not to use any of our names."

"I've been around the block a few times," Jack replied. "No worries."

"Tell her the ransom is one million dollars."

"One million!" Jack exclaimed.

"Don't you think she's good for it?"

"Oh, she's good for it."

"Good." Her eyes slowly drifted down toward his crotch, then back up to his face. "Why think small when you can think big?"

First rule of undercover: don't make enemies. Jack grinned, pretending to like her attention. "Good point, but what about my cut, then? I should get more than the two hundred and fifty that Derek and I talked about."

"I agree. And you will. My idea is that we get half the ransom, and you get the other half. It's only fair that you get back what they took from you."

"Oh, man, that'd be great!" Jack replied enthusiastically.

"Thought you'd like it. The mother will probably need a couple of days, although it would sure be nice if she could get it by tomorrow."

"It's a lot of money to get together that quick."

"It's just that tomorrow's my birthday, and that'd be a hell of a way to celebrate. We'd have more than a few *slaintes* around the punch bowl, then."

"You're Irish?" Jack replied.

"You bet. Green will be the colour of the day."

"The green ones are only twenties," Jack said. "The hundred-dollar bills are brown. Why think small when you can think big?"

Celeste threw back her head and let out a short laugh. "Ooh, you sound like my kind of guy."

Jack frowned to try to restore some seriousness to the conversation. "I just hope everything goes as planned. Derek said you have some experience doing this?"

"That we do," Celeste assured him. "Don't worry. This isn't our first gig." She waved her hand toward the hangar. "When the money drop is being made, Skye and I will be watching from the air."

Thought so. No wonder our people got burned when Chung tried to pay the ransom.

"We'll put the mother through lots of hoops," Skye said. "The old lady won't realize it, but Derek will scan her to make sure she isn't carrying anything she shouldn't be. If she did go to the cops, we'll know it."

Celeste studied Jack's face. "You told Derek that you're certain the mother won't call the police."

"Of course I'm certain. That's why I have no qualms about phoning her."

Skye glanced at Celeste. "So we won't need to be giving her a reference."

"A reference?" Jack asked. *As in David Chung.*

"Never mind. It's not important." Celeste then gave Jack a hard look. "We'll be keeping a close eye on you. If I think for a moment that you're getting any ideas about leaving and trying to take all the ransom for yourself … well, that isn't going to happen."

"No worries. All I want is my half mil back. You guys deserve to get the rest." He paused. "So what time is it going to happen?"

"Right now. We'll all go in the van, and you'll call the mother when we're about twenty minutes away from here. After that we'll toss the phone. You'll use a different one for each subsequent call."

"Now? Don't we have to grab Mason first?" Jack asked in confusion.

Celeste looked at Derek. "You didn't tell him?"

"This was your idea. I thought you should be the one to explain things," Derek replied.

"I see. Come with me, Jack. We'll go in the trailer for a moment."

Jack followed her up the steps, and Skye tagged along. Upon taking his shoes off and entering the trailer, Jack saw the kitchen in front of him, with a table, four chairs, and a bench. The living room to his right contained a sofa and two upholstered chairs. Celeste motioned for him to follow her down a hall to his left.

The first room they passed on the right was a washroom, followed by a bedroom that contained a bed butted up against the wall and desk against the opposite wall. On it was a computer with two monitors.

The next room was the master bedroom, which took up the entire end of the trailer and had an ensuite bathroom. A king-sized brass bed decked out in red satin sheets with black pillowcases was butted up against the wall to his right.

Jack tried to act nonchalant when he noticed the mirrored ceiling above the bed and the black leather riding crop on the dresser. *To each their own. Consenting adults and all that.*

"Take a look," Celeste said, unlocking the padlock of a storage trunk beside a tall dresser.

What's she keep in there, sex toys?

Celeste opened the lid and stepped back, watching Jack with curiosity.

Oh, fuck, it's a body!

A woman had been jammed into the fetal position in the trunk. Her wrists were fastened behind her back with zip ties, as were her ankles. Strips of duct tape covered her eyes and mouth. She moaned and twisted her head.

Good … still alive. Then Jack gaped in horror as he realized who the woman was.

Alicia!

CHAPTER FORTY-SIX

Laura had arrived at the triple one office at 8:30 a.m. Her undercover part of the operation was over, but her excitement at the prospect of the kidnappers being arrested had made for a sleepless night.

Her first call was to the Emergency Response Team commander to ensure they'd be hidden in position at the Silver Hills Cemetery no later than 10:30 a.m. Mason wasn't detailed to arrive at the cemetery until 3:00 p.m., but in the event the kidnappers arrived earlier, she didn't want to take the chance that they'd spot ERT setting up. She was pleased to discover that ERT had already scouted out the area and would be on their way shortly.

She then called Hawkins to confirm that he'd be the spotter in the airplane and airborne by noon. Moments later, Special O confirmed that, as per instruction, they wouldn't risk doing any mobile surveillance on Derek Powers, but they would put someone in position to monitor the storage facility where he kept his van.

Her next call was to Rose to let her know that everything was set to go, with arrests anticipated at the cemetery around 3:00 p.m.

She thought about phoning Jack, but knowing he'd
likely had less sleep than her, she decided to leave it a
while longer.

At 10:00 a.m. she put on a pot of coffee. Fifteen minutes later, she was feeling irritated that Alicia still hadn't
arrived at work. The night before, Laura had told her she
didn't have to start until 10:00 a.m., but when Laura mentioned she'd be in by 8:30 a.m. herself, Alicia had eagerly
said she'd come in early, as well.

Laura phoned Jack, but was immediately switched to
voice mail. *Probably in the shower.*

She looked out the window at the parking lot. Alicia's
own car was there, but not the BMW she was currently
driving. *Okay, Alicia, where are you? This isn't the day to be
goofing around.* She called Alicia's number and listened to
the ringback tone before she was forwarded to voice mail.
The message she left was curt. "You're late!"

At 10:45 a.m., after another unsuccessful attempt to
reach Alicia, Laura called Connie.

"Hey, Laura," Connie said cheerfully. "We all set?"

"Yes, as far as I know. Haven't talked to Jack yet, but
Derek called him last night and said everything is still on."

"Great. I'm going to be in my office, so call me when it
goes down. We'll be getting search warrants for everyone
involved."

"Listen, Alicia should've been in to work by now. I left
her a message, but she hasn't returned my call. I'm worried. Is she the type to be late?"

"No, quite the opposite. Usually arrives early. Are you at your new office?"

"Yes."

"Any chance she misunderstood and went to your old office?"

"She should still be answering her phone. Would you happen to have her address?"

"Yeah, I've been to her place. It's a townhouse in Langley."

Laura jotted down the address. "That's only twenty minutes away. I'm going to drive over for a look."

"It's probably nothing, but let me know, will you? I've got a soft spot in my heart for that kid."

"I didn't know you had a heart, Connie," Laura teased. "Maybe she forgot her phone at home, realized it on the way over, then went back to get it."

But Laura was more than a little concerned twenty minutes later, when she reached Alicia's townhouse and saw the BMW parked in the carport. She got no response to either ringing the doorbell or pounding on the door.

Laura called Alicia's number again and this time heard ringing close by. She discovered the phone inside Alicia's purse, along with her gun and police identification — underneath the BMW.

Oh, man, oh, shit! She phoned Jack immediately. *Still no answer? What the hell happened?*

CHAPTER FORTY-SEVEN

"What the fuck?" Jack yelled, turning to face Celeste as she flipped the lid of the trunk shut. "Who the hell's this? What's she doing here?" he spluttered.

Celeste seemed taken back at how enraged Jack was. She glanced at Skye before clicking the padlock closed and motioned with her head for Jack to go back down the hall.

Jack strode down toward the kitchen, followed by Celeste and Skye. Peter and Horace stuck their heads in from the porch while Derek looked from behind.

Jack turned to face Celeste. "Who's she?" he asked, jerking his thumb toward the bedroom while trying to hide his panic.

"Her name's Ally," Celeste replied. "She's Mason's sister, and from what I've heard, she's mommy's favourite."

"How — how'd you find her?"

"Skye and I were up in my Cessna helping Derek when Mason met her two nights ago. It wasn't difficult to follow her home. Her car was basically the only one on the road. This morning, Derek, Peter, and Horace caught her when she was about to leave."

"I thought we were going to grab Mason," Jack said.

"The sister is better," Celeste replied. "First of all, she's an innocent pawn, so mommy dearest is more apt to comply. Second of all, it leaves Mason free to collect some of the money he stole, or at least to contribute whatever his take was, along with the cash he got for selling his car."

Jack glanced at the people around them, wondering how many of them were packing guns. *What are my chances? Not my chances — our chances.* He eyed Celeste. "What you say makes sense."

"It's the best way."

Jack looked at Derek, Peter, and Horace. "What did she say when you grabbed her?" *You obviously didn't look in her purse, or we'd both be dead already.*

"Not much," Peter replied. "Horace and I hid alongside her carport, and when she came out to her car, I stuck a gun in her ribs and told her to keep quiet. Derek drove up in the van and we shoved her in and taped her yap shut. She didn't really get a chance to say anything."

"Any chance you could've been seen?"

"Naw, there are hedges up the sides of her property. Plus we wear masks that make us look like old people. Even if anyone did see, they'd think we were taking her to church or something. The plates on the van were hot, and we switched them after we got back. No worries. Took us less than a minute from the time she walked out the door."

Jack looked toward the master bedroom. "Can she get enough air in there? What if she suffocates?"

"We've used it before," Celeste said. "Enough air gets in."

"Are you sure? She looked really stuffed in. If she gets a blood clot or something, her mother will go berserk. Probably spend every dollar she has to track me down. I think it'd be better to tie her to a kitchen chair."

Celeste appeared to mull it over.

"Maybe he's right," Skye said. "The ones we kept in there before were a lot smaller. They could squirm around. She can't."

"Okay, but not until after we make the call," Celeste replied. "That should only take about an hour. She'll be okay until then."

"Also, it'd be best to let me deal with her after that," Jack said. "They obviously know I'm involved, so there's no point letting her hear anyone else's voice."

Celeste nodded. "Good idea. The less she knows, the better." She grinned at him. "So you want to *deal* with her, do you?"

"I mean, she'll need food and water."

Celeste looked annoyed. "She can last a couple days without it."

"Yes, but the better we treat her, the more inclined her mother will be to sweep everything under the carpet afterward. Not to mention she'll probably need the toilet, otherwise it could get smelly."

"He's right about that," Skye said. "Remember how much it stank before?"

Celeste made a face. "Okay, you can babysit her when we come back. You'll be sleeping in the room next to us, so we'll tie her to a chair in there. I don't mind you taking the tape off her mouth to see if she needs something, but

I'll be the one to cut the ties on her hands and feet and go with her if she's using the toilet."

"Sure, I understand," Jack replied.

Celeste gestured toward the door. "Let's go make the call."

Okay, Rose, you might be in for a surprise. You're about to play the mother of a twenty-seven-year-old kidnap victim. Say the wrong thing and there'll be two more vacancies to fill in the office.

CHAPTER FORTY-EIGHT

Alicia felt immense relief, if not joy, at the sound of Jack's voice when the trunk was opened. *He knows I'm here. A quick call when he gets a chance and I'll be rescued. Everything will be okay … everything will be okay.*

She recollected the events a few hours prior. She had taken the keys from her purse, admiring the BMW as she approached, wondering if she could afford to buy it.

Then the force of a gun being jammed into her ribs had made her gasp.

"Don't scream, you stupid bitch, or you're dead." The man spoke in a whisper, but his tone was deadly.

Another man grabbed her wrist, and she dropped her keys as a black van pulled into her driveway.

"Turn around like everything's okay and get into the van," the man with the gun ordered.

She glimpsed their faces and saw their masks. Masks that had been described to her by Jia Chung when her son was kidnapped.

It's them! My gun ... my badge! If they see that ... She dropped her purse to the ground and kicked it underneath the BMW.

Her action caused one of the men to chortle. "We're not fucking purse snatchers, you dumb broad. Hurry up, bitch, and get in the van."

She had done as she was told and been relieved when the two men did likewise, leaving her purse behind.

A sudden cramp sent a stab of pain through her leg, bringing her back to her current situation. She tried to press her feet against the side of the trunk to alleviate the cramp, but there wasn't any room.

Jack will get help. It shouldn't be long.

CHAPTER FORTY-NINE

Horace drove the van, with Peter in the front passenger seat. Jack sat on the bench seat behind, and Celeste made a point of sitting beside him. Derek and Skye sat in the row behind them.

"I don't want the mother to start giving us any proof-of-life bullshit," Celeste said as they drove toward the Trans-Canada. "All that does is help the cops try to find her. Make it clear to her that if she wants proof of life, we'll send her some fresh body parts. Got it?"

"Got it," Jack replied.

Twenty minutes later, they parked at a small shopping mall in Abbotsford. Celeste handed Jack a phone. "Okay, cowboy, time to do your thing, but hold the phone so I can listen."

Jack was more than a little nervous, wondering if Rose knew yet that Alicia was missing. He made a point of hiding the phone number he tapped in, which seemed to amuse Celeste.

When Rose answered, Jack spoke quickly and harshly, hoping to prevent her from saying something that might alert Celeste.

"You don't know me, but my name's Jack. This morning we kidnapped your daughter, Ally, because yesterday Mason robbed me of five hundred thousand dollars."

Silence followed. Celeste looked at him and raised her eyebrow.

"Are you listening to me?" Jack yelled. "Mason actually thought he could get away with robbing me! The bastard's been selling me cocaine for years, but yesterday, for whatever reason, him and a bunch of guys beat the shit out of me and stole five hundred thousand dollars!"

"Is this — is this some kind of joke?" Rose replied.

Good, she's playing along. He was relieved, though he knew the panic in Rose's voice was genuine. "No, it's not a fucking joke! If you don't believe me, try calling Ally. I guarantee she won't answer. Then talk to Mason. Get him to tell ya what he did."

"Oh, dear, Ally. Is she ... did you hurt her? Can I speak to her?"

"No, you can't fuckin' speak to her until you pay us. You make any more demands like that and we'll be sending you her body parts."

"Oh, God, no! I can't believe this is happening. Please don't hurt her!"

"We haven't hurt her ... yet. That's up to you. If you ever want to see her again you'll round up a million bucks in hundred-dollar bills."

"A million dollars? Okay, yes, whatever you want. Please, don't hurt —"

"You go to the cops, or tell anyone other than Mason, and she's dead. Tomorrow, when you see your bankers or financial advisers, make up a story or tell them you want a cash gift to surprise your kids with. Your daughter's life depends on you keeping your trap shut. Got it?"

"Oh, God, I was worried he might be involved in drugs."

"I said do you understand? Don't go to the cops! And get me my million bucks!"

"I will. I have investments and money in several banks. I can get it all by late tomorrow if I get some money from each place."

Celeste whispered in Jack's ear, and he passed on the message to Rose. "I'll phone you back at one p.m. tomorrow with further instructions. Tell Mason not to bother trying to call me. I don't even have my phone with me."

"Yes, okay. I'll get the money," Rose replied.

"What's your first name?" Jack asked. "Is it Rose? I think that's what Mason said it was."

"Yes, it's Rose."

"Tomorrow! One p.m.!" Jack yelled, then ended the call.

"You did good," Celeste said, her face still so close that he could feel her breath.

"I think it went okay," he replied. He held the phone so Celeste couldn't see the screen as he retrieved the call history and deleted Rose's number before handing it back.

Celeste smiled, then gave him a squeeze on the inner thigh before moving away. "Sounds like I really will have reason to celebrate my birthday tomorrow."

"Hopefully it'll be a party we'll never forget," Jack replied.

* * *

Rose had barely entered the triple one office when Jack had called. After he'd disconnected, she sat down, stunned, then looked up at the sombre faces of Laura, Mason, and Connie. "You heard?"

"We heard you. Is she okay?" Laura asked.

"It sounds like she is for now," Rose replied. "They're demanding a million, and Jack said he'll call me tomorrow at one p.m."

"Is he with Alicia?" Connie asked.

"I don't know."

"But he's seen her?" Mason queried. "Was he there when they grabbed her?"

"I don't know. He said she was okay, so I'm sure he's seen her."

"Will we arrest them when they pick up the money?" Laura asked.

Rose grimaced. "The location of the money drop won't be under our control. If something goes wrong, like it did with the Chung kidnapping, they might kill Alicia. Jack, too, if he's there and tries to stop them. Same thing if we grab Derek and try to get him to talk."

"We could try tracking Derek through his phone, but I bet it's turned off," Laura said.

"I'm sure it is," Rose replied. "Jack told me he didn't have his phone with him."

"So they don't trust him," Mason noted.

"Evidently not."

"Safer to pay them, then wait until she's released and the two of them are safe before making any arrests," Connie stated. "Jack's bound to know where they live or something that'll lead us to them."

"There's something else to consider," Laura said. "What's to stop them from murdering Jack and Alicia once they have the money? In their minds, the police would go after Jack and maybe presume he skipped the country."

"Especially if neither of their bodies is found," Mason noted gravely.

CHAPTER FIFTY

Jack followed Celeste and Skye down the hall, carrying a kitchen chair.

"Set the chair down beside the trunk," Celeste said. "We can drag her back to your room after."

As soon as Celeste unlocked the padlock, Jack opened the lid and pulled Alicia upright so she was on her knees.

"You don't know me," he said, "but your brother, Mason, ripped me off for half a million bucks yesterday. We've grabbed you to hang on to until I get my money back."

Alicia made an unintelligible sound that was muffled by the duct tape over her mouth.

"I called your mother, Rose. She hopes to have my money by tomorrow afternoon. Behave yourself and you won't get hurt. The sooner we get our money, the sooner we'll let you go."

Alicia didn't respond.

"You're going to be tied to a chair," Jack said as he lifted her out of the trunk. "Before that, do you need to use the washroom? A woman will need to go with you. Do you need to go?" he repeated.

Alicia shook her head.

Skye cut the zip ties binding Alicia's ankles together with scissors he'd taken from the kitchen, then he retied each ankle to one of the front legs of the chair with more zip ties. Another zip tie was used to fasten her already bound wrists behind her to one of the chrome pipes extending down the back of the chair.

They then dragged her in the chair to Jack's room, shut the door, and returned to the kitchen, where Derek, Peter, and Horace waited.

"Okay, it's time for lunch," Celeste announced. "Skye and I'll make some sandwiches. Corned beef okay?"

Lunch? I feel like throwing up. "Sure," Jack replied as he approached the counter. "Can I help? Slice the meat or something?"

"Uh-uh," Celeste replied. "Go sit down. I prefer that you keep away from sharp objects while you're here."

Jack rolled his eyes. "Think I'd grab a knife and attack all you guys, then collect the ransom myself?"

"The thought has crossed my mind."

"I'm sure you guys are all packing pieces, and believe me, I'm not dumb enough to bring a knife to a gunfight."

"Glad to hear it, but Skye and I can make the sandwiches. We don't need any help."

"Then I'll bring a glass of water to our guest."

"Okay, you can do that. I'll get you a plastic cup. Put the tape back on her mouth when you're done."

Jack entered the bedroom, bypassing Alicia, and looked out a sliding glass window. All he saw were fields of stubby grass from which hay had likely been cut the month before. A look at the window itself revealed that a large nail had been hammered into the window track to prevent it from being opened.

The computer was turned off, and there was no doubt in his mind that it was password encrypted. He whispered in Alicia's ear. "It's me. I'm alone and I brought you some water. I can take the tape off your mouth, but not your eyes. I think it's safe for us to communicate, but keep it to a whisper. They hadn't planned on you being in this room with me, so I don't think it's bugged. If I hear or see someone coming, I'll dig my fingers into your knee. In future, always wait for me to whisper the okay before saying anything."

Alicia nodded, and Jack peeled the tape from her mouth.

"Where am I?" she whispered.

"In a mobile home on an acreage halfway between Abbotsford and Chilliwack. Five bad guys involved: one woman and four men. Derek and Peter are two of them. The woman, Celeste, owns the trailer and is the leader. Her partner is named Skye, then there's another guy by the name of Horace. Celeste is a pilot and has a plane stored in a hangar beside the trailer."

"A plane? Is that how I was burned over Tommy Chung? Maybe the other night, too, when I met Mason in —"

"Probably." Jack paused. "It's pretty barren outside. Not much for cover if we escaped and tried to run. They also have a pit bull living under the trailer that's off leash at night."

"So we're stuck until Rose gives them the money?"

"Maybe. Rose gave a believable enough story, saying she could come up with the money by tomorrow. In the meantime, this bedroom is the one I was told to use. I talked them into letting you stay with me, but you'll have to go back in the trunk each time we leave to make a call."

"I'm sorry I let them take me," Alicia said tearfully. "This is all my fault."

"I don't see it that way. You let them take you to get proof that they're the kidnappers. Once we're free, I'm recommending you for commendation."

A flicker of a smile crossed Alicia's face.

Maintain your humour, kid, you'll need it.

"Two guys with guns and masks grabbed me when I went out to the car," Alicia explained. "A third drove up in a black van at the same time. I got the plate number."

"You're incredible," Jack said, hoping to boost her confidence. "Most people would be too busy crapping their pants to think of the plate, let alone remember it."

"Maybe you'll get a chance to grab one of their guns? That might be safer than the ransom drop, especially if they're using a plane for countersurveillance."

"Since I've been with them, I haven't seen anyone with a gun. Don't know if they're simply well hidden under their shirts or in ankle holsters, or if they've got them stashed. As far as ransom goes, I'm confident that Rose and Laura will handle it properly. My guess is they'll pay the money and wait until we're free before making arrests." *Or they'll arrest Derek if we're murdered, but there's no need for you be thinking of that.*

"What's to stop them from murdering us and keeping all the money for themselves? In theory, the police don't even know about them."

I guess she did think of that. "That's a possibility, but I haven't had any vibes to that effect."

"Vibes?" Alicia sounded dubious.

"I've been doing this for a long time. Lots of people have tried to kill me, and I've been around people before they murdered others. Generally, there are subtle signs, such as detachment."

"Lack of eye contact or something?"

"Yes, although sometimes it's the opposite. Touching someone more than usual with the idea of portraying friendship while reassuring themselves that the intended victim doesn't suspect anything."

"And if you do sense something, what then?"

"Then we'll have to take different steps."

"Like what? Grab a knife and stab one of them to get a gun?"

"Unless they'd already tried to kill me, I'd probably be charged with murder if I did that. It'd be hard for me to say that I killed someone because I thought they *might* kill me. I'd need proof."

"What proof? A bullet in your head, like Leo?" she added sarcastically.

Jack couldn't tell if she was angry or scared. *Probably both.* "We'll cross that bridge if we come to it, but at the moment I think there's less risk in chancing it that we'll both be freed once they get the ransom. Besides, with my luck, if I did stab someone, they wouldn't have a gun."

Alicia paused. "Doesn't look like we have a choice at the moment."

"Here, have a sip of water," Jack said, holding the cup to her lips. "Let's hope by tomorrow night I'll be offering you an olive soup."

Alicia drank the water down, then Jack put the tape back over her mouth and returned to the kitchen. He sat with Derek at the table as Celeste and Skye brought them sandwiches and water. Peter and Horace both ate their sandwiches in the living room while playing a video game and drinking cola.

Following lunch, Celeste addressed Derek. "Take Jack and those two" — she nodded toward the living room — "out to the hangar and play arcade games or something. I need to talk to Skye, then I'm going to lie down. I feel a migraine coming on, and I could use some quiet."

Perfect. A chance to look around.

Jack followed Derek into the hangar through a side door. Closest to him and on his left was a red Corvette. Nosed in beside it was a Cessna 172.

"Nice car," Jack commented. *Another plate to memorize.*

"It's Celeste's," Derek stated. "Skye had one, too, but sold it about a week ago. Don't know what he plans on getting now."

"And the plane?" Jack asked. *Okay, two plates and the call letters for a plane.*

"The Cessna belongs to Celeste, too."

On Jack's right, along the end wall was a row of six arcade games, with a fridge planted in the middle. Past the fridge was a workbench upon which sat two drones. He decided to amble over for a look. *Disposable cellphones, facial recognition software, an airplane, drones …*

"Perfect for countersurveillance," Derek said, gesturing at one of the drones. "I've got another one in my van."

"Nobody could make a move without you knowing about it," Jack noted, hoping the sick feeling he had didn't show on his face.

"You got that right. There are some zones that Celeste can't fly into, but we still manage to cover everything."

"Impressive. You guys really are professionals." He wandered over to the far side of the plane. "I'd love to own one of these. Of course, I'd need to learn how to fly first," he added.

Derek chuckled. "Yeah, that might be a good idea."

Jack opened the door to the cockpit and looked in.

"Four-seater, high wing," Derek said. "Can fly slow and land or take off on a dime. Ideal for what we use it for."

"Yeah, perfect." *Too perfect.*

They finally had the answer to how Alicia had gotten burned during the Chung kidnapping. The bad guys had been using a plane and drones to monitor the areas. Seeing the same car show up at different locations would have been a dead giveaway.

"Hey, anyone want a beer?" Peter asked, opening the fridge and taking out a Pilsner.

"Yeah, me," Horace replied. Jack and Derek both declined.

"Looks like Peter and Horace have already latched on to their favourites," Derek said, looking toward the arcade games. "Do you play?"

"Not really."

Derek smiled. "Me neither. But it'll help pass the time."

Jack pretended to enjoy a driving game as he contemplated what to do. *Will Rose let the money go without trying to do any surveillance? Will she even get permission to let it go? Tommy Chung might've been lucky compared to what they'd do to Alicia ... and me.*

He eyed the backs of the three men as they played the arcade games. Peter's and Horace's shirts were hanging out, but he didn't see any telltale bulges. *Are their guns locked in the van? Or in the master bedroom? Derek looks to be unarmed. Then again, all of their pants are baggy enough that they could be wearing ankle holsters.*

From where he was, he scanned the workbench for potential weapons. A few screwdrivers and a hammer hung from hooks on a piece of plywood behind the bench. *Great, some sick bastard made an outline on the plywood behind each tool so you can see if anything's missing. And I thought I was Type A. Probably not a good idea to bring a screwdriver to a gunfight, either.*

Also on the workbench was a box of motor oil, a jug of antifreeze, and windshield cleaner — but it was something underneath the workbench that caught his attention.

There are hooks on the wall holding a jacket and ball cap, and yet a set of coveralls is spread out over something underneath the bench. Something that someone decided I shouldn't see?

"Hey, Jack," Peter whispered.

Jack turned and saw Peter pointing a pistol at him. He felt his body tense, then realized the pistol was attached with a cord to the arcade game.

"Kapow!" Peter said. He gave an evil grin, then returned to playing his game.

That makes me feel so much better.

CHAPTER FIFTY-ONE

Alicia heard someone enter the room and hoped it was Jack.

"Hey, I bet you're lonely," Celeste said. "How about we have a little fun to pass the time?"

"What fantasy are you thinking?" a man asked.

Fantasy?

Celeste sounded cheery. "It's always me being the dominator. How about you dominate for a change?"

"She is pretty," he replied. It had to be Skye.

Oh, God. No.

"I know," Celeste said. "She does it for me, too. Drag her back to our room and let's have some fun."

Whatever you're planning, please don't. Jack, where are you?

Alicia felt her chair being tipped backward as she was dragged into the next room.

"Hang on," Celeste said. "Give me a chance to wiggle out of these jeans and enjoy myself."

Alicia heard the sound of a zipper and a moment later felt the brush of silk panties across her face.

"Hey, baby, do you like how I smell?" Celeste asked.

Alicia stiffened. She heard the bed squeak as Celeste lay down on it. "Okay, start the show," she said.

Alicia twisted her torso violently when Skye stood between her legs, but was unable to stop him from undoing the top of her blouse and unfastening her bra.

"Ooh, you're a fighter," he said, digging his fingers deep into her breasts in a twisting motion.

She squirmed and strained at the bonds, begging him to stop, but through the tape it came across only as a muffled cry.

"Oh, yeah. Real, too," Skye commented as he continued to grope. "These aren't store-bought."

Oh, God. Please stop.

Skye continued for a moment longer, then released his grip.

"Hey, not so fast," Celeste said. "I'm not even wet yet. Don't rush. Be nice to her. Stroke her nipples. See if you can make 'em hard. Get her to want you."

Alicia felt him massaging and stroking her breasts with his fingers, pausing intermittently to lick her nipples.

"Oh, yeah, does that feel good, baby? Come on, lean into him." Celeste's voice had gotten husky. "Let yourself go. Sway into him … you know you want to."

Alicia remained rigid, and eventually he stopped.

"She doesn't want to play," he said, then undid the rest of her blouse.

She heard him take his pants off, then felt his legs straddle her body as he stood over her. His fingers caressed the sides of her face, then he used his hands to clamp his penis between her breasts as he slowly pumped his body.

"Ah, a titty-fuck isn't doing it for me," Celeste said a moment later. "Come on, you can do better."

"Okay, but I need a little insurance," he replied, briefly stepping away. When he returned, he grabbed her throat with one hand and peeled the strip of duct tape from her mouth. "Be a good girl," he said, bringing his penis toward her mouth. "You know what to do."

"Try it and I'll bite the end right off!" she spluttered.

"Ooh, I think she means it," Celeste said. "You better be careful."

Skye's grip on her throat tightened, and she started to gag. "I thought you might say that," he said. She then felt the cold muzzle of a pistol in her ear. "You ready to die, little girl?"

"You might need me alive for the ransom," she retorted in a tone whose confidence surprised her.

The bed squeaked as Celeste approached. "Put the gun down," she said. "I've an idea."

Skye obeyed. "I don't believe you'd really bite," he said. "Not if you want to live."

You're going to kill me, no matter what. I know it. She felt the knob on her lips and clenched her teeth.

"Open up," Skye said, digging his thumb into her throat.

She started to choke and opened her mouth.

"That a girl," he said.

Go ahead. Blow my brains out. I don't care anymore.

She bit down as hard as she could. As her teeth sunk in, she shook her head wildly from side to side like a dog trying to rip gristle off a bone.

CHAPTER FIFTY-TWO

"Settle down!" Derek said, after Peter and Horace started roughhousing and bumped into him. "You've each had four beers. We need clear heads tomorrow."

"Four?" Peter questioned. "Naw, I think it was only three."

"It was four. Look at the fucking empties on the bench," Derek replied.

Peter pointed to the bottles and started to count them one at a time, then screwed up his face and started over again.

"It's eight," Derek stated.

"Yeah, yeah, okay," Peter replied. Then, in an apparent attempt to change the subject, he said, "So, tomorrow's Celeste's birthday. Who do you think will be making her birthday wishes come true?"

"Personally I think she favours Jack," Horace said. "You see how she looked at him when they met?"

"Yeah, I noticed," Peter replied. "Bet you noticed too, eh, Jack?"

Peter and Horace looked at him with silly grins. Even Derek looked amused.

"Okay, guys, let me in on the joke."

"Let's just say that Skye and Celeste have a real open relationship," Derek said.

"What do you mean by open?" Jack asked.

"She enjoys other guys, and I think it turns Skye on," Peter said.

"For sure it does," Horace said. "He likes to watch, but I don't care."

"You've had sex with her while he watches?" Jack said.

"Well, one time I was doin' it to her on the sofa and I look up and he's standin' there with his hand down his pants," Peter replied. "Horace and me both have had her. It's like we're all … what did the hippies call it? In a commuter."

"A commune," Jack said.

"Yeah, that's what I said." Peter looked at his brother. "Except for Derek, 'cause women don't turn his crank."

"You guys have had too much to drink," Derek stated. "You should watch what you say."

"Aw, come on," Peter said. "You saw the moves she was makin' on Jack. He's gonna find out, anyway."

"I think I already figured out that she enjoys sex," Jack said.

"Enjoys sex?" Peter laughed. "That's an understatement. She likes to tie you up and then tease you until you're begging for it. Damn near drives you nuts trying to hold your load."

"You call it teasing, but the fucking riding crop scares the shit out of me," Horace said. "It hurts."

"She's used a riding crop on you?" Jack repeated.

"Yeah, she does like her toys," Peter said. "Sometimes she wears a black leather mask, a leather bra, and tight leather shorts."

"That turns me on," Horace said. "Makes her seem wild. Kind of catlike." He glanced at Derek. "How about you? Your friends do shit like that?"

"None of your business." Derek looked disgusted. "Christ, you both sound like a couple of goofs. Have at it, I'm playing a game," he said, turning his back to everyone.

Thank you for not sharing your exploits.

"Better than what Skye lets her do," Peter said, ignoring his brother's comment.

"Fuck, yeah," Horace said. "She's one wild ride, though. I think Skye lets her peg him with a dildo to keep himself from being thrown off."

"You guys are shitting me, right?" Jack asked.

"Maybe," Peter admitted, "but I've seen him so sore he had trouble sitting down, so somethin' was goin' on. Once she got Horace and me trussed up at the same time, then teased us to see which one she'd choose. The last one to keep his dick standing up won ... and that was me."

"She sounds like quite the girl," Jack noted. "Wonder if Skye's ever brought her home to meet his mom?"

"More like his dad," Derek replied, not bothering to take his eyes off the game.

Peter and Horace guffawed, and Jack pretended to join in. Then he had a horrible thought. "I wonder if she swings both ways?" he asked.

"For sure she does," Horace said. "I've seen her drooling over girly magazines more than most men do." He eyed Jack. "Where you going?"

"Back to the trailer. I, uh, need to use the toilet."

CHAPTER FIFTY-THREE

Alicia didn't hear a scream or taste any blood as she bit down. What she got was the taste of rubber, and she spit it from her mouth.

"Holy fuck!" Skye commented. "Glad I didn't shove my pecker in there."

"The fucking little whore!" Celeste uttered. "She damn near took the end off my favourite johnson."

Alicia found herself hyperventilating and tried to control her breathing.

"Think you can be defiant and in control, sunshine?" Celeste hissed. "You're lucky I don't have my boyfriend rearrange your face with a bat."

An image of Greg Dalton lying in a parking lot flashed into her mind, and she gasped some more. Celeste was close enough that Alicia could feel the heat from her breath on her face.

"Let me teach you a little something about who's the master," Celeste continued.

Before Alicia could utter a sound, the tape was placed back over her mouth. Next, her chair was tipped backward onto the floor so her face and torso pointed up toward the ceiling.

"Your turn to watch and learn," Celeste said to Skye, who grunted in response.

Alicia tensed when she felt her jeans being unzipped and yanked past her knees along with her panties. She begged Celeste through muffled sobs to stop. A moment later she felt Celeste's breasts against her face, then felt her tongue darting and licking her navel before moving onward.

"Work with me, baby. Come on," Celeste urged. "Let yourself go. Relax and enjoy. You'll like it. Come on."

Although her feet were still tied to the chair, Alicia was able to clamp her knees together.

"Want to be that way, do you?" Celeste said. "I told you, I'm the master. You will please me … one way or the other."

Celeste changed positions and sat on Alicia's shoulders, facing the opposite direction. She felt Celeste's bare thighs on either side of her head. She gasped as Celeste savagely grabbed her by the hair with both hands, pulling Alicia's head tight to her body. She smelled the odour and felt pubic hair on her nose as the fleshy mound enveloped her face. Soon she couldn't breathe, and panic set in as she madly tried to free her nose.

"That's it! That's it!" Celeste said, urging her to struggle. "Oh, yeah. See?" she said. "Like riding a wild pony. Giddy up, little pony."

"I love it," Skye replied.

Alicia's panic turned to terror as her body demanded air. Then, in a semiconscious state, she realized Celeste had backed off and given her a moment to breathe. Her nostrils flared as she quickly tried to inhale.

She lost track of how many times this process was repeated, but eventually Celeste's primal utterances faded — as did everything else.

When she awoke, she'd been dressed and was upright in the chair, being dragged back to the other bedroom. Then they left her alone.

How could this happen? Why? Her chest heaved as she sobbed behind the tape, then another horrific thought came to mind. *Oh, God, what if people find out at work? That's all anyone will think about when they see me.* She envisioned people talking about her behind her back. *I wish I'd died.*

CHAPTER FIFTY-FOUR

Jack entered the trailer with Derek a few steps behind. He felt relieved to see Celeste and Skye sitting in the living room. "Feeling better?" he asked.

Celeste smiled. "I feel much, much better. Thanks for asking."

"He needed to use the toilet," Derek offered, as if by way of apology.

"First door on the right," Skye stated.

Jack made a pretense of using the bathroom, then came back out. With a nod toward the rear of the trailer, he said, "I better check on our guest."

"She appeared to be asleep when we saw her earlier," Celeste stated.

"Still, I'll check. She hasn't eaten. Should at least get her to drink more water and see if she needs to pee or something."

Jack entered the bedroom and realized a moment later that Celeste and Skye had followed. He handed the plastic cup that Celeste had given him earlier to Skye, then motioned for him to get water.

Skye took the cup and disappeared down the hall without hesitation. The action didn't go unnoticed. Celeste regarded Jack, then, with a nod toward the hallway, said, "Yeah, he's a good little lap dog. Something tells me that you're not of that breed."

"What breed am I?"

"I'm not sure. Perhaps time will tell."

At least you don't think I'm a police dog. Jack touched his lips with his finger, then pointed to Alicia as a warning to Celeste that she should be careful not to be heard. He knelt beside Alicia. "We came to give you some more water."

Alicia didn't move, but she stiffened when he touched her cheek to pull the tape from her mouth. *Why so jumpy? You know it's me.*

Skye reappeared with the refilled cup, and Jack held it to Alicia's lips. She drank at little, then turned her head.

"Would you like some more?" Jack asked.

Alicia shook her head, then bowed her chin to her chest. *You look as if you've given up on life.*

"Would you like a sandwich or to use the toilet?" Jack asked.

Alicia shook her head again, seemingly afraid to speak.

Has she had too much time to worry and now she thinks she's going to die? Damn it, kid, get a grip. If you think that way, you'll end up that way.

* * *

Jack took a seat in the living room on the sofa with Derek and Peter. Celeste and Horace sat in the upholstered chairs as Skye prepared spaghetti in the kitchen.

While waiting for the water to boil, Skye opened a bottle of red wine and poured glasses for everyone. It was a chance for Jack to assess everyone's mood, including whether or not anyone was avoiding eye contact with him or sneaking furtive looks.

No signs of distancing — then again, anyone psychotic enough to go along with chopping off a child's fingers, murder, and beating in a man's face with a bat probably wouldn't get stressed over killing me.

During dinner, everyone seemed friendly, though hyper, which he knew was due to the excitement of what tomorrow would bring. Eye contact was also strong — perhaps too strong, when it came to Celeste.

By the time dinner was over, the six of them had finished three bottles of wine, and Skye was cracking open a bottle of Irish Mist liqueur.

Jack decided to check on Alicia. He was allowed to go alone, although Celeste made a point of adjusting her kitchen chair so she could see down the hallway.

Once in the room, he quickly removed the tape from Alicia's mouth, but kept one hand on her knee, ready to squeeze if anyone approached.

"We can talk. Are you okay?" he whispered.

"I'm fine," she said quickly.

"You don't seem fine. Did something happen you're not telling me about?"

"Nothing happened."

"Okay, then what's got into you? You seem worse than —"

"How would you feel if you were me?" she snapped. "Tied up in here and —"

"Keep your voice down," Jack cautioned. "Try to hang in there. Tomorrow it'll all be over. Rose will pay up. You need to be strong."

Alicia remained silent.

"Is there anything I can get you? Maybe some food?"

"No."

"Bathroom?"

"I said no! I want to sleep. I just want to be left alone."

Jack placed his hands firmly on her shoulders to make her brain focus. "I get it. Blindfolded, scared, it'd be easy to give up hope. But we'll get out of this. Trust me on that."

She didn't respond.

"I'll be back to check on you in a little while." He put the tape over her mouth and returned to the kitchen, where Derek, Skye, and Celeste were all seated at the table with lowball glasses filled with ice and liqueur in front of them. Peter and Horace sat on the sofa holding their glasses.

Celeste looked at him and raised an eyebrow.

"She doesn't want anything," he said, squeezing behind the table to sit on the bench across from her. "Just asked to be left alone."

"Here ya go!" Skye said, sliding a glass of liqueur across the table to him.

"*Slainte!*" Celeste said, giving the Irish toast.

Everyone gulped their drink and Skye started to refill the glasses, but Jack covered the top of his. "Thanks, but no."

"Come on, you're part of this team, aren't you?" Skye chided.

"Yes, give us a toast," Celeste added.

Jack relented and raised his glass. "An Irish toast comes to mind. May we get what we want, may we get what we need, but may we never get what we deserve."

Celeste laughed. "Perfect!" She blew him a kiss before downing her drink.

"Hey, Celeste, all right if Horace and I play some video games on the TV?" Peter asked.

"Go ahead. No more booze for anyone, though. We need clear heads tomorrow."

"I'll clean up," Derek said, getting to his feet and taking dirty dishes to the sink.

"I'd help, but the kitchen is off limits for me," Jack said, hoping to convey disappointment at not being trusted.

"Maybe tomorrow night you can help," Celeste replied. "Speaking of which, I want to talk to you about tomorrow."

"I'd like to know who'll be doing what, where, and when."

"You'll be making the call to the mother at one p.m.," Celeste noted, "and if she has the money together, you'll phone her again in two hours and give her a location. That'll give the rest of us time to set up. At that location we'll leave another phone for her to use. Then we run her around and make sure she's not being watched and that she doesn't have any bugs or GPS locators hidden on her."

"You and Skye will be up in the plane?" Jack asked.

"Yes."

"And me? Will I be with Derek in his van?"

"No, because he won't always be in his van. He'll be the one who checks for bugs when we send the mother for a walk. You'll be with Peter and Horace."

"Once we know it's safe and have got the money, we'll all meet here," Skye added.

"After that, Peter and Horace will take Ally and drop her off someplace," Celeste said. "Then it's a simple matter of calling her mother and letting her know where to find her."

"Sounds good," Jack said.

Celeste gave a warm smile. "Once you get your share, Derek can take you back to your hotel, or you can stay and celebrate with us."

Jack faked a smile. "A double celebration. Your birthday, as well."

Celeste was thoughtful, and her face became cold. "If, for any reason, mom doesn't have the money together, I want you to scare her. Tell her she has exactly twenty-four hours to get it. For every hour she's late, I'll cut off one of her daughter's fingers. After ten hours, I'll start on her toes."

"Yep, that ought to scare her," Jack replied. *You should've said to tell her that I'd chop off the fingers, not you. A Freudian slip?* He knew he was staring into the eyes of the person who had mutilated Tommy Chung.

"Got it?" Celeste asked.

"Got it."

She sat back in her chair. "So there we have it." She made eye contact with Skye and gave a subtle nod.

Skye cleared his throat. "I almost forgot. I need to use the computer in the spare room. There's someone I need to talk to online."

"Better slide Ally back into our room," Celeste cautioned. "Jack and I'll help."

Jack followed Celeste and Skye into the bedroom. He tapped Alicia on the shoulder and said, "We need to take you to another room so someone can use the computer in here for an online chat."

Alicia went rigid, but didn't respond.

"Hang on a sec," Skye said, "I gotta grab something from my room." He returned a moment later, then he and Jack tipped back Alicia's chair and dragged her into the master bedroom.

Jack was about to follow Skye out of the room, but Celeste grabbed his wrist and held him back. Skye went into the next room and shut the door.

"I want to talk to you … privately," she whispered.

"Privately?" Jack asked. He gestured to Alicia. "She might hear."

"I mean without those … boys in the living room listening in." Celeste closed the door, then glanced at Alicia. "As far as our guest goes … this should do the trick." She turned on some Latin music, and under the slow-tempo sound of bolero, led Jack by the wrist to sit beside her at the edge of the bed.

Jack glanced up, caught their reflection in the mirrored ceiling, and moved away slightly. "What is it?" he whispered.

Celeste kept her voice low. "When we first met, I teased you a little."

"Oh?" Jack replied.

Celeste's eyes took in his body, then drifted back up to his face. "When I checked you out and said why think small when you can think big."

"I think I remember that."

"You think?" Celeste snickered. "I caught the smile you gave me," she added, snuggling closer. She gently squeezed his inner thigh. "Would it be presumptuous to say I think you're attracted to me, too?"

Actually I think you're a slut.

"I do find you appealing, but you've got a guy ... and he's in the very next room."

"Skye doesn't mind," she murmured. "We have an open relationship."

Jack felt her give his groin a gentle squeeze. *Oh, no, you don't!* He grabbed her by the wrist and pushed her hand away. "I have a girlfriend," he said, abruptly getting to his feet.

Celeste looked amused and grabbed his wrist again. "That doesn't bother me. A foursome would be okay," she teased.

"Sorry, but I'm a one-woman kind of guy," he replied, giving his wrist a jerk.

She held on. "Maybe that's because you've never had me."

"No, but I've heard a few stories."

"Stories?"

"Relating a preference for bondage, which I'm not into."

"Boys like to talk," Celeste said scornfully. "That's why I call them boys." She studied Jack. "But you're no boy. You're a real man. Someone, I bet, who knows how to please a woman."

"My woman, yes." He glanced at the door. "We should go."

"Doesn't what I say interest you at all? Use your imagination a little. Imagine someone so turned on, wanting you so bad, being fully under your control. Having them beg for you to touch them, caress them ... make love to them."

"Sounds erotic, but —"

"Did the boys tell you about my outfit?"

"They mentioned a riding crop … which really doesn't do anything for me."

Celeste gave an unladylike snort. "That's only for show. I'd never really hurt anyone." She gave a nod toward Alicia. "Do you find her attractive?"

"She's pretty," Jack admitted.

"I can see some men not wanting to perform with another man watching, but what about another woman? Bet I could make her horny if I put on my outfit and had her watch us get it on. What do you think?"

What do I think? I think it's obvious you don't plan on letting her live afterward. Perhaps not me, either … or does that depend upon my performance in the bedroom? He forced a smile. "You're messing with me, right? You couldn't do that — she'd see your face."

"Believe me, she'd never say anything. Especially after she's joined in."

"How do you know she'd want to join in?"

"Trust me on this. I'm a good judge of character. Besides, why should you care? She already knows you."

I'm not stupid. You do plan on killing her.

"So? A little ménage à trois?" Celeste prodded. "Think you could handle two women at the same time, Jack?"

"I'm not that much of a stud. Come on, enough. Let's —"

"Imagine yourself lying here, pleasing her and making her cry out with pleasure as she sits on your shoulders … while I sit behind her and take you in. Pleasing you ever, ever so slowly." She paused. "Ever bring two women to orgasm at the same time, Jack? It's wild."

"Thanks, not interested," he replied, pulling his wrist from her grip and turning toward the door.

"Shame," Celeste replied angrily. "She'll have to settle for just me."

Jack spun on his heel. "Don't even go there," he warned.

Celeste looked taken back. "Wow ... seems like I hit a nerve," she replied, glancing at Alicia, before regarding Jack with suspicion.

"It's my ass on the line! I'm the one making the phone calls. Her mother won't go to the cops only if she isn't harmed. You do anything to her and they will go to the cops!"

"Ally wouldn't be the type to say anything. She'd be too embarrassed."

"Not a chance I'm willing to take."

Celeste eyed Alicia.

Damn it, what do I do? No way I'm leaving you alone with her. "Look, I'm sorry," Jack said. "I don't know you that well and you really caught me by surprise. Tonight I feel stressed to the max. Sex is the last thing on my mind."

"That's funny, I'm the opposite. The more stress I feel, the more I want to have sex. It makes me relax."

"Not me. All I can think about is getting the money tomorrow. Place half a million dollars in my hand and I'll be a lot more amiable."

Celeste's face brightened, and she got up off the bed. "Define amiable."

"Well, I know it's your birthday tomorrow. I'd sure hate to disappoint a lady on her birthday." *But you're no lady.*

Celeste ran her hand up the front of his jeans. "Promise?"

"Definitely."

"Then I'll hold you to it." She cupped his groin and smiled.

"Let's go. Tomorrow will be a special day … for both of us." Jack nodded toward the door and she led the way out of the room.

When they were part of the way down the hall, Skye emerged from the guest bedroom. "I'm done."

He and Jack dragged Alicia back to Jack's room before rejoining the others in the living room. Peter and Horace looked at Jack with knowing grins. He decided to ignore them.

"Turn off the game," Celeste said. "Make sure there's nothing on the news."

The news was uneventful. An hour later, Jack said he was calling it a night. Once inside his room, he closed the door and removed the tape from Alicia's mouth.

"Did you hear what happened?" he whispered. "When Celeste and I were in the master bedroom with you?"

"The music was a bit loud. I know the two of you were on the bed. Did you … you know, her and you?"

"Christ, no! What kind of person do you think I am? I'd never do that."

"Oh."

"But the ransom has to go ahead tomorrow. Would you like any food or water? Maybe use the bathroom?"

"I'm not hungry, but I'd like some water. I also need to pee."

"I'll get you some water and tell Celeste. She made it clear she won't let you go to the bathroom alone."

"Will you be there? Outside the door, I mean?"

"Yes, I'll be around to keep an eye on you. Celeste swings both ways, and I'm sure she meets the definition of a nymphomaniac. If she tries something, stomp your feet, and I'll kick the door in if I have to."

"They'd probably kill you if you did."

"Probably is a chance I'm willing to take."

Minutes later, Celeste used the kitchen scissors to temporarily free Alicia's hands and feet, then took her to the bathroom before returning and securing her to the chair.

Jack whispered in Alicia's ear as soon as they were alone. "Did she say or try anything?"

"No. Just asked if I was done and that was it."

"You're trembling. You weren't a moment ago."

"I'm cold."

Jack wrapped a blanket around her, then moved her chair closer to the wall and wedged a pillow behind her back and head. "I feel bad leaving you in the chair while I sleep in the bed beside you."

"I'm fine where I am. I'm — I'm glad you're here."

Jack didn't undress, but lay on the bed and tried to analyze what he should do in the different circumstances that could arise. *Will Rose let them pick up the money and hold off on any arrests until we're safe? Will Ottawa allow her to do that? If they do try to make arrests, will we be safe? What if they spot surveillance, or what if some of them are arrested, but the plane makes it back? Bet they'd kill Alicia. Even if the ransom is paid and Alicia is freed, I've still got the slut to deal with. What then? Fake appendicitis to get out of sex with her? That wouldn't go over well …*

He listened as Celeste and Skye murmured in their bedroom, then heard Peter telling someone he'd take the first shift.

His thoughts returned to Peter pretending to shoot him in the arcade. There was something in his smile afterward, like he had a secret and was toying with Jack. *Do they plan to kill us both?* Then there were the coveralls under the bench rather than hung up on a hook. Was he being paranoid? Had they simply been tossed there? He remembered how the coveralls appeared to have been laid over something. *No, they weren't tossed there. Trust your instincts.*

CHAPTER FIFTY-FIVE

At 6:30 a.m. Jack quietly slipped out of his room and went down the hallway.

"You're up early," Horace said from where he sat in a kitchen chair.

The noise awoke Derek, who was asleep on the sofa. He tossed a quilt off himself and sat up. Peter was stretched out in a sleeping bag on the floor. Derek gave him a nudge with his foot.

"I couldn't sleep," Jack said. "Too keyed up." He glanced at his wrist and frowned. "Also I lost my watch. The pin that holds the strap in place keeps coming out. I'm thinking it might've fallen off while I was playing arcade games. I'm going to pop out to the hangar and take a look."

"I'll go with you," Derek said, getting to his feet. "Give me a sec to chain Diego up first."

In the hangar, Jack made a pretense of looking around the floor near the arcade games. "I was also looking inside the Cessna," he noted. "Mind checking it for me while I look over by the drones?" He moved toward the workbench.

While Derek walked over to the far side of the plane, Jack had a couple of seconds to peer under the coveralls below the bench. It was more than enough time to see what the kidnappers were planning. *A shiny new pickaxe and shovel, with the price tags still on the handles. Guess they don't plan on sharing the ransom.*

"Not here," Derek announced.

"Not here either," Jack replied. "Hopefully it'll turn up somewhere."

"I'll get Horace to look in his van later. How about some coffee?"

"Great idea."

* * *

Not until an hour later did Jack have the opportunity to speak with Alicia in private and tell her what he'd discovered.

"They're going to kill us once they get the money," Alicia said matter-of-factly.

"My thoughts exactly," Jack said. "Somehow I need to stall Rose from paying, then figure out a way for us to escape."

"I think there's a gun in the other bedroom."

"What? You didn't mention it before."

"Uh, I forgot, but when they first put me in the trunk, I heard one of them — Skye, I think — tell Celeste to hold on a sec before closing the lid. I heard him go to a dresser or something, then he came back and stuck a gun in my ear and threatened to kill me if I made any noise or tried to escape."

"I bet as a precaution that's what he took out of the room last night before Celeste made a pass at me."

"Maybe that's a good thing. She might have shot you when you didn't do as she wanted."

"I think I handled it okay, but you're right. Probably in their eyes I've served my purpose. They could get your mom's phone number from you directly, and one of the others could contact her. With all the equipment they have, there must be something for altering a voice over the phone."

"So what're we going to do? They could kill us both at any time."

"I'll try and gain everyone's trust and convince Celeste to keep me around. I'm hoping I already took care of that with the promise I made to her about tonight."

"To have sex with her," Alicia replied matter-of-factly.

"Once I get her back in the bedroom, I'll put a sleeper hold on her and gag her. Then tie her up and look for —"

"But if Skye has the gun and decides to use this room like last night, what then?"

"I'll need to ensure that he's out of commission first. See to it that he's incapable of responding or using a gun before I take out Celeste. Then, with luck, I can go back and get the gun from him if need be."

"How will you do all that without someone seeing and putting a bullet in your back?"

"I have an idea. Might take a little Irish luck."

CHAPTER FIFTY-SIX

"Happy birthday, girl!" Jack said, raising his coffee mug when Celeste entered the kitchen wearing a cream-coloured silk nightgown and fuzzy pink slippers.

Celeste smiled. "Thanks, let's hope it will be," she replied. She poured herself a cup of coffee before joining Jack, Skye, and Derek at the kitchen table. Peter and Horace were in front of the television playing a video game, as usual.

"How's our guest? I heard whispering from your room this morning."

"You did. I learned some things," Jack said. "Our guest has a sister by the name of Laura."

"Why'd she tell you that?"

"She's worried about her mom being able to come up with all the money so quickly, since she's starting to suffer from senility or dementia."

"Shit, that's all we need," Skye said.

"The good news is that this Laura is married to some rich dude and could likely chip in a couple hundred grand right away. I'm sure both Mason and Laura will be there when I call. I think I should talk to Laura and put a little pressure on her."

"Is there any chance of Laura going to the police?" Celeste asked.

"I asked that." He smiled. "Her answer was 'not if she wants to remain in Mom's will.'"

Celeste thought for a moment, then shrugged. "So nothing really changes. Talk to Laura instead. If they have the money, then great. Get her to deliver the ransom. If they don't have it … well, you know what to say."

* * *

The rest of the morning was spent sitting around the kitchen table discussing various money drops and routes for the ransom payment. Jack had little to say about the matter, but he pretended to be pleased when Peter announced that he'd found his watch on the mat in the bathroom.

Lunch consisted of peanut butter and jam sandwiches, then Celeste announced that it was time to put Ally back in the trunk so Jack could make his call. Once that task was completed, everyone started to exit the trailer.

Out on the porch, Jack tapped Celeste on the arm and motioned for her to wait as the others walked toward the van.

"What is it?" she asked.

"Because of you, I couldn't sleep all night. I kept think-ing about what you said to me." Jack shook his head for effect. "Talk about my imagination running wild. You don't know how many times I wanted to get up and knock on your door."

Celeste smiled. "I was thinking about you, too. Very much looking forward to tonight."

"What you suggested damn near drove me crazy afterward. Thinking about bringing two women to orgasm at the same time …"

"So you've changed your mind about including Ally?"

"I gave it a lot of thought. I mean … if I please her, what's she going to say? That some guy aroused her and she wanted more?"

"Exactly. She's not going to tell anyone about it."

"We should keep her blindfolded, though. It would still be better if she never saw your face." Jack tried to sound enthusiastic. "I can hardly wait."

"Good. Anticipation is all part of it." She kissed him, and he let her slip her tongue into his mouth as she pressed her body up to his. "It sounds — or, should I say, *feels* — like I'm going to have a good birthday one way or the other." She looked at him coyly as she stepped back.

"About your birthday. I want to talk to Skye and get him or someone else to go out and get some stuff. Let's have a party. Everyone is feeling the pressure. It would be good to have something to take our minds off of things, especially if it takes longer to get the money. I'd also feel better if everyone was partying and not paying too close attention later, when you and I slip away to the bedroom. Less of an audience, if you know what I mean."

"I could go along with that."

"I'll do the cooking. Sort of my way to thank everyone for helping me get my money back. We'll need some balloons — green, of course. I have a delicious recipe for ribs, and I also make a great Caesar salad. If you're real lucky, I might even make my secret punch, providing someone can pick up the booze for me."

Celeste looked pleased. "Write out a list of what you need when we come back from making the phone call, and I'll have Horace get it all." She raised an eyebrow. "Secret punch, huh? What's the secret?"

"It's my version of a jade cocktail. I won't disclose the exact recipe, but I can tell you that it's jade green and a great aphrodisiac."

"Really?"

"It really livens up the, uh, senses."

"Well then ... that's definitely something we'll have to try."

* * *

Sitting behind her desk at the triple one office, Laura glanced at her watch as Rose and Mason arrived. It was 12:00 p.m.

Rose had added some grey to her hair and slapped on an abundance of makeup to make herself look older, old enough to portray Alicia's mom when she delivered the money. Normally Laura might've teased her, but nobody was in the mood for humour today. Instead, she said, "You look good. Ten years older, for sure."

"Who knew that'd be a compliment," Rose replied sardonically.

All eyes turned to the door. Connie Crane, Ned Hawkins, and Inspectors Dyck and Crimmins had arrived together.

Laura wheeled in extra chairs from Jack's office.

"I've obtained the money," Dyck said as he sat down. "A million bucks, all in hundreds. It took nine banks to get it together. It's in a safe at my office."

"And Ottawa?" Rose asked.

"Spent most of last night on the phone. Approval came through this morning. The ransom can be paid with the hope of recovering it after our people are safe."

Laura exchanged a glance with Mason and Rose. They all breathed a sigh of relief that Jack and Alicia's safety would come first.

"I sincerely hope the money can be recovered," Dyck added.

Because your career will be over if it isn't.

"Any changes since yesterday?" Crimmins asked.

"Not a word from Jack," Rose said, sounding stressed. "Special O has had a watch on Derek Powers's address. Neither he nor his brother have been seen. Same for his office. His surveillance van is still in the underground lot and hasn't moved."

"We also have the tactical teams on standby," Laura noted.

"So they'll be ready to go once our people are freed and can tell us where to go," said Crimmins. He turned to Rose. "I still don't like the idea of not having you in sight of any ground surveillance." He glanced at Hawkins. "Having you up in the air is one thing, but a lot could go wrong that you wouldn't be able to see. Constables Short and Dalton are prime examples."

"I'm not worried," Rose said. "I'll hide a pistol in my car, but even that I don't think is necessary. It's Alicia and Jack we need to protect. The best way to do that is to pay the money and hope the kidnappers follow through with their promise."

Crimmins nodded.

"Or, with luck, to have the plane spot where they go and get ERT to do a raid. Hopefully one that doesn't turn into a hostage situation," Dyck said.

Laura checked her watch. *Forty minutes to go. You could cut the tension with a knife.*

"Anyone like a coffee?" Mason asked.

Laura's stomach felt acidic, and coffee was the last thing she wanted, but she decided that anything to pass the time until Jack called would be better than sitting in silence or trying to make small talk. Everyone else wanted a coffee, as well. *Guess I'm not the only one.*

It was exactly 1:00 p.m. when Rose's phone buzzed. She put it on speakerphone.

"Before you say anything, shut up and listen!" Jack said harshly. "Is Ally's sister, Laura, there?"

Oh, man. Something's not right. Why does he want to speak to me? Rose was looking at her for a response, so Laura nodded.

"Yes, she's with me," Rose said.

"Let me speak to her."

Laura pulled the phone toward her. "This is Laura."

"Ally tells me your mom is suffering from senility, so let me make this perfectly clear to you. If you deliver the money, your little angel in the full moon will be returned exactly as she is. Fuck with us and things will go real bad for her, do you understand?"

Angel in the full moon? Laura stared blankly at Rose as her mind raced. *That's the English translation for the name of the Vietnamese girl Jack and I tried to save years ago. She ended up being murdered. Pay and Alicia will end up exactly as she is … murdered.* Laura swallowed the mixture of bile and coffee which slid up her throat.

"Are you listening to me?" Jack yelled. "Do you understand?"

"Yes, yes, but it takes time to get that much money. Our investments require a minimum of two or three business days." Crimmins poked her arm and turned his palms upward, asking what she was doing. She glared at him and mimed slashing her throat with her index finger, then continued. "We also have to go to different banks because we don't want anyone to know how much we're taking out or for what reason."

"I'll give you until one p.m. tomorrow. After that, for every hour you're late, Ally will lose a finger. After ten hours we start on her toes. You got that?"

"I'll have it by tomorrow. Please, please don't hurt her. We're doing our best. Honest. We —"

Laura stopped talking after Jack had ended the call.

"What the hell are you doing?" Crimmins demanded. "We told you, we've got the money!"

Laura explained what Jack meant when he'd mentioned an angel in the full moon.

"So he's saying that they intend to kill Constable Munday once the ransom is paid?" Crimmins said.

"Yes, I believe so."

"If Sergeant Taggart is warning us that they're going to murder Constable Munday, I believe we can rest assured that he believes they're going to murder him, as well," Dyck stated. "There's no way he could even pretend to go along with it. His resistance would mean he'd be killed, too."

"I agree," Laura said. "I'm sure his script was laid out for him. When he squeezed in the bit about the angel in the full moon, I think he was taking as much risk as he dared."

"So where does that leave us?" Mason asked. "If we pay the ransom, they'll both be killed, yet if it's not paid by tomorrow, they'll start cutting off body parts."

"It doesn't leave us with much choice," Rose said. "Tomorrow we'll have to pay the ransom, then try to follow whoever picks it up."

"I see another potential problem," Hawkins said. "Whoever picks it up could be some chump who doesn't even know where Jack and Alicia are."

"So what are we supposed to do?" Rose eyed Laura. "You know Jack the best — what do you think?"

"Jack stalled for a reason ... perhaps only to give themselves time. I think we need to be prepared to pay tomorrow and make the arrests, but I've got a feeling that Jack and Alicia's survival is dependent upon whatever he plans to do between now and then."

"Maybe he has a plan or is hoping an opportunity will arise to call for help," Crimmins suggested.

"Maybe," Laura replied.

"I'd better call Assistant Commissioner Lexton and let her know," Dyck said. "She wanted to be kept up to date."

Especially if any bodies turn up, which is quite likely. Laura felt nauseous. Was it from being pregnant? *Who am I kidding? It's from worrying that the bodies that turn up might be Jack and Alicia's.*

CHAPTER FIFTY-SEVEN

Celeste looked surprised when Jack handed her the cell-phone back.

"Aren't you going to delete the number first?" she asked.

"It's time we started trusting each other." He winked, then added, "I want you to know I'm a stand-up kind of guy."

She looked amused for a second, but then her face grew serious. "I think the issue of trust will resolve itself after we get the money."

Meaning the status quo remains in effect. "I'm sorry that they couldn't come up with it in time for your birthday."

Celeste seemed indifferent. "I expected it to take a couple of days. It usually does. What's this angel in the full moon bit?" she asked curiously.

"I wanted something to pull at their heartstrings a little, so I asked Ally what pet names her mom had for her.

She said 'the angel in the full moon' was from a family camping trip. Something to do with her going out at night and pulling the pegs out of Mason's tent."

"I see. That was a good idea. It'll make them think fondly of her and provide further motivation." Her face hardened. "However, don't do anything like that again without running it past me first."

"Sure, no problem."

* * *

Once they were back at the trailer, Alicia was removed from the trunk and tied to the chair in Jack's room. Jack didn't have a chance to speak to her alone, but did tell her that he'd spoken to Laura and had been told they'd have the money tomorrow.

He then sat down with Horace and Skye at the kitchen table to write out a shopping list for the party. Celeste sat on the sofa watching television with Derek and Peter, but from her furtive glances and smiles at him, Jack could tell she was pleased about all the attention she'd be getting.

Some of the items Skye said they had on hand, but not others, including romaine lettuce, pork ribs, hoisin and honey garlic sauce, a birthday cake, and balloons. For his punch, Jack requested a bottle of crème de menthe, a bottle of white rum, a small bottle of Cointreau, lime juice, and six fresh limes.

Skye reviewed the list and stated he'd pay for everything. He handed a wad of cash to Horace.

After that, Jack found a chance to talk to Alicia.

"It's me, I'm alone," he whispered.

"Did they go along with your party idea?"

"Yes, Horace is picking up the stuff. He said he'd be back in an hour."

"So you're going to do it in an hour?"

"I need to prepare the ingredients, plus get the poison. It'll take time."

"What if you're caught?"

"I'll tell them my plan was to take the money for myself. There's still a possibility that they'd let you live."

"You know they wouldn't."

"I know. I was hoping you didn't."

"I'm not as naive as you think," she said bitterly. "If you do get away with it, once everybody starts getting sick, they'll know something's up."

"It takes a couple of hours to take effect, depending upon the person's size and how much they drink. Skye is small. If everyone drinks the same amount, he'll be the first to feel the effects. At about the time I think he's ready to pass out, I'll take Celeste to the bedroom. I'm sure that at that point, Skye will use this room. Then all I need to do is stall a little with Celeste to ensure he really is passed out and won't come in on us, then I'll slap a sleeper hold on her. After that, I'll gag her and tie her up, then look for the gun. If it looks like Skye has it, I'll slip back and take it from him."

"What about me?"

"I'll come up with something to cut the zip ties. I'm betting we'll also find a cellphone somewhere in the master bedroom to call in the cavalry."

"Do you think this'll kill them?"

"It takes at least twelve hours for actual death to occur, but again that depends upon size and the quantity drunk.

If my idea works, they can be saved if they make it to the hospital in time."

"If that happens, do you think Celeste and Skye will confess to ... everything?"

"Possibly. They'll probably play the blame game and point the finger at each other, try to make themselves look like the victim somehow. They've done other kidnappings, so a good defence lawyer would worry about that coming out in court. It would be better to cut a deal to get their client a reduced sentence in exchange for testimony."

"Oh," Alicia replied, sounding even more sad.

"Is there something you're not telling me?"

"No," she answered bluntly. "Nothing."

"Then why ask only about Celeste and Skye? Don't you mean all of them?"

Alicia paused, then explained, "They're the only ones who've dealt with me since I've been here, and Celeste is the ringleader. I guess her name popped into my head first."

You're not telling me something. Perhaps something you feel too much shame or embarrassment to talk about? Oh, shit, those fucking animals ... what did they do to you? He looked at Alicia and sighed. *I'll leave it for now. You're under enough stress.*

* * *

After Horace had returned with the shopping, Jack prepared the salad dressing at the kitchen table under the close scrutiny of Skye while Derek washed the lettuce. His next step was to make the punch.

"Some ingredients need time to blend," he said, using a measuring cup to pour two cups of rum, half a cup of Cointreau, and a generous splash of lime juice into a bowl. "It also needs to be refrigerated before you add the rest."

"Did you forget that?" Skye asked, pointing to a cup of crème de menthe that Jack had set aside.

"I'll be putting that in the freezer and turning it into a green slush."

A moment later, Jack shut the refrigerator. He turned to the counter and tore open the packages of ribs. "If someone would hand me a butcher knife to cut these into sections, I'll wrap them in foil with a couple of ice cubes and steam them in the oven for a couple of hours." He gestured to the limes on the kitchen table. "Also I could use a paring knife. I forgot to cut up a couple of the limes for the punch."

"I'll cut the ribs and wrap them in foil," Skye informed Jack, giving him a gentle push on the shoulder to move away.

"Do you really think I'd run amok with a butcher knife? Give me a break," Jack said sarcastically, returning to the table.

"Like Celeste said, everyone will feel better once we get our money," Skye retorted. "I'll section the meat, you slice the limes."

Jack examined the paring knife Skye handed to him. The blade was no longer than his little finger. "Are you sure? This looks pretty deadly. Could be a weapon of choice in a gunfight."

Skye didn't seem amused, but Derek flashed a smile.

Jack sliced up two of the limes and dumped all the slices into the bowl in the fridge. The other limes he set aside for later, then watched as Skye put the ribs in the oven before washing the butcher knife and putting it in a drawer.

"I've got a little time before I need to add more stuff to the punch," Jack noted. He looked toward Peter and Horace in the living room watching television with Celeste. "Anyone up for some arcade games?"

Upon receiving an affirmative response from Peter and Horace, Jack picked up the bottles of rum, crème de menthe, and Cointreau. "These need to be put in the freezer," he commented, going to the refrigerator.

This was a risky part of his plan, as he knew Skye would be keeping an eye on him to ensure he didn't go near the knife drawer.

What Skye didn't notice was that Jack put only the bottles rum and Cointreau into the freezer. Nor did he notice the slight bulge in the front of Jack's pants and under his shirt when he excused himself to go to the bathroom.

Despite having turned on the bathroom fan, Jack was relieved that nobody else went in immediately after him. The smell of the crème de menthe he'd poured down the toilet lingered.

He glanced at Celeste as he followed the others out onto the porch, knowing she was the most likely one to spot the bulge of the hidden bottle.

She flashed him a smile. "How's that secret punch of yours coming along?"

"Hopefully, it'll do the trick," he replied with a wink. *The thought of leaving you two alone with Alicia makes my skin crawl.*

"When can I try some?"

"In about an hour and a half. I'll be back shortly to work on it some more. Dinner will be ready an hour after the punch is."

"Sounds great."

"I suggest you get some rest," Jack replied, "because you'll need it once the party starts." He grinned.

"I'm really, really looking forward to it," she replied, then mimed a kiss.

Jack caught the eager look on Skye's face as he flirted with Celeste. *Guess what, you sick bastard, you're the smallest. With luck, you'll be the first to die.*

* * *

"Man, I'd love to learn to fly someday," Jack exclaimed upon entering the hangar. He pretended to admire the Cessna and turned to Derek. "Do you think it'd be okay if I sat in the cockpit for a moment to see what it feels like?"

"Yeah, go ahead. The keys aren't in it, but don't touch anything, anyway."

Derek, Peter, and Horace were distracted by the arcade games and didn't notice when Jack grabbed a jug off the bench on his way to the Cessna. Three minutes later, he left the crème de menthe bottle in the cockpit — only now it was filled with antifreeze.

Antifreeze was a deadly poison. Three ounces was enough to kill most people, and the initial symptoms were similar to being drunk. It also had a sweet flavour, but that was something Jack hoped to mask with the other ingredients.

He'd already done the math in his head. *There's enough in the bottle for each of them to have five ounces. The lowball glasses hold about four ounces, along with ice. If the drink is half antifreeze, I'll need them to drink two glasses each.*

There was a problem with this plan that Jack was well aware of. It'd likely be several hours before anyone lost consciousness or went into a coma, but before that, some of them might be vomiting or displaying other signs of poisoning. If everyone got sick, they'd suspect him. What he wanted was to convince Celeste and Skye to drink more, then separate them from the others before any suspicion was roused.

Forty minutes later, Jack suggested they get back to the trailer and blow up some balloons while he finished making the punch.

"Already?" Peter complained. "I'm on my best game ever."

"Go ahead and finish it," Jack replied. "I'm going to go sit in the cockpit again."

CHAPTER FIFTY-EIGHT

Jack put the punch bowl on the kitchen table and fussed over it, ladling some of it into a glass and pretending to sample it, then repeating the process as he added more ingredients, conscious that Skye was watching.

"Okay, it's ready," Jack announced. He ladled out the mixture into the lowball glasses and had Skye deliver them to the others, who were seated in the living room. He also took that opportunity to pour some of the crème de menthe he'd set aside earlier into his own glass before entering the living room.

Celeste smiled at him. "Saved you a spot," she said, patting the sofa cushion.

Jack glanced at Skye, who went to get a kitchen chair for himself, then returned Celeste's smile and sat beside her.

Jack cleared his throat, then raised his glass in a toast. "Happy birthday, Celeste ... and don't forget, an Irish

woman is never drunk as long as she can hold on to one
blade of grass and never fall off the face of the earth."

"That's supposed to be an Irish man!" Celeste exclaimed, but she laughed.

"To you," he said, then gulped his drink down.

*Score one for Celeste. One for Skye ... although it looks
like he didn't like it. Derek only took a sip. Same as Horace.*

"Yeah, I'll have another one of them," Peter said.

"You can have mine," Derek said, handing his brother
the glass. "A bit too sweet for me."

"I'm going for another one, as well," Jack said, standing
up. He looked at Celeste.

"Why not," she said, handing him her glass.

Jack reached for Skye's. "Uh, thanks, no," he said.

"Come on, you're part of the team, aren't you?" Jack
chided.

Skye grinned. "Guess you owe me that one. Okay, one
more."

Jack was a little slower to consume his second glass,
but by the time he did, Skye and Celeste had finished, as
well. Horace's original glass was still half-full, but Peter
had finished Derek's drink and already helped himself
to a third.

*Damn it, slow down, you idiot. If you pass out, Celeste
and Skye will be giving me the hairy eyeball when they start
to really feel the effects.*

By the time dinner was over, Skye and Celeste were
beginning to slur their words. When Peter stood up, he
stumbled and had to grab the wall to keep from falling.

*Son of a bitch. He's out of it. Celeste and Skye aren't quite
there yet. We need to keep the party going for a little while*

longer. Even though everyone else was finished eating, he speared another section of ribs as Peter staggered toward the bathroom.

Celeste glared at Horace. "How much did the two of you drink out in the hangar today? I know we're having a party, but get real. We have a job to do tomorrow."

"Nothin'," Horace replied. "I swear."

"Yeah, I'll bet."

The sound of Peter vomiting came from the washroom.

"Real nice," Celeste said. "Get him out of here. Grab his sleeping bag and put him in the hangar to sleep it off."

"He's my brother, I'll look after him," Derek said, then looked at Celeste. "Nobody had any beers in the hangar." He raised the half-full beer he'd been drinking and said, "This is the first beer I've had."

"Same for me," Horace said, indicating his own bottle.

"I think that punch was stronger than it tasted," Derek said, eyeing Jack.

"It is pretty strong," Jack acknowledged. "Sorry, maybe I should've warned everyone."

"Yeah … I can feel it myself," Skye said. "I won't be having any more, that's for sure."

Peter lurched out of the washroom and Derek steadied him by the arm to lead him outside to the hangar. After a few minutes, Derek returned. "He's passed out. It had to have been really strong."

Jack smiled apologetically, then slowly finished off the last piece of rib on his plate. He was conscious of Celeste staring at him from across the table and knew that to reach for more food now would make her suspect that he was stalling.

"I wonder if this would be a good time for you and me to check on our guest?" Celeste said, as Jack wiped his fingers with a paper towel.

"Uh, might be a bit early," he replied. "We haven't had your birthday cake yet." He felt her toes search out his groin under the table and squirmed back in his chair.

Celeste looked bemused at his discomfort. "I prefer to have my cake afterward," she said, rising to her feet. "Derek and Horace can do the dishes when they're done their beers." She looked at Skye. "Aren't you supposed to have an online chat with someone?"

"Oh, right ... I'll need some privacy," Skye replied, his head swaying slightly.

CHAPTER FIFTY-NINE

Jack followed Celeste and Skye down the hall, all too aware that Derek and Horace were watching him from where they sat at the kitchen table.

Upon entering Jack's room, Skye sat down heavily on the bed.

"You all right?" Celeste asked.

"I've got a splitting headache," he replied, massaging his temples with his fingers.

"Come with me," Celeste said. "I've got some Tylenol in the bathroom. I could use one myself."

Drugs and poison ... that should be a good mixture to speed things up.

Celeste looked at Jack. "Wait here."

He waited until the two of them had entered the master bedroom, then whispered in Alicia's ear. "Everything's going well. Skye won't be awake much longer."

A moment later Skye reappeared in the doorway and gestured with his head toward the master bedroom. "Go on in, she, uh, wants to talk to you." He held the door jamb to steady himself, then continued down the hall to the kitchen.

His shirt was tucked in a moment ago and now it's not. Got a gun in your waistband? In your condition you'll be lucky not to shoot yourself.

Jack tipped Alicia's chair back and dragged her into the master bedroom. As he did, he saw Skye talking to Derek and Horace. From the bit of conversation he picked up, they were telling him that they felt okay.

"Close the door, Jack," Celeste said, emerging from the ensuite. She was wearing a black leather mask, a black leather bra, tight black leather shorts, and knee-high leather boots.

Jack closed the bedroom door, then gestured to Alicia. "Do you have the scissors?"

"This isn't your fantasy, Jack. This is my birthday, and things are going to be a little different."

"Oh?"

"Take the tape off her eyes. I'm saving her for a grand finale, but I want her to watch."

"But she'll see you."

"We've been over that. I'm willing to risk it. Hurry up."

Jack peeled the tape from Alicia's eyes and saw the fear in them. He heard the door of the room next to them closing. *Good, Skye's back. Bet he passes out within twenty minutes at the most.*

"Leave your underwear on, but take off everything else and lie down on the bed," Celeste ordered.

Hell, no!

She opened the bedroom door a crack and called out to Skye. "You okay in there?"

He mumbled an affirmative response, so Celeste closed the door and turned her attention back to Jack. "Why're you still standing there? Get undressed."

"Maybe you'd like to take 'em off for me?" Jack suggested, nodding for her to join him where he stood beside the bed.

"No, you do it."

Jack slowly started to unbutton his shirt, then smiled at Celeste, his fingers hesitating over the last couple of buttons.

"My fantasy doesn't include a striptease," Celeste said. "Come on, off with it. I want you on the bed. Why are you stalling?"

"Pleasure comes from anticipation," he replied.

"I've been anticipating all day. Hurry up!"

Can I get away with choking her out now? He glanced at his watch. *It's only been three minutes. I need to stall.* He took off his shirt, jeans, and socks, then sat on the edge of the bed in his boxer shorts. He smiled and patted the sheets. "Get over here. Let me really put you in the mood."

"I'm already in the mood," she replied, opening a dresser drawer. She took out some items and tossed them on the bed.

Jack looked at the short black leather belts. *No fucking way.*

"Do your ankles first, then one of your hands," she ordered.

"No, I'm not into bondage. The idea of it freaks me out."

Celeste shook her finger like he was a naughty child. "It's my birthday, Jack. You said yourself it'd be a shame to disappoint a lady on her birthday. Now do what I command!"

"But the idea of being tied up is like a phobia for me. I wouldn't, uh, be able to perform."

"I'll be the judge of that," Celeste said testily.

"No, really. I mean it." *That's it, I'm not waiting. Time to put you out.* He stood up, then heard Skye calling out, asking her to come back in for a minute. *Damn it, now what?*

"Where do you think you're going, Jack? Stay here, I'll be right back."

As soon as she left, Jack took the paring knife from out of his jeans and cut the zip tie binding Alicia's wrists to the back of the chair. He hadn't yet had time to cut the one around her wrists before Celeste reappeared.

"What're you doing?" she demanded.

"She was trying to say something," Jack said, slipping the paring knife into Alicia's hands before turning around. It was then he saw that Celeste was pointing a gun at him. "What the hell? What's that for?"

Celeste glared at him suspiciously. "My headache is getting worse and I'm starting to feel sick. I also get the distinct impression that you're stalling, for some reason." She gave a nod toward the door and added, "My partner's feeling worse, though he hasn't been sick or passed out like —" she glanced at Alicia "— like the young guy." She paused. "You poison us somehow, Jack?"

"No! What the hell? The ribs might've been a little off, but that's not my fault." He paused. "Now that you mention it, I don't feel all that good, either." *Who would, with a gun pointed at them?*

"But who passes out from food poisoning? With the young guy, who knows? Maybe he did drink too much, but my partner didn't. If he passes out in the next hour, you're going be praying for me to kill you long before I actually do."

"You're being paranoid. Can't you see I've been looking forward to tonight as much as you?"

"If that were true, you wouldn't be stalling. Get your ass back on the bed and tie each ankle, with the strap overlapping the crossbar and one of the vertical bars at the foot of the bed. Space your feet about shoulder width apart. Then tie one hand to the headboard. After that, I'll finish the job."

"This is ridiculous. Why are you blaming me for —"

Celeste cocked the gun and aimed it at his face. "Do it!"

Jack got on the bed and picked up a strap. As he tied his left ankle, he said, "You won't shoot me. This is silly. Put the gun away and come over here."

"I won't shoot you? For your information, I shot a guy just last month. Believe me, I'm not afraid to do it again!"

"You did?" Celeste didn't respond. "Okay, fine, but you're going to see that we probably just ate something that was off," Jack said with assurance. As he bound his right ankle, he glanced at Alicia, who was to his right. Their eyes met and she looked down at her own ankles before staring at Celeste.

Jack understood. She couldn't cut those ties without Celeste noticing. Another concern crossed his mind. When he'd cut the zip tie binding Alicia to the chair, one of the cut ends had sprung out wide. If Celeste saw it, she'd realize what was happening.

"That one's not tight enough," Celeste said, gesturing to his ankle. "Pull it tight!"

Jack tightened the belt further, then slipped the end through the loop to hold it in place. Both of his feet were secured. He flashed a smile to pretend he didn't mind. *Keep her talking. Lower her guard.*

"Now your hand," Celeste said.

"Okay, but tell me," Jack said, as he picked up the two remaining belts, "what's in store for her? Obviously it's not my fantasy, but you said you were saving Ally for later. Let me enjoy some anticipation, too."

"She'll be a treat for you and my partner later — if he's okay," she said, frowning.

"Of course he'll be okay," Jack said quickly. "Come on, tell me what you've got planned," he said, stringing one of the belts through the bars on the headboard on the side closest to Alicia. He held the belt in place with his wrist before turning to look at Celeste.

Celeste smiled. "For starters, I'm going to tie her face down on the bed, with her feet at the headboard and her face overlooking the end."

"Oh?"

Celeste then addressed Alicia directly. "Then I'm going to sit in that chair, hold your face up by your hair, and watch while Jack and my partner take turns fucking you up the ass." She paused, relishing the look of fear on Alicia's face, then turned to Jack. "Don't worry, she's not the type to kiss and tell."

"Forget that! Turning her on is one thing. That I'm willing to chance, but to do that …" He shook his head. "Any idea what happens to rapists in jail? If a riot breaks out, they're the first ones who get —" He let the belts fall off the side of the bed and made an unsuccessful lunge for them. "Oops."

Celeste took care to aim the gun at him as she moved past Alicia toward the fallen belts. "Twist away from me and turn your head," she commanded.

Damn. "Sure, but first … what makes you think Ally won't tell anyone?"

Celeste smiled in response, while behind her, Alicia used the paring knife to cut away at a zip tie around her ankle.

"Because she and I already know each other pretty well." She studied his face for a reaction.

"Help me!" Skye screamed from the hallway. A shudder through the trailer indicated that he'd crashed into a wall before staggering into the master bedroom.

Celeste's mouth fell open.

Skye pointed at Alicia as he stumbled in. "Look out! She's getting free!"

As Celeste turned, Alicia sprang up and tried to stab her in the neck. Celeste jumped back and the knife left a long, bloody slash down her leg.

"You bitch!" Celeste screamed over the sound of Derek and Horace charging down the hall.

Jack made a grab for the gun while delivering a solid punch to the side of her face with enough force to break her jaw.

She let out an anguished cry as she fell. At the same time, Derek burst into the room with his gun drawn. He was the first one Jack took a shot at, though the shot missed. Derek did an about-face and crashed into Horace as the both of them tumbled back out of sight.

Jack pointed the gun at the doorway. Beside him on the floor, Skye was screaming. Alicia, with one foot still tied to the chair, had toppled over on him, and she was wildly stabbing at him with the knife while Celeste cried out from the bottom of the pile.

"Alicia! Enough!" Jack said. "Cut yourself free!" He kept the pistol pointed at the doorway as he undid the belts around his own feet. A quick glance back told him that Celeste wouldn't be a threat; she'd crawled out and was sitting in a corner, cupping her broken jaw in her hand. Any movement she made would cause her extreme pain.

Skye lay in the fetal position beside her, staring at the defensive wounds on his hands. Several more puncture marks were visible on the back of his shoulder.

Alicia crouched on her knees, her body trembling as she held the knife above them. She still hadn't removed the tape from around her mouth.

Jack got on the floor beside her, still aiming the pistol over the top of the bed. "Peel the tape from your mouth," he said.

Alicia didn't move, so Jack reached over and yanked the tape off, then turned his concentration onto the doorway. "You okay?" he asked over his shoulder.

"No! She stabbed me!" Skye said, easing over to sit beside Celeste. "I'm —"

"Not you, asshole! Shut the fuck up!"

"I'm — I'm okay," Alicia said.

Like hell you are. You're going into shock.

"I'm bleeding all over," Skye said, slurring his words and gawking at his bloody hands.

"Derek Powers!" Jack yelled. "Ally and I are both undercover RCMP officers. You're going to be arrested for kidnapping. Don't up the ante to attempted murder!"

"Bullshit!" Derek replied. "You're nothing but a fuckin' dope dealer!"

Sounds like they've retreated to the kitchen. "We've had your phone bugged. We heard Peter talking to you about a drug deal by saying he was selling golf clubs. After that, we watched you set up on our undercover operator in your surveillance van at Brentwood Town Centre."

"Shit. He really is a cop," he heard Derek say.

"Got some more bad news for you!" Jack shouted. "I poisoned your brother with antifreeze. If you don't get him to a hospital within a few minutes he'll be dead!" He glanced at his watch. *Actually he's probably got another six or seven hours, but no need to tell him that.*

"Oh, fuck," Skye whimpered beside him.

Jack tried to listen as Derek and Horace argued. Derek wanted to save his brother, but Horace wanted to stay and kill them. A few minutes later, Jack heard movement behind him and turned to look. Skye had slumped over.

Celeste stared wide-eyed at Jack.

"You'll both be dead if I don't get to a phone," he told her.

She pointed to the dresser while still supporting her jaw with one hand. "Second drawer down, between my underwear," she mumbled.

Seconds later, Jack tapped in Rose's number.

She sounded annoyed when she answered, maybe thinking it was a wrong number or a telemarketer.

"It's Jack. We're both alive but need help."

"Where are you?" Rose shouted.

"Somewhere on an acreage about halfway between Abbotsford and Chilliwack. I've got a gun and am in a bedroom with Alicia at the back of a mobile home. There are two bad guys somewhere else in the trailer with guns who want to kill us. One is Derek Powers and the other is a guy by the name of Horace. He drives a black van."

"You know his plate?"

"Yes, but he doesn't live here."

"Damn it," Rose said, "give me a sec to grab another pen."

"Hurry, the battery's almost dead."

"Keep talking."

"Two more bad guys are in the room with me, but out of commission."

"Out of commission? You mean dead?"

"On their way to being dead."

"Jesus … okay, I've got a pen."

Jack gave her the licence plate number to Horace's van.

"Uh, okay. I take it you don't know your exact location?"

"No, it's in a rural area south of the Trans-Canada. Got a pit bull roaming around outside, as well."

"Which —"

"This phone's almost dead. I think I should call 911 while I still can. I'll call you back when I find another phone or recharge this one."

"Don't go yet! At least tell me which exit you took to get off the Trans-Canada —"

The sound of the dog barking underneath the trailer told Jack it was time to quit talking. "Gotta go. Someone's about to attack," he whispered, then ended the call.

"Jack!" Derek yelled from the kitchen. "Talk to me, man! Are Celeste and Skye okay? Do you want me to call an ambulance?"

Talk so that Horace can shoot me from underneath the trailer? Not fucking likely.

"Don't make a sound," Jack whispered in Alicia's ear. "Horace is underneath us."

They sat in silence for several minutes while Derek kept trying to get them to talk. Eventually Jack heard him swear and run from the trailer. By then, Celeste had slumped over. The hand she'd used to hold her broken jaw in place had fallen to her lap, and her mouth gaped open. *Hope you die, you bitch.*

CHAPTER SIXTY

Jack heard Derek yelling from outside, near the hangar, followed by the sound of Horace scrambling out from under the trailer.

"Sounds like he's leaving," Alicia whispered.

"Maybe," Jack replied, picking up the phone. "I'm going to call 911. They'll be able to trace my call." He stabbed in the numbers, then cursed. "The battery's dead." He looked at Alicia. "Sit tight. I'm going to try and see what they're doing."

Alicia grabbed his arm. "Don't leave me," she said anxiously.

"I won't. I'll turn the lights off and peek out the window. At the same time, I want to grab my clothes and get dressed."

Alicia gestured to Celeste and Skye. "In the dark, what if … what if they're faking it and they try something?"

Jack knew from the sound of the voices that Derek and Horace were far enough away not to be a threat. "Okay, if it'll make you feel better, hold this." He handed her the pistol and added, "Keep an eye on Celeste."

He grabbed Skye by the ankles and dragged him on his back toward the end of the bed. Skye moaned, but his eyes never opened. Seconds later, Jack used the belts to bind Skye's hands to the brass railings on the footboard.

Celeste was next. She cried out in pain and pawed at her jaw as Jack dragged her into position. Seconds later, she too was stretched out on the floor and tied up beside Skye.

The voices outside had come closer, so Jack took the pistol from Alicia, then turned the bedroom light off and shut the door to block the light from the hallway. He then stood back from the window so his face wouldn't be illuminated by a yard light.

Horace was helping Derek load Peter into the van. Once that was done, Derek stayed in back with Peter, Horace jumped into the driver's seat, and the van roared off. *Good, they're all gone. We're safe.*

Jack turned to look at Alicia. *Sorry, I'm going to lie to you now, but I think someday you'll be glad I did.*

"What are they doing?" Alicia asked, getting to her feet.

"Stay down," Jack whispered. "I think Derek is taking his brother to the hospital, but I can't see Horace. He might be under the trailer again, perhaps hoping we'll think they've all gone, and then he'll try to kill us. He probably doesn't know we have a phone, or he wouldn't even believe us if I told him."

"So what do we do?"

"We stay put and wait. Once my eyes adjust to the dark, I'll rummage around and see if I can find a charging cable."

Jack got dressed. Once his eyes adjusted, he saw that Alicia was sitting on the floor with her arms wrapped around her knees, trembling. "Try to relax," he said. "If Horace decides to burst in on us, he'll have to shut off the hall light first or face looking into a darkened room while silhouetted in the light behind him. If he does shut the light off, we'll know, and I'd kill him before he gets to us. His only other alternative is to try and shoot us from underneath the trailer."

"So you think we're safe?"

"As long as he can't pinpoint where we are by listening to us. Sit quietly and I'll look for the phone charger."

"Okay," Alicia whispered.

Jack then looked through all the dresser drawers. "Can't find it," he said. "I think we'll need to wait until daybreak." He took a blanket from the bed and wrapped it around her shoulders. She cuddled up beside him when he sat down.

Over the next two hours, Jack checked Celeste and Skye's pulses every fifteen minutes.

Eventually Alicia whispered, "I can't stand it! I'm sure he's gone. I haven't heard a thing."

"Or maybe he's lying in wait, thinking that Derek and Peter might return from the hospital. Do you want to watch these two while I go out to the kitchen? Maybe the phone charger is there. Hopefully that isn't where Horace is hiding."

Alicia paused. "I think you should wait another hour."

Another hour dragged by, then Jack said, "Wish me luck." He then crept down the hall to the kitchen and returned to the bedroom a minute later, the phone charger dangling from his hand. "Got it!"

Rose answered her phone after the first ring.

"We're okay," Jack said immediately. "Did you get the name to the licence plate I gave you?"

"Yes. It's registered to a Horace Romano, with an apartment address in Abbotsford. He isn't home, and we staked out his address."

"You got this number on your call display, or is it blocked?"

"I've got it."

"I'm hanging up. Call me back immediately and I'll let it ring several times."

"Why?"

"I'll explain when you call back." Jack ended the call, then yelled out, "Horace Romano! If you can hear me, I've got a phone. If you're close enough, you'll hear it ringing. I've already given them your plate number. It's over! Go stand under the yard light with your hands on top of your head — otherwise our sharpshooters will kill you."

The phone started to ring, but there was no response to indicate Horace was around.

"Okay," Jack said upon answering, "I think we're safe and I found the phone charger."

"Where are you? We've been going nuts! Why didn't you call 911?"

"I tried … the battery died. Let me tell you where I am."

"Are you still at the mobile home?"

"Yes, in a bedroom at the rear of the trailer. Derek's car is parked in the yard and there's a hangar close by with a Cessna inside and a red Corvette. Where are you? Are you —"

"At your bloody office! We all are! Give me your location!"

Jack gave her the call letters for the Cessna and the licence plate number for the Corvette. He told her they belonged to a woman by the name of Celeste, who was the ringleader of the group. "She's unconscious and tied to the foot of the bed beside me," he added, "along with her partner, a fellow by the name of Skye."

"You said there were two others trying to kill you. Derek and Horace."

"Yes, Derek's brother Peter was also in on it. I poisoned him and I think Derek took him to a hospital not long after I first called you."

"You poisoned him?"

"Yes. Same as Celeste and Skye. I got them to drink antifreeze, but Derek wouldn't drink any and Horace only had about two ounces, so he's probably okay for a few more hours."

"Where's Horace?"

"I'm not sure. I think Derek used his van to take Peter to the hospital, but I don't know if Horace was driving. I'd heard him arguing earlier about wanting to stay to kill us. He might still be lurking around, possibly under the trailer."

"Okay … Laura's handed me the plate info on the Corvette. Registered to a Celeste O'Brien. Rural address. It was her birthday yesterday."

"Yeah, it was quite a party. I would've called you, but I was sort of tied up."

"I'll let the Emergency Response Team know where you are. They'll likely be there within thirty minutes. We'll also check the hospitals."

"It'll be light in a couple of hours. Alicia and I are safe. Tell ERT that if they want to set up a perimeter, then hold off until daybreak, it won't be a problem."

"I'll let them know."

"Have them phone me when they're set up. We don't need anyone getting killed by friendly fire."

"Will do."

"Listen, I think I heard something under the trailer again. I'm going to hang up. I'll call you later."

"I didn't hear anything," Alicia whispered after Jack ended the call.

"Probably the dog, or maybe the wind," Jack said.

Almost another hour passed before ERT called Jack to inform him that they had set up around the trailer and also secured the hangar.

"It'll be daybreak soon," Jack noted.

"Yeah, if you're sure you're safe, we'll wait until then. We've also got the dog master with us, but seeing as you said there was a pit bull living under the trailer, he's not inclined to put his dog in harm's way unless he has to."

"I agree. Let's wait."

Thirty minutes later, Jack checked Celeste and Skye's pulses.

"No pulse on either!" he said, then started administering CPR to Skye.

Alicia simply stared at him, stunned.

"Damn it, get to work on her!" Jack ordered.

Alicia didn't move.

"What the hell? I'm giving you an order. Start CPR!" he stated, still pumping on Skye's chest.

"No," she whimpered, "I can't."

"What do you mean, you can't?"

"You don't understand." She started to sob. "They did stuff to me."

"Stuff?"

"They assaulted me … sexually. The both of them. I was too ashamed to tell you."

Jack didn't slow down as he continued to administer CPR. "Alicia, I'm sorry, I truly am, but you need to get a grip. It's not you who should feel shame. If they survive, you'll have your day in court, and it'll be up to a judge to decide their punishment. They're not a threat to us now. Our job is to try and save them."

Alicia hung her head and sobbed.

"Do it!" Jack yelled.

Alicia crawled over to Celeste and started administering CPR.

Minutes later, the phone rang and Jack answered, holding it in the crook of his neck as he continued CPR.

"We got 'em!" Rose said. "Horace and Derek have been arrested at the hospital. Peter is unconscious and the doctor doesn't know if he'll make it or not. Horace is being treated, but is cuffed to the bed."

"So Horace did go with them," Jack commented. "That's good news. Call ERT for me and tell them to come in. Alicia and I are doing CPR on the two we got here."

"I'll call them and be there within ten minutes myself. Laura and Mason are with me."

Moments later, the ERT commander checked Celeste and Skye for a pulse, then shook his head. "You're wasting your time. They're both dead."

Jack looked grim. He stood and wrapped his arm around Alicia's shoulder, then glanced at the ERT commander. "The pit bull?"

"Safely secured. We used a dog catch pole."

Jack went outside and He turned to face Alicia upon seeing Rose's car billowing dust as it zoomed along a gravel road toward the acreage.

"Sorry, Alicia, I'm sure you were looking forward to your day in court," he said facetiously, nodding toward the trailer.

Alicia looked puzzled, but didn't reply.

"Are you okay?" he asked.

"I will be … I need time to process, but I'm okay."

"I think we better get you to a doctor."

"Is that necessary?" she asked. "I mean, there wasn't penetration. I'm upset. But …" Her eyes sought his. "Does everyone need to know?"

"That you were sexually assaulted?"

Alicia nodded.

"Seeing as the perpetrators will never do it again, I'm happy not to mention it and to leave it out of my statement."

Alicia looked relieved. "Thank you."

"But there's still a possibility that some people might find out," Jack said. *Especially if, as I suspect, Skye was watching and recording everything.*

Alicia frowned. "You think the other three knew about it? That they'll talk?"

"Yes, that's a possibility, too."

"Too?"

"Why do you think Skye made a point of going into the next room earlier?"

"He had to have a chat with someone online. Obviously he didn't want me to hear."

"Yeah, that's what he said." *Poor kid. No use freaking you out any more than you already are. Especially if I'm wrong.*

CHAPTER SIXTY-ONE

A few hours later, Lexton saw Rose through the open door of her secretary's office and waved her in.

Rose's conversation was short as she explained how Taggart's plan had gone astray and how he had believed that the kidnappers were going to kill them both, so he'd tried to poison them all.

Celeste O'Brien and a Skye Cunningham had succumbed to the poisoning. A third man by the name of Peter Powers was expected to survive, but with serious brain, liver, and heart damage. Two others, Derek Powers and Horace Romano, were in custody.

"What about Miguel Hernández?" Lexton asked. "The person who we know supplied photos of our undercover operatives to Derek Powers. Was there any evidence on Powers's phone?"

"No, he was obviously expecting to be arrested. They seized his phone, but it was missing a SIM card."

"I see. So, back to the trailer. You're telling me that because Sergeant Taggart saw a pickaxe and a shovel, he jumped to the conclusion that they were going to be killed, then tried to murder everyone?"

"I think murder is a harsh conclusion," Rose said. "We need to get all the facts."

"The facts according to Sergeant Taggart's statement," Lexton replied.

"Derek Powers is being interviewed as we speak. Horace Romano will be interviewed shortly. It's too early to be judgmental. Corroborating evidence to support Sergeant Taggart's statement may come to light."

Lexton tried not to let her emotion show. "I appreciate that the arrests took place only this morning." *After I get the full reports from I-HIT, I'll take the appropriate action.* "You can go."

A moment later, Lexton went to her safe and removed her file folder marked *JT.*

You murdered two people and turned another into a vegetable because you saw some tools? They were in a hangar, for Christ's sake. You'd expect to see tools in a hangar.

She jotted some angry comments in the file, then returned it to her safe.

* * *

At 7:15 a.m. on Wednesday morning, Jack answered his phone at home.

"Did I wake you?" Mason asked.

"No … apparently guys my age get up early."

Mason chuckled. "I'm at the airport to catch a flight back to Toronto for court. Should be back in Vancouver on Friday afternoon."

"Good. Be careful what you eat. Keep away from those dirty utensils."

* * *

It was 9:30 p.m. Wednesday night when James Deacon, alias Fat Boy, the sergeant at arms of the Devils Aces motorcycle club in Hamilton, answered his door.

He wasn't impressed by the man who flashed an RCMP badge. "Show me your warrant," he demanded.

"I'm not here for that," the cop replied. "I'm here because our homicide squad out in B.C. has a suspect for the murder of one of your guys, and they want me to talk to you."

"Leo? They know who shot Leo?" Fat Boy asked.

"Yeah ... a Leo Ratcliffe."

"Come on in."

"No, come out to my car, where I've got the file."

Fat Boy got into the passenger seat. The cop was holding his stomach and rocking back and forth behind the steering wheel. "What the fuck's wrong with you?"

"Mild case of food poisoning. Shit," the cop muttered, clenching his teeth a moment before reaching into the back seat to retrieve a briefcase. "Okay, there's a picture I want to — shit!" He dropped the case and grabbed his stomach, rocking some more, then he started the car and put it in drive.

"What are you doing? Where you taking me?"

"There's a gas station two blocks from here. I need to use the can."

At the gas station, the cop took a deep breath, then said, "I think I'm okay at the moment." He opened the briefcase and removed a file folder, along with a yellow writing pad and a pen on a clipboard, which he placed on top of the console. He then took a couple of surveillance photos out of the file and handed them to Fat Boy. "His name is Miguel Hernández. Do you recognize him?"

"Nope," Fat Boy replied, scrutinizing the photos carefully.

"He lives in North Vancouver at the moment and works for the Sheriff's Services in the courthouse."

"He's a sheriff?" Fat Boy asked in surprise.

"I think he spends more time smuggling dope in for whoever Satans Wrath wants him to. You sure you don't recognize him? He might've had a beard before. Originally he's from Mississauga."

"That's only about thirty minutes away," Fat Boy noted.

"Look carefully. It's been ten years, so he might've changed a lot."

"What makes you think he shot Leo?"

"Can't, uh, give you any more information than I already have," he said, patting the file folder. "That's confidential. We just wondered if you knew him or if any other Devils Aces were out in B.C."

"I don't recognize him and nobody else from the chapter is out there."

The cop started to rock again. "Looks like we're done. I'll drive you — shit, wait here, I gotta use the can."

The cop was barely out of sight when Fat Boy opened the file and read the report. It said how Miguel Hernández had been smuggling dope for Satans Wrath for years, and that he knew they were at war with the Devils Aces. The report went on to say that Hernández had recognized Leo in a strip club called the Hedonic Palace and followed him home one night.

A confidential informant identified only as a stripper told the cops that Hernández had bragged to her about doing something really big for Satans Wrath and that he expected to get a lot of money. Later another informant inside Satans Wrath told the cops that Hernández killed Leo, hoping they'd reward him for it. Apparently Satans Wrath refused to pay because they hadn't sanctioned the hit.

The last paragraph in the report caught Fat Boy's attention. It concluded that there was insufficient evidence to arrest Hernández and said there was a rumour that he planned to quit the Sheriff's Services and move away. It also listed Hernández's current address.

Fat Boy glanced up to ensure the cop wasn't in sight, then helped himself to the notepad and pen.

CHAPTER SIXTY-TWO

Jack was at home Friday at noon when he received a call on his undercover cellphone.

"Bruce, it's David Chung."

Oh, good, he still thinks I'm Bruce.

"You'll never believe what's happened! I just had a visit from a Sergeant Hawkins of the RCMP."

"Oh?"

Jack listened as David told him that the RCMP had done an undercover operation and caught all the kidnappers. Also that one of the kidnappers had confessed and was co-operating with the police.

"There were five of them," David went on to say, "and two were killed, including the one who cut Tommy's fingers off. Two others who were involved have been arrested and one of them has confessed and is co-operating with the police. The third one won't be charged because he's now severely brain damaged."

"That's great news," Jack said, after David had provided more details about how some of the kidnappers had been poisoned. "Does the RCMP know about me?"

"No … and I didn't tell them."

"Thanks. My wife is extremely distressed and wants to put it all behind us. I don't think she could handle going to court."

"I understand. It's strange though, they knew about Andy Zhao and the other Chinese family I told you about, but they never mentioned you."

"Maybe the guy who's confessing now got out of it before they took my son," Jack suggested.

"That might explain it."

"I hope it doesn't come out. I'm really worried about my wife. We've even sold our place and are moving back east at the end of the month."

David expressed his condolences and well wishes, then said, "There's something I feel awful about. There was a young policewoman involved in the investigation from the beginning. Jia and I sort of blamed her for what happened to Tommy. Turns out that she was involved in the undercover operation and was actually kidnapped by them and held for almost two days."

"They didn't realize she was a police officer?"

"No, she was undercover. Jia and I want to meet with her to apologize for how we treated her, but Sergeant Hawkins said she probably was suffering from extreme stress and wouldn't be available to see us. He also said she's been transferred to some special undercover unit where the officers like to have anonymity."

"He told you she is suffering from extreme stress?"

"Yes."

Hawkins knows what happened to her.

"Jia and I are thinking we'll write her a letter instead."

"That sounds like an excellent idea. A letter is something she could hang on to, and it'd mean more than a quick verbal apology."

* * *

Late Friday afternoon, Lexton nodded cordially to Dyck as he and Connie entered her office.

"You said you have something to show me?" Lexton said, eyeing the laptop that Connie had brought with her. She gestured to an area in her office where a cluster of upholstered chairs were gathered around a coffee table.

"I'd requested Staff Sergeant Wood to attend," Dyck said. "I told her we had some evidence from the trailer that concerns her people."

"Yes, I'm here," Rose announced, striding in. "Sorry if I'm late."

"You're on time," Lexton said. "Take a seat." She saw Rose glance furtively at Dyck. *Probably worried about what they've discovered about Taggart.*

"To start with," Dyck said, "one of the suspects, Horace Romano, has confessed and given a statement in the presence of his lawyer, and he's willing to testify against Derek Powers. He told us he acted as a lookout when Skye Cunningham, accompanied by Celeste O'Brien, beat Constable Dalton with a bat."

"Does he know how Constable Dalton was identified as an undercover operative?" Lexton asked.

"No, he said someone tipped off Derek Powers, but Horace has no idea who that was. He also identified three children who've been kidnapped in the past two years and said he was present when Celeste O'Brien chopped off Tommy Chung's fingers using a meat cleaver. He said it was also O'Brien's plan to murder Sergeant Taggart and Constable Munday immediately upon receipt of the latest ransom."

"So Sergeant Taggart was correct in his belief," Rose noted. *Point taken. No need to throw it in my face.* "How did they select their targets?" Lexton asked.

"Both Celeste O'Brien and Skye Cunningham sold real estate," Connie said, "which is how they met. Apparently they selected their targets by the price of the home they owned, with a preference for Chinese immigrants based on a belief they'd be less likely to call the police. It wasn't an accurate assumption, but after they'd made the Chungs an example to scare the other victims with, that didn't matter."

"Do we know how the rest of the group met each other?"

"Celeste and Derek Powers were friends since high school," Connie replied. "Horace Romano was simply a friend of Peter Powers and was involved in the drug trade with him. Apparently when Derek was studying criminology, he and Celeste used to joke about how to get away with criminal acts and discussed different strategies."

"And then the joke became not a joke," Lexton observed.

"Exactly," Connie replied. "Besides kidnapping, Romano said they were planning to rob an armoured car this coming Christmas at one of the malls."

"I presume Romano, through his lawyer, has already cut a deal for a reduced sentence?" Lexton asked.

"His lawyer was smart enough to know that cutting a deal would taint his client's evidence," Connie said. "At this point no deals have been made, but no doubt the lawyer hopes Romano's co-operation will be taken into consideration when he is sentenced. Crown is expecting him to receive a ten-year sentence, while Derek Powers is looking at fifteen if he pleads guilty. My understanding is that his lawyer will go for that."

"I take it you have something else?" Lexton asked, gesturing to the laptop.

"Yes, we recovered this footage from the trailer," Connie stated, opening a video on her laptop.

Lexton felt confused. "Pornography?"

"Taken surreptitiously," Connie replied. "Give me a minute to fast forward to, uh, what you may find relevant."

"Forensics found hidden cameras monitoring the master bedroom in the trailer," Dyck stated. "It's believed that, with the exception of Celeste O'Brien and Skye Cunningham, the other participants didn't know they were being filmed. It was all hooked into a computer in the next room."

"This is it," Connie said sombrely. "Alicia … I mean, Constable Munday, was sexually assaulted by O'Brien and Cunningham."

Lexton viewed the footage in silence, pursing her lips in an effort to control her emotions as her eyes welled.

"She never told me," Rose lamented, looking visibly shaken.

"There's more footage from the next day," Connie said. "You can see Alicia after being dragged back into the room by Sergeant Taggart. A moment later O'Brien is seen pointing a gun at him … I'll let you watch."

"Everything ties in completely with their statements," Dyck said, "with the exception of the sexual assault on Constable Munday. She never mentioned that in her statement."

In the video, Lexton watched Jack gain control of the gun, then tie the two suspects to the end of the bed. "Okay, then they were rescued later," she noted, expecting Crane to stop the video.

"Skip ahead to the end," Dyck said to Crane. "I think the assistant commissioner might find that part of interest."

When Lexton saw Taggart ordering Munday to perform CPR, she realized that her mouth was hanging open.

"Ultimately, they weren't successful," Dyck noted, "but under the circumstances, I think it quite extraordinary that they displayed such strong principles after what had taken place."

Lexton found herself at a loss for words. She glanced toward her safe and felt ill about what it contained.

"What should we do about Constable Munday?" Dyck asked. "Obviously she left something very serious out of her statement, but under the circumstances …"

"Her brain may have blocked it out," Connie suggested. "The omission may not have been intentional."

Still distracted by what she'd viewed, Lexton paused to collect her thoughts. "She'll need professional help," she noted. "Perhaps stress leave, as well."

"I'll take her aside and talk to her about it," Rose said. "I got my masters in psychology. I think I could help guide her to whatever she needs."

"Good." Lexton eyed each of their faces. "I don't know who else knows about this, but I believe it would be in

Constable Munday's best interests if anyone who does keeps their mouth shut."

"Only one person in Forensics knows what we found on the computer," Connie said. "She's already promised me that she'll keep it to herself."

Lexton sighed. *God, this has been a long week.* She dismissed everyone from her office, then retrieved the *JT* file from her safe. On her way out, she handed it to the secretary.

"Tracey, toss this in the shredding bin before you lock up."

* * *

It was 11:00 a.m. the following Monday when Inspector Dyck called Lexton to inform her that someone had shot Miguel Hernández in the face earlier that morning when he answered his door. He also said there were no suspects for the murder yet.

"Goddamn it!" Lexton blurted. She lowered the phone from her mouth and yelled, "Tracey! Did you shred that file I gave you on Friday?"

"Sorry, not yet," her secretary replied.

"Good. Don't!"